Mourner's Bench

Sanderia Faye

The University of Arkansas Press
Fayetteville
2015

19 18 17 16 15   5 4 3 2 1

Designed by Liz Lester

♾ The paper used in this publication meets the minimum requirements
of the American National Standard for Permanence of Paper
for Printed Library Materials Z39.48–1984.

Library of Congress Control Number: 2015938421

For Granny, the true storyteller
and Dr. Maya Angelou, who gave me the confidence to write.

#BLACKLIVESMATTER

ACKNOWLEDGMENTS

My deepest appreciation to Mrs. Carr, my high-school English teacher, for suggesting that I become a writer. I will be forever grateful to Oprah Winfrey for every show she did about finding your passion and following your dreams. I am thankful to the Phoenix College Creative Writing Department. I am more than grateful to Arizona State University Creative Writing Department, where I wrote the first draft of this novel: Alberto Rios, Jewell Parker Rhodes, Ron Carlson, Neal Lester, Melissa Pritchard, Demetria Martinez, Paul Morris, Keith Miller, and Mark Richard. And to my classmates, Robert Nelson, Mentor, Michael Guerra, and Tayari Jones, for setting the highest standards and encouraging me to follow her. Thank you to the University of Texas at Dallas, Arts and Humanties, where I finished writing and revising the manuscript: Professors Clay Reynolds and Matthew Bondurant and doctorial classmates Latoya Watkins, Bryan Gillian, Jessica Miller, Vanessa Baker, and Susan Norman.

I appreciate walking, and writing, in coffee shops with David Haynes, founder and faculty at Kimbilio Fiction; and thanks to faculty ZZ Packer; the Kimbilio advisory board, especially Darryl Dickson-Carr and Matthew Johnson; the Kimbilio fellows; and my roommate and reader, Christi Cartwright. Thank you to Hurston/Wright Writers' Workshop faculty Agymah Kamau and Terri McMillian and to classmates Ravi Howard, Dolen Perkins-Valdez, and to Erica Williams, who graciously read the manuscript from its first draft until the final copy. I am eternally grateful to Dennis Lehane and Sterling Watson, founders of the Eckerd College Writers' Conference Writers in Paradise, and to its dedicated faculty and my classmates, Christine Koryta, Michael Koryta, and the B&B'ers, Kathy Gillet, Damaris Hill, Charlie Clark, Ben Pfeiffer, and Anna Michels. I am especially thankful to Justen and Sarah Ahren, founders of the Martha's Vineyard Writers Residency and to my supportive housemates and friends Elizabeth Gould, Stephanie Smith, Sara Goudarzi, Anna Sequoia, Jenny Klion, and Nan Byrne. Thank you to Vermont Writing Center, the Dairy Hollow Writers Residency, Alison Taylor Brown at the Village Writing School, Chocolate Secrets, and Wordspace Dallas, especially Karen Minzer and Charles Dee Mitchell.

I am most appreciative to Jane Ryder and Peter Gelfan at The Editorial Department, and also to editors Shonell Bacon, Thomas Bernardo, and Carol Sickman-Garner. I am thankful to Crystal Wilkinson, Tananarive Due, Ethelbert Miller, Verne Moore, and Rosalyn Story for their generous notes on the novel and to Angela Ards for answering my desperate call for a summer writing partner. Many thanks goes to Dennis Cordell and our monthly Sunday book club members. I am grateful to my friends, Carolyn Bolden, Shalamar Muhammad, April Burris, Chris Evans, Cindy Banton, Diane May, Rosalind Jones, Sharon Green, and Stephanie Bush. I am honored to have the most supportive family, my aunts, sisters and brothers, and numerous cousins who are actually sisters and brothers, especially Willie Dixon, Pearl Dale, Eddie Carr, Jean Anderson, and Earnestine Shelton, Melvin Sanders, and Ciperanna Mayo.

I am indebted to Jennifer Wallach for believing in this novel and for not giving up until she found a home for it. Larry Malley, former director, and Julie Watkins, former editor at the University of Arkansas Press, had faith in and took a chance on this book before it was finished. Many thanks to the current director Mike Bieker, who kept his word and followed through until publication, and to his phenomenal staff who answered every question and was patient and generous with a first-time novelist. Thank you to the blind readers for their suggestions, which made this a better book. I have not experienced anything that compares to Arkansas hospitality. Thank you for taking good care of my novel.

I am most grateful to my hometown of Gould, Arkansas. I am thankful to the Student Nonviolent Coordinating Committee, the Arkansas Chapter and organizers Laura Foner, Robert Cableton and Tim Janke, and to civil rights attorney John Walker. Words cannot express my gratitude to Mrs. Carrie Dilworth for her many years of service to pursing equality for African Americans. I appreciate the tireless work and activism of my mother, Mayor Essie Dale

Cableton. I am indebted to my church and community for insisting that my best wasn't good enough, and continuously raising the bar higher. I gave many of the characters their names out of respect for the role they played in my life.

Many years have passed since I began this journey, so if I did not mention your name for any number of reasons, please know that I am truly grateful for your encouragement throughout the years.

MOURNER'S BENCH

RESILIENT FOLKS

CHAPTER ONE

We've Got to Move

INDOOR PLUMBING WAS the last significant change in Maeby, Arkansas, before my mama left town. For as long as I could remember, my family and other colored folks kept our pigs, chickens, cows and all other animals in our backyards, and a little further back, a ways from the gardens, sat the outhouses. The all-white city council threatened to take the animals away from us if we didn't clean up our yards and do something about that horrific smell. We didn't pay them no mind, talked about it after they drove off in their city cars. Reverend Jefferson may have brought it up in one of his sermons, but generally, we went on back to minding our business and so did they until the next time they felt up to performing their civic duties.

Then one day the city council members decided to make good on their promises. They bucked up and passed an ordinance that required us to remove all the farm animals outside of the city limits, and to get it done in no time flat. Just for the sake of it, they told us that we must tear the toilets out of the outhouses and replace them with flushable ones. All the grown folks were in a huff about it, especially over the toilets, but since I'd never seen or heard of one, I reserved my passion for when I would know what I was getting upset about.

I thought about the girl, Ruby Bridges, who Esther said was around my age. She was making plans to integrate the elementary school in New Orleans. I imagined her mama pressing the pleats in her dress over and over again but never able to get them to lie straight. And the boys and girls at Central High School who should be near graduating by now, but still wasn't able to fit in like they did at the colored school. I heard one girl couldn't take it any longer and walked out on the others. I would never do that. Reverend Martin Luther King Jr. crossed my mind. He led the civil rights movement throughout the South. Esther told me stories about how she planned to join up with them one day. According to Esther, colored folks won the right to sit at the front of the bus in Montgomery, Alabama. They chose to walk to work instead of ride the bus for 381 days. With all the protesting going on throughout the country, we, the folks in our town, except for Esther and a few others, were more worried about our toilets and farm animals than integrating schools and demanding equal rights.

Esther, who never agreed with anybody, sided with the white folks. She never stopped complaining about how funky the animals smelled. She was always holding her breath or pinching her nose. Said we should live more like people in the big cities like Chicago and New York. She strutted around the house like a cutting horse with her thick, black ponytail resting on her butt calling us all country bumpkins.

"Just 'cause you sneak over to Sister Tucker's store and watch that TV and read newspapers from Chicago and New York don't make you no better than us," Muhdea said.

"I read the ones from Washington, DC, too," Esther said, which started an ongoing argument between them.

"You wouldn't have so much to complain about if you kept your head in the Bible instead of in the ways of the world," Muhdea said.

Muhdea shook her head as if she felt sorry for her, and I didn't know which one of them to side with. When Esther tried to pull me too far into their argument, Granny would beckon and send me to get her spit cup or some other trivial item. When I returned, they would be working in unison as if not only a few minutes before they'd been heated at each other. When Esther turned her attention to me, she made up stories after reading the encyclopedia, the newspapers and the Bible and told them to me. "One day we're going to travel the world to continents like Africa and the North Atlantic," she said.

When my grandmama, whose name was Mozelle, but we called her Muhdea, short for Mother Dear, and my great-grandmama

Granny weren't around, she pinned the hem of her dress above her knee with straight pins and painted her lips with red food coloring. I eyed her like a mother hen watched her baby chicks. She was prettier than every girl I ever seen, even the ones on TV. Sometimes she sat me across her ankles, legs stretched halfway across the floor, and lifted me up as if I was on a seesaw. During those infrequent fun times, she tried to teach me to call her Mama, but every time she said "Mama," I called her "Esther" till she finally looked as if it wasn't fun to her any longer and scooted me onto the floor. In some ways, she favored Muhdea, dark complexion, full lips, and in others, she featured Granny and her Cherokee heritage, high cheekbones, long legs and funny-colored eyes. All put together, she didn't look or act like the rest of us even though Muhdea said she was homely 'cause she hadn't filled out yet. "Never seen a girl so flat after she done give birth," Muhdea said. Granny wasn't filled out and neither was I, "rail thin," Granny called me, but it would take three truckloads to haul Muhdea's hips. I was the spitting image of Granny, "as if Esther didn't have nothing to do with it," folks said.

When the council members came around, they couldn't believe we hadn't caught TB or some other incurable disease. They shook their heads when they saw the maggots in the toilet as if they never seen them the last time they came around. Muhdea wondered why would they go sticking their nose in there every time as if it would change just 'cause they didn't like it. Weren't nothing in there any of their business anyway. Mr. Sam Ray Blackburn, the white owner of the dry goods store on our side of town, held his breath and cussed at us.

"Damn crying shame," he said. He pinched his nostrils together after his breath gave out. "Can't y'all smell this shit?"

Folks rolled their eyes at him but remained quiet for fear of a night in jail. Esther might've said whatever she pleased to us, but when the white men came, she was on our side. She sashayed up to them and held her nose as if they were the ones who smelled, and without saying a word, she turned and switched away. Lord knows she could switch her small hips from side to side, and her thick black ponytail bounced back and forth. Granny adjusted her toothbrush every time she saw Esther switching and told her it was what got her in trouble in the first place.

"What trouble?" I said.

"Not the kind you need to know nothing about," Granny said.

It was after I heard them tell me so many times what I couldn't know that I started keeping a list of things I wanted to find out. I wrote so many pages that I started keeping them in a notebook. *Why did switching get Esther in trouble?* was my first question.

Whenever the white men came around to warn us about the smell, over the next few weeks, some cow, or pig, or good laying hen came up missing. We locked the livestock up tight at night but that didn't help. Granny said the men only came around to scope out whose animals were the best to come back later and steal them. Some of the colored ladies who cleaned for the white people saw their very own pigs slaughtered and cleaned in the their backyard. They were certain some of the meat ended up at Mr. Sam Ray Blackburn's store and was sold back to us.

"They might as well take them when they come over here," Esther said. "There ain't one thing any one of us can do to stop them."

"Well, it's the principle," Muhdea said.

"Ain't no principle in stealing," Granny said.

I paid close attention to the three of them all the time. Close enough to know I didn't understand them at all. They never agreed, but then again they did. Granny was the one I mimicked the most, the one I wanted to be just like. I believed she sat on the right-hand side of God and He whispered in her ear. I learned not to mimic Esther as much though. One day Granny caught me in the bedroom mirror trying to move my tail from side to side like Esther, and she slapped me in the back of the head, not hard, but hard enough.

"Sarah! Don't let me catch you doing that no more," she said.

I just about jumped up to the ceiling. "I ain't doing nothing," I said.

"Just don't do it no more," she said. "'Fore you end up like your mama." She hit the back of my head again. "Listen to your Granny if you want to stay out of trouble."

I wasn't trying to disobey her; I only wanted to know why Esther got into so much trouble. As far as I could tell, my hips didn't stick

8

out as far as hers yet, and my hair refused to cooperate. I attributed my hair's behavior to the head full of plaits and the array of colored rubber bands twisted at the end of each one of them. I watched Granny, Muhdea and Esther as if I was an outsider. They wouldn't allow me into their trio, not yet anyway. So I stayed quiet and out of their way. I could see and hear them but they didn't hear or see me.

Then after a couple of weeks of disappearing hogs, chickens and cows, we went on back to living as if nothing had happened. We pitched in and helped replace whatever they took to whomever they took it from. Then five or six months later, some other white person would be offended by the smell, and the white men would show up on our side of town again.

Esther and Uncle Robert were always someplace where they didn't have any business, hardheaded, disobedient, contrary. Folks said he was a tall, cool drink of water. Uncle Robert wasn't our blood relative. Muhdea took him in when he was a boy like she did with other kids. Some lasted and some didn't, but Uncle Robert stayed. Granny said he minded her better than Esther did but he was head-strong, and 'cause of that, he would learn plenty of lessons in life. I figured learning was a good thing, so it was okay to pattern myself after his behavior.

One day Esther was up there lurking around the combined jail-house, utility house and city hall being disobedient. She was prob-ably on some mission for our town activist, Mrs. Carrie Dilworth, Maeby's own version of Reverend Martin Luther King Jr., but Granny said she was nobody's reverend. Granny tolerated her from time to time, but they weren't friends and nobody knew the reason why. Anyway, Esther overheard the city council pass ordinances that would require us to get our side of town up to code by the end of the summer, which meant removing all animals except housepets out of the city limits and upgrading to flushable toilets, either outside or inside the home didn't matter except they must flush.

Esther was out of breath when she got home and told us about it. Muhdea got ahold of the pastor of the First Baptist Church, Reverend Jefferson, and he put the word out to meet at the church at seven o'clock sharp.

"Make sure at least one person from every household, and

each church denomination, Baptist, Methodist, Protestant, Jehovah Witness and Pentecostal, meet with us. If what Esther heard is true, we ain't got much time if we going to get all this done before revival," he said.

Esther gave the papers to Reverend Jefferson, and he took the copies as if he was the one who stole them from the city hall. Mrs. Carrie reminded everybody that Esther risked life and limb to get the papers.

"We should be proud of her," she said. "The least they would've done to her if they caught her would be to lock her up for God knows how long."

Mrs. Carrie talked slow and deliberate. She spoke to children and grown folks in the same manner, which was trying on me. It would be easy for me to fall asleep halfway through one of her sentences if I hadn't been taught to respect my elders. She and Granny looked so much alike they could've been first cousins. They were about the same height, but Mrs. Carrie's face and body were wider, and she wore her hair pulled straight back while Granny wore hers with a part down the middle and plaited on each side of her head. Mrs. Carrie spoke before the meeting started for she wouldn't be allowed to voice her opinion during a church meeting. Neither Esther nor Granny cared for that rule, but Reverend Jefferson was pretty good at running all other church business so Granny overlooked it, but Esther let her voice be heard whether anybody was listening or not.

Reverend Jefferson called the meeting to order. He stood at the podium in the pulpit still wearing his overalls. He rubbed his work-beaten hands across his face and head. The other preachers, including the jackleg ones like Mr. Stith, sat in the chairs behind him, except for the one female preacher, Miss Ora Bea, who sat on the front pew next to the mothers of the church. Reverend Jefferson began the service by reading a scripture from the Bible and delivering a prayer. Then he opened the meeting. "Well," he said. "It's good we know in advance. We knew that this day was coming and now it's upon us."

It was the first time I'd seen grown folks in church wearing their work clothes instead of their Sunday-go-to-meeting ones, and all of us kids were still wearing our play clothes. The deacons prayed.

It seemed like regular church, but nobody preached and the choir didn't sing. Reverend Jefferson told us what to do in the same manner as he gave us orders from the Bible.

"First, I need everybody to make a list of the type and number of animals that need to be moved. Second, whoever got room on they farm to house some of these animals give your name to Reverend Stith and let him know what type and how many you can hold."

By the time he was done, most of the deacons had instructions to come to church on Sunday with a compiled list including carpenters who had free time, where to go for supplies for the toilets, trucks for hauling and everything else Reverend Jefferson and the men could think of.

"You know where to find me if we missed anything," he said. He began his speech to close the doors of the church but then he stopped right after he got started. He scratched the deep wrinkles his forehead. "Go on 'bout your business as usual," he said. "Don't let on we heard nothing. They want us to be caught off guard. They want your livestock. We don't want to lose as much as a chicken with this move. Now, the one thing we not going to do is forget the Sabbath. We will continue to keep it holy."

The church clapped, and "Amen" roared through the crowd. Reverend Jefferson said a closing prayer and dismissed us.

Every preacher and deacon present struggled with at least two or three lists they were responsible for compiling by Sunday. During the week, there weren't very many men in town. All able-bodied men were off working, laying highways or putting up big office buildings throughout Arkansas and as far away as Georgia. The ones like my granddaddy, who was a foreman for the colored highway crew, worked all over Arkansas and were able to come home every weekend. Some of the others could only get home once a month, if that.

When the men were home, we made it nice for them, cooking, ironing, behaving, drawing bath water, and even Esther wore her dresses below the knee instead of pinned up. Miss Ora Bea and Mrs. Carrie were the exception. They weren't respectful of the way we treated the men. They gave them lip on any day of the week, and insisted on never taking a backseat. I didn't know what seat Mrs.

Carrie took at the Methodist Church, but at First Baptist Miss Ora Bea sat right on the pew next to the mothers. She might've called herself a preacher, but nobody else in town referred to her as reverend or pastor like they did Mr. Stith and the other men. I liked her though, and she knew her Bible. Granny said so and she liked her too. I believed Esther wanted to pattern herself after Miss Ora Bea and Mrs. Carrie but she wasn't old enough yet.

Uncle Robert gave Esther half of his lists to complete. It was reported that the other men shared their lists with the women as well. No way we could get it all done unless everybody helped out. I followed Uncle Robert around while he worked on his list. He was always in town on account of his illness. He didn't look sick most of the time, but he did take to his bed on occasion when he didn't take his medicine. They called his illness "Sugar." It was the kind folks didn't say out loud like when Granny called me to bring her the sugar for the cake, the tea, the Kool-Aid. When they talked about Uncle Robert's "Sugar," they whispered in each other's ear as if his "Sugar" was a secret. He preferred to act as if he were as healthy and strapping as the men who went off to work, and that's how I treated him except for them occasions when he took to his bed, and then I waited on him hand and foot. Orange juice seemed to make him feel much better.

Mr. Stith gathered up the lists and Reverend Jefferson gave every household their marching orders. He requested that the men come home every weekend till all the work was done. Their biggest project was the toilets. The men could start cutting down trees and preparing and treating the wood, but they needed to be careful, put everything away, and they couldn't be caught taking or bringing nothing from the country till we got the word from the city council. He didn't want the white folks to catch on to our plans like we did theirs, so the other preachers needed to make sure they didn't have any tattlers in their mix. He told the owners of the juke joints to keep their customers in line, and he gave Bro Hollin instructions to keep an eye out for his field hands and the folks who didn't go to church or to the juke joints like him. We were going to meet every Sunday after church service, Christians and sinners alike till we got the job done.

"Reverend Stith got the major list," he said. "Y'all check in with him regularly. We moving a few animals at night, little by little, so nobody will notice it."

I was with Esther when she met with Mrs. Carrie and Reverend Jefferson on Back Street, in front of Mrs. Carrie's house. They didn't believe he should start moving any animals to the country.

"We can win this in court," Mrs. Carrie said. "These ordinances they passed are illegal."

Reverend Jefferson disagreed with her. "Whenever this go down, Carrie," he said, "you do what you have to do, but I ain't risking the little bit these folks got over your shenanigans."

Mrs. Carrie protested. Esther wasn't allowed to talk back to her elders. In the end, he walked on down the road and left Mrs. Carrie in the middle of her sentence.

We got the word from the white people a few weeks later. Most of the folks had complied with Reverend Jefferson's orders. When the city council summoned Reverend Jefferson, Mr. Stith and a few other preachers to a meeting, they put on their Sunday-go-to-meeting suits, walked uptown together, and brought back the orders from the council to us.

Mrs. Carrie rustled up a few folks from the low end of town to protest the ordinances, including Esther, Miss Ora Bea and Bro Hollin. While we were obeying Reverend Jefferson and the white masters, she sought the advice of an NAACP lawyer. I reminded myself to look up NAACP in the encyclopedia.

"Mrs. Carrie, me and the others going to picket at the city hall," Esther said. She stood in the middle of the living room floor, right after supper, and said it as if she were delivering the church announcements. "Will you join us, Robert?"

"You can't be sure how your plans will turn out," he said. "There's a lot of physical work to be done and only a few men around here to do it. I want to support you and I want you to win, but just in case you don't, I wouldn't feel right if I stood by while folks lose all their belongings."

Esther flung her head around before she walked out the door and said, "I can't believe you, Robert. For real."

The following day every man, woman and child got to work doing whatever they could, laboring day and night to finish the projects. I ran back and forth helping everybody. By now, I could hammer a straight nail as good as anybody else. I worked alongside Granny most of the time unless Muhdea or Uncle Robert needed me. I rounded up the animals and put them in the cages we built out of chicken wire. Uncle Robert rode on the back of the trucks with the men, and they transported the animals to the farms. While we were running around fixing toilets and moving livestock, Esther switched out the door and said she was going to the city hall. Muhdea and Granny both shook their heads. Like Uncle Robert, I knew my place was to help Granny and Muhdea, but I sure did want to know what it meant to picket the city hall. It wasn't unusual for Esther not to take me with her. She never did for me what I saw other mamas do for their kids. Granny combed my hair, laid out my clothes, and chastised me.

Then a few weeks later, out of the blue, Esther announced that she was leaving town on the Continental Trailways bus. "I got an art scholarship," she said. We were all at the table eating breakfast, getting ready for another long day's work.

Uncle Robert wasn't surprised, and he said as much. "I knew it. You always been a good artist," he said. "I'm proud of you."

Esther was always drawing and painting pictures that looked like us. She painted the stained-glass windows at the church. Her other seven sisters lived in Kansas City. She was the only one who never left town. Granny shook her head as she always did when it came to Esther. Muhdea left out the back screen door and slammed it behind her. Esther had better be careful. Slamming doors wasn't a good sign.

That night as she packed her suitcase Esther told me she was leaving the next morning. "I'm doing this for us. I won't be gone long," she said. "You understand?"

"I guess," I said, but I didn't know why she was leaving when we still had so much work to do, or why she was explaining it to me. She finished packing, and we walked to the living room, where Muhdea lit into her.

"I know it's more to it than what you letting on," Muhdea said. "Robert, what you know about this?"

He tried to explain that Esther had been applying to art colleges every since she graduated from high school. "Ain't nothing here for her. You have to let her go."

The next morning Muhdea came into the kitchen and told me to come with her. "We walking your mama up to the highway."

We all went, Esther, Muhdea, Granny, Uncle Robert and me. Uncle Robert carried Esther's brown-striped suitcase. We crossed the churchyard and took the trail between Mr. Buddy's and Mr. Matthew's white houses. We passed by the city hall on our way to Highway 65. Esther stopped to say goodbye to Mrs. Carrie and the four other folks who were walking around in a circle carrying signs with slogans written on them. Miss Ora Bea said a prayer for Esther. Bro Hollin wished her well. He told her not to take any wooden nickels. It was my first time seeing the other man and woman, and nobody introduced them to me. Both of them told Esther she made the right decision.

As we walked away, they waved at Esther for a good while. I read a couple of the signs aloud: "Livestock deserve equal rights," and "Our animals are our pets too."

"Are they picketing city hall?" I said. "Is carrying a sign all it is to it?"

"No," Esther said. "It's more meaning to it than what you can see but I don't have time to explain it now. Robert, will you tell her for me later?"

We walked with Esther on up to the highway. We waited a while before we saw the bus speeding toward us. When Esther and Uncle Robert saw it coming, they flagged it down. The man in uniform pulled over to the side of the highway, got off the bus, took Esther's suitcase, and placed it in the luggage compartment. She held my face between her hands and placed her nose close to it. Her eyes were big, and today they were a grayish blue and light brown. They changed colors all the time. She smelled like lavender. I couldn't recall ever being that close to her.

"Be good, Sarah, till I come back and get you," she said and kissed me on the lips. I wondered why she acted so sappy with me. "Don't forget me, and don't believe everything Muhdea and Granny tell you. Go to Robert when you have a question."

I watched her as she got on the bus, waved to us, and blew kisses as the bus pulled out onto the highway. We never kissed or blew kisses before, and acting sappy out in public was uncalled for.

"Your mama always got to show out," Muhdea said when we turned back toward home.

"Well, we'll miss her," Granny said. She wiped her eyes with the back of her hands.

"We sure will," Uncle Robert said. He placed his hand on my shoulder. "Alright, Sarah?"

Granny caught hold of my hand and squeezed it. "Sarah be just fine," she said.

I looked up at Uncle Robert and told him as if he didn't hear her. "Granny said I'll be just fine."

At church that Sunday, Muhdea told Reverend Jefferson Esther had left town. "We put her on the bus yesterday." He already knew.

"We'll add her name to the prayer list at every service," he said. "Don't you worry, sister, God will watch over her and keep her safe. She resilient likes the rest of us folks. We fall down but we gets up. For show. We resilient folks."

The only services where they didn't call Esther's name for prayer were Baptist Training Union and Wednesday-night Bible Study. I reckoned she would be alright 'cause the whole church prayed for her at eight services per week, and we prayed at home too. I figured the church members who always laid hands on Esther and me, prayed to God to relieve us of our sins and sprinkled us with holy water most every time they saw us would continue to bless me and lay hands on me even though Esther was gone.

By the time we finished constructing toilets and herding livestock like the men on the TV show *Rawhide*, it was almost time for revival. We didn't lose even a chicken, as Reverend Jefferson prophesized. White folks said they could finally tell the smell of our town from that of the paper mill. We moved the last of the pigs to the farm the day before revival started that August, 1959, which was a blessing 'cause whether we finished or not, all things except the Lord's work came to a complete halt during revival.

I admired the new commode in our outhouse. We started calling it a restroom and began using store-bought tissue instead of news-papers and brown paper sacks. A few weeks after revival, the white people held a parade in honor of the clean fresh smell in the air. In time, the parade turned into the annual Turtle Derby and people gathered from all over the state to our fairgrounds to watch and bet their money on painted turtle races.

CHAPTER TWO

I'll Come See You

MUHDEA STAYED MAD most of the time after Esther left town. Before, her anger was split between the two of them and now all of it plus some extra was geared toward Uncle Robert. I talked back to her and acted out at church so she would fuss at me instead of him, but she didn't. Granny tried to get her to watch her tongue with him. Folks hired him to do handy work and landscaping around their homes after the animals were gone. Some of them chose to build a bathroom onto their house. If Muhdea was on a rampage when he came home from working, Granny met him at the door and warned him to come back after she went to bed. Soon he began coming home late at night and at times was gone for the entire weekend.

It didn't take long before he started acting like he did before the city passed the ordinance. Granny said he chose the Devil over his medicine. She found both of them in his dresser drawer. Folks said Uncle Robert was "a cool drank of water," over six foot tall, and could pass for a white man if he wanted to, the thought of which pissed him off. But he started to look haggard, worn out. His clothes hung on his body and dark circles formed around his eyes. His color got darker too. When he did come home on Friday and Saturday nights, he tried to climb the walls. I saw him attempt it with my own eyes and pleaded with him to stop.

"You can't climb no wall," I said as I pulled the bottom of his shirt. "You ain't no roach or ant. Get down from there."

"Go away, Sarah," he said. "Hide under the bed. I got to go after them." He scratched off the wallpaper with his nails.

"Settle down before you lose your mind," I said.

Granny brought him a can of orange juice from the kitchen and poured it down his throat. She was the only person who could get him to quiet down. Muhdea quit trying months ago. We sat on the couch and rocked with him till he fell asleep. Afterward, Granny sent me for a quilt to cover him with. The next morning he didn't remember any of it. I found him in the kitchen making coffee before he went to work. Muhdea came in and sat at the table. She spoke to him in a kind voice, which startled me.

"Robert, the Lord lives in this house, and I won't have you disrespecting Him," she said. "Nobody here, and especially not Sarah, need to see you the way you was last night. You act like you don't believe me when I say I ain't putting up with your foolishness much longer, so you better start acting like the man I know you can be."

He straightened up after that night, and Muhdea lightened up on fussing at him for every little thing he did. We were glad to have him back. He filled up the empty space Esther left. I believe Granny and Muhdea were beginning to miss Esther a lot less. I rarely heard anyone call her name except for when the church emcee called the names on the prayer list. Then a few months later, Uncle Robert sat us down to tell us the big news. He was jumping off the rafters with excitement. I braced myself wondering if he was going to climb the walls again.

"I've joined up with the Nation of Islam," he said, as if we knew what he meant. "And I'm moving to Little Rock with my brothers."

Muhdea wasn't clear on whom he was joining up with, or why he decided to leave town.

"Little Rock?" she said. "Why you got to leave, and who is this Nation?" She looked as if she'd found two identical pieces of a puzzle but neither one of them fit. "It's just too far away, Robert. I don't know these folks, never heard of them. You, Granny?"

Me and Granny shook our heads.

"What is it, Robert? We should talk to Reverend Jefferson before you make any rash decision. How did you hear about these folks?" She strutted back and forth across the living room floor as if she was trying to catch time.

"My mind is made up. This is the best thing for me. One of the brothers is picking me up tomorrow," Uncle Robert said. He was as calm as Peter was when he walked on water.

"Brothers? You ain't got no brothers," Muhdea said. "Maybe a couple of sisters. What's got into you, son?"

"The Honorable Elijah Muhammad is the Messenger, and Malcolm X is one of the ministers. Haven't you heard of them?"

Muhdea tapped her foot. He better hurry up and turn it around if he didn't want her mad at him again.

"No, I ain't heard of them. Is that what you been doing? Running up behind folks you heard talk? What is it, boy, a cult, another type of religion? I swear, if I hadn't raised you and Esther myself." She raised both hands over her head as if she wanted to give up. "Do they believe in Jesus?"

I hoped for his sake they did. I scooted to the edge of my seat.

"Not in the same way you do," he said. It wasn't till then that I noticed that all of his pretty hair was gone. His head was bald, and he wore a dark suit and bowtie. I pointed at him, trying to bring it to Granny's attention, but she shook her head, no.

I gripped my seat and waited. Whites, coloreds and Christians lived in Maeby, and not Muslims, Jews, Catholics or people of any other religion. That day Uncle Robert told us as much as we wanted to know about the Nation of Islam, which wasn't much. It was a religious movement spreading rapidly throughout the country, empowering black people. He spoke highly of their leader but focused more on a man who was quickly becoming the voice of the Nation, Malcolm X. Uncle Robert studied the Holy Qur'an with a few brothers from Little Rock. His last name, Jones, was no longer fitting for him, which cut me deep 'cause our last names were the same. His last name was now X till he earned another one. They believed Jesus to be a prophet, but He wasn't the Son of God. I thought Muhdea would pop a blood vessel when he said that. One of their goals was business ownership, and his teacher and the members of the mosque helped to financially support his purchase of a ceramic shop. He didn't know the Holy Qur'an through and through like we did the Bible. It was new to him, but he believed in it whole-heartedly. He took it seriously, and we should, too.

That day we sat there dumfounded as he carried on about his brothers we'd never met. Even the Nation's dietary constraints were unusual to us. Eating pork and catfish was forbidden, he told us. Muhdea asked if he also meant her pork chops. People came from all across the county to eat her pork chops, waited for her if they arrived before her shift started at the café, and would go buy the meat if they ran out of it.

Muhdea and Granny pleaded with him. Granny even pushed me to ask him to change his mind.

"You told Esther that you would look after Sarah," Granny said.

His face grew long, and sadness covered it. I thought he was going to cry, and I would've done anything for him not to do that.

"It's okay with me if you move away. I'll come see you," I said.

Those were the last words spoken that night. The next day Uncle Robert packed up his belongings in boxes and waited for his brothers. Muhdea was at work when they got there. Granny watched them as if she wanted to snatch the box away from him. Uncle Robert rubbed her back with his hand.

"Don't," Granny said and walked away from him.

"You be a big girl, Sarah," he said. "I'm only a couple hours away if you need me."

We didn't walk him out to the road. Instead, we sat on the couch and stared at the wall. I didn't feel much different after Esther left home, but Uncle Robert leaving left a hole in me. Within two years Muhdea's hardheaded, contrary, disobedient children were gone, and we didn't know when or if they were ever coming home again.

SUMMER 1964

CHAPTER THREE

Your Mama Called Last Night

IT WAS THE summer of 1964, and I was eight years old. Granny measured me against her body. My head touched the top of her elbow. "You growing like a weed," she said. "All legs like your mama." All legs like you, I thought. It was hard for me to picture Esther. She sent us a letter every few months but she wasn't able to make it back home since she left. Whenever she wrote that she was coming, one thing or the other always came up, and she didn't make it. I figured since over a year ago the mothers quit sprinkling holy water and laying hands on me that it was 'bout time I get baptized and take responsibility for my own sins. No telling what Esther was doing up there in Chicago. Granny and Muhdea thought she wasn't up to any good. The church must've believed she was living a life of sin since her name remained at the top of every prayer list. Uncle Robert's name was also on the prayer list too, but only at the eleven o'clock and the Sunday-night service. His was in the middle of the list, probably 'cause he came back every few months and folks could see he was doing fine even if he still talked all that foolishness. I practiced the speech I planned to say to Granny and Muhdea about why they should give me permission to sit on the Mourner's Bench come revival. As long as I could come up with reasons why they wouldn't agree with me, I knew it wasn't ready so I rewrote the weak portions of my argument.

Last month Reverend Jefferson preached on the sins of the mother and father. He said the mother and father needed to be Christians, to be baptized and forgiven for their sins on account of they carried the sins of their children till the child turned thirteen.

"Now think on that," he said. "If you passed on while you was still living in sin and your child wasn't of age, all his sins would come rushing in on him." He woke me out of my sleep as he always did when he got to whooping and hollering near the end of his sermon. "That ain't no way to treat your children. And you can't just talk the talk, you gots to walk the walk just like Jesus."

Right after he said that, he opened the doors of the church. "Anyone out there who is living in sin, any of you that's been backsliding, pick up your net and follow Jesus right now."

A couple of backsliders moseyed down to the front of the pulpit, and some others went up for prayer. The other sinners, who weren't baptized, knew they would have to wait till revival, where they would ask God to show them a sign as an indication He had forgiven them of their sins. Sit on the Mourner's Bench till He revealed their sign to them, get up before the church, give their testimony, and get baptized the following Sunday at the Jericho River. Afterward, they were required to live a life without sin like Jesus did when he walked the earth.

Although I knew all about sin, Reverend Jefferson's words struck me that day. He lit a fire under me, and I was bound and determined to not let another revival pass without getting my religion. At First Baptist, children started praying when they turned twelve and were baptized by age thirteen. But as I pondered on what Reverend Jefferson said and searched the Bible for the scriptures (it would be shameful if anybody knew I didn't know my Bible), I came to believe that if Esther was on eight prayer lists, my soul was at risk of going to Hell. I needed to hurry up and take responsibility for my sins. Neither Esther nor me was living like Jesus did, and I knew what happened to folks who lived and died in sin. Reverend Jefferson clearly said the mother and father and not the grandparents. Muhdea and Granny should've insisted that I get baptized. They knew my salvation was in jeopardy, and we shouldn't be biding our time, waiting for Esther to come into the house of the Lord. Granny and Muhdea didn't even want to speculate on what she was doing without their guidance. So, after I studied on it, and wrote the questions I didn't know on my list, I made up my mind to ask Granny if I could start praying and asking God to forgive me for my sins.

I practiced my speech the same as I did my vocabulary words and reading. I read for hours every day, every chance I got, whenever I wasn't doing chores, changing children's clothes and caring for babies. Sometime after Esther left, my aunts started bringing their babies home for us to care for till they could find better jobs in Kansas City. We looked after nine children. I made up stories and read them to the babies. Granny told me a man she knew named Louis Armstrong practiced the horn till he became better at it than everybody else. "Seems like you like reading and writing as much as he did that horn, so we giving you as much time as we can spare to do it. But we expecting you to be the best in your class."

Granny and Muhdea asked me to read the Bible and the Sunday-school lesson to them every Saturday evening. I carried a Bible everywhere I went just in case anybody else wanted to hear me read, but nobody ever did except Sister Tucker. Folks thought I carried it 'cause I was planning on becoming a saint. Sister Tucker was our only neighbor who'd gone to college, and she told me that if I could pronounce every word in the Bible, I would be able to read anything else with ease, even foreign languages. Reading could take me places in life and in my mind. Knowing my Bible served two purposes. I wanted to be a saint like Muhdea, and I wanted to be an expert at reading like Mr. Armstrong was at playing his horn.

My reading expertise paid off when Mr. Matthew Graves, superintendent of the Sunday school, asked me to be its acting secretary. He told me Sister Tucker was getting on in years, and since, for the last year, I sat next to her when she read the minutes and because I read the minutes on fifth Sunday, I was his first choice.

"Do you think you can take it on?" he said. "I already spoke to Muhdea 'bout it."

He and Muhdea kept their heads together plotting church business, with her being the head mother and him the superintendent and head deacon. The secretary wrote down the business of the Sunday school in a meeting book, counted the collections from each class, and read the minutes to the congregation. "I'll sit with you until you get the hang of it," Sister Tucker said. I said yes to her sitting with me for a while till I caught on, but I knew how to do it. I coveted her position from the first time I read the minutes.

"I ain't saved yet," I said. "Can I do it if I ain't a member?"

"It'll be temporary," Mr. Matthew said. "You'll be alright till we find somebody."

After I agreed to be the acting secretary, I wrote on my list to find out the difference between temporary and permanent members. Why did I have to be saved to become a member of the church? Was doing a temporary assignment similar to Esther carrying my sins till I turned thirteen? I also added a page with two columns and started keeping a tally of when I did or didn't sin. My best friend, Malika, who kept a notebook too, disagreed with me keeping a tally.

"Nobody adds up how they behave," she said. "I ain't keeping up with that."

One of her aunts, who lived in Chicago, named her Malika, and I got sick of hearing her talk about it. She believed it was so special to have a name that meant "queen."

"My aunt said that whenever the white man calls me by my name, they'll be calling me queen," she said. "That's how little they know about who we are, African queens. And even if they don't know it, they'll be calling me one."

"That don't mean you no queen though," I said.

I wished that my name meant something. When I complained to Granny, she told me I was named after Sarah, in the Bible, one of God's favorites. I knew the story of Sarah, and I shared it with Malika.

"Malika might be an African queen, but she ain't God's favorite," I said.

We argued about our names and the extra pages I added to my notebook, which we called "Things I'll Know When I Get Grown." I'd picked up a penchant for cussing from Granny, and I made a check whenever I said a few unkind words. Mainly, I kept track 'cause Esther's credit with the Lord was pretty bad, and I needed to know where I stood with Him.

I got to liking being the acting secretary so much that if both Jesus and the Lord asked me to give it up, I'd hide it behind my back, and they'd have to take it from me, which I knew was a sin. Granny and Muhdea supported me more after I started to read in public. They made all kinds of allowances for me when my head was stuck in a book, but I still did all my chores, and I didn't take advantage of them. It didn't occur to me till later, but as I studied on it, I decided to include becoming the permanent secretary in my plea to Granny to let me get baptized.

As far as I could tell, we were all fine. Muhdea said it to folks all the time when they inquired about our day, our health and our mamas. Although Esther didn't come home or send for me to come live with her as she promised, she was still my mama, as Muhdea reminded me whenever folks mentioned it to her. She was in school and would do better, when she found a job that paid more money. The first time Muhdea told me that 'cause Esther changed her mind after she wrote that she was on her way, and I believed her, and I cried on Granny's chest till she told me to dry my tears. She didn't ever want to see me cry over nobody who didn't keep her word to me again. When Esther kept promising over and over that she was moving back home, I quit paying her any mind. I wouldn't have paid much attention to it, but Granny interrupted me while I was reading and she sounded serious.

Granny called me with a sense of urgency in her voice. I was sitting at the kitchen table practicing reading the Sunday-school lesson and every now and again making a note on my list of "Things I'll Know When I Get Grown."

"Sarah," Granny said. When I didn't answer, she called again. "Sarah, come in here and let me talk to you for a minute."

I tucked my notes between the pages of my Sunday-school book, bumped my knee on the corner of the old wood table, peeped out the window into the backyard and counted six cousins ranging from ages three to five, with their hands clasped as they circled the slop can playing Ring around the Rosy. They seemed fine. What could she want? I would normally have an idea and prepare an answer ahead of time. Maybe she wanted me to change one of the babies' diapers.

That wasn't a good enough reason to stop me from studying. I'd talked to Muhdea earlier in the week about me getting my religion at the upcoming revival, but we didn't settle on nothing. She wouldn't have approached Granny about it, not yet anyway.

My other three cousins were asleep in the baby pen, an old patched quilt concoction fixed in the middle of the living room for as long as I could remember. Granny rubbed her hand up and down the cracked, orange vinyl davenport we called a "deb-nit." She caught hold of a string of the silver duct tape we used to patch the hole, wrapped it around her finger and pulled it out.

"Sit down right here beside me, baby."

I eased down next to her, away from the crack with the wire sticking up. My mind was still on the lesson about David and Goliath.

"What you say got you so caught up in there?" she said.

"It's just the Sunday-school lesson."

"Well." Granny stalled and resituated her toothbrush.

"What you need?" I said. I began rebraiding one of her long, mixed-gray plaits.

When she didn't try to grab the plait away from me, I finished and then turned the palms of her hands face up to see if she wanted play a game of Slaps. She wasn't interested. I could tell something was wrong, and hoped I wasn't the one who done it. I tried to yank the toothbrush out of her mouth. If the other kids were here, we'd take turns, but we weren't ever quick enough to grab it before Granny turned her head, or gripped it with her three brownish teeth, two at the bottom and a loose one up top.

I made Granny's toothbrushes from the thin branches of the Nellie Stevens holly trees. I cut two inches off the branch for each toothbrush. Then I shaved off the bark and boiled them in water. When they became soft, I chewed one end till it frayed. Granny stirred the frayed end in her snuff jar and put it in her mouth.

"Hand me my snuff, baby," Granny said.

Was that all she wanted? I thought. She called me in here to get her snuff. I felt her forehead.

"You feeling sick?"

"Why you ask?" she said.

"No reason." She wasn't ready. I waited. I wanted to tell her to stop slow-poking around and tell me. David and Goliath were waiting on me in the kitchen.

She wound the couch string around the tip of her finger till it was red. Since she wasn't getting to the point, my mind wandered off like it did at school when I knew the answer way before the rest of the class. I tried to control the nervousness hammering up and down my stomach.

"Sarah." She rubbed my thigh. "Ain't but one way of telling you this and that's to go ahead." She stopped for a few seconds and gazed across the living room.

"Go ahead, Granny. I'm listening."

"Well, Mozelle." She paused for a long time, then started over. "Your grandmama said . . ."

"Muhdea?" I said.

Granny never called Muhdea by her first name even though she was her daughter. Why was she stuttering around the issue? What did I do that was so bad?

"Muhdea, Mozelle," she said as if I were making her mad. "How many grands you think I'm talking bout?"

The nerves battling in my stomach jumped up to my throat and out of my mouth. I regurgitated everything I knew and I didn't say one word of the speech I wrote.

"Me and Muhdea talked about the revival. I didn't ask her to come to you. Ain't no decisions been made. No need to get into it today."

Granny snickered a bit and covered her mouth with her wrinkled fingers. "Hush, gal, you telling on yourself." She twisted my plait. "That ain't what this is 'bout, but don't think I ain't heard the whispers."

Why was she slow dragging? She promised to spit it right out. Reverend Jefferson's sermons were shorter than this. Then, as if it came from unstuck in her throat, she blurted it all out.

"Muhdea told me this morning that your mama called her last night at Sister Tucker's store and said she's coming home."

"Esther?" I said.

"What is it with you today? You act as if you don't know nobody," she said.

I was thinking on how to hurry Granny along and get back to David and Goliath, but Esther's name wiped it right out of my head.

"When she coming?"

"It might be as early as this week or the next," Granny said.

"She bringing another baby home? I bet she bringing a baby and going right back up there like my aunts do," I said.

"I don't think it's nothing like a baby," she said. "At least I hope not, but you can't ever tell with your mama."

A redbird sat on the window sill. Perspiration ran down both our faces. One of the babies turned over on its side and yawned.

"Granny, you my mama now, right?" I said.

According to Reverend Jefferson, we were supposed to mind our mama first before our grandmama. The Bible said to honor thy mother and father.

"Will I have to mind her, let her comb my hair, and call her mama?"

Most of us called folks by whatever name everybody else called them. Nobody insisted on it one way or the other. We just fell into it, and stuck with it. Most everybody called my grandmama Muhdea and my great-grandmama Granny. Mostly only strangers or white folks ever said their real names, Mozelle and Pearlie.

"I'll do my best to stand between y'all," Granny said. "She's your mama and ain't no changing that. You have to behave yourself, obey her."

"Why do I have to? She ain't been here. And she never told me the truth about why she didn't send for me," I said. I got more and more riled up as I talked. "Can I just roll my eyes at her? Do I have to mind her?"

All I could think of was how things changed since Esther left home. Folks didn't pray over me no more. The superintendent of the Sunday school selected me as the acting secretary. I was ranked first in my classes. The school decided I was too smart for my class and double promoted me from the first to the third grade.

"Did Muhdea tell you anything else? Can we pray she don't come?"

"No, that's all Muhdea said. Since she called, I think you better prepare for her this time." She wound the couch string around her finger again. As if I weren't there, she said, "Lord, I hope Esther Mae don't get mixed up with Carrie Dilworth and them freedom workers."

"Freedom workers? You talking about the folks in town from SNCC, the civil rights workers?"

"Who? What you say they name is?" she said.

"SNCC," I said and told her what each letter meant. "Student Non-Violent Coordinating Committee. Folks been talking about them, but ain't nobody I spoke to heard much from them."

"Freedom, civil rights, whatever it was you said, makes no differ-ence to me. It all spells trouble." She wandered off again. Then she told me I could leave. "You go on back and finish reading your story."

Folks said Mrs. Carrie Dilworth brought three SNCC organizers to town. As far as I knew, a few folks spotted them at Mrs. Carrie's, but the whole town was up in an uproar about them. Folks said it was two boys and a girl. The girl and one of the boys were white, and the other boy was colored. Reverend Jefferson called them "the evil among us." No Christian should get mixed up with evildoers.

I stood at the kitchen door pondering on what Granny told me. Ever since Esther left home, I had worked right alongside Granny, taking care of babies, cleaning, gardening, chopping wood, helping the kids with homework, and listening in on grown folks' conversa-tions till they caught me. I overheard whether the grocery money was short, and if Deacon Macon's breath smelled at church last Sunday.

"Sarah," Granny said, breaking my thoughts. "Don't you sass your mama when she gets here. You hear?"

"Yes, ma'am," I said but didn't mean it.

I sat down at the table, closed the Sunday-school book on David, opened my notebook of "Things I'll Know When I Get Grown" and replaced the pages I hid under my Sunday-school book.

I turned to the next page and placed ten checkmarks under the Hell column for wishing my mama wasn't coming home. Then I flipped back to the page of "Things I'll Know" and wrote question number sixty-six, *Why do mamas leave their babies?* Number sixty-seven, *What happens to the daughter when her mama comes back home?*

I dragged my book satchel to the table and placed the books in it one by one. Seemed as if they gained weight. I'd always imagined David skipping to the ring to meet Goliath. Reverend Jefferson had preached about the weight of the stones many times. As I picked up each book, I imagined David as he chose his weapons. I wondered if the stones grew heavier as he got closer to Goliath. Was the tension in the sling tighter than ever before? I placed the last of the five books in my bag, still thinking about David, when it occurred to me that God had anointed him, and if God could protect David from Goliath, I was sure He could save me from Esther. All I needed to do was get baptized, so I could be responsible for my own sins. That way I wouldn't have to answer to Esther. Then I'd receive my marching orders directly from God. It seemed to me that God wouldn't make me mind her if she wasn't minding Him. If she was behaving herself, Reverend Jefferson would take her name off at least half of the prayer lists. I decided to beg Granny to let me get baptized. Not only would God protect me from Esther, but I could become the permanent secretary of the Sunday school too and gain ownership of my own sins.

CHAPTER FOUR

We're Going to Make a Mosaic

I LOOKED IN the backyard for the kids 'cause I didn't hear them playing. My heart raced a bit when they weren't there. Then I heard their voices coming from the side of the house. I rushed to the front door so I could head them off from going out to the road and send them to the backyard. I looked toward the church, and nothing. I saw a redbird flitting around on the roof. I blew it a kiss for love 'cause it was bad luck if I didn't. What a great sign, I thought. I'll ask God to send two redbirds sitting side-by-side atop of the roof of the church as a sign for His forgiveness for my sins. I rarely saw two of them together. It would be a true sign. But redbirds could bring bad luck too if you didn't perform rituals for them, so I decided against it.

My cousins ran from the side of the house toward the church ground. I yelled at them, "Come back here. Granny, hurry up. Help me. They running 'cross the road."

Granny opened the screen door, and I saw a woman walking down the trail. One of my cousins grabbed hold of her suitcase. I vaguely recognized the brown stripes. They wrapped themselves around her legs, almost wrestled her to the ground. *Have they lost their ever-loving minds?* They knew better than to accost a stranger. Who was that woman anyway, wearing hot pants and switching like that around here? I slowed to a walk. My, wasn't she tall and pretty, charcoal black, with hair down to her waist. Granny was right behind me, both of us calling the kids to come back.

"Get back here. You going to get a whipping," I said.

As we got closer, I realized the woman was Esther. I picked up my speed, and then I started running to meet her the same as the other kids were doing. Granny did, too. Before I reached her, I remembered and backed down, but Granny went on to greet her and grabbed her suitcase from my cousin.

"Esther Mae," she said. She patted her shoulder. "You made it home. Good Lord, she home."

I WATCHED HER. A few times, she almost caught me staring her down. When she walked toward the kitchen, I was right on her heels. Granny called her name, and she stopped suddenly. I was able to back up before I bumped into her. Before Granny could ask me, I told her I was on my way to the kitchen, and before she could ask me what for, I said to get some lye soap. What Granny wanted with Esther was more important than calling me out. And since I wasn't on my way to get soap, and revival was lurking in the back of my mind, I went on to the kitchen and picked up the soap as if God couldn't see right through me even if Granny chose to ignore why I needed soap in the middle of the day. I eased out to the backyard in case it dawned on Granny that I'd told a story.

I couldn't keep my eyes off Esther. I knew she was up to no good, and I'd rather see it coming than be caught off guard. She started dragging me up and down the road behind her. I wanted to go, but I didn't want to either. If I went, I could keep an eye on her, but Granny needed me at home, and Esther kept me out for hours. Granny was left to do my work and hers. When we were together, Esther took the liberty to talk to me and ask me questions about myself that I didn't care to hear or answer, most of them geared around why I was so serious all the time, and why I cared so much about religion as if I were an old woman.

"Come on, Sarah," Esther said when she came out to the backyard.

I'd stopped asking her where we were going 'cause that led to a long lesson on her being the mama and me the daughter. I didn't understand what me wanting to know where I was headed had to do with her being my mama. It was my body trailing up behind her, and I had a right to know, and decide if I wanted to follow her or not. Of course, she didn't see it that way, so I found myself in places where

I'd rather not be, like listening to her, Miss Ora Bea, and Mrs. Carrie talk for hours about the difference between the feminist movement and the civil rights movement, and why a colored woman should show allegiance to the civil rights movement. Esther disagreed with Mrs. Carrie. She argued that a black woman must demand both feminist and civil rights. Mrs. Carrie Dilworth said she'd been an activist way before Esther was born.

"I was there during the Elaine murders," she said. "And I traveled throughout the country on behalf of the Southern Tenants' Farmers Union, so you might think I know more about organizing than you. Our strength is in being focused on the bigger picture. We need to have an equal playing field before we can make any other demands."

Miss Ora Bea, the preacher, agreed with Mrs. Carrie. She played with her ponytail, which lay across her shoulder, plaiting, unplaiting and replaiting the tail of it over and over.

"When we get civil rights, it will take care of the women, too," she said.

It was the worst thing she could've said to Esther. "They are exclusive, not one and the same. Why can't you see that?" She stood up and said it as if standing would help get her point across.

They went round and round for hours on how to achieve one or the other or both, and I wondered how children's rights fit into it 'cause all I wanted to do was go home and I couldn't. I erred on the side of Mrs. Carrie. Esther couldn't argue with her history. I didn't see how anybody took Esther serious strutting around in them miniskirts and hot pants, showing way too much skin, and smoking them Winston cigarettes.

Malika was visiting her sister in Chicago, and I wished she was home. Folks said when they saw one of us, they saw the other one, but that was during the winter. Every summer she left town right after school let out. We could've struck up our own debate as to what we thought they meant, but to sit and listen to them go over the same thing was way too much for me by myself. And whenever I dozed off, or they thought I wasn't paying attention, one of them said I needed to hear this or did I hear that, did I understand.

I did want to know why these feminist women were so different and demanded more than a regular colored woman, but I didn't ask, for I knew it would lead to another hour or two of explanations, in which they would've been honored to break down every detail. I remembered enough of their conversation to tell Granny and Muhdea, and I wrote what I didn't understand on my list of "Things I'll Know When I Get Grown."

"They just like the sound of their own voice," Granny said. "Don't pay them no mind."

Granny couldn't figure out what Esther was up to by what I told her, but she still asked me every time I got home. "They say the same thing every time? You sure you ain't leaving out nothing?"

She inquired about the SNCC organizers, but I hadn't seen them. Mrs. Carrie said they were at her old two-story house. She'd donated it to the cause. The SNCC organizers were down there fixing it up, and it would be ready to hold meetings soon.

Esther added a new project, something we could do together that was supposed to be a lot of fun for both of us, picking up broken, colored pieces of glass off the side of the road. She swore I was going to love it, our first mother-daughter project.

"We're going to make a mosaic," she said. She noticed my blank stare. "Oh, you'll see. You're going to love it."

She was more upbeat and perky than folks were around here. Maybe it was 'cause we worked all day, and she flipped around town, like a catfish on a carving table, running her mouth.

We walked up one road and down the other picking up glass. Some folks started saving pieces of glass for her. They kept the glass · till she stopped by to pick it up the same as they saved slop for our hogs. Maybe they thought she'd give them a piece of the mosaic like we did our meat after we slaughtered the hogs. Or maybe they wanted to see what it took so much glass to make. She told me to come up with some ideas for a design. How could I come up with a design for something I had no idea what it was? I only owned the encyclopedias up to the letter H, and school was closed for the summer, or I would've looked it up.

I didn't enjoy walking down the roads during the middle of the day with temperatures skyrocketing, looking in ditches, pulling back weeds, prowling through trashcans for colored glass. I figured I wouldn't enjoy anything we'd do with it after we collected enough to make whatever she called a mosaic. She promised to show me pictures of ones she'd made. "I prefer it if you use your imagination. What comes to mind when you look at the glass?" Nothing, I thought.

More folks started saving pieces for her, which led to longer talks in hot kitchens and on front porches listening to secular music, a blind boy called Little Stevie Wonder and a man named Smokey Robinson mostly. I took to sticking a book in my panties and going to the restroom to read it while they talked. I was sure they wanted to ask Esther what was wrong with my bowel and why it took me so long. I knew they wouldn't ask out of respect, but they thought it and talked about it amongst themselves after we left. One time Mrs. Martha Murray sent her boy to get me.

"What you do in there for such a long time?" he said.

"None of your business," I said.

"Come on, Sarah, tell me. I know you can't just be using it. You taking a nap or what? I can't see how you stay in there so long with the way it smell and all."

I slapped him on the back of the head. "None of yours," I said. He eyed me as if to say he'd just open the door and see for himself. "I'll poke your eyes out if you ever look," I said. I knew it was in his mind, and if I kept it up, he'd open the door one day.

WE'D BEEN GONE most of the day, and Granny couldn't do all of my chores. When Esther turned in the direction away from home, I asked her if I could go on back to the house.

"Granny can't do all the work by herself," I said. "She probably needs help with the children by now."

"Do you ever have fun?" she said. "You should be playing, not worrying about chores."

"Granny is old," I said. "We got a system. You breaking the chain."

"Granny doesn't have to do it. She does it because she wants to.

My sisters can come home and take care of their responsibilities the same as I have."

I tried to excuse what she'd said. Maybe the sun was getting to her. She wasn't wearing a hat, and the sun can fool you sometime. Had she forgotten that she'd been gone for years? If she was calling me her responsibility, I begged to differ. If she called me that again, I wouldn't be letting her off the hook. I eyed her up and down.

"Can I go?" I said. "I'm real hot, getting dizzy."

"If you're feeling sick," she said.

Before she changed her mind, I took off running toward home.

"I thought you were feeling dizzy," she yelled.

I kept running as if I hadn't heard her.

As soon as I opened the door, Granny handed me a hollering baby. "Where y'all been?" she said. "Where's your mama? I got to get supper on, and I could use a hand."

"She kept going the other way," I said.

"Give her this bottle. Check and see if she wet. She been crying like that all day. She got the rest of them fussing, too. Where did you say your mama went?" she said as spit flew over my face. She pinched the toothbrush between her lips, which made her sound like cards flapping on bicycle spokes.

I changed the baby's diaper. She settled down after she got enough milk in her. I got the other one changed and fed. They should've been fed and changed a couple of hours ago. Everything at our house ran on time. Granny said it was so many of us it would be a catastrophe if we got off schedule. I didn't know what she meant, but the way we were running around trying to put things back in order, this must've been one. Muhdea would be home soon, and we hadn't shucked the corn or peeled the peas, and catching a hen and plucking it was out of the question. Granny gave orders, and I followed them. By the time Muhdea opened the front door, I could barely tell how badly things had been out of order a few hours ago.

At supper, Granny told Muhdea she needed to have a talk with Esther. If she wasn't going to help out, she couldn't take me traipsing up and down the road behind her.

"What y'all doing out there all day?" Muhdea said. "I hear she got folks picking up glass. Somebody going to get hurt fooling around with broken pieces of glass. You hunting for glass, too?"

I nodded.

"You washing your hands real good before you eat, I hope. You ain't eating over nobody's house is you, Sarah? Folks need their food. Your mama ain't taking folks' food, is she?"

I shook my head. Esther had drunk many cups of coffee and eaten plenty of cake and sandwiches, but not me. Only people who didn't have nothing to eat at home ate at other folks' houses, except the pastor on Sundays, but Esther and them folks on the low end was doing it like they were at a social engagement.

"I'm sorry if you enjoying yourself with your mama, but I got to put a stop to y'all going out every day. Do you understand we need you here?"

I nodded.

"You okay with that?"

I nodded again. Sometimes it was best to stay quiet. Muhdea seemed to look more tired since Esther came home. She rubbed the wrinkles in her forehead. Looked as if they had gotten bigger. Her eyes were red from the poison they sprayed on the cotton. It was one of the reasons Granny didn't let me go to the field, and why she called us all inside the house when the airplane sprayed for mosquitoes. Muhdea changed into her white café uniform, so she'd be ready to head to her second job after supper.

I hadn't found out what Esther was up to, but I didn't think the mosaic was all of it. Muhdea's decision was fine with me, but Esther might not take it too well. If she had been here to see how messed up the house was, she wouldn't take me out again just to show folks she was my mama. Most of them already knew that as long as she was in town Granny and Muhdea wouldn't interfere. They knew their Bible. Muhdea would have to ask if it was alright with her for me to stay home. Children obeyed their parents. Muhdea obeyed Granny, and I obeyed Esther, but Esther didn't mind nobody, not even God.

I tried to remember things about Esther before she left town, but all I could recall was that her hips and her hair switched from side to side and somehow that got her in trouble. Everything about her was new to me, from her painted face and nails to her proper talk.

The following morning, after Muhdea had a private talk with her, she strutted out to the backyard wearing a white miniskirt and a pink halter top. Granny told her she needed to cover herself.

"That ain't no way to carry yourself. You attracting the wrong kind of attention."

Esther told her not to worry about what type of attention she got. What she wore shouldn't have anything to do with who she was.

Granny turned her attention toward me. "Don't you ever use your looks to entice folks," she said. "It ain't pretty."

I was confused as to why she said it to me, when Esther was the pretty one. It was the first time I knew Granny to be wrong.

"You staying here today," Esther said. "Is that alright with you?"

I nodded. She hadn't asked me if it was alright when she took me with her even when I told her I didn't want to go, but now she wanted my opinion, wanted me to disagree with what Muhdea had told her.

"You sure?" she said.

I nodded.

"You can go with me on Wednesdays when Muhdea doesn't work at the cafe."

That evening Muhdea brought home ice cream, chocolate and Neapolitan. I called it Napoleon. Her boss gave it to her when it was outdated and too old to serve to customers but not too spoiled for us. It tasted the same as it did when I saved a nickel and bought a cone at the malt stand. Muhdea gave me an extra spoonful or two for one thing or the other I'd done to help her. All my cousins ate theirs fast, but I savored mine. I placed it in my mouth the same as when Granny fed it to the babies, in small sips. Muhdea believed it would taste better if I took a whole spoonful. I tried it that way, but it wasn't for me. I tasted the cool milk on the tip of my tongue and let the flavors ease down my throat. Chocolate was my favorite, but Napoleon came close. I placed all three flavors on the tip of my spoon and held my head back as it slid across my tongue. Wasn't any use in asking nobody to trade with me. They liked ice cream as much as I did, and so did Granny and Muhdea.

"Yours is melting," Granny said.

"I know. I like it like that, too."

"You show act strange when it comes to your ice cream," Muhdea said. "I don't think I ever seen nobody who likes it as much as you."

Esther walked in the kitchen, then sat next to me, and rubbed her hand across my hair.

"Your mama likes it, too, but I think you got her beat," Muhdea said. "Esther, you remember when you jumped on a boy twice your size for knocking your cone out your hand?"

Esther smiled. "You made his mama buy me another one."

I placed another spoonful in my mouth and licked the spoon after the ice cream was gone.

"Esther's favorite was Napoleon. You still eat it?" Granny said.

"My favorite," she said.

Muhdea told her that she'd saved her some, but she'd better eat it now before it melted. We sat a long time with spoons clicking against bowls and teeth. Even the babies were quiet.

When I got up Wednesday morning, Esther had already bathed and fed the babies. The other kids were at the breakfast table chowing down a meal that was generally reserved for Sunday mornings. Granny stood at the stove holding a coffee cup on a saucer, the only one we owned that wasn't chipped, and it matched. She called it a china cup, and even I wasn't allowed to touch it. I admired how dainty it was, white covered in pink flowers with green leafy stems. I asked Granny if she had bought it in China with the way she carried on about it. She told me to think about what I'd asked and draw my own conclusion. I preferred to think she had traveled by boat and was only able to bring back a cup and saucer that was worth a lot of money.

I took my seat at the table, amazed that I slept through so many activities. The coals in the stove were raked and thrown out. The kitchen was cool. I'd missed at least an hour's work.

"Where's Muhdea?" I said.

"She went to the farm. One of the pigs is giving birth. She be home directly," Granny said.

"Wish she'd taken me with her," I said.

Esther handed me a plate with much more food on it than I could eat in one sitting. I ate all of it 'cause some poor child in Africa was starving.

On the days I didn't follow Esther, she told me to place all of the pieces we'd collected on the picnic table out back and sort them by color and size. I overheard Granny and Muhdea's objections. They worried whether one of the kids would swallow a piece or cut themselves with it. They told them to play in the front yard till Esther finished her project.

"Hurry up, Sarah, you're going with me today," Esther said.

"We waiting on Muhdea to get back?" I asked.

"Granny will be fine until she gets here."

I checked in with Granny with my eyes. She gave me the go-ahead.

Folks were so glad to see Esther. In between talk about glass, chickens, children and weather, Esther slid in some of the messages I'd heard her say to Mrs. Carrie and Miss Ora Bea. She used another tone, not her citified one, with most of them. "We can't let the man keep us down. He's using the pigs to do his dirty work." I didn't care for her or Uncle Robert calling folks pigs. She was slick. Folks didn't know she was trying to pull one over on them, or like me they couldn't figure out what she was trying to pull and went along with her till she showed her hand.

"We ain't caring what them white folks doing 'cross the track," Bro Hollin said. "Why you so interested in them?"

Bro Hollin was the field foreman and a man who stood up for what was right. He hauled folks to the field and watched over them till the man came and paid them. Esther'd pushed a little too far, so she skated back. She was good at planting a few seeds here and a few there, then sliding out when she pushed the wrong button. She told them that she'd worked as an artist in Chicago, painted stained-glass windows. She'd painted two windows at First Baptist Church before she left, so we understood what that was, but none of us knew how to make a mosaic, and we were all too proud to ask her again. We felt as if we were a part of something new and exciting, something from the city, which was better than anything in the country.

We left them and headed toward the white side of town. If it were anybody else except Esther, I'd ask where we were going, but I'd learned my lesson about asking her questions unless I wanted to hear a long sermon. I followed along like a trained mule. Coloreds only went to the white side of town on Saturday mornings. We strolled past the juke joint. Mr. Leonard and Mr. Trucks were sitting outside on a bench. Mr. Scrap, the owner, held his head out of the window. Esther asked if they'd been down to help out at the two-story house. "We'll come if you there," Mr. Leonard said.

"I'll meet you down there after supper," Esther said.

All three of them grinned, showed all their teeth. Granny said they would follow her to California if she told them to. I kicked up dust, and Esther gave me a cross look. We waved at the Methodist preacher and a few men helping him get a bird's nest out of the steeple of the church.

"Where you headed, Miss Esther?"

She waved to them as we waited to cross Highway 65 and head over to the café. They stopped working and were watching her when we turned the corner. My first thought was how happy I'd be to see Muhdea, but then it occurred to me that she didn't work days at the café, and it was her day off. When we got to the café, we stood at the window. Nobody came to take our order. Esther talked about the restaurants in Chicago filled with black people, not coloreds. She'd been commissioned to paint pictures for some of the finest restaurants in Chicago.

"It wasn't easy in the beginning, but I stayed in school and I worked hard," she said. I must've got caught up in her telling of the paintings, how she conceived the ideas, wondering what she meant by organic, and before I knew it, we were talking. Talking the same as if it was with Granny or Muhdea.

"What is a mosaic?" I said.

"Oh, Sarah, I'm sorry. I thought you understood. No wonder you don't seem excited about the project." She fanned away a few mosquitoes. "It's too damn hot out here," she said as she continued to tell me how she'd started making mosaics and what they were.

She made it all sound pretty, beautiful, as if it were the only thing in the world to do with your life.

"All them folks that's been helping you will want to come see it, and Granny won't like that."

"Do you always worry?" she said.

I changed the subject 'cause what she called worrying I called respect for others especially if it was their house, and I enjoyed listening to her stories and didn't want her to stop.

"Did you make a living at drawing mosaics and painting windows back when you were in Chicago?" I said.

"Yes, of course. My work is displayed in some of the finest buildings and churches throughout Chicago as well. I even had a showing once. My proudest moment was as one of the artists for Reverend Martin Luther King Jr.'s March on Washington in August of 1963. Remember when I sent you a postcard of the White House?"

She'd been commissioned to draw pictures of all the people who were on stage. She drew so many pictures her arms and hands were tired. At one point, she ran out of paper, and one of the men rushed out to get her some more. She looked like a different person when she told that story. Like a woman that should be at the White House and not one standing at this café window getting eaten up by mosquitoes.

"Did you tell Muhdea that you went to the White House?"

The excitement drained from her face. "Yes. Yes, I did, but she doesn't understand."

"She was probably worried," I said. "I'm sorry she didn't say she was proud of you."

She changed the subject. "Remind me to show you the pictures from the march," she said. "I was able to sneak away with a few of them."

She rang the bell again. "Where are they?" She wiped sweat from her face. Checked her underarm. Honeysuckle and hamburgers mingled together with the still air. It was too hot for birds to chirp. Only mosquitoes could stand that heat. Then right in the middle of

46

one of her sentences, Esther caught my hand and said, "Come on, we're going in."

Esther caught my hand and walked us through the front door of the café. We stood inside the door of the café and stared at four rows of tables covered in yellow and white daisy tablecloths with yellow vinyl chairs. To my right was a long bar with the same daisy covering and with sweets on glass cake plates, and yellow bar stools. It was cold inside. I rubbed my arms up and down. Within a few seconds, a lady wearing the same color apron as the tablecloth, with white hair pinned up in a bun, and her skin the same color as her hair, rushed up to us.

"What you doing in here, Esther? You can't be in here. Mozelle don't work on Wednesdays," she screeched.

"We want two cones of ice cream, chocolate," Esther said.

She sat on one of the stools at the counter and crossed her legs. Two deputies were at the other end, eating. Esther noticed that I was hesitant to sit on the stool, and it was raised, as if a tall man sat there before. She picked me up and sat me on the stool beside her. The white lady placed her hand across her heart, and said, "Well, I declare." One of the deputies moved in front of the white lady, Mrs. Cox, the owner, and took hold of Esther's arm.

"Esther Mae, you done come back here prettier than you left," he said. The white lady sneered, rolled her eyes. He changed the tone in his voice. "Don't make me have to run you and little Sarah over to the jail for trespassing. Y'all go on back round to the window, and Deborah will come round there and serve."

Mrs. Deborah Brown, Malika's mama, had worked in the kitchen with Muhdea for years. She was the kind of lady who was scared of most everything, so Esther and me propped up on stools ordering ice cream would scare her right out of her white uniform.

Esther called the white lady by name. "Mrs. Cox, two cones of chocolate ice cream, please."

The deputy's eyes roamed up and down Esther's long legs. "Come on now, Miss Esther. Go on and let me finish eating."

Esther looked as if the last thing in the world she wanted to do was move. She stretched, crossed her legs, uncrossed them and crossed them again. He watched every move she made, looking at her legs as if he were trying to figure out how to handcuff them instead of her wrist. He seemed more nervous than I did. I rubbed my arms to warm up. How did they get it so cold in here? I thought. And then, just like she had decided to walk through the front door, she got up and started to walk out, me in tow.

"We'll be coming back," she said. "And the law says I have as much right to eat in here as you do. Next time you should check it out rather than my legs."

He took his right hand off his holster and drew his fist back at Esther. "I ain't above hitting no colored woman," he said.

My arms were down to my side, and I balled up both my fists. Esther saw this, and caught me by the hand, and we walked out of the door. Mrs. Deborah beckoned us to the back door of the kitchen and handed us each a cone of chocolate ice cream.

"Keep your money," she said when Esther reached to open her purse.

My hand was shaking. I'd heard tell of folks going to jail in other cities, but I never thought I'd be one of them. No wonder Granny and Muhdea didn't want me traipsing up and down the road behind Esther. And they knew us by name, too, knew Esther was a trouble-maker. All that nice talk around painting pictures and making mosaics just to reel me in to trouble. I stomped my feet on the rock road, and kicked up dirt as I licked my ice cream. She kept trying to talk to me. Trying to explain.

I finished off the cone and licked my hand. Esther gave me the rest of hers.

"You know how there's always a water puddle in front of the hydrant in the backyard?" she said.

I was done listening to her. Didn't she know? She'd probably gotten Muhdea in trouble, too.

"I'm going to draw a design on the ground, and we're going to cut the glass into small pieces to fit the design. The design is a mosaic. We're using glass, but you can make one from shells, pictures, stones, almost anything. It's going to be pretty, you'll see."

"Why you do that?" I said.

"Do what?" she said as if she didn't know what had just happened. "I left when I realized you were afraid. I should have explained what I was doing. I wasn't thinking."

I could give her a sermon on what happened to people who weren't thinking or listening. Instead, I told her I wasn't afraid.

"Oh, I'm sorry then," she said. She tried to wipe the ice cream off my mouth, and I pushed her hand away as I finished off her cone. "You've heard me talk about equal rights. Well, the café is a place where if we spend our money we deserve to be treated the same as a white person.. Do you understand?"

I didn't want to hear it. Reverend Jefferson had warned us they'd try to catch us off guard and get us to sin. I didn't think it would be my own mama. I wanted to tell her I didn't like what she'd done or how she'd tricked me, but when I thought about it, tears came to my eyes. I choked up. "I'm telling Granny," I said. "I don't want their ice cream. Sister Tucker got ice cream at her store, and she ain't trying to send nobody to jail for coming in there to buy it." I took off running toward home, outrunning the butterflies but not the mosquitoes. They ate my legs up.

CHAPTER FIVE

I Want Permission to Sit

I MIGHT BE a whole lot of things, but a fool wasn't one of them even if Esther treated me like I didn't have no sense. I was her project, and she didn't let go after a week like Muhdea said she would. She wasn't going to trick me again like she did with the ice cream. I started dodging her, tried my best to stay out of her way. If she was making the beds, I washed the dishes. Instead of studying at the kitchen table, I went out behind the smokehouse to read. Granny knew I was back there and sent me a cup of cold water by one of the children when the sun was at its highest. I appreciated it. Muhdea said I was being stubborn and unreasonable. I always read at the kitchen table, and she wasn't taking time away from her work to pacify me. Esther didn't realize anything had changed. She had been in Chicago for so long she didn't know much of anything and wasn't trying to learn how we ran the house. When Muhdea asked her what she'd been doing with her days, she told her to wait and see. She had plans. Muhdea said she needed to get a job 'cause she never heard tell of plans putting food on the table.

One or the other of Esther's friends swung by the house most every day before noon, and they ran the streets till way past suppertime and sometimes late into the night. Mrs. Carrie or Miss Ora Bea stopped by for her, too. We knew what Mrs. Carrie was up to with them SNCC organizers, but we couldn't figure out Miss Ora Bea's agenda. I couldn't see Esther coming out of them hot pants and wearing a long purple robe. Miss Ora Bea wore robes prettier than Reverend Jefferson's, but she still wasn't allowed to preach or sit in the pulpit. Maybe it was a sin for jackleg preachers to be in the pulpit like it was for kids. I wrote it on my list. Why did Mr. George

Stith, who didn't have a church home or a robe, sit in the pulpit with the other ministers and preach when the pastor was absent and on certain special occasions?

Esther had been home most of the day. If I hadn't been getting ready to sit on the Mourner's Bench, I would've lost my patience with her.

"Sarah, let me wash your hair. Sarah, come help me wash the dishes. Sarah . . ." she said.

Finally, I crawled behind the bed. I studied the Sunday-school lesson before it was time to read it to Granny and Muhdea. I waited for one of them to call me like they did every Saturday after we settled down from eating supper. When I finished loading my book satchel with every piece of reference material associated with the lesson, it came to me that nobody had called, so I collected my bag and went to see what was keeping them.

Maybe I was so wrapped up in my own head I didn't hear Esther. I was standing in the middle of the living room before I realized what she was doing. Words flew out of my mouth before I could catch them as if I'd never been taught any manners.

"What the hell you doing? Why in God's name are you reading to them? You trying to mess up everything I do?"

I eyed Granny. She was probably thinking that she hated she'd taught me how to cuss. She'd said it was pretty much the only thing that would show I meant business. This old boy used to hit me hard in the middle of my back every day after school. One day Granny told me to put a Coke bottle in my book satchel and gave me the words to say when he tried to hit me. On that day, when he got close enough, I eased the bottle out of my book satchel, set the bag on the ground, and wrapped my fingers around the neck. As soon as he looked as if he were about to draw back his fist, I turned around and faced him, holding the bottle straight out toward his head. "If you hit me one more damn time, I will beat your ass like you stole something," I said and stared him down.

Granny told me to put as much emphasis as I could on "damn" and "ass," and to say it slow, and to never take my eyes off his. "Don't be afraid. I be right down the road watching," she said. "Don't move your eyes till he back down."

I did exactly what she told me, and he backed down, said he'd just been playing with me, he didn't know it hurt. I took the liberty of cussing him again, and it felt good. I felt strong. Granny laughed when I met up with her and told me to never cuss again, but once I had a taste of it, I couldn't quit. I made so many checkmarks for cussing I might as well give it its own page.

On that day, I rolled my eyes at Esther. My eye socket was sore from cutting my eyeball so far over to the corner. I'd practiced in the mirror how to make my stare look meaner.

I stood in the middle of the living room and braced myself for a fight. "Granny, why you letting her read for y'all?" I held back the tears.

No way was I going to cry in front of Esther. I tried to compose myself like Uncle Robert had taught me. He never lost his temper. He'd learned how from the Nation of Islam. Esther had asked about him quite often since she'd been home. She wondered why he didn't come down from Little Rock, and I wondered, too. Granny's toothbrush was situated in the corner of her mouth, her chin propped in between both hands, her elbows rested on her knees. Muhdea was bowing her head up and down so often I thought it might fall off and roll across the floor. Esther sat on a stool with her long legs sprawled across the floor. She wore those red hot pants and a silver and red top. She brushed the hair from her face and pulled it back like a ponytail, but when she held her head down to read, it fell around her face 'cause she didn't have a rubber band wrapped around it.

"Granny," I yelled. I dropped my bag to the floor and placed my hands on my hips. "What's going on in here?" I gave each one of them a different dirty look and eye roll. "What's Esther doing? Why you and Muhdea letting her do it? Don't nothing belong to me no more?"

"Get hold of yourself, gal," Granny said.

"What you mean get hold of myself? You ain't told Esther to get hold of herself one time since she been here, and she been disobeying you and Muhdea."

"What you talking about, Sarah?" Muhdea said. "Your mama don't mean no harm."

"Yes, she do, Muhdea," I said. My voice broke, so I stopped talking till I collected myself.

"Why do you think that, Sarah?" Esther said in her proper voice. "I'm your mother. I wouldn't hurt you. Why are you so upset? I don't understand."

Esther lowered her eyes to look innocent. I'd seen Allison on Sister Tucker's TV give the same look on *Peyton Place*.

"Here, take the book. Go ahead." She held the book out to me.

It wasn't the Sunday-school book like I thought it was. I felt it in my throat, worse than a lump of butter.

"Here, you finish reading it to them," Esther said.

I was wrong, but by then momentum was on my side. "I don't want it. I don't want you to be my mama. I don't want you here. Why don't you go back to where you came from? Go today and leave me alone."

"Sarah," Granny and Muhdea said.

I kicked my book satchel across the middle of the floor, ran to the bedroom, and slammed the door. My head thumped so hard I couldn't cry. I eased down on the floor beside the bed.

"God, please don't let Esther come back here. I might hurt her for real." She came in the room running her mouth. I kept my head down. No way was I going to let her know how bad my head hurt, pounded. I couldn't hear her even if I'd wanted to. Granny generally came to see about me whenever I had a problem. Where was she? I was too old to cry. The only place I could go where I hoped Esther wouldn't follow me was outside to the restroom.

I asked her politely, "Will you excuse me please? I got to go."

"What?" she said. "Just give me a chance, Sarah. If you're worried I'll leave you again, don't. I have plans for us, baby, wait and see."

Polite didn't register with her. I made my voice sound even more country, which she hated.

"I got to pee," I said. "I's be right back."

"Sarah." She called my name as if I shocked her.

"I got to go now." I said it real mean. So mean she moved to the side to let me pass by her.

"We'll talk about this later when you're not so emotional," she said.

I kept walking. She was the one who was emotional. I got to the living room, where Muhdea and Granny were still sitting in their same seats. Even though my head was banging, I gave them one last eye roll before I slammed the back door. I needed a BC powder.

I sat on the toilet seat, dry, couldn't make myself pee. How many checkmarks would I have to place under the Hell column for what I'd done, maybe the whole page? I sat there and prayed.

"God, I know I ain't been saved, but I need help. Please tell Esther to stay away from me 'cause she's going to make me lose my religion before I get it. Not to mention my position as acting secretary. Tell Granny it will be alright for me to sit on the Mourner's Bench. Please don't let her believe that I'm too young." The pee finally came.

"I can do everything thirteen-year-old girls do, and some things I'm better at than grown folks. I wouldn't ask you if it wasn't urgent. My standing in the church and in Heaven depends on it. I know it's a big request coming from a sinner, but I'll make up for it after I get saved.

"After I get my religion, I'll be good, I'll quit cussing, and I'll even carry Esther's sins for her till she straighten out and get off the prayer list. I know I ain't supposed to beg, but I'm begging for my salvation. Amen."

Granny wasn't going to let me show out the way I did earlier and not chastise me. I kept my distance from her for the rest of the day. I stayed busier than a mama blackbird preparing a nest for her new babies. I changed diapers that weren't wet, fed kids who weren't hungry, played hopscotch with the girls and marbles with the boys.

Muhdea left for work at the café, and only God knew where Esther had gone. Granny hadn't cornered me yet. Maybe she was waiting for me to think about what I'd done and figure out a solution. I'd gotten pretty good at sorting out most things on my own.

"You getting grown right before my eyes, Sarah. Pretty soon I won't have nothing else to teach you," Granny'd said. Now Esther was back trying to undo all the growing up Granny taught me, and I wasn't going to let her do that. She'd have a better chance roping a steer at the prison rodeo. Whenever I finished thinking it through, I'd find Granny and tell her what I'd learned and how I'd do it differently next time. After she'd heard me out, she'd wait awhile, let me stew in it, and finally say, "Alright then."

When it came time to do the real work, I was already worn out, and Esther still wasn't home. Me and Granny heated water and bathed the children in the number-two washtub, babies first, girls next and then boys. The ones who were big enough got out of the tub and put on their own pajamas. I sang to the babies.

"What?" Granny said. "You talking to me?"

"Singing is all," I said. I knew she was waiting for me to talk about what happened, but she'd have to pull it out of me. I wasn't sorry for it, and I sure wasn't ready to change.

I walked on back to the bedroom to settle down the babies. One went straight to sleep, but the other one was a little antsy. I told him the story of David.

"I can't hear you. Speak up if you need me," Granny said.

"Talking to the baby," I said.

I tried to sort out the day. Was I wrong? What would I do next time? 'Cause according to Granny, there was always a next time to get it right. How could I place the blame squarely on my shoulders? I couldn't see straight for getting mad all over again, which didn't do nothing for my headache. I searched in every corner and couldn't even find an empty BC powder packet. I still didn't want to tell Granny my head had been hurting all day. She'd make me lie down, and I wasn't going to let her do all the work by herself.

When we were done, I sat down next to her on the davenport. I looked away from her so she wouldn't notice my red eyes. We sat in silence. First time that day. She waited for me, but I wasn't bringing it up. I'd waited for the right time to talk to her about my religion, and I might as well bring it on up. If I caught her off guard, she might let me do it.

"I've been thinking," I said.

She turned toward me as if to say it was about time, she'd been waiting most of the day.

"I been praying and asking for guidance," I said. "I can't confirm any certain answer from God, but I do believe He's laid it on my heart." I paused 'cause I'd repeated the exact words I'd heard many times in other folks' testimonies. Granny didn't check me on it. I kept going. "I've talked it over with Muhdea and Mr. Matthew. Sister Tucker advised me, but I came to my own conclusion." The church would've said "Amen."

"I know I'm not thirteen, but I'm old enough. I can handle responsibilities, and I'm a good acting secretary for the Sunday school. You should come see how well I read to the whole Sunday school. Folks clap sometimes. Muhdea can tell you."

Granny held on to my words the same as she did when I read to her. I cleared my throat, which she hated.

"I decided this for myself. You told me every person was responsible for her own salvation, so I want you to give me your blessing to sit on the Mourner's Bench come revival."

CHAPTER SIX

They Called It an Anxious Seat

I EYED GRANNY every day and she did the same to me, but neither one of us mentioned the revival. Took me days to get my nerves up again, but I planned to get an answer from her that night after we prayed and settled into bed. We used to be the last ones to go to bed before Esther came back home. Trying to wait up for her before we locked the door turned out to be a feat for both of us. That night wasn't any different. Muhdea made a remark concerning Esther's absence, and then said she was tired and went to bed. We followed her soon afterward. I slept in the bed with Granny. We kneeled down beside the bed and said our prayers every night. Granny prayed aloud first.

"Father, here we are once more and again. Thank you for waking us up this morning clothed in our right mind, with a reasonable portion of health and activities in our limbs."

Then she nudged me, and I thanked God too. "Father, we come before you with our heads bowed, leaning on your everlasting arms. I thank you that last night our bed was not our cooling board and our cover was not our winding sheet."

After we prayed aloud, we continued to pray silently for a good while. I finished way ahead of Granny but stayed on my knees till she was done. Once we got settled in bed, I didn't wait. I brought it up. I gave her my reasons for wanting to get saved now. She asked me a few questions so she could judge whether I was bound and determined. Finally, she told me it was Esther's decision to make and not hers.

"You know your mama got the last word," she said.

"Yes, ma'am, I know. Don't understand it, but I know."

"Can't see no reason why she'd have a problem with you getting your religion. Be respectful when you talk to her. She means well, Sarah."

"Should I apologize for the other day?" I said.

"Probably, but make up your own mind. You know what's right."

"Granny?" She knew I was going to ask her something she wouldn't want to answer, so she tried to stir me away from it.

"Ain't you tired, Sarah? We had a long day."

"Just one more thing. I believe it'll help me a great deal."

She sighed. I crossed my fingers and toes.

"Tell me how you got saved again. I can't remember the whole story."

"You know it better than I do. Stop telling tales," she said.

"This the last time I'll ever ask," I said.

"Now that's a tale, too, but since you trying to get your soul ready, I'll do it this time. You better not fall asleep on me either," she said.

I'd heard her testimony more than one hundred times, but I never tired of listening to it. I propped myself up in bed. I wanted to stay awake, and I prayed Esther wouldn't come home and interrupt us. She slept in the same room with us but in another bed.

"Well," Granny said, "I sat on that Mourner's Bench. Well, it was no bench. The deacons took white chairs with three slats across the back and a straw seat from the back of the church, lined them up facing the pulpit, and called it a Mourner's Bench. We sat there all week praying to God for the forgiveness of our sins. Back when my mama got her religion, they called it an Anxious Seat. Ain't much changed between then and now except the name.

"First, I picked a sign and then asked God to reveal it to me. I asked Him to let Mr. John Freeman sing 'I Need Thee Every Hour.'"

I smiled as Granny sang, "I need Thee, O I need Thee. Every hour I need Thee, O bless me now, my Savior, I come to Thee!"

"My mama chose the same song as her sign when she got saved. I knew beforehand I wanted Him to show me the same sign," she said.

"All the other mourners had testified and was sitting up in the choir stand with a white band tied around they head. See, the white band signaled that God had forgave them of they sins, and they was ready to be baptized on Sunday. It was Saturday night, the last night of revival. I was at home getting ready, and my heart was heavy. Six nights, I'd listened to the preacher and mourned for my sins, and nobody sang my song. I feared God wasn't paying me no attention, but I continued to pray the whole time I was putting on my clothes. Took me longer to get ready that night than ever in my life. I couldn't get the knot twisted right in my stockings, so they kept falling down. Then I looked in the mirror and my slip was hanging. I finally got out the door, late, and headed toward the church.

"And still, I walked mighty slow that night—I mean, I all but crawled to the church—constantly in prayer. I handed my life over to God one more time before I rounded the front of the church and eased up the stairs, one step at a time. As soon as I reached for the doorknob, the choir started singing. So I put my ear close to the door, afraid to listen. It was an old hymn. I don't like it to this day. Now I had myself a dilemma. Should I go on in or wait for the choir to start the next song? I stood there with my ear pressed against the door a good five minutes before Sister Tucker came up behind me and forced me on through the door.

"I dragged myself up to the last chair, the only one left of what was the Mourner's Bench. I was so into prayer that not only did my mind keep repeating 'I Need Thee,' but my entire body shook with the words of the song. Ain't never had that feeling before or since. And no sooner than the bend was in my knee, right before my hindpart touched the wicker in the seat, Mr. John broke out singing 'I Need Thee Every Hour.'"

She turned to me. "Oh, Sarah, you should've heard him. I'm just as sure today as I was then that I levitated right up to the front of the church, shouting, 'Thank you, God! Thank you for finding me.' I got my religion at last."

When Granny finished, I lay quiet next to her as if I were asleep. I prayed silently. I asked God for the same sign He'd given Granny and Granny's mama. I was certain it was the right sign for me. Not even two redbirds could match her sign. Then I whispered, "Please, God, don't let Esther sin no more till I get saved."

I SAT ON the steps holding one of the babies. The other kids were playing jump rope in the yard. Esther hadn't surfaced yet, but I knew she'd push open the door soon, mouth running like the Mississippi River about nothing I wanted to hear. I wouldn't be shocked if that was the reason her name was at the top of the prayer list at church. She wasn't nothing like me, Muhdea or Granny. We knew how to keep our mouths closed.

The baby was fussy. I'd given her a bottle, changed her diaper, walked back and forth across the yard, but couldn't quiet her down. When Esther walked out on the porch, I placed the baby across my shoulder to see if I could get her to burp.

"Is she wet?" Esther said.

I acted as if I didn't hear her.

"When did you last check?"

I placed the baby across my knee and stared out at the road as if I were expecting Jesus. I'd taken care of this baby since her mama left her with us, and Esther thought she had the right to question me. What was her problem? I knew this baby better than she did or ever would.

"Sarah, you had to work like a little woman for a while, and I understand that, but I'm home now. Let me handle the adult stuff, and you can be a child. Give me the baby, and go play with the other kids."

Esther had to be kidding. I wouldn't trust her with the baby if she wasn't fussy.

"Don't you want to play?" she said.

I tried to find the words that would make her go away and leave me alone, but every sentence that popped into my head would get me in so much trouble if it came out of my mouth. Hopefully, she'd leave me alone before God started paying attention to my thoughts. The baby must've felt my frustration too 'cause she started screaming as if I'd pinched her or stuck her with a pin. I got up and went into the house without saying a word to Esther. Granny was in the living room. I handed the baby to her, and she quieted down as soon as we made the exchange.

When I came back to the porch, Esther was out in the road helping the other kids draw lines for a hopscotch game. I sat on the steps and watched. She tried to get me to come help them. I wouldn't, so she came and sat next to me. She told me I was too young to be acting so old.

"Fifty-year-old mind in an eight-year-old body," she said. "You need to play, have fun, act your age, stop being serious."

I did play, have fun, and Granny said I was wise for my age, always been that way. There wasn't nothing playful in praying for a sign from God. No wonder her name was forever on the prayer list at church. Even though I didn't have her permission, I had already gone into revival mode, immersed myself in goodness and prayer.

She insisted I go down the road with her. I prayed she'd leave me alone while I was in meditation. I watched as she told the kids to go play in the backyard. She didn't want them follow her. Lured them back there with two Pixy Stix, grape and orange.

Muhdea came outside and yelled for her to come back and help with the housework.

"Esther, we ain't finished cleaning yet," she said. She followed us down the road. "You need to come on back in here till we get done."

Esther picked up her step and turned the corner as if she hadn't heard Muhdea. I turned to go back, and she told me I'd better not. "Speed up," she said.

Muhdea hollered at her a few more times. "Esther, Esther Mae. Y'all come back here. I know you hear me."

I was conflicted. I wanted to go and see what Esther was up to in the streets, who had she been meeting up with, why did it take most of the night to get it done, was she up to no good, would she bring shame to the family again as Muhdea had speculated. She said Esther should move to the low end with the folks who acted like her and leave us respectable folks alone. I also wanted to obey Muhdea, but she'd told me to mind Esther.

Esther caught my hand and started skipping. I skipped to keep up with her. We stopped at Mrs. Carrie's house. Why was she stopping here? It was the first of the month, and Mrs. Carrie would be out delivering commodities.

She told me she was going to buy me new school clothes, the

kind the girls wore in the city. I hoped it wouldn't be like her hot pants and miniskirts.

"Will you get me a doll and an Easy-Bake Oven?" I said.

"No child of mine is going to raise babies and keep house. Haven't you had enough of that already? I'll buy you a set of paintbrushes and an easel, and the rest of those encyclopedias," she said.

I enjoyed keeping babies and couldn't wait till I was old enough to cook. If I wanted to paint, she'd insist I do something else. Since she was in a good mood, I figured I'd try to interrupt her and bring up revival. I hated Granny was so gung-ho on my getting Esther's permission to sit on the Mourner's Bench.

"I got a question," I said. She acted as if she didn't hear me and kept right on talking. Maybe my voice was too low. We reached Mrs. Carrie's porch before I got up the nerve to say it louder. Esther knocked and knocked at the door. For some reason, I didn't want to tell her Mrs. Carrie's whereabouts. Let her knock. Let her figure it out on her own.

"Carrie ain't home," Bro Hollin said as he walked past.

"Hey, how you doing?" Esther said. "Have you seen Mrs. Dilworth?"

"She all the way down on the low end. Got the commodities stacked on the back of her truck," he said.

"I guess she left early," Esther said. "I'll cut through the alley and catch up to her."

"If you planning on riding with her, her truck is packed," he said as he continued down the road, his overalls rolled up and a tool belt wrapped around his waist. I wondered why he wasn't in the field.

"The work you doing at the house is marvelous," she said.

He gave her a wide grin. "I's looking forward to seeing your work too."

She caught my hand. "Come on, Sarah. We have to hurry."

I didn't feel right about it. I felt Muhdea pulling for me.

"Can I go back home?" I said. "I got a stomachache."

"Sarah," she said. I knew she didn't believe me. "I guess. Go ahead."

I heard Esther's voice in the wind even after I'd gotten home, but Muhdea's tone drowned hers out.

"Your mama just might drive me crazy one day soon," Muhdea said when she saw me. "Where is she?" I hunched my shoulders. "See if that baby will take a bottle, then come help me in the kitchen. Didn't you hear me yelling at you to come back?"

Granny came out of the kitchen with the bottle and saved me from having to answer. I laid the baby next to the other babies in the quilt-patched baby pen, which I was told used to belong to me. I folded a diaper and propped the bottle on it so the milk would flow into his mouth. While I was still getting the baby situated, Aunt Sally knocked at the door. Not my kin, but we all called her Aunt Sally.

She delivered the news in town. Good, bad or indifferent, she was the first to get the news and spread it throughout. She let herself into the house.

"Muhdea, you in there?" she called.

We were supposed to be good to her 'cause she knew voodoo. She'd fixed a potion for Uncle Jab to get him to marry her, and she'd helped other women trap their husbands, too. Muhdea told me to stop listening to gossip, but I still didn't eat or drink nothing she gave me.

Granny sat on the davenport, and Muhdea dragged over to the rocking chair and sat in it. Aunt Sally kept talking.

"Carrie Dilworth will be here directly." She appeared to be out of breath, and sat down next to Granny, away from the duct-taped seam with the wire sticking out.

"Whew," she said. "Carrie was just on my street. I came to warn you. She got them people with her, too."

Granny rubbed her hand up and down the duct tape that covered the crack in the couch. She made the hole wider when she caught hold of a string, wrapped it around her finger, and pulled it.

"What people you talking about?" Muhdea said.

"Them folks Revered Jefferson been warning us about. You know, them civil rights workers."

"You sure that who it is?" Muhdea said as she wiped her hands on her apron and then straightened her wig.

"Yeah, Mozelle. She got a white gal riding right up there in the front seat with her. A white man and a colored boy riding in the back of the truck with the welfare rations. They can't be up to no good." She patted her chest as if it would lower her blood pressure. "I had to rush over here and let you know ahead of time." Her eyes widened as if she were surprised, which was how she always looked, excited, surprised. She talked fast as if the words had to get out of her mouth before they dissolved into spit.

I'd been anxious to see the people who had Reverend Jefferson so fired up. If Malika was in town, we'd have come up with a way to meet them by now. A few folks in town said they'd seen them. I thought Reverend Jefferson had scared them away from our end of town. I knew he had me afraid to look them in the eye.

The news didn't seem to rile Muhdea as it did Aunt Sally, but sometimes it was hard to tell with her. Muhdea believed in hiding her true feelings in front of most people.

"Well, Sally," Muhdea said. "We can't let Carrie upset us. Best thing to do is to pay her no mind. Listen to her and be respectful, but don't take it in. Remember what Reverend Jefferson told us. If they can't get folks stirred up, they'll leave and go someplace where people might want to start a ruckus."

I couldn't tell what Granny was thinking. She hadn't mumbled a word, or chewed any harder on her toothbrush.

"I know you right, Muhdea," she said. "But I can't be as calm as you, and I don't think other folks will be either. Like I said, a white girl and a colored boy is with her. Take it like you want to, but don't say I didn't warn you."

Granny told me to go get Aunt Sally a glass of water. She swallowed it down in two gulps and asked me for another one.

"She'll be here directly. I'm heading on out to warn the rest of the folks before Carrie make it down their way," Aunt Sally said. "It'll be a shame for them to get caught off guard like we did on our end."

It was hard to believe anybody caught Aunt Sally off guard. She knew most things before they happened, a pregnancy, a proposal of marriage, an unexpected check.

"You go on then, Sally," Muhdea said. "I appreciate you letting us know. We be ready for her when she get here."

I handed her the second glass of water, but she waved it away. Muhdea closed the screen door behind her and watched while Aunt Sally walked out the yard and down the road.

"You be careful out there in that heat," she said. "They said it supposed to get up to a hundred today."

Aunt Sally waved her hand in the air.

"Hey, Sally." She turned around and started walking back toward us. "You see Esther Mae down there?"

"Yeah. Her and Ora Bea was standing in front of Baily Chapel Church earlier. Ain't seen her since."

She waited as if to see if Muhdea would ask her another question. Muhdea waved her off.

"You watch out for her now, Mozelle. Don't let them talk you into signing up for nothing. Tell everybody you can beforehand."

Muhdea came back and sat next to Granny. "What you think Carrie's up to with them white folks?"

Granny didn't say nothing.

"I think most of us at First Baptist won't get mixed up with them," Muhdea said.

Granny picked up her snuff off the shelf.

"In Heaven's name, what she doing with Ora Bea?" Muhdea said. "I like Ora Bea well enough, but in a different way, she causes Reverend Jefferson just as much grief as Carrie. Always asking him to sit in the pulpit and if he'll let her preach," Muhdea said.

I braided the end of one of Granny's plaits that had come loose. Muhdea became more riled as she talked, but she'd calm down and put on her face before Mrs. Carrie got here with them visitors.

"Now, Esther." Muhdea scratched her wig. "I almost wish she would've stayed up north. Can't ever count on her to do the sensible thing."

I never knew Muhdea didn't want Esther to come back home. I daydreamed about her sisters calling and telling her they'd found the pot of gold at the end of the rainbow, and she needed to come and help them spend all the money. If me and Muhdea teamed up, we might be able to convince her to leave town. Or maybe she'd sign up with them civil rights folks, and leave with them when the white folks and Reverend Jefferson ran them out of town.

Muhdea and Granny sat and talked as if I weren't listening. With grown folks' conversation, children became invisible.

"Don't trouble yourself over Esther," Granny said. "She ain't even told us why she back here. I don't expect her to stay even though I can tell she wants to." Then she turned on me. "Sarah, don't think I don't see you over there taking this all in. You keep your little fast tail away from them people, too." She spit in the cup and wiped the dribble off her top lip with the back of her hand.

I opened my mouth to speak, but she stopped me.

"I don't want to hear it. You stay in this house when Carrie gets here. Don't set one foot outside that door."

All I wanted to do was get a good look at the SNCC organizers since I'd never seen one before. Reverend Jefferson had already said they were doing the Devil's work so becoming aquatinted with them wouldn't do nothing but hurt my chances at getting my religion.

CHAPTER SEVEN

Visitors with the Commodities

WE DIDN'T HAVE to wait too long. It was less than thirty minutes before Mrs. Carrie drove up in front of our house with the community rations packed in the bed of her green and beige Chevrolet truck. She delivered them every month, and folks walked over from all four streets to pick up their food. Our streets weren't paved and didn't have signs with names written on them like Markham or Carol Lane as they did on the white side of town. We had gravel roads, and we named them ourselves. The main road in between the church and Sister Tucker's store we called Front Street, the one behind our house Back Street, while ours was called Jones Street 'cause most of our family members lived on it, and east of the church was Side Street. We usually gathered in the road in front of our house, and kids played and grown folks talked while we waited for Mrs. Carrie. That day, nobody came out of their houses to pick up the government surplus of hash meat, pressed-ham loaf, rice, cheese, butter, powdered milk and eggs.

We grew most of our food in the garden, like whippoorwill, purple hull, crowder and black-eyed peas, and cabbage, turnip, collard and mustard greens, and every other kind of vegetable that survived the heat, weeds and insects. We raised cows, hogs and chickens in the country, except for a few laying hens we still kept in the backyard. Whatever we didn't grow or raise, we bartered for with our neighbors. For instance, some folks traded poultry and pork with Bro Hollin for beef. Reverend Jefferson included all of the items in the church announcements. During late summer, the commodities helped stretch our meat and vegetables while we waited to slaughter livestock in the fall. We canned the vegetables and cured the meat. We kept the meat in the smokehouse out back.

Mrs. Carrie blew her horn two or three times. She hadn't ever had to blow it before. She put you in mind of Granny, tall, thin, long mingled gray and black hair and the high cheekbones of an Indian. They could be mistaken for sisters or at least first cousins. They weren't any kin, but they both had a lot of Indian in their blood.

I stood at the screen door. Muhdea walked past me. "Don't you come out here," she said and gave me the eye.

I was sure every household had heard the news from Aunt Sally and was waiting to take their cue from Muhdea. Reverend Jefferson had business at the county seat and wasn't in town. I wondered if Mrs. Carrie had planned it that way. Even Sister Tucker hadn't hobbled across the church ground on her cane, as much as she liked a reason to talk. She made too much money at the store to qualify for the rations, but she came every month anyhow, and we shared our food with her regardless of what the government said.

Muhdea welcomed them. "Hey, Carrie," she said. "Who you got out here with you?" She dried her hands on her apron.

Granny came and stood beside me, and we watched and listened to the commotion outdoors. Muhdea's friendliness wasn't considered phony. It was our way of being kind to visitors whether we liked them or not.

Mrs. Carrie got out of the driver's side of the truck first, and then two men hopped off the bed of the truck. A white girl slid off the front seat on the passenger's side and stretched. When Esther slid out behind her, me, Muhdea and Granny had a coughing fit. I looked for Muhdea to beat the snot out of Esther right there in front of company when she recovered. Granny didn't go snatch the hair out of her head either, which she'd threatened to do on a number of occasions. Muhdea finally raised her head and proceeded as if Esther hadn't shocked her.

"I'm sorry about that," she said. "Something must've gone down my windpipe."

They all chuckled, but I knew wasn't nothing funny to Muhdea. I meshed myself against the screen door as if I were privy to a fight between Cassius Clay and Sonny Liston. I was just like most colored folks and kept forgetting he'd changed his religion, and his name to Muhammad Ali. Mrs. Carrie acted as if she didn't notice the coughing fit and continued once she knew Muhdea was fine.

"Hi, Mozelle," she said. "These are the SNCC organizers I've been telling you about for months. They work for the Student Non-Violent Coordinating Committee headquarters in Atlanta." Mrs. Carrie looked regal with her hair pulled back in a bun, and she stood up straight and confident as if she meant business.

Muhdea looked back at us as if to ask if we were paying attention to this mess. Esther stood next to the white girl. She moved her hands as if she were fixing her lilac and white minidress. She'd got ahold of some makeup since I left her at Mrs. Carrie's house earlier, and painted her face like a Jezebel. The two men stared her up and down, from her high-heeled white shoes up her legs to her minidress to where her ponytail lay across her chest. Esther captivated all the men that way. Muhdea and Granny said it was a pity she didn't know what to do with it. She looked striking in her getup.

"Where's everybody?" Mrs. Carrie said. "Mozelle, can you let them know we're here? It would be nice if Esther didn't have to introduce everybody twice."

Her voice sounded stretched, as if she were getting irritated. She pulled a handkerchief out of her light blue purse with a gold snap and wiped the sweat off her forehead. Then she used it to fan away the mosquitoes. The hotter it got, the stronger the honeysuckles smelled. Bees swarmed around the pink roses in our yard, and I thought I saw a wasp near Esther's head. It was the heat of the day, and nobody should be standing around outside without a hat on and a towel to fan the mosquitoes.

Muhdea must've finally given a signal. Mrs. Carrie looked around as if she expected to see the people walking down the road. Instead, they all came from across the church ground, out of Sister Tucker's store. Our neighbors, two to three of them paired together, walked toward the truck. Mostly older women and children too young to be in the field, like Mrs. Mary and her son Junior. Sister Rebecca clacked along on her cane with Sister Ruth, and Mrs. Rachel dried her hands on her apple-covered apron. She'd been washing dishes. Sister Tucker hobbled beside Mr. Peter. She was overweight and didn't walk often. He still had the pruning shears in his hand. Everybody looked as if they'd stopped during the middle of doing their work. We'd been cleaning the house and feeding the babies before Aunt Sally disturbed us. I couldn't recall a time I'd stopped by anybody's house and they were sitting around doing nothing. When they reached the truck, Esther and Mrs. Carrie seemed to perk up, and she continued with her introductions.

"You all know Esther," she said. "She's come home to share her expertise with us by leading our grassroots efforts and managing the overall operation." She caught hold of her hand. "Esther, why don't you take over from here?"

Esther brushed her dress with both hands again as if she were trying to rub out invisible wrinkles. She cleared her throat.

"I will go ahead and introduce you to my family first." She rubbed her hand across her hair and looked at Muhdea from under her eyes, afraid to hold her head up, I imagined. "Well, this is Mrs. Mozelle Jones. We all call her Muhdea."

I eyed Granny. Muhdea wouldn't like that Esther was telling strangers her nickname.

"She practically runs First Baptist Church. She works in the fields during the day and at the Roadside Café in the evening. She is the head cook for the elementary and high school during the school year." She looked at the white girl. "There is a lawsuit pending with the courts against the school board. Mrs. Carrie has petitioned for full integration of the schools, and we're waiting for their decision, although I believe separate but equal schools are the only way to go."

Our schools were already separate, but why would Esther think we weren't equal to the white school? I was probably smarter than any student they had over there. Nobody around here wanted to mix with them. What was she talking about?

"But let me get back to Muhdea," she said. "She is raising her grandchildren because my sisters had to leave town to find jobs to support them. We want to bring jobs here. Mothers need to be home with their children. She is a devout Christian and a pillar in the community. She has made sacrifices that wouldn't ever be required of a white mother."

Esther talked about Muhdea as if she were somebody I'd never met. I stood up straighter. Granny smiled. Nobody'd told me Esther left town 'cause she couldn't get a job around here. Granny nudged me in the side, interrupting my thoughts.

"She trying to talk proper, but we know she more country than a syrup sandwich."

That was a good one, but I couldn't fall out laughing like I wanted to. All I did was smile and nudge her back.

"Standing in the door is Granny, my grandmother, Mrs. Pearl," Esther said.

She was giving up too much information. Them folks didn't need to know what we called Granny or Muhdea. They didn't know us.

"Granny is the matriarch of our family," Esther said. She twisted her shoe heel in the rocks and looked in the direction of First Baptist Church.

Esther acted as she'd forgotten that she was introducing Granny and started with me. "Standing beside Granny is my daughter, Sarah. They can't see you, baby. Come on out here."

Why did she call me? She knew better. Muhdea would've brought me out with her if I were supposed to be out there. Esther knew that, too. She hadn't forgotten our ways. I looked to Granny for her okay, and I didn't want to get in trouble with Esther. Granny hesitated, and then nudged me on out the door, but I could tell she wasn't happy about it. Muhdea gave me the eye again as soon as I stood next to her. I was used to getting the eye from Granny, but I didn't know how to read it from Muhdea. Esther caught my hand and pulled me next to her. I wasn't wearing my school clothes from this morning. I'd changed into my work skirt and blouse, which I could tell she didn't appreciate. She placed her hand atop of my head as if I belonged to her. She introduced the white girl.

"This is Gail Lehrer," Esther said, still fidgeting with her dress. "She came all the way from New York City."

Muhdea shook Gail's hand. She was a little woman and wore a sundress covered in daisies. Her hair was light yellow and long. I wondered if her hair was the same color as the ladies' on TV. Sister Tucker let me watch her black and white set sometime. She'd bought a cellophane cover and put it over the screen. It turned the black and white pictures colored, which changed all the time. On one station, the actors' faces were red, and then were green when the commercial came on. We never knew the true color of their clothes either, but it was a colored TV all the same.

The SNCC men wore tee-shirts that read "Power to the People" and "I'm Black and I'm Proud."

"This is James Harel. He's from Maine," Esther said. James wore wire-rimmed glasses and jeans and a tee-shirt with a picture of a black fist and the words "I'm Black and I'm Proud."

"Hello, Mrs. Jones," he said. "It's a pleasure to be here. Thank you for inviting us."

"The pleasure is all mine," Muhdea said.

Esther smiled and caught hold of the other man's hand. "Rutherford, come up here. What are you doing all the way back there?"

Rutherford walked around and greeted Muhdea.

"This is Rutherford Johnson," Esther said. "He's from Georgia."

He looked scrubby and wrinkled. He picked at the bumps on his skin and scratched his beard as if he were trying to get bugs out of it. Jeans and tee-shirts seemed to be the uniform for men in the civil rights movement. Esther finished making introductions of all the folks who were gathered. She called them by name but didn't tell who they were as she'd done with us. Now that Esther had properly introduced everybody, we were allowed to talk to each other. We were southern country folks with plenty of rules and regulations. One being that women couldn't talk to men till after they were properly introduced. Esther turned the focus back to Mrs. Carrie.

"We can't ever forget that she is the reason we're here," she said.

Gail approached me. "We're starting a Freedom School," she said. "I'm going to teach Negro history. Do they teach it at your school?"

"Yes, ma'am, well, no, ma'am, not much," I said. I'd learned all about Negro history from Sister Tucker, but my teachers did make us remember a few dates about slavery for the test.

"I have books written by and about Negroes," Gail said. "Would you like to see them sometime?"

"Yes, ma'am," I said. I checked in with Muhdea with my eyes to see if I was saying too much.

Esther didn't seem like the same person as she talked back and forth to the civil rights workers and the neighbors. She acted as if she were the lead turner in a double-dutch contest, and Mrs. Carrie was holding the other end. The civil rights workers told us we were fortunate to have them here. Other cities needed their help. Mrs. Carrie's long history of service throughout the country as far back as the Elaine murders, and the STFU, was the reason SNCC had chosen our town. We should also be happy that Esther had returned home to lend her expertise. She'd worked tirelessly in Chicago, and even traveled with Reverend Martin Luther King Jr.'s entourage. No wonder she remained on so many prayer lists.

"Mrs. Dilworth has worked a long time. Actually, all the way back before the Elaine, Arkansas, murders," Esther said. "With God's help, we will make concrete lasting inroads this time. These people have left their colleges and their families to be here with us."

It sounded like the same old stuff Mrs. Carrie told us every month when she delivered our commodities. Nobody listened to her. We needed change. We owned much less than the white folks. We must demand equal rights. They were going to do whatever it took to help us receive our rights. The white folks went to good schools with proper heating, new books and new athletic uniforms. The twist here was Esther and them SNCC organizers. What did she have to do with all of this? Had she known the SNCC organizers in Chicago? Whatever her reason, it wouldn't be near as important as the trouble she was going to be in as soon as this meeting broke up.

"You have worn, outdated books and wood stoves," James said as if we didn't already know it. "I was taken aback when Mrs. Dilworth showed me the school. Buildings brought here that were damaged in the move from the Japanese refugee camp. How can you learn in buildings with such horrific history?"

We all knew the story and where they came from, but he must've just heard about it 'cause he looked as if he were going to cry. A few people gasped, he looked so pitiful.

"There are actually rats living in there. Aren't you afraid they're diseased? I am. I will be working to change such inequality," James said.

Now he sounded just like Mr. Sam Ray Blackburn and them. What was he going to steal from us? How was he going to help us if he was afraid of rats? Nobody around here was scared of them. If he couldn't handle rats, what was he going to do when he felt the wrath of Reverend Jefferson and Mr. Michael James King, the chief of police, and not to mention Mr. Sam Ray Blackburn, who ran most everything?

"Have you heard about the Civil Rights Act that Congress passed this month? Does anybody know what that means for you?" Rutherford said. Nobody answered. We already knew about that, too, had talked about it at a church meeting. "We will explain what it means for you, and what we are going to do to enforce these rights," he said.

They sure were planning to do a whole lot. Did they plan on living here for the rest of their lives? He wiped the sweat off his face with the back of his hand. A couple of grasshoppers jumped out of the Johnson grass into the bed of the truck. I picked a leaf of honeysuckle and squeezed the juice in my mouth. The smell burst through the air. Gail looked as if she were trying to recognize what it was.

"Ask yourself, why do you live on one side of the tracks and them on the other?" Rutherford said as if he were a preacher.

We didn't covet our neighbors' goods. How much longer was Granny going to put up with this chatter?

"We're going to organize, but first we are going to finish remodeling Mrs. Dilworth's house she has so graciously donated." His voice was raspy, as if he smoked.

"We're living upstairs and we are building a library, Freedom

School and meeting room downstairs," James said. He spoke in a soprano voice, not alto like Rutherford.

If they could fix up that old run-down, falling-apart, unpainted house of Mrs. Carrie's, I was sure they might be able to get us some new books. Not one person from town except Esther had said one word, asked one question.

"How would you like to attend the all-white school?" Gail said. I'd never heard a voice like hers. She rolled her O's and R's in a way that made it hard to understand what she said.

"I'm fine at the colored school, ma'am. We don't mingle," I said.

I heard the screen door squeak, and knew Granny was coming for me, but instead she walked to the truck and searched for our rations while James was still talking.

"Glad you decided to join us, Pearlie," Mrs. Carrie said.

Granny acted as if she hadn't said a word. She took the sack with our name on it out the bed of the truck and gave Esther the eye.

"Stay away from Esther. You hear me, Carrie?" Granny said while chewing on her toothbrush.

"Pearlie," Mrs. Carrie said.

"I'm warning you, Carrie, and you know why, too."

Granny took the commodities and strolled back to the house. Some of the folks turned their whole bodies around and watched her till she disappeared behind the door. Granny had had enough, and she wanted to send a signal to Mrs. Carrie to stop holding folks' food hostage, and to Esther to keep her mouth shut. All the folks wanted was to get their food and go home to their chores. Not one of them was as brave as Granny. Plus Esther, Mrs. Carrie and them civil rights workers were wasting their breath. Reverend Jefferson had told us not to pay them no mind. I looked across the church ground onto Front Street and saw a police car coming around the curve. It was upon us before I could let them know. I stretched my neck to see who was behind the tinted window. Muhdea caught hold to one of my plaits and pulled it back in place and me closer to her. The driver rolled up and eased down his window. They were riding four deep.

"Hey, Mozelle," Mr. Michael James King, the chief of police, said.

Nobody I knew ever called him Chief King or Mister or any other name. We always said his full name when we talked about him outside of his company, and in his presence, we said sir, like "Yes, sir" and "No, sir."

"Carrie, what you got going on here?" Mr. Michael James King said.

One of the two deputy police was sitting in the back seat on the passenger's side, the owner of the Esso station sat next to him, and Mr. Sam Ray Blackburn was in the front seat.

"Delivering commodities," Mrs. Carrie said.

"Young lady, ain't you on the wrong side of the tracks?" he said to Gail.

"And the wrong part of the country," Mr. Sam Ray Blackburn said.

Gail took a step toward the police car as if she wanted to get close enough for them to hear her answer. Before she could mumble a word or get any closer, Esther placed her hand around her waist and eased Gail behind her. Esther walked toward the car.

"We're finishing up here," she said. "Almost done."

"I heard you was back in town, Esther Mae," Mr. Michael James King said. "You keeping out of trouble?"

"Starting it," Esther said, placing her hand on one hip.

Muhdea cleared her throat. Mr. Michael James King focused his attention on her.

"Mozelle, how you and little Sarah doing? I figured you'd be in the field today." he said. He looked at me as if he were peeping over his eyeglasses, but he wasn't wearing any.

"You growing quicker than that Johnson grass, girl. I don't know why Mozelle ain't taking you to the field yet," Mr. Sam Ray Blackburn said, and the other men in the car nodded. "Esther Mae, I know you ain't been to the field in that getup." He eyed her from bottom to top.

"She'll be ready soon." Muhdea smiled between her teeth.

Before she could respond, Mr. Sam Ray Blackburn changed the subject.

"Can we give you a lift, little lady?" he said.

I thought he was talking to me and was about to say no, thank you. I wasn't going anywhere.

Instead, Esther spoke up. "We're about finished. Just a few more packages to hand out." She picked up a sack and gave it to Mr. Peter.

He smiled and gestured to the men in the car as if to say she was telling the truth.

"Alright, Carrie, I'll be circling back through here," Mr. Michael James King said.

Gravel crackled under the weight of the tires.

"We'll be finished by then," she said.

As the car window rolled upward, Mr. Sam Ray Blackburn said, "Little lady, if I were you, I would catch the first thing smoking back to where you came from. We don't mix in these parts."

Folks half-waved at the car as it cruised down the road. James picked up his speech as if he hadn't witnessed what happened.

"There shouldn't be any white-only and colored-only signs to keep us separated," he said.

"Looks like rain, Carrie," Mrs. Mary said.

There wasn't a cloud in the sky. Any other time Mrs. Carrie would've known what she meant.

"Esther, why don't you go help Granny in the kitchen?" Muhdea said.

"In a minute," Esther said. Then she turned to James as if she were mad at him. "Why are you telling these people things they already know? They aren't stupid, you know. You're telling them about equality when they aren't aware of inequality. Integration isn't going to work here. Most people here like their lives the way they are now. They don't feel as if they're missing out on anything."

Esther was in a heap of trouble. Just wait till Reverend Jefferson heard about what she'd said. Muhdea nudged me toward the house. I got the hint and went inside to help Granny. She was taking cans out of the sack and slamming them onto the table.

"They ain't Moses, and we sure ain't the children of Israel," Granny said. "How them young folks think they will lead us? Men and women who ain't married. White and colored living under the same roof. Carrie opening a big can of bait, and they might get out and crawl all over Maeby. And your mama," she breathed slow and hard. "I ain't got the words I need for what I want to say about her."

"What did Mrs. Carrie do? Did y'all have a falling out before?" I said.

I knew Granny and Mrs. Carrie respected each other, but they also stayed out of each other's way. Me and Malika had talked about why we thought they weren't close, but all we came up with was that one was Baptist and the other Methodist, which didn't answer nothing. We both wrote that on our lists.

"Wouldn't be Carrie if she wasn't stirring up something. Her and your mama mean well. It just never turns out right."

I wished she'd stop saying "your mama." Granny was my mama as far as I was concerned, and Esther was Muhdea's daughter.

"What you mean about that, Granny?"

She didn't answer me. She was done talking. I walked to the screen door to see if the police had come back. Granny called me. I didn't answer.

"Can't you hear me, gal?" Granny said. "You don't need to be listening to them folks anyhow."

Rutherford asked for volunteers to come down to Mrs. Carrie's old house and help them change it from an eyesore to a community center. Nobody raised their hand. Folks remained quiet out of respect, and because Mrs. Carrie was holding their rations hostage.

"What kind of help do y'all need? Break it down for them," Esther said in a voice similar to the people who lived around here, not citified.

I walked on back to the kitchen. Granny handed me a can of hash meat, and I put it on the shelf, wood planks nailed to the wall. We kept canned and dry goods on one side of the wall and dishes, pots, and pans on the other. I put the cheese and eggs on the other shelf.

"I'm sorry, baby, hand me back that can of hash." She took down a pan to cook it. "Mozelle will be out there all day messing with them people. Carrie act like she don't know we got things to do, and the others is too ignorant to tell her they got to get supper on the table. They families will be hungry when they get home from the field."

I handed her a can of hash meat.

"The last thing we need is for your mama and Carrie to be in cahoots. Esther wouldn't be studying them if that old straggly-beard colored boy wasn't part of it."

She struck a match on top of the stove, and then lit the kindling and coals inside the oven.

"Granny, what if things will be different now that Esther is leading them, and she got them other people to help her and Mrs. Carrie? Our stuff is worse off than the white folks'. Their side of town looks a whole lot better than ours. Ain't no place to write our name once we get their leftover books, and half the pages be torn out."

"You or Esther ain't telling me nothing I don't already know. We make do, child. We make do, and we be fine without Carrie bringing this mess here. You deserve better, but I don't want no heap of mess. What Carrie doing might turn families against each other. It may even start a rift 'tween folks and the church. You see what I'm trying to tell you?"

I didn't see, but I was sure if Granny said it, she was right. She wouldn't take up time trying to explain it if it wasn't important. Folks in our town got along fine, and I'd be alright if I never got a new book or sat in a café. I stacked the rest of the food on the shelves. While we talked, it struck me that if Granny was right, this might turn me and Malika against each other.

"Granny, what about Malika? Will this turn only grown folks, or can children turn on each other, too?"

"It'll be a bad thing if children get caught up in grown folks' mess, but Esther seem to think this fight is 'bout you. You remember what happened to them little girls in Alabama. When you bring in folks from the outside who don't know our ways, ain't no telling what might happen. We take each day as it's given to us. Right now, she ain't here, so no need of worrying about it. We have to wait and see how all this pans out. Ain't no telling what may happen around here with a white woman and a colored boy under the same roof.

The whites won't like that at all." She shook her head as if she were trying to shake something loose in her brain. "The Christians won't like it either. If Carrie wanted to start some trouble with the whites and coloreds, she done went and got a whole heap of it now."

I decided I would write Malika to tell her what took place. Maybe we could put our heads together and figure out how to get around this mess. Muhdea came in the kitchen and started peeling Irish potatoes for supper.

"Carrie still out there?" Granny said. "What she waiting on? Mr. Michael James King to come back and haul them all off to jail?"

"She finally gave the folks their packages. They left as soon as she handed them over. Esther Mae is still out there though."

"Oh, Lord," Granny said.

"Oh, Lord is right. I figure I'll tell her to keep her distance later tonight," Muhdea said.

I walked back to the screen door and looked outside. Sure enough, Esther was laughing it up and running her mouth like an open hydrant with Mrs. Carrie and the SNCC organizers. All the folks were gone. As Mrs. Carrie pulled off, and Esther walked toward the house, the police car crawled down the gravel road. Esther had better be careful when she talked to Muhdea. She was in a whole bunch of trouble.

CHAPTER EIGHT

The Devil Is Busy

ESTHER STRUTTED IN the house as if she'd given the high school commencement address instead of shaming her mama in public. Muhdea waited till the next day, after she'd discussed what Esther had done with Reverend Jefferson, before she confronted her. I was surprised he didn't want to sit down with her. One of Muhdea's rules was to never speak to anybody out of anger, wait till the anger passed. You can't ever take back what's been said, so walk away and come back later. So her voice sounded natural when she sat across from Esther in the living room where we could all see and hear. I knew it meant she was sending a message to all of us, Granny included.

"Esther Mae," she said, her hands clasped, elbows dug into her thighs. "You a grown woman. I've tried to tell you what to do most of your life, and you defied me. I'm tired. We all tired of your antics. I thought you wanted to come back here and be a mother to Sarah, make amends. I'm done with it. If you plan to keep living in my house, you will abide by my rules. This ain't no threat, Esther. I know I said it before, but I mean it this time. You gone too far. I suggest you stop thinking about yourself and put your efforts into helping others and getting right with the Lord." Her eyes roamed over Esther for a long time before she said, "That's all I have to say. I'm wiping my hands of the whole situation. You let me know what you decide, and if it ain't to act right, then maybe you should catch that bus on back to where you came from."

I thought Muhdea and Esther would go at each other like wild hogs, but Esther didn't say nothing except "Yes, ma'am," and waited for Muhdea to raise her head to dismiss her. Both of them had a fiery temper. Me and Granny exchanged looks. Had Esther backed down without a fight, or was she up to something? Muhdea wasn't playing. She'd better be careful.

I TRIED TO approach Esther several times, but . . . well, she was busy. Every time I attempted to ask her if I could sit on the Mourner's Bench, my instinct told me to keep my mouth shut. Granny had taught me about instinct. Like if a white lady asked me an inappropriate question, don't follow my instinct and cuss her out, but if two white men approached me, follow it and run like hell. She should be as proud as Muhdea was of me for wanting to come to the Lord. Wasn't that what every mama wanted for her child?

She was in more trouble than ever after that stunt she pulled with Mrs. Carrie and them civil rights workers in front of most of the First Baptist members. Muhdea was too stunned to look at her. She held her head down whenever anybody mentioned her name. Even though Esther needed prayer more than ever now, she wished Reverend Jefferson didn't have to call her name at every service. I wondered if folks would start back sprinkling holy water on me and placing their hands across my forehead. I tried to keep my distance from her as much as I could to keep folks from remembering that she was my mama and not Muhdea and Granny. Every time one of them said, "Y'all could be twins," I cringed.

I figured it was a good idea to ask Esther while she was vulnerable. I didn't know how to win her over like I did with Muhdea and Granny. I didn't know her or her ways. If Granny asked for her toothbrush, I knew she'd take the long way around to explain why she'd said no. Muhdea resituated her wig or her stockings before she answered yes. After I caught on, it didn't sting as bad. I braced myself for the answer before they told me. I'd never asked Esther for permission to do anything, so I studied her and bided my time, which was running out. Revival was starting in a couple of nights.

I caught up to Esther while she was in the garden Saturday morning. She had pulled the tarp from over the plants, but she hadn't folded it properly and put it away. We have to cover the plants on the days the city sprays for mosquitoes. Even though they don't spray enough to kill them like they do on the white side, 'cause we can see the fog when they spray over there, Granny don't want none of it to get on us or on her plants. We all hated spray days 'cause we had to come inside before the sun went down.

I folded the tarp and put it away. Then I got my hoe and took the row of squash next to hers. Neither one of us seemed to know how to be with the other. I pulled away the weed that was choking a plant and sprayed the plants with vinegar water; I cleared my throat and held my hand out so she could see the Johnson grass.

"Glad I got this. It would've killed that poor squash."

"Probably," she said.

What could I say to that, probably? I laid the weeds between the rows and kept chopping, waiting for an in.

"Whole church is excited about revival. You going?"

"Probably not."

She was always trying to talk to me, and now I wanted to strike up a conversation, and she ain't got but two words, probably and probably not. What had gotten into her? Had Granny told her what I was up to? I tried again.

"This would be your first one in a good while. Folks will be expecting you."

"Folks always expecting stuff they won't be getting."

"It'll be a good time to renew your faith," I said.

What had crawled up her panties? She didn't even look up at me, or acknowledge my presence.

"You don't care how it will make Muhdea look?"

"Sarah, why are you fishing?" She pushed back her straw hat and sunglasses. "Who cares what folks think?"

I pushed mine back on my head. It fell on the ground. I picked it up as I scrambled for words.

"Folks will talk if you don't go. Muhdea cares what they say."

"Do you care?" She paused and looked directly at me.

"They ain't talking about me, they gossiping about you," I said. I twisted my mouth as I did when someone was getting the best of me. We'd gotten clear off my reason for talking to her, and she was making me mad.

"Well then," she said.

"So that's it? You staying at home?"

"Pretty much," she said and wiped the dust off her legs.

I unwrapped another weed with my hands. She told me to use the edge of my hoe. I used what I wanted to.

"Well, I'm going. They got a powerhouse preacher, and Reverend Jefferson said we're going to have a good time. I guess you don't want to have fun with us."

"Going to church is fun to you?"

What kind of question was that?

"What do you get out of it?" she said.

Again, I didn't answer. Didn't feel like she'd agree with me if I did. I sighed.

"Esther."

"Mother."

I sighed again.

"What you got against the church?"

"What do you really want to ask me, Sarah?"

"Nothing. Trying to strike up a conversation with you is all. Just figured I'd help you with the gardening."

"I'm not stupid, you know."

I wasn't getting anywhere with her. I believed she knew what I wanted. If I didn't bring it up, she couldn't tell me no. I hadn't expected her to one-word me. I thought she'd be chattering away as always. Maybe she'd run out of Chicago stories. Maybe she thought she'd break me since I wanted something from her. Not a chance of that happening.

I chopped a while longer, giving her a chance to get on my good side, but she stood fast. She wasn't going to make it easy for me to ask her. I wasn't sure if she wanted me to ask. We played around with talk for a few more minutes. She treated me like I'd treated her since she came back home. When she tried to get on my good side again, I would remember this. I cut down a couple of plants. Gardening required careful attention, and I wasn't paying it any. I chopped down more plants. Esther called my name as if I'd cut her.

"Esther?"

"Mother."

"Then I guess you ain't planning on minding Muhdea? I guess you packing your bags again, huh?"

She acted like I wasn't talking to her. I waited a few more minutes, cut down a few more plants, put them in my pocket.

"Pick up my row from here. I got to go," I said.

I left before she had time to say anything, like where you going. Time wasn't on my side. I needed to go off to myself and pray. The other kids had been in prayer all year, and here I was asking God to do overtime for me. With all that was going on between Muhdea and Esther, I might need him to do triple time. I went on back behind the smokehouse to pray, ask for my sign, beg for forgiveness. God needed to forgive me quicker than it took to make Folgers instant coffee.

SUNDAY-NIGHT REVIVAL ROLLED around quicker than a chicken ran when it was chosen for supper. Reverend Jefferson rose from his oversized chair in the pulpit and approached the podium. He grasped each side of the wood and took a long breath. I'd made up my mind to take my seat even though I'd never asked Esther. With all that was going on and my failed attempt in the garden, I'd never found the right moment to approach her again. I felt as if I didn't have much to be concerned about. She wasn't coming to revival anyway, and if she did, nobody would care whether I had her permission or not. After she'd disobeyed Reverend Jefferson in public, the church members would understand how urgent it was for me to get baptized. Within the next weeks, I needed to seek forgiveness of my sins and receive a sign from God as proof. I wasn't off to a good start.

"Welcome. Welcome one and all to our summer revival," Reverend Jefferson said. "Before we get down to our purpose, which is to honor the Lord, I must take care of a little matter. I hate to bring this up when we have honored guests here in the pulpit."

He scratched his head, rumpled his gray hair and adjusted his glasses. What matter could he be talking about? I'd figured out how much time it took from him beginning service with reading the Bible verses to closing with opening the doors of the church, which was more than long enough, and now he wanted to add another matter.

"Y'all all know Carrie Dilworth done gone out and got herself mixed up with them people, SNCC." He sounded out each letter. "I don't know what they plans is."

He rubbed his hand across his hair from back to front.

"Not to worry though, I'll get to the bottom of it. I been told it's three of them staying at her old two-story house on the low end of town. Two whites and a colored. One of the whites is a girl. Some of you done made their acquaintance. Carrie brought them around when I was gone up to Cotton Plant on church business. And from what I hear, one of our own is mixed up with them. All we can do is continue to pray for Sister Esther Mae."

The church clapped.

"I ask the church to hold Sister Esther Mae up to the Lord every day. She is gone astray, and only the Lord can bring her back into the fold."

"Reverend," a woman said from the back of the church.

"Reverend," a different woman said.

"We don't want the marches and the boycotts. No good has come out of it in other places. Nothing but sadness in Alabama and Mississippi. If it wasn't a sin, so many folks wouldn't have got hurt," he said.

"Reverend." I recognized Mrs. Mary's voice.

"Sister, I have the floor now. Can't it wait?" he said.

We all turned our heads to look at Mrs. Mary, who stood up.

"No, sir, it can't," she said.

We turned back toward him, but right before, I noticed a white woman sitting on the last row of pews, near the corner.

"We got guests back here," she said.

"I acknowledged that, Sister Mary," he said.

He was turning colors under his dark skin. He couldn't see who sat on the back row from the pulpit, but he wouldn't want to be up there talking about folks and not know they were in the building. I wanted to stand up and tell him since Mrs. Mary seemed as if she couldn't spit it out, but it wasn't my place. Then one of the deacons spoke up.

"She trying to tell you the civil rights workers is sitting back there on the last row," he said.

"Thank you, deacon, for letting me know," Reverend Jefferson said. He continued as if he wasn't ashamed. "I already welcomed them, sister. Please take your seat, and let me get on with the service."

For the first time, I noticed how the podium swallowed Reverend Jefferson. Only his head, his short neck, the top of his shoulders and his small hands were visible. He was too far into his message to turn back. He looked over his shoulder at the other five pastors sitting in much smaller straight-back chairs, three on each side of his over-stuffed whale of a chair, which he would graciously hand over to the guest preacher after he introduced him.

"As I was saying," he cleared his throat and grunted, "I'm telling you what the Bible says, and whoever is within listening distance is welcome to hear. Ain't no shame in that, is it? Amen."

"Amen. Amen, Reverend," roared through the church and collapsed like lines of dominoes.

"We gets along fine with the white people in town. I can see why some folks might think we need more, but that ain't what I'm going after right now. A much bigger problem is looming down there, and regardless of the occasion, we know what's right is right. Shouldn't no men and women be living under the same roof unless they kin or married. That's what the Bible says."

He held up the Bible. The church clapped long and loud. He threw his head back, confident the church was on board.

"And the members of First Baptist won't be getting involved with Carrie's mess," Reverend Jefferson said.

The church stood and clapped, and I did too, relieving my behind from the hard, wood pew. We'd been raising money for a while to buy red cushions to match the carpet. Every time we came close to having enough money, something came up and we started over again. We always left one dollar in the piggy bank as startup cash. Reverend Jefferson told us it was easier to add to a dollar than to start from nothing. The last time we used the money to help pay Mr.

Peter's hospital bill, and the time before that was to help pay a boy's college tuition. Reverend Jefferson said he'd spend the last dollar on a child's education.

He preached for a while from Luke 2:41–52. Even Jesus strayed away from His parents to learn and teach. Reverend Jefferson motioned with his hands for us to be seated. Rutherford, the colored civil rights worker, was the only person left standing.

"May I address your statements?" he said. He scratched his beard. His voice was distinct, a twang of country and a lift to it like city, but not proper like Esther's.

"This is not the time or place, young man," Reverend Jefferson said.

"But you've made it the time and place, sir. I deserve a chance to address your comments."

Somebody needed to pull his coattail. He couldn't talk back to Revered Jefferson. I looked around to see if anybody was back there who would hurry up and let him know before the Lord smacked him upside the head. What church did he attend in Georgia where they hadn't taught him basic manners?

"You may set up a time to see me later, sir, but tonight we're here for revival, and we don't want to stray no further away from our purpose than we already have. Amen, church."

"Well now," Mrs. Mary blurted out, then covered her mouth with her hand as if she was surprised she'd said it alone and aloud. Reverend Jefferson dismissed Rutherford without another word, left him standing in place, as he went on with his message.

"We got a dynamic speaker here with us tonight. He came all the way down here to help these sinners come to the Lord."

Rutherford remained standing as if Reverend Jefferson were going to change his mind and give him a chance to speak. He had plenty to learn, and he was supposed to be here to show us how to live.

"Since we've taken up so much time tonight, I'll just get right down to business," Reverend Jefferson said. He cut his eyes at Rutherford. Then he held his mouth wide open and held his head back, which we all knew meant a powerful song was coming. He belted out two words, "Precious Lord," and the choir picked it up immediately.

That Rutherford was in a lot of trouble. He'd caused Reverend Jefferson to shorten his introduction by at least fifteen or twenty minutes.

As the choir sang, the church halfheartedly joined in, and Rutherford remained standing. Reverend Jefferson raised his hands for the church to stand and sing louder.

"The doors of the church is open," Reverend Jefferson said. "Please stand, church. Let the Lord hear you. Let your voices break through the rafters."

He held his head back even further and sang a verse: "Precious Lord. Let me stand. I'm tired. I am weak. I am worn."

He checked to see if the other ministers were up out of their chairs and singing.

"All you who have a desire in your heart to be saved, please come forward as we sing," Reverend Jefferson said and raised his arms higher and wider, and I didn't know what the plan was.

He whaled out another verse of the song. Then one of the other ministers whom I hadn't ever seen before picked up the lead. The three civil rights workers and a few other people from the low end of town walked toward the door. Well, if the folk from the low end were advising them, no wonder they hadn't learned any manners. Eyes made contact back and forth throughout the church as they walked. How would Reverend Jefferson handle them? He kept right on singing as the cardboard fans donated by Brown's Funeral Home, where we all had burial insurance from the day we were born, fanned faster, the choir sang louder, and the amen corner praised the Lord with different versions of "Thank you, Jesus," and "My Lord."

Not even a long-standing sinner would walk out when the doors of the church were clearly open. The civil rights workers didn't tip out with one arm held high and forefinger pointed up, which signaled all else had failed, and they had to be excused this minute. They walked to the front of the church, past the pulpit, the Mourner's Bench, and right on by the mothers. Ingrates, I thought and was sure the rest of the church felt the same.

Rutherford reached for the doorknob, but Esther opened the door from the other side before he even touched it. She shook hands with them, and they whispered back and forth. What could they be whispering about? I wondered. I included her name in the ingrate pile right along with them. She might've been gone for a good while, but she had home training. She better hurry up and recall it before Reverend Jefferson came down from the pulpit and reminded her.

They finally left, and Esther slid between the pews on the mothers' side of the church, which she knew was meant for them and for very old ladies in good standing with the Lord. Muhdea would hear about it from the ladies and the mothers, and I hoped to be hiding in a corner listening when she told Esther about herself. Esther took her seat, then realized she was the only person seated and stood up. Reverend Jefferson motioned for us all to be seated.

"Thank you for joining us, Sister Esther Mae," Reverend Jefferson said. "Since you seem to know more about what's going on than the rest of us, why don't you shed some light on it for us? What exactly are you expecting to accomplish hanging 'round with the wrong folks?"

Esther looked around the church before she stood up. At least she'd had enough sense to not wear them hot pants to church.

"It was a rhetorical question, Miss Jones," he said.

The whole church laughed. He quieted them after he finished laughing. It wasn't right for him to call Esther out that way. I refused to laugh. Although it was funny, I held mine in.

"Excuse me," Esther said.

"No need to get your draws in a bunch," he said. "Church, you see how busy the Devil is tonight. Have a seat, Esther."

She didn't. He went on with the service in spite of her protest. The church turned their attention to him. "Amen" and "Praise God" rang out over Esther's voice. She did what he expected her to do. She stormed out of the building.

"As I said, the Devil is busy tonight."

Reverend Jefferson and the five other ministers—each dressed in a different bright-colored velvet robe, with gold trim down the front all the way to the hem—held out their arms as if they were trying to coax a baby to them. "Come to the Lord." Each one of them took a turn at the podium between the choruses of "Every Time I Feel the Spirit," by Mahalia Jackson, Granny's favorite singer.

"Please come. Let the Lord in your heart tonight."

They spread out around the pulpit, and one walked out into the audience. "Come to Jesus," he said.

Miss Ora Bea stood off to the side and invited the sinners to come too. If the choir would just sing "I Need Thee Every Hour" right now, I could bypass the Mourner's Bench and go straight up and testify. Then Esther could act any way she pleased, sin if she wanted to, 'cause she wouldn't be the proprietor of my sins no longer.

Mothers dressed in white from head to toe, including nurse's shoes, stockings and caps, added more chairs to the Mourner's Bench, white high-back ladder chairs with sea-grass seats, at the front center of the church. I heard the sea grass scratched welts on your behind as the nights of revival wore on. Some talked about mourners who joined church early just so they wouldn't have to sit in one of them chairs another night. The seats were supposed to remind the sinner of the wrath of God. Some mourners padded their behind with paper sacks, but it made such a noise the mothers sent them to the toilet to remove it. Mothers had keen eyes and instincts. One rarely got away with anything around them.

Before all the commotion, I decided to make my intentions known. I wasn't going to be the first to get up, but I hadn't planned to be the last either. I pretty much knew the mourners would be all the boys and girls who would turn thirteen before the next revival. The sins of the child belonged to the parent till the day she turned thirteen. First Baptist Church required children to be submerged underwater during their twelfth year. Children took most of that year to review their sins and begin to ask God for forgiveness. As the revival came near, they prayed to God to give them a sign as proof of His forgiveness. All playing and everything else that could be associated with the Devil ceased and desisted during revival so the mourners could hear the Lord speaking to them. For as long as I'd been going to church, God had answered prayers, women had made baptismal gowns during the weeks as sinners came to the Lord, and ministers had baptized all of them at the Jericho River on Sunday after the revival ended. Parents hoped and believed for their child's salvation. I felt as if some of the parents, whose child acted as if the Devil had hatched her, would be more than happy to pass their child's sins on to her.

I wasn't as bad as most of them who would come forward that night, but I was worse than a few of them, and Esther's arrival and what I was about to do put me right up there at the top. I still can't say with any amount of certainty why some religions hold parents accountable for their children's sins. I imagined the age has to do with the age of Jesus when His mother Mary found him at the temple.

The young folk were guaranteed to come forward, but we never knew how many backsliders or grown folks who'd never been baptized would take their seats. Miss Lilith felt that she needed to repent and be baptized every year. I planned to take my seat sometime before the returning sinners angled their way up to the chairs. I'd run up and get in front of them if I had to.

"All who want to get saved come on up and sit on the Mourner's Bench. The mothers done prepared for you. Come on up," Reverend Jefferson said.

Crazy Abigail popped up first. The church praised her with a few "Thank you, Jesuses," but it wasn't out of the ordinary for Abigail to be the first to volunteer for everything. I expected folks to shout when they realized I'd taken a seat. Mark and John, the superintendent's sons, angled toward the chairs, heads down. They'd better look up before they took their seats. Mark was the oldest, but they were only nine months apart in age, so John would be thirteen before the next revival. They sat right in front of me, and I almost caught John's hand and walked with them, but I couldn't move my feet.

Reverend Jefferson said, "Praise be to God. Deacon Graves got to be mighty proud of his boys."

Their mother stood next to the chairs and greeted them even though she was a member of the Methodist church. Deacon Graves held her hand. Tears rolled down her face, and Deacon Graves praised Jesus aloud and raised his free hand. Dinah Anderson, who sat on the pew behind me, walked up with two other girls. Her mama was one of the mothers. She grabbed and squeezed her silly, blocking the other girls' mamas from reaching them. Mrs. Anderson raised her hands to the sky and cried out, "My Lord, Thank you, Lord."

Sinners took their seats one by one. Reverend Jefferson changed the song to a more upbeat tune. I couldn't stop one leg from shaking and couldn't move the other one. Everybody in church was standing except me. I lost sight of Muhdea in the sea of folks gathered around the mourners. I hadn't told her or Granny about my final intentions. Maybe my legs didn't know, and I didn't know what their plans were either 'cause they sure weren't cooperating with me.

The lady who sat next to me tapped me on the shoulder and motioned for me to stand up. It wasn't proper behavior for me to be seated when the whole church was on fire.

"If there is anyone else that's out there thinking about it—come, please come while the choir sings," Reverend Jefferson said.

Even the backsliders except for Lilith beat me to the bench. All the preachers and mothers gathered around the sinners. All but three chairs were taken. After the visiting preacher took the podium, I'd have to wait till he finished his sermon if I didn't go soon. I wouldn't want to be the person whom the mothers went back to the choir room and got chairs for. Some folks didn't make up their minds till after the sermon. They generally didn't attend First Baptist, but were from surrounding churches throughout the county.

The church was on fire. Mrs. Anderson led the shouting, and I missed my chance at having the people shout for me. She flung her hat in the air, and Mr. Matthew Graves caught it. Afterward, like every Sunday, Mrs. Anderson threw her glasses across the room, and spun around and around, then ran toward the preacher. Deacons positioned themselves to catch her before she reached him. Once she'd sidestepped them and tackled Reverend Jefferson head on. We played a game to see who would be the one to catch her glasses. She threw them in the other direction every time, and then we ran to pick them up, till the deacon put an end to it before one of us kids broke her glasses. If she cared whether they got broken, she'd keep them on her face, but I couldn't say that to the deacon.

Reverend Jefferson quieted the church. I'd better go now. "Please take your seat," he said. "Bow your head, close your eyes and let's pray for these poor sinners."

As soon as he began to pray, I got enough courage to walk to the front and take my seat. All eyes must've not been closed 'cause when I was about to take my seat, Muhdea gave me a tight hug and lifted me off my feet. She spun me like Mrs. Anderson had twirled herself earlier. I'd never seen her shout. As surprised as I was, I wanted her to put me down. The other mothers joined Muhdea and started shouting all over again.

At the end of the prayer, Reverend Jefferson gave the podium over to Reverend Isaiah Rich and sat in the chair where Reverend Rich was sitting.

"Father, I stretch my hands to thee," Reverend Rich belted out, and the church repeated. "No other help I know."

Anybody who sang that song meant business. If Rutherford had stayed, Reverend Rich would've saved his soul. Reverend Rich started out slow—announced his text, his verse, and eased into his sermon about Jesus and His disciples. He wanted them to follow Him and become fishers of men. I knew the story from Sunday school. Mrs. Anderson came over, handed Crazy Abigail a paper napkin to spit out her gum and gave her a warning look. I'd better be careful not to nod off. If she'd caught Abigail, who was the slickest of all of us, she'd have no problem catching me.

Reverend Rich was in full steam, sweating and then wiping it off with his white handkerchief. His voice got louder as he got more wound up.

"One by one the disciples laid down their nets and followed Jesus. Paul laid down his net. Luke laid down his net." At the top of his lungs, he yelled, "Are you willing to lay down your sins for Jesus? 'Cause if you don't . . ." His voice trailed off.

I watched him preaching Hell and damnation. He was black as night, and all of his teeth were gold. Every time he opened his mouth and flashed those big gold teeth, I wondered if the streets in Heaven were paved with the same type gold. When I kneeled to pray, my eyes met Esther's. She stood at the front door patting her foot.

CHAPTER NINE

The Hand Is Quicker
Than the Eye

SISTER TUCKER MADE me stand next to her and count change for everybody who bought candy, washboard cookies, hoop cheese and whatever else while we waited for the storm to pass. I added, subtracted, multiplied and divided the price of items and figured the tax in my head, couldn't use my fingers. Sister Tucker said I'd thank her when it helped me get into college. I might thank her later, but right now, all I wanted to do was pay for Granny's snuff and go home.

"I'm proud of you for taking your seat," she said.

"Thank you."

"I'm glad Esther is back home so she can see it. Did she tell you her testimony yet?"

It was customary for parents to sit their child down and tell her how they got saved. Granny and Muhdea had told me their testimony, but I didn't know if Esther even had one. Since she didn't know I was going to take my seat, there wasn't any reason for her to tell me hers. Muhdea went on and on about how happy she was for me. I kept quiet and waited to see if Granny would give away to Esther that she'd told me to ask her for permission. Esther clenched her jaw, but even she didn't want to spoil Muhdea's mood. Granny waited till we were on our knees next to the bed ready to pray. She didn't chastise me or tell me I still needed to consult with Esther. She asked me if I thought I'd done the right thing, if I thought God would be pleased with my behavior, then the next day she gave me all of the other kids' chores and told them they could go play. I put my head down and got to work. As a rule, whoever sat on the Mourner's Bench was excused from everything except prayer. Nothing should interfere with God's plan. Granny was disappointed with me, or she wouldn't be placing obstacles in my path. I'd make up for disobeying her by being the first to get my sign and testify. She'd be proud of me then.

"No, ma'am, she hasn't told me her testimony yet," I said. "I'm sure she'll get around to it." Esther was expected to help me cross over to the other side.

Sister Tucker looked as if she was confused. Why wasn't Esther helping me? I wasn't worried. How could a sinner advise another sinner?

"I'm sure she'll get around to it. She may have forgotten the significance since she was away for so long," she said. "You listen to as many testimonies as you can. The more you hear, the more it'll become real to you."

She proceeded to tell me hers again. I mouthed it along with her, as did the other three customers, while they waited.

I left the store and walked across the First Baptist Church ground with my head hung down. Sister Tucker had reminded me of how much wrong I'd done. She'd given me a two-for-a-penny caramel kiss as my pay for hours of counting without making any mistakes. I hated going to her store. Every day except Sunday, Granny sent me to buy snuff, chewing tobacco, potted meat, pressed ham, Spam and other stuff she said she needed and sometimes already had on hand. I made change for myself and everybody else that came in the store, and they seemed to always trickle in for hours whenever I was there. Sister Tucker even did what ifs. What if I take away a pound of hoop cheese and add a box of saltines, what would that add up to? Don't forget to add the taxes.

If Granny caught me with my head down, she'd be mad. A young colored girl should always hold her head up high unless a white person was talking to her: never look at them eye to eye. I would've stared one down that day. Instead, I stared up at the clouds, which were hanging lower than my head, ugly black clouds shaped like a bugle. They dropped so low it felt as if I could reach up and touch the tip of them. My mind treaded back to the bags of Bugle chips clipped to a red metal stand at the store. Sister Tucker could've given me a bag of Bugles or a box of Cracker Jack.

I kicked a big rock across Front Street and up onto the church ground. I heard a car on the road behind me and turned to see Uncle Robert's black Cadillac cruising down Front Street. My head lifted, and I took off running to meet him. We hadn't seen him for a while, and everybody wanted to know what he'd been doing. Esther asked about him every day as if he should've made a special trip home to see her.

I ran across the church ground, skidded on the gravel road in front of our house, came to a dead stop on our front porch, then opened and closed the screen door like somebody who lived in a house and not in a chicken coop. If I had run straight through and slammed the screen door, Muhdea would've whipped my hind-part till I couldn't sit down.

I heard their loud voices before I eased the screen door all the way closed. I knew their conversation concerned Uncle Robert's new religion. Not one thing about them Muslims was alright with Muhdea, but Uncle Robert kept trying to convince her that he was better off as a Muslim. He would've had a better chance convincing her that we weren't colored. They argued at everything from what he ate to what pictures she chose to put on the wall. She believed he would've come back into the fold by now. Unlike with Esther, she was too ashamed to add his name to more prayer lists.

Uncle Robert stood in the middle of the living room with a stack of pies. He said they were good for her health, same as the beans from the garden. She wanted nothing to do with any Muslim food.

"Don't bring your mess up to me," she said.

"Just try it," he said. "It taste like potato pie."

"If I wanted potato pie, I'd make myself one," she said.

They were off and running. He had only been home for two minutes, and she was already lighting into him like a prizefighter. Muhdea's voice was loud, but Uncle Robert's was calm, which made her get louder.

"Go on now, boy. I ain't got time for your foolishness."

He set them on the coffee table, and went to the kitchen to get a knife. When he got back and attempted to cut one of the pies for her to have a taste, she lost it.

"Where's my holy water, Granny? Sarah, go get it. You know the shelf where I keep it."

I straddled between wanting to taste Uncle Robert's pie and obeying Muhdea.

"I'll have a taste soon as I get back," I said.

"The hell you will," Muhdea said.

I returned with the holy water. Muhdea doused him in it as she prayed in tongues. He stood there and took it as if he'd suddenly found himself in the middle of a Holiness church.

Granny didn't generally intervene unless things had pretty much got out of hand. Now she grabbed Muhdea's wrist.

"That's enough, Mozelle," she said. "He don't deserve this. They jest pies."

She turned to Uncle Robert and gave him the eye. He placed the wrapping paper back over the pies and walked out the door with them. In Muhdea's eyes, he was a rabble-rouser, worse than Carrie Dilworth and now Esther. She didn't understand and didn't try to understand his dress, his prayers, his diet, nothing. Far as I could tell, much of the Qur'an was similar to the Bible. It was when Uncle Robert called the white people pigs and said some other hateful things that I disagreed with.

Uncle Robert owned a ceramics shop in Little Rock where he made and sold whatnots and pictures. He brought us black ceramic dolls, bowls, vases, cups and any other thing he pottered, the ones that weren't perfect. Muhdea placed his knick-knacks all around the house even though she thought his dolls were too dark and their hair was way too nappy. Hadn't he ever heard of a pressing comb? Wasn't displaying his whatnots good enough? Why did he always push her too far?

He was tall, rail thin, and could almost pass for white, and we had the same last name, Jones. She was crazy about him, not having any boys of her own, but they always argued. Granny said her world wasn't orderly unless she was fussing at him and Esther. Granny said Muhdea wasn't mad at Uncle Robert. She was mad at herself for insisting he leave her house not knowing he'd join another religion and move out of town. Muhdea twisted her head from side to side and made eye contact with me or Granny whenever she could. I read it as her asking me if I could believe what that boy she raised had the nerve to say in her house. Maybe she pleaded with the Lord to take him or wished he'd stayed and climbed the walls, but whatever she thought, she didn't say it right then. What I didn't understand was why Uncle Robert encouraged her. Smoke came from the kitchen. Uncle Robert came back in the house just as Muhdea realized her beans were burning. Uncle Robert watched her as she went to see about her food.

"I got some new copies of *Muhammad Speaks* in the car if you want to see them. Sarah can read it to you," he said.

No, I thought, please don't put me in the middle, but I did want to read them. She let the Jehovah Witnesses leave copies of the *Watchtower*. I read their pamphlets, but he knew Granny and Muhdea weren't interested in me reading nothing but the Bible to them. Although Granny did ask me to explain to her the little bit I understood about the Nation of Islam. I didn't tell her about the nasty things Uncle Robert said about white people.

I needed to pray to God to give me my sign tonight, so I grabbed my Chatty Cathy doll and went out to the front porch. Not long afterward, Uncle Robert followed me. We sat on the steps for a while without talking. Me, him and the clouds looked weary.

"What you been up to, Sarah?" he said.

I waited, tried to gather my thoughts before I spoke. He was a grown man, and I knew my place, but like Sunday-morning shouters, I couldn't hold my peace.

"Uncle Robert, you got to stop believing in all that foolishness," I said. "What if Muhdea tells you to stay away from here for good? What if you die? You going to Hell? Jesus don't play. He made it clear in the Bible who going to Heaven and who ain't." I stood up and pleaded with him. "Why don't you stay down here and sit on the Mourner's Bench with me and renew your faith? We can get baptized together."

"You haven't been listening. You're more intelligent than this," he said as he rubbed his forehead. "Now they're brainwashing you." He shook his head from side to side as if he believed I was on Muhdea's side and not his.

"Oh no, sir, not me. I'm getting my religion on my own. I've been listening for God all by myself. I'm old enough to carry my own sins, and I ain't planning on moving till I get the sign from Him even if I have to wait till He knocks me down on the ground like He did Paul."

Uncle Robert rubbed his hand back and forth across his eyebrows. I wanted him to take my word for it.

"I know you don't believe me, but ain't nobody brainwashing me," I said. "Granny told me to go into prayer and wait to hear from God myself. She don't even know what I asked Him to show me. You see, ain't nobody trying to do nothing to me except God."

"Slow down, Sarah. Sit here, honey. It's going to be alright." He took hold of my hand. "I know all about Christianity, but after seeing how it enslaves blacks, I made the choice to change to a religion that empowers me. Don't worry though. Jesus isn't going to banish me to Hell, and neither is Muhdea from this house."

I was getting riled up like Muhdea. "Ain't no choice, Uncle Robert. Baptist is all there is. I don't know what you mean about empowering you, but Baptist is the only ones going to Heaven, nobody else."

Uncle Robert rubbed my shoulder to settle me down. He chuckled a bit. Chatty Cathy sat next to me. He eyed her up and down.

"Now tell me this. Where did you get that little ugly, white, one-eyed doll?"

"You can't change the subject, and she ain't ugly, Uncle Robert. Mrs. Cox at the café gave her to me. Granny made her dress out of leftover quilting pieces. She's Chatty Cathy. The new ones can talk but mine can't, so I make up the words for her."

Uncle Robert looked at me as if I were telling him I believed she was alive. After Muhdea gave her to me, I read in the Sears and Roebuck catalog that she could walk and talk. She said phrases such as *I love you* and *You're pretty*.

"She wouldn't have given it away if she could talk and had both blue eyes," he said.

Before I could defend Mrs. Cox, Muhdea came out to tell us supper was ready. A little later, we got up to go in the house. He pulled my plait as he got up. "How good are you at playing checkers?"

"You know I'm the best around."

"Why?" he said.

"I know my opponent, anticipate his moves and attack. You taught me that."

"It's strategy, Sarah, and you can use it to win at checkers and in life."

He was serious. I knew checkers, but I never compared it to living. I'd have to think on that, write it on my list for later 'cause my religion was all I could ponder right now. He told me Chatty was about the most ugly doll he'd ever seen, and she probably wasn't much better looking when she was new.

"If you promise to let me put her in the trash barrel, I'll make you a doll and bring it to you the next time I'm home."

I told him he could as long as she could walk like Chatty. He said he couldn't promise me that, but she'd be pretty. He promised to come to my baptismal and bring the doll with him. I promised to give him Chatty Cathy after I saw the other doll.

Esther came running down the road as if she saw Jesus. "Robert, Robert, you're here," she said as she wrapped her arms around him.

I knew my time with him was up. Esther took over whenever she showed up, plus they'd been missing one another. They whispered and grinned all during supper. Muhdea held her peace mostly 'cause Granny kept telling her to with her eyes.

After I finished eating, I excused myself from the table and went out by the water hydrant to pray, beg God to send me the sign I'd asked Him for. Uncle Robert kissed my forehead on his way out to his car. He reached behind my ear and pulled a Bo dollar, which white people call a silver dollar, from behind it. I grinned and asked him, as always, "How'd you do that?" I had a mason jar filled with silver dollars he'd been pulling from my ear ever since he left home. "The hand is quicker than the eye," he said. We walked out to his car. I followed behind the car down Side Street till he turned left onto Front Street. Then I ran up to the top of the church steps and waved goodbye to him for a long time. I should've gone back home to finish praying, but I stood and waved at his already gone car. Then I remembered I didn't want to do nothing wrong in case God decided to give me my sign that night, so I ran back to the house, before anybody realized I wasn't out back praying.

CHAPTER TEN

In Remembrance of Me

MUHDEA AND GRANNY washed, and Esther rinsed. I did whatever one or the other told me to do, from filling and emptying the tubs with water, to wringing and hanging the clothes on the line. Even though it was work, I loved washday. As long as I didn't forget my place, I could tell stories and crack jokes right along with the grown folks. Neighbors stopped by to borrow lye soap, and this and that, but mostly they talked about who had a good crop and the fattest livestock, what they heard was happening on the low end of town, who was sick or needed help, and what their children were doing. It didn't dawn on nobody that I should've been in prayer and not working, so I helped out like I did every weekend

We washed clothes on Saturdays. Everybody helped: me, Esther, Granny, Muhdea and my cousins who were big enough. We laid a board across two quilting horses, placed two #2 washtubs atop of the board, put a bar of lye soap in the bottom of one of them, filled a foot tub with water, boiled the water on the stove, poured boiling water in the tub to wash the clothes and cold water to rinse them. It took two people to carry the foot tub. We changed the wash water at least six times before all of the clothes were pinned on the wire clothesline. We washed the whites first.

That Saturday they talked about the civil rights workers. A few folks had been down to the two-story house and reported it was now being called "The Hall." Bro Hollin had joined up with them. He lived across the street from us, but wasn't a member of any church. He clarified for us what the others had guessed or overheard. He backed away from the tub to keep from getting wet as he filled us in on what he knew.

"Yeah, they come up with the name so everybody feels welcome. We been making shelves, tables and desks for the Freedom School," he said.

"What's the Freedom School?" Muhdea said. She and Granny wrung a pair of pants as tight as possible.

"Well, according to Gail, the white girl, they teaching the kids about colored history."

"When they planning on teaching it to them? School fixing to start up in a few weeks."

"She been teaching a few kids who live around there already. Both your sister-in-law's kids been over there. She ain't got the books in yet, but she using her own."

"I still say," Muhdea said. We all stopped in place. "Who she plan on teaching when school starts?"

"No need to get a tone with me, Mozelle," he said. "She having an afterschool program or something like that. Right, Miss Esther?"

We'd all gone back to the washing by then. Esther cut her eyes at Bro Hollin. It was quick. I only saw it 'cause I was standing directly in front of her. He caught it. Muhdea had her head down.

"I still say, Hollin . . ." Muhdea said.

Bro Hollin cut her off. "I don't know everything, Mozelle. Why don't you come on down there and ask the girl yourself? I got to be going. Plenty work to do at my house."

Esther walked around the corner of the house with him. Granny and Muhdea kept talking about the Freedom School.

"Do they teach you colored history at school?" Muhdea looked at me.

"Some," I said. "I learned most of what I knew about colored history from Sister Tucker and Uncle Robert."

"I imagine they teach as much as you need at the school. No need in teaching it over again at no Hall," Muhdea said.

Esther came out the back door with a glass of ice water. She took a sip and set the glass next to her tub.

"They're going to teach more than history. The plans are to teach black literature, art, writing and other courses that aren't being taught at school," Esther said.

Muhdea bit her bottom lip and turned her hip. Esther should've let it go, but she didn't.

"Why?" Muhdea asked as she held a pair of white cotton bloomers in her hand.

"Take Sarah. She's smart. She knows more than children her age and most adults. But she has to learn about her own history outside of the classroom setting. Everybody should know as much as Sarah, and Sister Tucker shouldn't be her only source of information."

"You trying to say Sister Tucker's learning is wrong?" Muhdea said. She pushed the clothes down into the water, grabbed a dress and scrubbed it on the washboard. "I believe if they needed it, the school would teach it."

Me and Granny kept quiet. I wiped sweat off my eyelid. Lye water splashed in my face. I closed my eyes to keep the water from getting into them.

"It's our history. The school requires us to know white history. If Sarah learns what her own people accomplished, she'll know it's possible for her to achieve more."

"So, now we're talking about what Sarah needs to know," Muhdea said as she scrubbed faster, shaking her head.

"Yes, Sarah, me, you and all black people."

I looked in the basket to see if there were any clothes I could take to the clothesline, but it was empty. I showed the empty basket to Granny, but she didn't pay it much mind. Took the toothbrush out of her mouth, checked the snuff, and put it back in the opposite jaw. I moved over and started helping her wash. Esther's tub was filling up with panties, bras, diapers and socks.

"So, now Sarah's black?" Muhdea said.

"You would know that if you knew your history."

"You throwing around what we need to learn like you know everything. Just 'cause you say 'black' and not 'colored' don't make you wise. Don't make you smart. You been here a little over a month. What makes you an authority on what we need or don't need to know in this house?" Muhdea picked up a white towel out of the rinse water. "This ain't clean, Sarah. Pay attention to what you doing."

It was between her and Esther. Why were they bringing me into their mess? Muhdea handed me the towel, and I placed it in the hot water and lathered it with lye soap. Esther took a swallow of ice water and chewed the ice.

"Are you saying I don't know what my child needs?" Esther tried wringing out a sheet. Muhdea stopped washing and helped her.

"You think you know what's right. You doing everything but ain't figuring out nothing before you act."

Each one of them caught hold of one end of the sheet and wrung toward the middle, one wringing tighter than the other when it was her turn. Muhdea put the sheet in the basket. Granny seemed as if she wasn't paying them much attention.

"That's just wrong. I don't know what you're basing it on. I want what's best for Sarah as much as you do. I may be more progressive in my thinking, and it may not come off in the same manner as yours and Granny's, but I put thought into everything I do."

Granny dried her hands on her apron and mumbled something about going in the house to check on the babies. I tried to follow her, but she closed the back door before I could slip through. Esther wrestled with a holey towel.

"Were you figuring or doing when you allowed Sarah to sit on the Mourner's Bench?" Esther said.

"Let's end this right here," Muhdea said. "We slowing down and we got a lot more work to do. Let's just say we both want what's right for Sarah and leave it at that."

The edges of Esther's hair started to sweat. She pulled it back in a ponytail. Last week she'd threatened to cut it all off and wear an Afro like Angela Davis. I thought Muhdea would throw a fit 'cause she loved hair but didn't have but a little bit of her own. She just shook her head and walked outside.

"See how you are. As soon as we get into it, you want to cut and run. Not today though. We're finishing this," Esther said.

Muhdea started humming a tune. I wanted to join in. Esther picked up another sheet. Muhdea reached over to help her.

"That's alright. I got it."

Muhdea backed off but kept humming. Esther swallowed hard. We stayed like that for a long time. Esther dropped the end of the sheet on the ground. She shook it off and put it in my tub. Then she cleared her throat. We took the clothes in the basket and hung them on the line. No wind. I liked it when the wind blew through the clothes. Tree leaves were still. Weeds were taking over the garden. We'd have to till the soil for planting soon. We changed the water in the rinse tub, and I poured hot water in the washtub from the foot tub. Esther cleared her throat, again.

"Sarah is going to the Freedom School on Monday."

My hand slipped, and the hot water landed on Muhdea's leg. She yelped. I set the tub on the ground. Granny came to the door. Esther doused Muhdea's leg with cold water from the glass of ice water she was drinking, and then she put ice in a towel and held it against Muhdea's leg. Muhdea walked back in the house with Granny to take care of it.

"I ain't going to no Freedom School," I said.

"Either you go or I pull you off the Mourner's Bench," Esther said.

"You can't override God," I said. "Maybe Muhdea and Granny but not God." I pushed and pulled the sheet she'd put in my tub, trying to get the dirt off it. I picked up the end with the dirt, lathered it, and scrubbed it between my knuckles.

"I'm trying to teach you how to make a decision, but don't test me, little girl."

"How you going to ask me to disobey Muhdea, the church and God? What kind of chokehold you trying to put me in?" I choked up. Felt like tears were in my throat and on their way up. I took my hands out of the tub and dried them on my dress. She bent over to put a towel in the basket. "I ain't going," I said. I walked in the house and slammed the screen door behind me before she could raise her head up from the basket.

Muhdea heard the door slam, and it was all she needed to yell at me. "This ain't no barn, Sarah. Take your narrow tail back to the room and pray. Do you think God answers the prayers of disobedient kids?"

I kneeled beside the bed like me and Granny did every night. If I told on Esther, it would only cause more yelling between her and

Muhdea. Granny was just sitting back and letting it unfold. I didn't know if she had a plan or not. Muhdea'd already told Esther she needed to make a choice. She didn't seem to care if Esther left town like Uncle Robert did. She may have been just putting on 'cause after today she knew Esther was still in cahoots with Mrs. Carrie and them, and didn't look as if she was moving nowhere. What if she moved, and took me with her? Muhdea would be hurt over that, and she couldn't stop her, not according to the Bible. Maybe that was why she hadn't said nothing else to Esther about it. What if God couldn't hear my request amongst all this ruckus? What if He didn't answer, and I wouldn't get a chance to be the secretary of the Sunday school? What if tomorrow was the last time I read the minutes? If it was my last time, I was going to read them as clear as the Heavenly angels sing.

That Sunday I read as if my voice needed to break through the Heavens to be heard. I held my head up and reached from deep down in my gut.

"Good morning," I said as if I'd never addressed the congregation before that day.

The years of being shy, called ugly, skinnier than a razorblade and twice as sharp, and mothers laying hands on me and praying for my soul were erased. I looked out at Muhdea, who was seated in the second row, center.

"These are the minutes of the First Baptist Church of Maeby, Arkansas."

Every class competed for two banners. The class who won hung the banner in their classroom till another class beat them. I recounted the money and the people twice before I delivered the announcements. Sister Tucker looked at me out of the corner of her eye. She stared at and graded me, then corrected me when I came to her store.

"The children class—Sister Martha Murray, teacher—present twelve—collected $4.57."

If Arthur Lee stuck his tongue out at me one more time, I would walk right over there and hit him upside his big head with this collection plate. He made faces and did whatever he could to make me mess up. If he got me mad enough, I'd point him out to Superintendent Matthew Graves.

"The intermediate class," I said, willing myself to remain calm, "Sister Mozelle White, teacher—present fifteen—collected $8.00."

I looked past Arthur Lee at the colors the sun made coming through the stained-glass windows. They reminded me of the colors in the kaleidoscope Uncle Robert had given me last Christmas, only more colors, and much brighter.

"The adult women class—Sister Tucker, teacher—present ten—collected $10.83."

The colors shone down on the dark brown pews and on top of the church folks' heads. Colors of the rainbow made different types of pictures on the ladies' hats and faces. It felt as if Jesus might slide down on the streams of colored light. I smiled to myself at thoughts of what folks might do if Jesus really did slide down those colors right into the church. There'd be more shouting going on, more than I'd ever seen before or since.

"The adult men class—Brother Elijah Allen, teacher and assistant superintendent—present six—collected $9.78."

The competition for the collection banner was mostly between the women and men classes, but about twice a year, our mamas gave us enough money so we'd win it. The adult classes separated the men and women, but the other classes included both girls and boys. I wasn't sure why they separated men and women when they reached a certain age. I would've preferred if they kept them nappy-headed boys out of our class.

"The grand total present today is forty-three students, and the total amount collected is $33.18."

Everybody looked up at and listened to my every word, waiting to see who would win the banners. I didn't stutter. I didn't make any mistakes. Sister Tucker wouldn't have anything to correct. She'd be proud of me. I prayed for my sign between each breath. If the choir sang "I Need Thee" during church service, it would count. I didn't tell God when they should sing it, only that they needed to sing it during revival.

"The attendance banner goes to the intermediate class—teacher

Mrs. Mozelle White —present fifteen. The collection banner will remain in the adult women class with Sister Tucker. They collected $10.83. Men class, good luck next Sunday." I smiled. "The lesson for today was taken from Genesis, chapter 21, God's promise to Sarah. Sister Tucker presented the overview to the congregation. We have to trust God to answer our prayers no matter how long it takes. Next week Brother Allen's class will give the review. This completes the minutes of the First Baptist Sunday school, Sarah Jones, acting secretary, and Brother Matthew Graves, Superintendent."

I looked out across the congregation. Next time we held Sunday school, I'd be a confirmed member. The superintendent would confirm me as the permanent secretary. I would've earned the right to carry my own sins.

"Now I'll turn it over to the superintendent, Brother Matthew Graves. Thank you, and God bless you as you go about your week," I said.

Brother Graves and I sat right next to the communion table with IN REMEMBRANCE OF ME carved in big bold letters on the front. Only members of the church were allowed to take communion. We sat behind the smaller collection table, right below and in front of the pulpit, looking out at the congregation. Muhdea gleamed with pride. If God were watching, He'd be proud, too.

I believed Reverend Jefferson was pulling one over on us when he said Esther would be addressing the congregation. The Sunday-school hour was over, and we were into the time for church service. He held on to the podium with both hands and then banged down hard on it with his fist before he spoke.

"We're running late, so we will just transition on over into our church service. Sister Esther Mae has an important message to relay to us. The next voices you'll hear after the prayer will be hers and Mr. Rutherford Johnson's." Reverend Jefferson raised both hands to quiet the congregation. "I met with them and the deacons earlier this week. Sister Esther may have strayed, but she's still one of ours, and it's only fair to hear them out. Amen?" He paused, scratched his head on the bald spot, and kept right on talking. "Don't get me wrong, It don't mean we have to do nothing just 'cause we listening to them. Amen?"

The church said, "Amen."

Esther looked so pretty. If she was white, she could've been on TV. She wore nice church clothes, a pink dress buttoned down the front, below her knees, and her hair was pinned in a bun, but her face was painted, and she wore red lipstick. She spoke first.

"As some of you may or may not know, Mrs. Carrie filed a lawsuit against the school board asking them to fund us separate but equal schools. We want our schools to be equal to the white school, meaning equal pay, equal facilities and equal equipment and books." She pulled on her dress and wrung her hands together. Rutherford stared a hole into her.

"I don't mean to take up much of your time." She sneezed. Sister Tucker pulled a handkerchief from her purse and handed it to her. Esther wiped her face with it and started again. "The courts reached a decision earlier this week, which was not what either of us wanted. Although the school board agreed to set aside bonds, it was for some future date that by the time we receive the money, it wouldn't benefit any of us here. The courts disagreed with that and made a decision based on the Freedom of Choice Act."

As she was about to explain what that meant, Rutherford took over. It showed on Esther's face: she didn't appreciate him interrupting her. He was long winded, and the only person who got away with that around here was Reverend Jefferson. He quoted the law chapter and verse, and we had no idea what he was talking about. Esther took over again and cleared it up for us.

"What this means to us," she said, "is our students will be able to choose whether they want to attend Maeby schools or Fields schools. For the first time, black students will be allowed by law to attend the white school. We'll need to select our best and brightest because like Central High School, they will not want our children over there, and it won't be easy on them. Right now, that's all we know. The NAACP lawyers are involved, and the next step, which I vehemently disagree with, is to file for total integration. We will update you as we have more information. Thank you for allowing me to take up your time."

She did a good job and spoke up right well. Reverend Jefferson continued his message as if what Esther and Rutherford told us hadn't stunned the whole church. He went right on back to talking about the revival and pulled the congregation away from equal rights to getting saved.

"Christians, Reverend Rich has been here since Sunday night. He's come to us in his own way all week. He raised our spirits with the message of Job and Isaiah. We were right there in the fiery furnace with him." Reverend Jefferson pulled out his handkerchief and wiped his forehead. "Three went in, but, oh glory, when the fire went out there were four 'cause Jesus was with them. Look up in the choir stand, and you can see God's children who were once sinners have now allowed Jesus to stand in the fire with them. We got a few more that need to heed the word of the Lord. Oh glory."

The church folks stood up and clapped for a long time. The four of us left on the Mourner's Bench couldn't do nothing but sit. Abigail had been up and testified earlier in the week, but after careful review, the mothers and deacons thought she needed to sit and pray awhile longer. I didn't believe she was telling the truth about getting her sign. I guessed the mothers must've figured it out, too.

I'd prayed all week for the choir to sing "I Need Thee" so I could go up to the front of the church and testify. Had the spirit forgotten about my song?

Only a few nights of revival left, and four of us out of the twelve sinners that started out were still on the Mourner's Bench. All the others were sitting in the choir stand with white bands tied around their heads, waiting on us. Both of Brother Matthew Graves' boys had given testimony that they'd seen a white light in their bedroom after they'd been asleep for more than two hours. Arthur Lee had caught a squirrel with his bare hands. Melvin Ray saw him catch it. Dinah's mama had told her one morning she could stay home. She didn't have to go to the cotton field. I'd begged Granny to let me go to the field every summer, and here was Dinah, not even wanting to go.

Why had God given everybody else a sign except me? Lilith wanted to be the last one to go up, so she could "show out." She was a backslider and didn't have to get baptized again, but she did every year. I guess she liked being dipped in the river. Last year it took her a good thirty minutes to testify, cry, shout and testify some more.

Crazy Abigail had her sign but was scared to go up again. As I was contemplating my fate, Simon Brown from the low end got saved. He gave one of the best testimonies I'd ever heard. He'd gotten his sign earlier that day and could barely contain himself till Reverend Jefferson opened the doors of the church. That left me, Abigail and Lilith on the bench, with me being the only one who hadn't been shown her sign.

THAT NIGHT REVIVAL ended without me getting my sign. If God was still on my side, I should've gotten it by now. Why didn't the Baptists sprinkle us like the Methodists did and get it all over with when we were babies? Esther walked with me to the road before she veered off with Rutherford.

"Sarah, there are so many reasons why you shouldn't be doing this," she said. "I've sat by quietly, but I see the pressure being placed on you, and I think you're just too young for it."

"You just don't like nothing we stand for," I said. "If it was something you wanted me to do like make that mosaic or go to that Freedom School, then that's fine with you. Getting my religion is what's expected of me. That stuff you want me to do is what's putting pressure on me and Granny and Muhdea."

"You being disrespectful," she said.

I guess Rutherford was tired of waiting for her. He told her to come on with him, and she went. When I got home, I sat at the kitchen table and went over and over every night's service in my head. Was there a break in the meeting where the choir could've sung "I Need Thee Every Hour" and I wasn't paying attention? No, that couldn't have happened; I would've heard it. I played every night of the revival in my head as I did when I studied for a spelling test, trying to remember if there was anything I could've done to steer things my way.

Muhdea opened the back door and lit the oil lamp.

"Sarah, you startled me, girl. What you doing sitting here in the dark?"

"Nothing," I said.

She had on her café uniform. Her wig was twisted. A piece of stocking cap stuck out from under it. She looked tired as she pulled a chair from the table and sat down. After chopping cotton every morning and then working at the café, she'd missed most of the revival. She set a greasy white bag on top of the table, took off her wig and laid it beside the bag. She untied her dirty white shoes, loosened the strings, and unknotted her opaque stockings before rolling them down into each shoe. She sat up and stretched for a minute before bending over and taking the stockings and shoes off together.

"Rough night at the café, Muhdea?"

"Aw, no more than usual. Hate I had to miss church tonight." She smiled at me. "Got a lady to work for me the rest of the week. I want to be there when you get yours." Her eyes widened. "You didn't get it tonight, did you, Sarah?"

"No, ma'am. No, ma'am. You didn't miss it."

"Oh, thank God."

"You probably won't ever see it either."

"Why you say something like that, Sarah?"

"I did everything," I said, fighting tears. "I've been good. I prayed. I don't even play no more. I do almost everything Esther tells me: get water, run to the store, change baby diapers, wash dishes. I ain't had no unclean thoughts that I know of. So where is my sign, Muhdea? Why ain't God given me my sign yet?"

She tore her hamburger in half and gave me a piece. It smelled up the whole kitchen. I was surprised the other kids didn't smell it in their sleep and come running. Muhdea and Mrs. Deborah made the best hamburgers in the world. Malika thought it was the grilled bread and pickles, but I knew it had to be the grilled onions and mustard. Wasn't nothing like having one of their hamburgers, French fries and a chocolate malt on Sunday afternoon.

"Hold your horses, Sarah. It ain't over yet. You getting ahead of yourself."

"I don't think so. Everybody else . . ."

"What I tell you about everybody else? If they roll down the levee and break their necks, you going to follow them? Think for yourself, Sarah. That's what your Uncle Robert say you so good at. You remember your Granny's testimony? When did she get her sign?"

"She got it on the last night." I took a bite of hamburger. "But, Muhdea . . ."

"Ain't no buts about God, baby. You asked him, and He'll deliver. It might not be in your time or mine. God works in His own good time. You can't question Him."

We sat awhile.

Esther came in the front door and was standing behind me listening.

"You want a piece of this, Esther Mae?" Muhdea said.

"No, thank you. Just listening in on you and Sarah," Esther said. "Don't you think it's too much for her, Muhdea? It seems to be taking a toll."

"She'll be alright. Jitters is all. It's almost over."

"I'll be fine, Esther. Don't worry. I'm not the only one the Lord hasn't answered yet."

If I'd known Esther was standing behind me, I would've kept my mouth shut. I chewed but couldn't half swallow the last bite of my hamburger for worrying about what she might do. I recalled Sister Tucker asking me if Esther had told me her testimony. Maybe I should've honored the tradition of mothers passing their testimony on to their daughters. I'd paid more attention to her sins, but maybe when she was little, she'd struggled the same as me and Granny. Muhdea had gotten her sign on the second night. She'd heard the voice of Jesus as clear as ice.

Muhdea told us she was tired and to not stay up so late. I had a big week coming up.

"Don't forget to blow out the light."

Esther and I hadn't ever been left alone in the house. I took it as a sign. Maybe whatever had happened to her when she was seeking salvation might give me some insight.

"Esther," I said, "you never told me your testimony."

"Oh, Sarah, it wasn't that big of a deal."

"Why would you say that?"

"You see everything as if it were a fairytale. I love how you see the good in everything, and you believe wholeheartedly. That's a gift. But there is another side to life, honey, and you still have a long time before you need to know about it."

"What other side? Is there another side to your testimony?"

She let loose her hair and then redid her ponytail and wrapped it into a bun.

"How old were you?" I said.

"I was thirteen. They baptized at the river. I almost drowned."

"Did they dunk you again? They say if you choke, you didn't get your sign. Was it the same when you got baptized?"

"It was the same, and no, I wasn't dunked twice." She loosed her hair again. "Sarah, I don't believe you're ready to understand. Let's say these are rituals, rites of passage. It doesn't happen to everybody the same way. You know that every religion doesn't baptize their members. Religion is complicated. It's not how you see it. What sins are you carrying that God would allow you to struggle night after night in humiliation sitting on the Mourner's Bench?"

I was getting riled. Why couldn't she just tell me her testimony? She was the buffalo side to our nickel, never seeing anything the same as we did.

"Can you tell me your testimony?"

"I don't have one."

"Are you saved? Did you get baptized?"

I surely had to take control of my sins if she hadn't been saved.

"Sarah, let's just say I am, and I did. It's late, and this isn't the night to get into it. Like Muhdea said, you have a big day tomorrow. It will be your first day at the Freedom School."

I wanted to blow up at her, but at times like this, I believed Granny and Uncle Robert had the right approach.

"Can it wait till after revival?" I said.

"No," she said. No explanation, just no.

"Esther, why don't you have a testimony? Just tell me that."

She held my hand. "We'll talk about it one day, sweetie. This isn't the time for it."

"I think it's wrong if you holding back on what I need to get my religion. I think it's wrong," I said.

I pushed my chair back. Nobody could have a decent conversation with her except them folks on the low end. Hopefully, God would look over her indiscretions and not take it out on me.

"I wish I could tell you everything, but I don't believe you're ready," she said.

If she knew anything about me, she would've known that was the last thing I ever wanted her to do. She could've fed it to me in a small spoon, took the stinger out before giving it to me, but to hold it out there like a toy and keep it from me was just plain wrong. Granny would tell me that she had her reasons, but I couldn't see any reason that would trump my salvation. She'd hurt me, so I figured I'd hurt her back.

"Esther, is the reason you won't tell me is what grown folks know about you, about why you left town, about the shame you caused and why everybody was praying over me, but nobody will tell me what you did? Did you refuse to testify? Is that the secret?"

Her faced turned mad, sad, hurt and threatening all at the same time. She eyed me, and I gave her the evil eye right back. God knows my salvation was in jeopardy.

CHAPTER ELEVEN

I Flunked It

STRAPPED WITH ALL of my feelings, I stood frozen in the door-way at the Hall, my feet rooted to the floor like a kelly weed in the field. I'd heard so much about this place, I was both scared and excited. If this was what Esther wanted from me, I wasn't going to fight with her during revival. Maybe if I pretended to be inter-ested, she'd leave me be till I got off the Mourner's Bench. Reverend Jefferson said Hell was a bottomless pit, and the way he talked about the Hall I believed it ran a close second.

Granny had told me to finish my chores and meet Esther down at the Hall. Her look said not to ask if I'd be able to go uptown first, or why her and Muhdea were letting me go in the first place, or any other question that I might've had.

"Yes, ma'am," I said.

I acted as if she'd given me all the details. I made a note in my head to write my questions about this day that was already starting out to be abnormal on my list later, in hopes I'd get the answers one day, 'cause Granny wasn't in no mood to answer nothing.

Here I was after having walked down to the Hall all by myself with all them things running around in my mind and still trying to take in a picture in my head of the redone Hall. Malika and her family lived across the road in their new Jim Walter home. I glanced over my shoulder at her house looking lonesome since she wasn't home. If she'd been there, I wouldn't be standing here. She would've run across the street and pushed me through the doorway pointing out every detail, showing off she knew more about the Hall than I ever would. I wished Malika would hurry up and come back home from Chicago. I felt alone standing here all by myself.

While I was still trying to make up my mind, Rutherford walked up, pushed me on through the door, closed it behind us, ambled on by, and left me standing a few steps from the door. He didn't speak to me, or say excuse me, or nothing. Like I cared.

The same old rose petal water-stained wallpaper was still pasted on the living room wall. Like ours, it had peeled halfway down the wall, and in some places, part of it was still intact all the way up. I wondered how that had happened. It wasn't like children played on the wall like we did the floor. Thick plastic covered the windows where they'd once been boarded over with plywood. The floors creaked. Two-by-four wood pieces and white poster boards lined the walls. Hammers, scissors, Elmer's glue, crepe paper, stencils, nails and a bunch of other stuff a second-grade class might need for a project lay in a corner on the faded wood floor, which needed stripping and staining. The house smelled old, wet and stuffy.

Esther swung the door open so wide it almost hit me in the back. Where was she coming from? She placed her hand on my back, slightly pushing me through the living room. We walked down the hallway. Three rooms lined the right side of the hallway, and a wall covered in the same wallpaper as the front room was on the left. I peeped in the first room.

Rutherford, Simon Bale, Bro Hollin, a man I only knew as Eatumup and some other men who didn't attend First Baptist Church and lived on the low end were sitting at a makeshift table talking. The table was a big piece of plywood that sat atop three horses. Granny used the same type horses when her and the ladies made quilts. About ten fold-up chairs were leaned against the walls. They acknowledged Esther and me, and carried on with their conversation as if we weren't still standing there.

Esther placed her hand on my shoulder and steered me to the next room. Somebody had started making bookshelves in the second room like the ones at the school library. Esther said it was going to be a library with all the books written by or about colored folks. Maybe I could loan them some of the books she'd sent me from Chicago till theirs arrived. No, that would be like her asking me to give up the plaits off my head. The books she'd sent were too easy for me, but I took care of them better than I did my baby cousins. I read them over and over to the kids even when they didn't want to listen. And when I finished, I wrapped them in worn-out diapers and placed them in the dresser drawer between my clothes.

"Where the books coming from? Why ain't they here yet?" I said.

Esther stared at me till I corrected my English. I wasn't at school, so why was she chastising me when nobody was there except us? She didn't always use perfect English, and it sounded too funny when she broke her verbs mixed with her too proper Chicago talk. Don't think I hadn't mocked and made fun of her in the mirror. Even though Granny laughed when she caught me, she told me it wasn't right and my mama would be offended if she saw it.

"The national SNCC office is sending the books. We're expecting them any day now," Esther said.

I wanted to ask her plenty more questions, but I didn't feel like having my English corrected, so I decided to wait and see who these colored people were who had written enough books to fill up a library. Over the years, Esther had sent me six or seven books, but all of them were primers except the one, which was a book of paintings. A picture of a stained-glass church window she'd painted, one of ladies named Fannie Lou Hamer, Ella Baker and Nina Simone. They were all gorgeous.

"We'll have afterschool classes in here," she said. "Gail brought enough books with her, and she has already started teaching."

I nodded as she talked as if I were mute. At the end of the hallway was the kitchen. Gail was sitting at the table, and Mrs. Carrie was standing at the sink. I wondered if the water was both cold and hot. I didn't see any water on the stove heating in a dishpan. Gail was surprised to see me. She jumped up out of her seat and hugged me. I backed away from her, not in a rude way but enough to let her know that she didn't have no business hugging me without my permission.

"You're finally here," Gail said. "We've been looking for you every day."

How could they have been looking for me when I didn't even know I was coming for real till Granny told me this morning?

"Sit here beside me," she said. "I'm so happy you're here. Your mother and Mrs. Carrie have been bragging about how smart you are."

I acknowledged her and then walked over to the sink and spoke to Mrs. Carrie, asked if I could help her with the tea when I really wanted to run my hand under the water. She didn't need any help.

"Can I wash my hands first?" I said.

"May I?" Esther said.

I cut my eyes at her. She knew better. Even when we were alone, it was embarrassing. I let it go. I felt the warm water run over my hands. Hot and cold running water, I thought. Over to the left of the kitchen was the bathroom. I peeped inside. There it was, an indoor toilet and sink. I wondered how long it took Bro Hollin to install them.

"Does it work?" I asked Mrs. Carrie.

"Go on in there and see for yourself," she said.

When I came out, I took my seat next to Gail and started reading. Mrs. Carrie asked if I wanted breakfast. She'd known Granny longer than me, and knew what my answer would be. Maybe she was just talking and wasn't expecting me to answer. I heard it was called chatter. I figured her mind was on something else, so I shook my head, no. Esther looked as if she were about to correct me again, so I spoke up.

"No, ma'am. Thank you very much. It was very kind of you to offer."

Esther smiled, patted my knee. In a family where manners meant everything, how could she have missed getting any at all?

Gail said classes started at eleven o'clock, and the other kids should be here soon. I prayed nothing would happen that would cause me to lose my religion, like what I would do if Esther corrected me one more time.

A few of the kids from the low end of town drifted in. Some of them ran through the house. Where were their manners, and why didn't Esther correct their behavior? I bit the inside of my lip. Miss Pastel and Miss Flora walked in the kitchen with their kids trailing behind them. They ducked to keep their heads from touching the top of the doorframe. Miss Pastel was dark, and Miss Flora was light skinned. They both were almost as wide as the door.

By the time class started, there were about eleven kids in all, ranging from ages five to sixteen. Esther and Gail broke the classes up by age. They taught the older kids first, and then the older ones taught the younger kids and they assisted. I was in Gail's class. She had three different sets of books. I hadn't ever seen any of them. They looked similar to our books at school except they didn't have ugly words written in them, weren't falling apart at the seams and didn't have any pictures of white people. Within thirty minutes, Gail had figured out I could read as well as or better than the older kids and moved me to the table with them. I liked her for catching on so quickly 'cause I sure wasn't going to tell her. Correcting grown folks would only lead to trouble for me.

After class, Gail asked me if I would help teach the adults how to fill out the voter registration forms. She pulled the forms from her bag and gave me a sample.

"Read it first," she said. "Then we'll go over what you don't understand. They have to be filled out perfectly, so ask me anything you don't know." She gave me the blank copies. "After you finish reading them, take the test," she said.

There was an "Application for Registration Questionnaire and Oaths," which included five parts, and several copies titled "Literacy Test," with a minimum of thirty questions each. The first instruction on the "Literacy Test" said it was to be given to anyone who could not prove she had above a fifth-grade education. I scanned the questions and wondered how many colored folk made it above fifth grade, and if they could pass the test.

The second instruction read, "Do what you are told to do in each sentence, nothing more, nothing less. Be careful because one wrong answer denotes failure of the test. You have ten minutes to complete this test."

What in the world: one question wrong, that wasn't fair. They'd still have an A if they missed . . . I counted the number of questions and divided in my head.

The questions seemed as if they were written to trick me. For instance, question number five: "Circle the first, first letter of the alphabet in this line."

I read and reread it, and then my eyes scanned back up to the top of the page and landed on "ten minutes," so I circled the A, but I thought it could also be the C. I guessed at many of the multiple-choice questions I didn't know the answer to outright, and a lot of the fill-in-the-blank questions stumped me. I wondered if I should've known the name of the attorney general, and 'cause I didn't know, did it mean that folks were just telling me a story when they said I was smart for my age?

I finished the test as best as I could and gave it to Esther. I thumbed through the books left on the table from our class. Esther came back in the room with Gail.

"We graded your test," Esther said.

"We don't want you to be alarmed," Gail said.

Be alarmed about what, it was just a test. I'd taken many tests and passed them all, pop quizzes, too.

"Remember they are designed for adults," Esther said. "We gave it to you so you would understand how much patience . . ."

"Why y'all beating around? You acting like I flunked it or something. Let me see."

I grabbed the papers out of Gail's hand before she realized what I was doing.

"Sarah," Gail and Esther said.

"I know I missed more than one question, but that's okay. Even if I missed five, it's still an A. It's silly for them to flunk you for missing only one question. That's crazy, isn't it, Esther?"

Gail sat in the chair next to me. "Sarah, let me explain," she said.

By then, I'd seen all of the red X's. I turned the page, and there were more X's.

"I flunked. I didn't pass. Look how many . . ." A lump formed in my throat. I couldn't speak or swallow. And when I did get my voice, I blamed both of them.

"Why y'all give me a test like this? I wasn't prepared. I never seen this material before."

Tears formed in my eyes and streamed down my face. I'd answered more than half of the questions wrong. I was going to the fourth grade and should've known the material. I'd never missed any questions on a test before, not even the ones given for honor students.

Esther placed her arms around me, and Gail dabbed my eyes with Kleenex. Both of them encouraged me to cry, get it out. The more they fussed over me, the harder I cried till I was whimpering like a baby.

"I'm so sorry. We should have explained it to you," Gail said.

"Don't worry about the test, Sarah. It's for grown folks, not kids," Esther said.

I pointed to the test. "I flunked."

They kept trying to console me. Neither of them could believe it had that type of effect on me. They stared at me while I cried and rolled my eyes at them.

Mrs. Carrie walked in and handed me a Popsicle. She took me to the bathroom and washed my face. We sat at the table. She waved away the onlookers.

"Go on back to your work. She'll be alright," Mrs. Carrie said. Esther and Gail attempted to walk toward us, and she waved them away, too. "What's wrong, Sarah?" Mrs. Carrie said. "Tell me what's got you so wound up."

She took the Popsicle from me and peeled off the paper as if it were a banana.

"They gave me them tests to make me look dumb," I said.

"No, they wouldn't do that, sweetie. Nobody wants to make you look bad. We're here to empower you, but those applications are meant to make potential colored voters feel worse than you did today. They're adults and can't pass the test."

She talked to me for more than an hour after she allowed Esther and Gail to join us at the table. Esther told me about the poll tax, threats and many other tactics to keep coloreds from voting. I vowed to learn every test backwards and forwards so I could teach other colored folks. I didn't want nobody to be at the registration table crying like I did.

"What's a poll tax?" I asked Esther.

"Taxes we pay on land we own. You see, only land owners who have paid their poll taxes are eligible to vote."

"What about folks who don't own land or haven't paid?"

"They can't vote. Even the ones who do own land have to pass a test like this or do some other ridiculous thing before they're allowed to vote."

"Can you vote?"

"The only person in this room who can vote is Mrs. Carrie."

I was dumbfounded. Mrs. Carrie went on to explain more of the rules to me and was still talking when Bro Hollin interrupted.

"We need y'all up front. They been beat pretty bad," he said.

Rutherford, James, Miss Flora and Miss Pastel were sitting in the chairs in the front room. Rutherford's lip was cut and bleeding. James' face looked as if it had been squished around in the gravel. Miss Flora was holding Miss Pastel's arm.

"He twisted it behind her back," Miss Flora said.

Rutherford was cussing and calling them crackers. Esther left and came back with a pan of water, towels and a first aid kit. They checked the wounds to see if any of them needed to be rushed to the hospital. Gail poured peroxide on James' face. He looked a lot better after she cleaned his wounds. I could've sworn he'd have to go to the hospital. They all tried to tell what happened at the same time. Mrs. Carrie finally calmed them down enough for us to hear.

According to them, Rutherford mostly, they'd timed it to take Miss Pastel and Miss Flora to register when the new clerk was at the window. A person was on watch at the office to let them know when the old clerk left the building. While she was checking the forms, the old clerk came back with the police chief and his two deputies. They couldn't figure out how she knew they were inside unless like them they had somebody on watch, too.

"Crackers outsmarted us this time," Rutherford said.

Esther rubbed salve on his lip. His jaw was swollen and growing. Somebody placed Miss Pastel's arm in a sling. They were known around town to be bold women whom nobody, woman or man, ever won a fight against. Other than one being light skinned and the other dark, they looked just alike, as tall as most men and weighing more than some. When they got a person down, they sat on him and dared him to move.

Miss Pastel swung at the chief, and one of the deputies grabbed her arm and pinned it behind her back. Miss Flora wasn't having it and bit him till he was in so much pain he let loose of her arm. They seemed to enjoy telling it. Fear eased out of the room as each one of them told their version of the incident. I laughed along with them as the tone changed from anger to good nature, but an uneasiness in my stomach caused me to want to run home to Muhdea and Granny, to our end of town, to First Baptist where folks didn't register to vote or get in fights. But if I left, who would teach them how to pass that test?

Later that evening, they held a meeting at the Hall. The men set out chairs and a podium up front. The lawyer John Walker from the NAACP, Mr. Bill Hansen, head of Arkansas SNCC, and Mr. Dick Gregory and Mr. Julian Bond, from the national SNCC office, had come down to speak to us. Our situation with the schools required immediate attention. After they all spoke, sounding like the newsman on the radio, they sat in chairs behind Esther while she stood at the podium and read off the names of the students that would be going to the white school. Esther said the Freedom of Choice Act required us to go to the white school. We were going whether we wanted to or not. She'd warned us at the last revival. Nobody'd believed her then, but it had come to pass. The Maeby Citizens for Progress, our grassroots organization, and the SNCC organizers had selected ninety-five of the smartest colored students to register to attend the white school. They hadn't asked me if I wanted to go. I liked my teachers and friends at the colored school. After she read my name, I eased open the door and slid out sideways. One of the other girls came out and stood beside me.

"Do you want to go?" I said.

"We don't know them. We'll have to cross the train tracks and the highway every day. You got anything to get us out of it?" she said.

"We could pretend to be dumb," I said. "We can make bad grades."

"They won't believe we all of a sudden started making bad grades. Miss Esther said it's the law. I don't believe we'll be able to outsmart our folks and them lawyers."

I peeped my head back in the door, and at the top of my lungs I said, "Why we got to go to their school? Why can't they bring their good books over to our school?" I darted right back out the door, walked off the porch, and before I knew it, I'd followed the rainbow down the road and toward the country. I passed the spring for the watering filtering plant. The shadow of a rainbow shone across the water. I turned around and followed the stream of colors. I kneeled at the spring, prayed to the Lord and asked Him along with sending me a sign to keep me from going to the white school. Nobody knew where to find me, so I trailed the rainbow to the other side, looking for the end where the leprechaun had left his pot of gold. If I could find it, we wouldn't have to go to the white school. I'd buy us a brand-new school with brand -new books.

CHAPTER TWELVE

I Need Thee Every Hour

IT WAS THE last night of revival, and everybody came, Christians and sinners, Baptists, Pentecostals and Protestants. Folks lined up in front of the church long before the doors opened. The only folks guaranteed a seat were the preachers, deacons, mothers and mourners. I got the word that Malika, the queen, was back in town, and she would be there. She'd stopped by to call on me, but Muhdea had told her I was in prayer and to come back when the revival was over.

When I saw Granny lay out her clothes on the bed, I figured she believed I would get my sign, but I was skeptical. She got all dressed up for church, which meant wearing panties, bra, stockings and a hat. She hadn't been to revival. Said she only attended church when it was absolutely necessary. Her business was already straight with the Lord, but sometimes she got the call to pay a visit to the church.

"You got the call tonight?" I said.

"You might want to get a move on, gal," she said, ignoring my question. "Muhdea left already with part of the kids, and me and the others getting ready to head out now."

"What about Esther?" I said. "Will she be there tonight?"

Esther hadn't been around much since she sashayed out the door after Muhdea told her to straighten up or get out of her house. Muhdea didn't hold her to it either, 'cause she show hadn't straightened up.

"I ain't seen Esther since before supper," Granny said. "You know how your mama is, no telling where she is or what she doing. Don't be surprised if her and Carrie try to ambush the service. If so, don't let it deter you away from your salvation."

"Did she say anything to you about me sitting on the Mourner's Bench?"

"No, ma'am. She been too busy dodging me and Muhdea."

She reached up over the orange vinyl davenport where I was sitting and picked up her snuff jar off the shelf. She swirled her toothbrush in her mouth and sucked the juice out before stirring it in the jar.

Granny checked every one of the twenty plaits on my head to see if I looked well enough to sit up front where folks would be staring at me.

"Hurry up now. You should've been the first one out of here."

I was scared. I wanted to grab her around the legs and cry out like I'd seen the white women do on the TV soap opera at Sister Tucker's store.

"Oh, Great-Grandmother. Please don't leave. We don't have to go over to that church tonight. Let's sit awhile and talk about it." Wiping tears from my eyes with the back of my hand and slinging them across the room, I begged her.

"What will happen if God don't answer tonight? What then?" I said.

I feared being one of the sinners I'd heard talked of but never seen myself who had to wait till the next summer's revival to be saved or travel over to a church in another county. Granny and Muhdea had told me not to get up and testify if I didn't have my sign.

"Granny, you think God will hear me tonight?" I said.

"You worry too much, baby. Everything will turn out just fine. God didn't give me my sign till the last night, remember."

"I know, but waiting ain't easy."

"Listen, Sarah, whether you get your sign or not, everything will be alright. Your life is ordered. You hear me?"

If Granny hadn't gone through just about the same thing when she was seeking salvation, I wouldn't be able to go over to the church. I didn't know what I'd do if I didn't get my sign. I was the only one who knew what I'd asked God to send me. Would I stay seated and wait for next summer with all the sinning Esther was doing? Half of the town, the church and every family member were disappointed with her. Would I try to fake it like Crazy Abigail and risk the mothers finding out?

"You going to be just fine whatever the outcome. Go ahead now. You don't want to be late," Granny said.

"I only got to put on my dress and shoes. I'll be right out."

"Pull the door shut behind you. You hear?"

Right after that everything went haywire. My dress wouldn't go over my head the right way. Granny had laid out my light blue dress with pink and green flowers. I liked it 'cause it looked like the ones she wore, gathered at the waist with lots of pleats. I wore a black patent-leather belt with it that matched my shoes.

When I finally pulled the dress over my head and looked in the mirror, my hair was messed up. Twenty plaits and not one of them lying down like it should. Short pieces stuck up like needles. I tried to smooth my hair down with my hands. When that didn't work, I hauled off and spit in both of them and tried again. Nobody would believe Granny had combed it less than two hours ago.

I thought a drink might help, so I walked in the kitchen to get a short Coke. Muhdea had bought a block of ice that morning in anticipation of my baptismal. I got one of the Cokes from out of the foot tub. I rumbled through the mix-matched silverware till I found an opener. On my way back to my room, I looked back to check the silverware drawer. Thank goodness, it wasn't hanging off its hinges. Taking a Coke wouldn't get me in as much trouble as Granny having to fix that drawer again.

Time was getting away from me, and I couldn't find my Sunday shoes. I glanced under the bed, full-sized feather mattress with springs on top of slats, no headboard, covered with a blue and white flower-appliqué bedspread. Next I checked behind the dresser with the cracked mirror. Only one of them was next to my everyday shoes at the foot of the bed. I couldn't bear the thought of sitting up at the front of the church with them beat-up old school shoes on my feet. I lay flat on the floor, and slid halfway under the bed. I saw my shoe stuck all the way back in the corner. Was the Devil playing with me? How had my shoe gotten back there? I'd half-swept that morning and hadn't seen it then. I crawled back, dragging the shoe with my fingertips, hoping I wouldn't get a splinter. I checked my dress in the dresser mirror. The front of it was covered in dirt.

I dusted the dirt off my dress, pulled "Things I'll Know When I Get Grown" out of the slit in the mattress and wrote, *Why does God let the Devil get in the way when you're doing your best to serve Him?* I stuck it back between the feathers and walked to the kitchen to take back the empty Coke bottle. We kept the bottles in the crate next to the can with the ten-pound sack of flour. The bottle read "Returnable 5 cents." Sister Tucker gave us a nickel for each empty one. On the way back to the bedroom, I turned around, grabbed another short Coke, got a small bag of salted peanuts from the cabinet and poured them in the bottle. I didn't shake the bottle and catch the spillover with my mouth like I generally did for fear the Coke might splash on my dress. I almost chocked twice trying to chug it down. Four tiny spots got on my dress. I swirled around and around so it would dry.

One more look in the mirror before I left. It wasn't much, and it blended in with the dirt, but there it was, way more than four tiny spots of Coke on my dress. I wiped it off as best as I could, spit in and then ran both hands across my hair again. I ran straight into Esther on my way out the door. She was blocking the way between me and the Lord.

"Hey, Esther."

She was the last person I wanted to see, dressed in pink culottes and shirt, thick black hair flowing loosely down her back. The Devil was playing another trick, so I better get away from her fast.

"We all over at the revival. Pull the screen door up close if you go anywhere else. See you when we get back."

She wasn't moving away from the door, so I skirted around her. Pushed the screen door up against her back and took off running toward the church. I heard her call my name, but I kept going.

I wondered how many people got what they wanted on the last day, at the last minute. How did it feel? Was it worth all the trouble? I only knew of Granny, and as many times as she'd told me her story, she never said how it felt, or what she thought on the days leading up to it. When the preacher asked for another song, and old man John struck up on "I Need Thee Every Hour," the church was already on its feet, ready to be dismissed. As soon as Granny heard the first bar of the song, she ran up to the front of the church, screaming and crying. "That's my sign, Jesus, that's my sign."

I reckoned it made her feel good, but she never said. She never said what she was feeling before that moment.

I tried to put the thoughts out of my head as I ran toward the church. I stopped running fast so I wouldn't smell like a piss-ant. If tonight was going to be my night, I sure didn't want the mothers backing away on account of the way I smelled. I looked up to God and saw two redbirds land on the roof of the church. I blew them a kiss for love and luck. If I'd asked for the redbirds as a sign, I could swing open the doors of the church and testify to everybody. I'd take them all outside to see it for themselves.

Since I hadn't asked God to send them, I stopped at the stained-glass window on the side of the church to listen to the choir sing. Esther had painted it before I was born, before she disgraced the church. I stood on my tiptoes to peep inside. I waited to hear the same song Granny had heard years ago, the one that propelled her mother out of her seat so many years before her.

"His Eye Is on the Sparrow."

Dag. I was afraid to be any later than I already was, but I took a chance and listened for the next song anyway.

I walked on around to the front of the church, and Sister Tucker was standing at the foot of the stairs.

"Sarah, I'm glad you came along. Help me get up these steps."

I took it as a good sign and refused to guess why I seemed to be there whenever she needed a shoulder.

"What you waiting on, Sarah? This is the last night."

What did she think I was waiting on?

Ask another question like that, and I'd ease up from under her arm. I wasn't no walking cane anyway.

"I ain't got my sign yet is all. As soon as I get it, I'm heading straight up to testify."

"Seems like I remember it taking your granny right up to the last minute," she said. "But don't worry. You a good girl. It'll all work out. We're all praying for you."

"You, too, Sister Tucker?" I said.

We made it to the top of the stairs and walked into the vestibule.

"Now, why wouldn't you think I'd pray for you?" she said. "You go on in now. I can make it from here."

"Thank you, Sister Tucker," I said. "For the praying, I mean." I felt a little better.

She waved her hand. I walked up front and took my seat along-side Crazy Abigail and Lilith.

Not long after I took my seat, Reverend Jefferson got up out of his red velvet armchair and glided across the thick red carpet up to the wide brown podium, where a cross was carved across most of the front.

"Three left," he said. "There were three in the fiery furnace till . . ." His voice elevated to a high soprano. "Till Jesus showed up. So don't be afraid, don't worry. God is in the saving business tonight." He reached down and picked up a glass of water. I knew there were a silver plate with a pitcher and eight glasses of water inside the podium. I'd set it there many times before. One glass for Reverend Jefferson and one for each of the six guest preachers, and an extra glass in case one showed up unexpectedly. Miss Ora Bea, an ordained minister, sat on the pews to my right with the mothers, wearing a purple and gold velvet robe. It was a sin for her to sit in the pulpit.

I hadn't found that verse in the Bible yet.

I felt a little bit better and sat up straighter in my seat. I knew the story of Shadrach, Meshach and Abednego by heart. Reverend Jefferson's face changed as if an usher had delivered bad news to him. Then he grinned so wide I could've counted every tooth. He set the glass on top of the podium and rubbed his hands across his red velvet robe with thick gold and black ropes hanging around his neck.

The pianist ran her fingers across the piano, and the choir, dressed in gold robes trimmed in red, hummed. Esther, the civil rights workers and a few folks from the low end strolled in and stood in the very back of the church. Esther still hadn't told them that men and women didn't sit together. I took her presence as a sign. God wanted all of them to be here, Esther, Muhdea and Granny, to see me get saved. Reverend Jefferson warned us about the enemy.

"You know some folks right in our mix are good at starting mess. God don't want us here at First Baptist to have no part in it. I mean it wholeheartedly. If you don't hear nothing else I say tonight, you hear this. Don't sign up to send your children across the highway. Our schools are good enough," he warned. Then he pulled a handkerchief from his robe pocket, wiped his forehead with it, and as if it were another day, he said, "Now let's get back to the reason we're all here. Let's get the rest of this flock saved tonight."

The entire church stood and clapped, even the three of us left on the Mourner's Bench, as the choir sang "Just a Closer Walk with Thee."

The choir hummed, and we bowed our heads as Reverend Jefferson prayed.

"Let us all bow our heads in prayer," he said. "Father, we come to you with our heads bowed and our hearts steadied on Jesus. Thank you, God, for the saved sitting in the choir stand tonight. And thank you, Lord, for the few little sheep we have yet to bring into your fold."

Whatever he said after that was lost on me. I couldn't stop thinking of Little Bo Peep's sheep. *Little Bo Peep lost her sheep and didn't know where to find them.* I stared up at his mixed black and gray hair and his eyes, believing he was right about Jesus saving us tonight. The spirit was back in the church, and Reverend Rich was at the podium.

"Please open your Bibles to the book of John, the twentieth chapter, verses twenty-four through thirty." He read all seven verses.

One of my favorite verses was that of doubting Thomas. He preached on through the night about how Jesus proved to Thomas who He was. Wasn't that proof enough for us poor sinners left on the Mourner's Bench? Reverend Rich begged and pleaded with us more than he had all week. He didn't have to preach no more fire and brimstone to me. All he needed to do was ask the choir to sing "I Need Thee Every Hour."

All three sides of the church had stained-glass windows except the back wall behind the pulpit and choir stand. Reverend Jefferson's office was on the left side where the deacons sat, and the choir room was on the mothers' side. Muhdea was sitting next to Miss Ora Bea, but I couldn't find Granny or the kids even though I almost turned all the way around when we stood up to sing. My eyes rested on the mural of Jesus and the white little children that covered the whole back wall. *SUFFER LITTLE CHILDREN AND FORBID THEM NOT TO COME UNTO ME* read bold capital letters on the bottom of the picture. Jesus leaned over to hand a flower to one of the children. He looked like a nice man.

As customary, one preacher passed off to the other as if they were in a track and field relay. I hunched Crazy Abigail in the side with my elbow to wake her up, and later she nudged me. Once or twice, the usher caught us both. The ministers seemed not to notice us at all.

"I'll try to wait on you, but I can't promise," Abigail said.

Lord, please, don't make me outwait Lilith. Come now. Abigail is about to leave me here by myself, I prayed.

Reverend Jefferson and the other preachers came down from the pulpit and stood in front of the communion table, an eight-foot-long, four-foot-high wood table with *IN REMEMBRANCE OF ME. LUKE 22:19* engraved in the wood in all capital letters. The deacons joined them. The mothers circled; some stood, and others kneeled down beside the three of us. Deacon Allen led a call-and-response hymn while we prayed.

"Father I stretch my hands to thee—hmmm," Deacon Allen sang.

I heard them repeat after him, and Mrs. Graves banged it out in my ear. Any other time, I'd be watching to see whose hands went up over their head or what pair of glasses would go flying toward the pulpit.

"No other help I know—hmmm," moaned Deacon Allen.

The church moaned after him, along with a few "Please, Jesus. I know you can." I felt the first inkling that my bladder was getting weak. Why did I drink them Cokes? I knew better. I knew to drain my bladder before service.

Please don't tarry, God.

"If Thou withdraw Thyself from me, oh whither shall I go— hmmm?" Deacon Allen dragged it out, and the church followed. I tried to lift up my head, but one of the mothers pushed it down.

"Stay focused," she said.

I'd go testify if they sang "I Need Thee Every Hour," or I might go to Hell if they didn't. Not to mention I'd lose my position as assistant secretary.

The mothers gathered closer around us. The different smells from their toilet water and powder blocked my breath. I caught a whiff of Muhdea's perfume, but I couldn't tell how close she was to me, and one mother wouldn't let go of my head.

The mothers, every one of them dressed as if she were a nurse, took my movements as a sign that I was receiving the Holy Spirit when I couldn't even keep my mind on God. I had something more important going on now. One mother placed her hand around my forehead, and another put hers on top of my head.

"He's working with her now," she said.

The rest of them were in deep, sincere prayer, calling on the Lord to come down here right now and save me, Abigail and Lilith, His humble servants. I turned my head from one side to the other trying to get around their white dresses and breathe. Abigail looked straight into my eyes.

"I'm going in a minute," she mouthed. "You ready?"

"Nope."

"Just go. You holding up Lilith."

"You got it this time?"

She rolled her eyes. Deacon Allen was about to wrap it up.

"Can you see Muhdea?" I said.

She shook her head, no.

"I got to do number one." I held up my forefinger.

Reverend Jefferson calmed the church. Everybody took their seats, and the mothers and us got up off our knees. I noticed Malika out the side of my eye before me and Lilith sat back in our chairs. She winked at me for good luck. Lilith gave me the cross eye, and I gave her one right back. She should've known I wanted it to be over.

139

She was the only one who seemed to enjoy being up here. Abigail remained standing. The choir started singing, not all out but mellow. Reverend Jefferson, Reverend Stith, our light-skinned, jackleg preacher, and Reverend Rich walked over to Abigail with their hands and arms opened to receive her.

Her grandma grabbed her, picked her up by the waist, let her go, and took off running up and down the church with ushers in tow. Abigail cried. I turned around to look for Granny. Where was she, the kids? Muhdea stood near me, and I reached out to grab her hand. The mothers moved. I touched one of the mothers' hands, who I thought was Muhdea.

"Just catch hold of Jesus," she said.

Me and Lilith got back on our knees, and they took Abigail up front to testify. She touched us both on the back before they tied the white band around her head and she took her seat in the choir stand with the others.

"Go on up," she mouthed.

I wanted to follow her, but the preachers would know it if I wasn't telling the truth. I lowered my eyes and said, "Tell Muhdea I got to do number one."

"You better listen to her," Lilith said. "What you waiting on? You can't outwait me."

She better be glad I was trying to get saved. I refolded my arms, placed them in the seat of the chair, laid my forehead on them, and prayed. Lord, let Muhdea come get me. I thought my prayer had been answered when I felt a tap on the shoulder. I thanked God for bringing Muhdea. When I opened my eyes, I realized whoever it was, wasn't wearing a white dress or the striped color Granny wore when she left the house. I assumed another member had come up to pray for me. I closed my eyes. She tapped me again. I wasn't doing anything wrong, so why was she tapping my shoulder? Maybe Abigail had told her to come take me to the bathroom. I raised my head and looked up into Esther's eyes.

Oh, Lord, where did she come from? I'd told Abigail to tell Muhdea, not Esther. She beckoned me to come with her. Would I have time to go take care of my business and get back before the choir sang "I Need Thee Every Hour"? With the pressure I felt, my only choice was to follow her and get back as fast as possible. I looked around again for Muhdea, anybody other than Esther.

"Come on, girl," she said. "I see you wiggling."

How did she know it wasn't the Lord working on me? "Where's Granny, Muhdea?" I stood up, and the mothers shuffled so I could walk between them. Abigail was in the choir stand soaking up all of the attention. Muhdea stood beside her. My legs were so weak I could've dropped to my knees. Reverend Jefferson started praying, the choir hummed, and I walked out the door with Esther.

"Thanks, Esther," I said. "I got to go real bad, but let's hurry up and get back before they stop praying."

We walked outside toward the restroom. We were near the window where I'd stopped earlier and listened to the choir sing. I slowed down again to listen for my song, my sign. The mosquitoes caught up to me and landed on my legs and arms. Without a towel, there wasn't much hope of them not biting me. Esther had been talking all along, but I'd been in too big of a hurry to hear what she was saying.

"I called you out here to talk to you," she said.

"What?" Talk to me about what? I followed the streams of green, red, blue and gold lights, which shone through the stained-glass window, with my eyes. When the choir lowered their voices, I heard folks shouting Lilith's name. I had to get going so I could get back in time to testify. I turned to continue to the restroom. Esther caught my arm.

"Didn't you hear me say I needed to talk to you?"

"Yeah, but I got to . . . ."

She mixed the proper city talk in with the country. "You too young. It's eleven o'clock, and you falling asleep in there waiting for a sign."

"No, no, ma'am, I'm a little tired but not sleepy. I been praying, everybody praying, even Sister Tucker," I said. "We know what we doing. I'm like Granny is all. She waited till the last night, but God didn't let her down. I'll get my sign when we go back, you'll see."

Every cricket, lightning bug, frog and mosquito seemed to be fighting with each other. If I'd been trying to catch a lightning bug, he'd have his dimmers on. If the insects weren't biting me, they were squealing or blinking. Was that how they acted after eleven o'clock every night?

"All I see is a child trying too hard. I kept quiet all week, but I can't allow this to continue," Esther said.

She could've been talking to the lightning bugs 'cause my mind was on getting back inside the church.

"You'll see, Esther. It's all figured out. I'm going to get my sign as soon as I get back from the restroom." I crossed my legs tight to slow down my urge to pee and started walking.

"Oh no, you don't walk away from me," Esther said.

She grabbed my arm. I pulled, but she held on tighter. I snatched it away, but she caught the other one. That's when I realized she was serious.

"Esther, I got to pee."

"I'm not buying that again. You must think I'm a stone fool. You're not going back in there, and you will obey me."

"Let me just go get Granny. She can tell you." The tone of my voice had changed from confident to pleading.

"It don't matter what Granny thinks, Sarah. I'm your mother."

Since when? Mothers didn't leave their children. I tried to make eye contact with her. I wanted to make her hear me.

"Esther, please, just let me go, please."

I couldn't stop the tears or nothing else from running. She held onto my wrist so tight it felt as if the blood would quit circulating. I hoped somebody, anybody would miss me and come looking for me. I prayed for Granny, the Lord, Muhdea to hurry up and save me from this woman.

I crossed my ankles, switching back and forth. Water began trickling down my legs. Esther kept right on talking. She didn't notice. Why was she doing this to me, why did she hate me so much? I was about to scream at her to let go of my arm when I heard the piano music. Nothing left for them to do but close the doors of the church. It was over. I hadn't gotten my sign. I gritted my teeth so I wouldn't yell at her. It was quiet for a moment. The mosquitoes quit biting me. I thought I heard the choir sing:

I need Thee every hour, most gracious Lord;

No tender voice like Thine / can peace afford.

My song. Oh my God, you heard me and answered my prayer. I jerked my arm away from Esther. That sudden move caused my water to break like the Arkansas Dam. Pee ran down my legs to my shoes. It splattered onto Esther's feet. She let go of my hand and jumped back.

"What the hell is wrong with you?" she said and slapped my face. I drew my hand back to hit her, but then realized she was my mama and rubbed my face instead. It didn't hurt, but it hurt.

"Look what you made me do," she said. She looked as if she were going to say she was sorry, but she didn't. "I bought these shoes at Lord & Taylor. It took me a year to save up for them." She brushed the shoes with her hand, but when she realized my pee was all over her hand, she stopped.

For the first time, it was quiet, and I heard the piano playing and the choir humming. I waited. It sounded like it was the right song, but was it? Yes, yes, the Lord had answered my prayer. The music was loud, and the song rang in my ear. The choir started out slow. They sang a few lines and then hummed the chorus "I Need Thee."

"It's my sign. I asked God to let the choir sing it," I said as I wiped away the tears with my dress sleeve. "Please don't play mama tonight. I'll be good tomorrow, and you can be my mama then."

She stood there as if she were lost in the woods. I walked toward the front of the church, looking back so I could run if she came after me. I'd reached the third step when I felt my wet dress touch my leg. I wrestled with whether I should go in or not. Jesus said come as you are, but Muhdea would have a fit if I stood up in front of the church smelling like a piss-ant.

Esther came up behind me. "Go on home and wash up," she said. "It's too late now."

I knew. I stomped down the steps and headed home, rubbing tears and snot off my face.

"Wait till I tell Granny you slapped me," I said. "You just wait and see."

CHAPTER THIRTEEN

I Know What's Best

ESTHER STEPPED ON my heel. She walked too close behind me. Couldn't she have backed off a little bit, given me a chance to collect myself, and empty the pee out of my shoes? I sloshed on to the house. It crossed my mind to slam the screen door in her face as if I didn't know she was right behind me, close enough for me to smell her perfume, White Shoulders. I'd sneaked a peak at it in her dresser drawer, wrapped in thin paper in a pink box with a woman on the bottle looking like her except she was glass. I'd sprayed it on my wrist. I didn't like the smell and still don't care for perfume.

She called my name several times as we walked. I all but ran. She asked me to wait, slow down, talk to her. If I hadn't thought I'd slip, I would've sped up, sprinted. I left the door open. She had to be on my neck to be able to catch the door when I left it open, or else I would've closed it so mosquitoes wouldn't slip in and torment me in my sleep. I smiled at the thought of smashing her like I would a mosquito, a gnat. She said my name again, pleaded with me to let her explain. I cut my eyes at her so fierce she should've been able to see it in the dark. My feet were wet, and so were my white nylon baby doll socks with the pink lace trim, and my patent-leather black Sunday shoes, not to mention my dress and satin white panties with pink lace trim. Granny would have a fit. I was too old to be peeing on myself.

Esther called my name. "Sarah. Please."

I strutted through the dark house with ease. She bumped into the coffee table, the end of the couch and demanded the matches for the oil lamp. If she was expecting me to answer, she must be crazier than a road lizard.

I slid down beside the bed. Thank goodness I'd developed a habit of not sitting on top of the bed. I'd finally gotten far enough away from Esther. It would take her a while to find the matches. I grabbed the towel hanging on the back of the door. I took off my shoes and wiped the inside of one with the towel. As I rubbed the mud off the bottoms, the memories rushed to the forefront of my mind. I swallowed hard, shook my head, rubbed my eyes, began peeling off my wet socks.

How could me or Muhdea show our faces at church again, or in town for that matter? We'd be a laughingstock. I would be the only girl in history to sit on the Mourner's Bench and not get baptized. I swallowed nothing.

"Sarah," Esther said.

I prayed Muhdea would come before she found the matches. I slammed the other shoe on the floor. Pee flew onto my face and across the room. I bit my lip. Sinner or not, I wasn't going to allow them mothers to start laying hands on me ever again. I'd gotten my sign. They couldn't hold me responsible for Esther's actions. Maybe Muhdea and Reverend Jefferson would intervene on my behalf, disobey the Bible and baptize me regardless of what Esther said. That thought brought me a smidgen of relief.

"Sarah, I know you hear me. Where are the matches? You'll be sorry if you don't answer me."

How much more sorry could I be than I already was? She'd done it all. There wasn't nothing left for her to do to me. She'd wrecked my whole life, and like a fool, I'd started to trust her a little bit.

Muhdea, I thought, please hurry home and straighten her out. I could testify at the river right before they baptized me, which would be an even more dramatic ending than Granny's or her mama's. It was only fitting since Granny's testimony had a better buildup than her mama's did. Esther still hadn't told me hers, and Muhdea's was simple. She believed it had reference to the resurrection. I didn't know why she hadn't followed the trend and asked for the same sign as Granny, and her mama, and me. I wondered if Esther had asked God to let the choir sing "I Need Thee Every Hour," and they hadn't sung it. Something bad had happened to her with the way she treated me. I saw why Muhdea refused to take her name off the prayer lists.

"Oh, shit. Sarah," Esther said.

Muhdea came through the door, calling my name and then Esther's. I crawled to the foot of the bed and wound myself into a knot. Tears flowed. I heard them bump into each other.

"Jesus, girl. Why you walking 'round here in the dark? Where's Sarah?" Muhdea said.

Esther mentioned the matches. Muhdea got them as she scolded Esther for not knowing where we kept them. I imagined the lamp lighting up the room and knew it wouldn't be long before they came after me. I wasn't moving, couldn't if I wanted to. Did I smell? How much time before I did? Granny's and the children's voices pierced my ears.

"Where's Sarah?" Granny said.

"What happened?" Muhdea said.

"Why didn't y'all come back in the church? Is she sick?" Granny said.

I waited to see what Esther would say to them. Would she tell the truth, or a story? Was she going to defend her actions? How could she defend slapping me? Maybe she'd leave it out, but I'd tell it. I'd tell it all.

"Sarah," Granny said as she walked down the hall.

I wound myself into a tighter knot.

"Wait a minute, Granny," Esther said. "Let me talk to her first."

Please keep her away from me. Don't let her tell you what to do, Granny.

"What happened between y'all?" Granny said.

"I'll tell you after I talk to her," Esther said.

Granny conceded. Esther opened the door. She kneeled down beside me at the foot of the bed with a towel and a pan of water. Her voice was soft like cotton, kind like a good mother's. Was I alright? No. What a ridiculous question. Was I alright after she ruined my whole life? Somebody come and get her before I do something to cause me to spend eternity in Hell. Save me. She peeled off my sock. Seemed not to care that they were soaked in pee. She talked to me caringly as she removed my other items of clothing. I lay there lifeless.

"I'm sorry," she said over and over again. "But I'm not wrong."

She washed my face first. As soon as she wiped away the tears, others replaced them. I wished I could have said what I was thinking. All my words formed a ball and caught in my throat. The more I tried to talk, the bigger the ball became till I thought I'd choke on my own words. I wanted to open my mouth, let one word unravel and slip out between my lips.

"I came home to be with you, to be your mother. That's all I want to do." She wiped my arms with the towel. "I've been caught off guard by many things. I'm doing my best to figure it all out."

She stretched me out enough to pull my dress over my head. I was almost naked, and I was too old to be naked in front of folks. But my limbs were limp, paralyzed. I couldn't stop her. I prayed for strength. Why did I think God would help me now, when he hadn't raised a finger in my defense back at the church? If I hadn't waited till the last night. If He hadn't waited till the last night. If only I'd told a story. They probably would've believed I saw two redbirds, lovebirds.

"I know you want to be baptized, but one day you'll understand why I stopped it. Why I believe it's the best thing for you right now. You have to trust me, Sarah. Your well-being is my priority. I care more for you than I do everything in life," she said.

As she reached for my Sunday panties, Muhdea and Granny came to the room. Granny picked up the stack of pajamas off the bed and handed them to Esther. She told her to go get the other kids cleaned up and ready for bed. Esther didn't put up much of a fuss. Maybe she was tired and sleepy, too. Both Granny and Muhdea went about taking care of me. My legs and arms relaxed a bit, but my words were still balled up in my throat.

"Can you tell us what happened?" Muhdea said.

I stared at her.

"It's going to be alright," Granny said. "Ain't nobody going to hurt you, and I mean that."

"I'm going to talk to your mama. I'll bring you a glass of water,"

Muhdea said. "All I want for your mama to do is straighten up and make amends, be a mama to you. Instead she's traipsing up behind Carrie and them strangers causing more confusion than she did before she left here."

"Don't get yourself worked up, Mozelle. Esther will figure it out. She's finding her way is all. Doing a pretty bad job of it right now, but she'll get there," Granny said.

"I know you right, but how much more do we all have to suffer for her growing pains, especially Sarah? She ain't a child no more," Muhdea said. "I'm going to talk to her 'cause it don't look like Sarah in no position to tell us what happened."

I tried to say she slapped me, said I couldn't be baptized, but all I could do was swallow nothing. Muhdea left the room. Granny finished what Esther'd started, talking to me, soothing me the whole time.

"How'd this happen? I'll need to wash all your clothes so they won't stain. I know how much you like this outfit."

She eased the gown over my head and pulled it down below my waist and then pulled down my panties. My body softened a little more. She kept talking without expecting any response from me.

"You and your mama got to learn how to get along. No point in placing blame now. It won't do nobody no good. Nod your head if you can hear me, Sarah."

I did.

"Do you feel sick? Just shake your head."

I did.

"Okay. I'm going to assume you just got your feelings hurt pretty bad, and you'll be alright." She pulled back the covers on the bed. "Go ahead and get in, rest your nerves. I'm going in here to see what Muhdea and your mama talking about. Shake your head if it's okay that I leave you alone."

I did.

Muhdea and Esther's talk escalated. Muhdea said she was at a loss for words as to how Esther could pull me off the Mourner's Bench on the last night of revival. Had she considered my feelings? Had she considered anybody's feelings other than her own? I could tell by the confidence in Esther's voice that she'd thought out her answer. She didn't stutter. Her speech was plain, clear, no hesitation. Muhdea hedged. Her words seemed lost, and when she found some of them, they didn't make much sense. I bet Esther had been waiting for the right time to spring it on us.

"I know what's best for my daughter," Esther said. "There is more to life than what's going on in this small town. You would know that if you woke up and stopped believing every word that comes out of Reverend Jefferson's mouth as gospel. He's holding you back, and you aren't even aware of it. If I can help it, Sarah will not be blinded by his and your dogma."

When I'd heard enough, I slid out of bed. My legs were like soupy grits. I pushed forward 'cause I wasn't going to let Muhdea take the brunt of what was meant for me. If she knew what Esther had done to me, she'd find her words and use them to cut Esther to pieces.

They didn't want me to be there, tried to send me back to the room, but I stood up to them. They were half scared to say too much to me in my fragile state. Granny helped me to the couch. Muhdea tried to calm her voice.

"I'm guessing you ain't planning on letting Sarah be baptized," she said as if it were a fact and not a question.

"I got my sign," I whispered before Esther could answer.

"You did? Really, Sarah? Praise God," Muhdea said. As if it meant anything to Esther. "You up to telling me what it was?"

My words began to unravel. "Same as Granny's," I said, not as a testimony, happy and excited. My words were monotone, flat and lifeless.

"The choir did sing it," Granny said as if she just recalled hearing it.

"I was standing by the window Esther painted when I heard them."

"'I Need Thee Every Hour,'" Granny said as if she were remembering a time long past. "I had no idea you chose it." She placed her arm around my shoulders. "We have to settle this tonight, Esther. Sarah been through enough."

Some of the air seemed to ooze out of Esther. She sat down next to me. Had we won her over? Would she say yes? She could be nice at times. She didn't talk to Mrs. Carrie and Miss Ora Bea the same way she did to Muhdea. There wasn't the strain in her voice, the sharp edge she used with Muhdea and sometimes with Granny. They talked to each other, laughed together, listened, agreed and disagreed without arguing. She sat on the porch and talked to folks for hours when we stopped to pick up colored glass. She didn't laugh like that with Muhdea. They were careful about what they said and how they said it 'cause if they touched up on the wrong subject, it would blow up like pulling the stem out of a grenade.

Esther wanted to do what was best for me, for our family. Her intent wasn't to cause trouble. I leaned in so I could hear every word. Maybe there was still a chance. My revival gown was hanging in the closet. I'd gotten my sign. She had to give in, or I'd die. I willed her to give me the okay. It seemed as if she were going to speak, but instead Muhdea spoke up.

"Do what's right for once in your life. Let her be baptized."

I felt Esther's chest rise again. Tension smothered the room. Esther's voice trembled.

"I'm right about this. If anything is ever going to change, it has to begin here," she said as she gathered strength. She held both my hands. "You can't be baptized tomorrow."

"What about my sign? How can you go against God's will?" I said.

"The choir sings that song at every revival, Sarah. It was only a matter of time before they sang it at this one," Esther said.

Muhdea sent me to my room. She told me that it was past my bedtime. I protested, but nobody was on my side. I left the door cracked so I could hear. Granny stayed out of it, but Muhdea and Esther didn't hold back. As always, it started with one situation, which ended up leading to their entire history. Esther was getting the best of Muhdea, but every now and again, Muhdea landed a few hard blows. Muhdea didn't pussyfoot around when she brought up Esther's civil rights work. She'd tried to wait for the right time and the right way to talk to Esther about it, but she was hot, and she wasn't careful that night.

"Why you come back here and join up with Carrie and them? Didn't you do enough in the past? I prayed that you'd made something of yourself up there," Muhdea said. Thinking I might hear what Esther had done before she left town, the reason her name remained at the top of the prayer list, I crawled down the hallway. I didn't want to miss anything. "Can't you be somebody I could be proud of, a mother Sarah would look up to?" Muhdea said.

"I'm doing that. Just because it's not the way you would do it doesn't mean it isn't the right way. And just so you know, I haven't joined up with anybody. You need to check your facts," Esther said.

Come back to the reason she left home in the first place. I inched closer, then backwards for fear they might catch me. After a while, I realized that it was more important for them to keep talking about Esther's involvement with the civil rights movement than her reason for not allowing me to be baptized. I'd almost backed up to the bedroom door when Muhdea told Esther she'd had enough. She was hardheaded, nobody could tell her anything, and that would be her downfall. Esther said her downfall was listening to her in the first place. Her advice hadn't ever worked out to her favor.

"What do you mean by that?" Muhdea said.

"You know," Esther said.

Muhdea gave Esther the same ultimatum she'd given Uncle Robert, after she swore it hurt her so badly she'd never say that to one of her children again.

"I tell you what, Esther Mae. I see now it ain't no helping you. I might not be able to tell you what to do, never have, but this is my house, and whoever lives in my house must abide by my rules."

"Be careful, Mozelle," Granny said.

It was as if she didn't hear Granny. She kept talking.

"If you don't stop whatever it is you been doing with Carrie, and if you don't let Sarah be baptized, then you disrespecting my home, and I ain't having it."

"If I don't, then what, Muhdea? I'll have to leave? You want me to leave?"

"You said it," Muhdea said. "This is your home as long as you do the right thing."

"You wouldn't know right if it walked in this room," Esther said, "but you've said it now. Don't worry. I'll get out of here by the morning. This time I'm taking Sarah with me."

The front door and then the screen door slammed. I knew it was Esther. Muhdea yelled for her to come back. "Come back here and finish this, Esther Mae," she said. "Don't you dare run away from me."

"This time I'm taking Sarah with me," Esther said again.

She was wrong to walk away and leave Muhdea in this dilemma. A decision needed to be made tonight. The baptismal was at eleven o'clock tomorrow. I leaned my head out the window and yelled after her.

"You come back here. You can't keep me from getting my religion. You ain't God." She kept pouncing down the road. "I'm getting baptized. You wait and see." She didn't break her stride, didn't look back, and that put fire inside my belly. "I hate you. I hate you a whole lot." And when she turned the corner, I yelled louder. "You ain't my mama. Muhdea and Granny my mama."

Later Granny came to bed. She knew I'd heard everything. She told me not to worry. She was sorry I'd gotten caught in the middle of Esther and Muhdea's battle.

"I don't want you to worry. We knew we were taking a chance with you sitting on the Mourner's Bench. Whether you get baptized tomorrow or later in life, everything will work out just fine," she said.

"Do you think she'll come around?" I said.

"Maybe not in time for you to get baptized tomorrow, but in time, next summer, maybe."

"You going to let her take me?"

She shook her head no. "We won't let her do that."

I cried. I cried inside my stomach till it jerked. I cried till there were no more tears. I cried 'cause I knew Granny might be right, or she might be wrong.

FALL 1964 AND WINTER 1965

CHAPTER FOURTEEN

Four Generations of Women Live in My House

ESTHER MOVED DOWN to the Hall with them SNCC organizers. She didn't take me with her, but she made sure I was down there all the time. I didn't mind as much since Malika was back home, and we were back to competing with each other over everything again.

"Thought Granny was going to let you come to the Greyhound bus station to pick me up," was the first thing she said when I saw her.

Granny had promised me and Malika before she left for Chicago that I'd be waiting at the Greyhound bus station when she got back. I'd bet Malika the Greyhound got off the bus and ran along beside it like it did on the TV commercial. She loved winning, so she took the bet. We debated over it, and the last thing we did before she left town was shake on it. I'd never been no more than nine miles from home. Mrs. Carrie was going to drive Malika's mama up there, and she'd told me we'd go to the capital, the Arkansas History Commission, Granite Mountain and some other sights. I'd made plans all summer. Granny didn't feel like I should be running 'round with Mrs. Carrie. She couldn't be sure if them SNCC people were riding with her, or if somebody might have it out for them and I'd get caught in the crossfire.

I told Malika all of this, and all she said was didn't nobody ride with her but her mama. I'd missed all the sights, and the greyhound didn't get off the bus, which started our debate all over again 'cause I still believed it did.

The second thing she said was, "What the hell was wrong with Miss Esther? Doesn't she know how you love the church?"

She cocked her hip to one side, and placed her hand on her hip-bone. We looked the complete opposite. I was tall for my age, and she was short for hers. I had way more hair than I'd ever need, and she couldn't get hers to grow, not even an inch. She cared about what she wore, and I could care less. But we liked learning everything there was to know, and that bonded us together like watermelon seeds.

"I tried to tell her. Muhdea and Granny did too. But she'd rather move down here to the Hall than let me get baptized. Granny said some folks don't know what to do with even a little bit of power," I said.

"What you planning?" she said.

"I got to wait till next summer. By then, we should be able to figure out how to get around her. I'm still mad though. She slapped me too."

I showed Malika how she did it. We sat on the steps of the Hall, and talked as if we were full grown. We wrote questions on our lists whenever we got stumped. I told her about me and Esther's trip to the café for ice cream. She told me they went inside and ate at restaurants all the time in Chicago. I reckoned Esther was telling the truth about that.

"Malika, you think we'll ever know the answer to any of these questions?"

She scratched her head like Muhdea did sometime. Looked like an old woman too. "Probably not," she said. "But it ain't hurting us to keep track of it."

"I think we will," I said. "I think we'll know it all by the time we get to Esther's age."

"You don't know what you talking 'bout. You just said Miss Esther didn't know nothing."

"I'll give you that one." We laughed. "Come to think of it, she should know better than to try and send us to the white school. They taking me and you out of our regular class and training us to go over there next year."

We were back to normal, but nothing else was, not with Esther threatening Muhdea to move me to the Hall with her every other day, and not with us kids going to the white school either.

THAT DAY ME and Malika met at the front gate of the school every morning as we always did. She was running late. When she got there I rushed her through the gate.

"Come on. I want to check my family tree again before the bell ring."

"You really should've included Miss Esther's name on it," she said.

"You just mad 'cause no matter who I include, you can't win."

We were getting into so many arguments and so much trouble over going to the white school our teacher had given us an assignment to make us appreciate the importance of family. She was our biology teacher, and grew prizewinning roses. She used them to teach us about family generations. She grew five generations of roses from one bud, rare even for roses. She assigned the class to draw "Our Family Tree." Whoever gave the best presentation and had the most generations in their family would win a yellow rosebud, and she would come to their house and show them how to plant it. She gave each of us a poster board, a cardboard tree with cutout leaves, crayons, paint and markers. We worked on it during class for weeks. We pushed our desks against the walls in a circle and put our books under the seats. We covered the brick floor with yellow, blue, red and green posters and toolboxes filled with arts and crafts supplies, including Elmer's glue and scissors.

At first, the assignment stumped me. Miss Brady had told us to be creative, but when I put Granny's name down as my mother and refused to fill in the left side of the tree, what she called the paternal side, 'cause I didn't know my daddy, not that I didn't know his name or see him around, but he didn't live with us, Miss Brady insisted that I at least knew his name and strongly suggested I fill in the paternal side. I told her Granny preferred not to even speak his name aloud, and so did I. I couldn't see where writing it was any different.

"I'll speak to Mrs. Pearlie," she said. Me and the rest of the class warned her it wasn't a good idea, and eventually she gave in and allowed me to only fill in my maternal side of the family tree. Most of the other kids had the same problem. Our families were mix-matched. Uncles lived with us who weren't our kin, women we called cousin who were friends of the family that fell on hard times, great aunts we called Mama Jean or whatever their first names were. I imagined it was easier to determine the generations of roses than it was human beings in Maeby.

We finished them a couple of weeks before me and Malika were to report to the gym to begin preparation to go to the white school. Neither one of us wanted to go. Every day two students presented their family to the class. On the day of my presentation, I stood before the class with my chest stuck out so far I thought my sweater might burst wide open. When I think of that day, my face still gets warm from the shame I felt. Me and Miss Brady stood at the front of the class, smiling. She, tall, color of chocolate cake frosting, with long thick black hair like a china doll, and me, long legged, three ponytails hanging down my back with different-colored rubber bands holding my hair together at the root and at the tip.

"Four generations of women live in Sarah's house," Miss Brady said.

She pointed to the sketch of my family tree leaning beside the blackboard, right under the calendar we'd made that read "Fourth Grade Class, October 1964." I stood on one side of my poster and she on the other side, pointing at each brown branch with a green leaf.

"Sarah, will you tell us the person you have listed on each branch of your tree?" she said.

"Yes, ma'am." I pointed with the ruler. "On the first branch is Granny, my great-grandmother. Her real name is Pearlie Hopkins. The next leaf is my grandmother, Mozelle White. We call her Muhdea." I'd left the leaf blank where Esther's name should've been. I pointed to the next branch. "The next leaf is for me, Sarah Jones."

Hands flew up in the air, almost every student. A few stood up, including Malika.

"Calm down, class. Take your seat. You will get your turn," Miss Brady said.

I wasn't expecting them to act that way. Malika raised her arm up and down as if she had to go to the restroom in a hurry. Miss Brady pointed to her first.

"Why didn't you include your mama's name?" she said.

Miss Brady looked at me. She seemed more curious than Malika. I stared at Malika, daring her to take it back, and gave the same stare to the rest of the class. Malika held her ground and dared me right back.

"Sarah?" Miss Brady said.

"My mama don't live in the house with us no more, but she still alive." I rolled my eyes at Malika.

"That ain't a good enough answer. Is it, Miss Brady?" she said.

"It's all I got, so leave it alone," I said.

I knew she wouldn't stop till she got the whole class stirred up. She'd been that way ever since we got double promoted from the first to the third grade, always trying to prove who was the smartest, and seemed to like it better when she had witnesses. The principal and teachers had tried to convince Granny to let me skip the first grade altogether, but she'd turned them down. After the first year, she went ahead and let me skip the second grade. Granny blamed Sister Tucker and Uncle Robert for teaching me too much.

Malika asked me question after question. She knew the answers. We'd talked it over. She tried to goad me. I wasn't falling for it, but it was too much for me when the other students got in on it, and she should've backed down.

"She told you," a boy said. "Leave her alone." He laughed.

"Ooh," some of the students said.

Miss Brady let them carry on without saying a word.

"She can't do that. Can she, Miss Brady?" Malika said.

"No, she can't. How can that be? It's as if she ain't got no mama. How can that be?" another boy said.

"She knows who her mama and daddy is," a girl yelled. "Make her write it on the tree, Miss Brady."

"My family ain't nobody's business in here," I said.

Miss Brady, frozen in place, pointed at the leaf.

"She mad at her mama. That's why she left her name off," a girl from my church said. "She mad 'cause her mama wouldn't let her get baptized and she peed on herself."

Miss Brady finally clapped her hands several times, bringing most of the class to order.

"Sit," she said with so much conviction I sat down in her chair. "Calm down, class. I'm sure Sarah has her reasons for not completing the assignment, but regardless, it doesn't give you a reason to ridicule her." She took down my board and looked at me emphatically. "Do you understand, class?" We all bowed our heads.

"She can't win now, can she, Miss Brady?" Malika said.

My chest lowered itself somewhere down near my feet, and shame spread all over me like chickenpox. Why did Miss Brady assign us that stupid family tree, anyway? Malika's hand went up again.

"Leave it alone," I said.

"Yes," Miss Brady said.

"I don't want the stupid rosebud. You can have it. I don't want to be your friend anymore either. You infiltrator," I said. I'd gotten that word from Rutherford. It sounded mean, and Malika knew I'd left Esther off my family tree on purpose. She knew I was the only one in class who had two great-grandmothers living. I didn't have to write in Esther's name for her to count.

The whole class looked at me as if I'd cussed when I used the word "infiltrator." I walked out of class, leaving all my belongings. Rutherford would get a kick out of it. It was cold. Miss Brady came out behind me, and I ran. When I got to the corner, I looked both ways and knew I had no place to go where I wouldn't be in trouble. Kids weren't allowed to get mad, to have an opinion about their life. All I could do was what I was told to do, and I didn't, and it caused me to lose my friend, do bad work in class, and get in trouble, so I went to the Hall. Maybe nobody there would notice me.

That evening at the Hall Malika tapped me on my shoulder. "Sorry, Sarah," she said. "Sorry for the whole thing."

She'd picked up my belongings after class and brought them down to the Hall with her. "Sometimes you don't know when to quit," I said.

"I promise I won't ever do that again. You my best friend, Sarah."

I tapped her shoulder, said "tag" and took off running to the backyard. "You better not do it again, and I'm getting you back too."

It wasn't ever that bad before or afterward, but we kept competing with each other even when later that semester we left our regular class and moved into the gym for our special "get ready for the white school" one.

WE TRIED EVERYTHING from faking that we were sick to pretending we didn't know how to spell, but nobody paid us any attention but us. We all reported to the gym to start preparing to attend the white school. Thick black theater curtains sectioned off each classroom. There were four groups of classes. Me and Malika were lumped in with the fifth- and sixth-graders.

During recess the other kids turned on us even more, called us stuck up, closed the circle, wouldn't let us in to play Little Sally Walker and hit us too hard when we played tag. One day a sixth-grader hit me in the back so hard I thought I saw Jesus. Malika got between us, and she drew back even further and hit her. Our teacher pulled us aside.

"I can try to put a stop to it," she said, "but I would rather teach you how to communicate. It's going to be worse at the white school, and communication skills will help you keep things calm until help comes or you can get away."

"Ain't no talking. If they hit me, I'm fighting," I said.

"That's not what your mother stands for now, is it, Sarah?"

"No ma'am, but I'm not lying on no ground, in a curl, when I'm wearing my school clothes. Are you, Malika?"

"I'm fighting, too, and I'll fight the ones that hit you, Sarah," she said.

"Well, I'll teach you anyway. You might change your mind."

PTA members, church members, fathers, mamas and grand-mamas drilled us in reading, writing and arithmetic every chance they got. Folks who ignored the civil rights movement, and ones who couldn't even read, became teachers overnight after Esther told us the whites were trying to devise a plan to keep us out of the classroom with them. They planned to place us in special education classes. The lawyer Walker filed another lawsuit to keep that from happening. Everybody on our side of town carried flash cards or memorized questions to ask us. Some didn't know the questions and the answers were written on the same page. We read the questions ourselves. If I didn't know the answer, I didn't have the heart to look at it. "I'll know it next time," I said, and they remembered.

"Name the seven continents, Sarah. Don't forget Africa now." They were not going to let their children be embarrassed over there across the tracks.

Being special was okay for a while, but I missed looking out of the window of my other classroom even though I had to look up and could only see the sky, and daydream about riding my bike on the clouds. Sometimes I dreamed me and Malika caught the train to New York like hobos with all our belongings tied in a red and white handkerchief. Looking at a thick black curtain wasn't the same as looking out the window. Plus, with only thirteen students, the teacher was bound to catch me if I drifted off. I missed all my other classmates. There wasn't anybody who needed help now. I stayed up later at night studying just to keep up with them.

I just quit going to recess altogether. In class and at home the teachers required us to speak the King's English. No more getting away with just writing it anymore. When I did go to the playground, I lost my calm every time. The last day I went to recess, Crazy Abigail started acting like the other kids.

"Y'all think y'all something 'cause you going to the white school," she said.

"Not me and Malika," I said. "We don't think we're anything."

"Yes, you do. You changed, Sarah Jones. You don't even talk the same no more." She placed her hand on her hip like we did when we played Little Sally Walker and yelled at the top of our lungs, "Put your hands on your hip and let your backbone slip," but she wasn't playing.

"Why you say that? That's stupid. We not even playing the game," I said.

She looked around and saw everybody looking. "Don't call me stupid." She hit me in my back. Stunned me. "I'm done talking to you, and everybody else is, too."

"You can't stop talking to me," I said

When she was a ways in front of me, she yelled back so everybody could hear.

"Don't ever in your life talk to me again."

Everybody laughed except one girl. I looked in her face and knew they'd planned it, and Abigail was right. None of them was going to ever talk to me again. I ran home. Esther walked down the steps. I told her what had happened through snot, sobs and tears, the front of my dress wet from wiping the tears with it. She wiped my face with the hem of my dress, and when it seemed as if I'd composed myself, she held my face between her hands.

"This is the last time I want to see you cry over this," she said. "You have a job to do, and from now on, you have to be strong." She was so close to me her hair hung over my shoulders, and I could have kissed her red lips. "There won't be any crying at the white school. Do you understand me, Sarah?" she said sternly. I was still mad, but I did know all the fun I had in learning was gone and might not ever come back again.

CHAPTER FIFTEEN

That's Blasphemous

RUTHERFORD TOOK ME and Malika across Highway 65 and the railroad tracks to the library almost every day. He didn't hold our hands to make sure we looked both ways for the cars or the train before we crossed. He drank from a paper sack, and when we asked for a swallow, he laughed and said no. Our one big mistake was mentioning to him that Mrs. Carrie had said somebody'd written a book with an article in it about Mr. Stith. The worst part of it was we were just messing with him, playing on his intelligence, as he liked to say. Mrs. Carrie did tell us about the book, but we made up the part about it being in the library.

"Mr. Rutherford," Malika said. "You read that book with Mr. Stith in it?"

While he was studying on how to sound smart, I added my two cents.

"Mrs. Carrie read it. Saw it in a library."

"What's the name of it?" he said.

"She can't remember," Malika said.

"She saw it in a library in Georgia. We just asked since you from there," I said.

He was not one to be outdone.

"Well, that's alright," Malika said. "Seem like something important enough to know before we go to the white school."

"Did y'all look for it at the school library?" Reverend Adam Moses said.

We realized they were taking us seriously and figured we'd better leave them alone. We left Rutherford and Reverend Adam Moses, minister at the Methodist church Malika and Mrs. Carrie attended sitting on the back steps passing the paper sack back and forth. We tried to hold our laughter till we got around to the front yard, but we couldn't. We burst out laughing as soon as we turned the corner, holding our stomachs and bending over it was so funny.

THE FOLLOWING DAY, as soon as we got to the Hall and put down our book satchels, Rutherford came and got us.

"Come on," he said. "Y'all going with me."

He didn't tell us where we were going till we were almost there.

"It's time we integrated the library. We'll use that book about Reverend Stith as a reason to be there. Y'all feel me?" he said.

It took all we had within us to keep from breaking down laughing. I turned my head in the other direction, away from Malika. Rutherford walked up to the counter, and the white lady at the desk looked as if she'd seen three convicts and turned her nose up as if we smelled like polecats. I sniffed under my arms to see if I was funky from the walk. Rutherford approached her similar to the way Esther had Mrs. Cox at the café.

"Miss, we're looking for a book, and we would like to register for a library card," he said.

"Mrs.," she said.

"Oh, pardon me," he said.

I thought we were about to have our first success. She seemed pleasant enough. Me and Malika held hands, but before Rutherford could complete his sentence, her attitude changed.

"Boy, you know better than to be in here. Go on," she shooed us. "Y'all get on out of here, or I'ma call Chief King.

Me and Malika headed for the door, but Rutherford gave us a look that stopped us in our tracks.

"Now, go on," she said as she picked up the phone.

"Call him," he said.

Me, her and Malika bucked our eyes. She turned her back to us and made the call. I stood on my tiptoes to try and see how the telephone worked.

Mr. Michael James King and two deputies showed up in record

168

time. They didn't ask us any questions. They placed Rutherford's hands behind his back, handcuffed him, and pushed him in the back of the police car. The chief told us to get in the backseat of the deputy's car.

"Take them home," he said. "I'll stop by the café and have a talk with their mamas later."

"They going to beat the hell out of him," Malika said.

We'd seen him and James come back from across town from aggravating the white folks bloody and swollen.

"We can't follow him up here no more," I said.

"We can if it gets us a ride in a police car," Malika said.

We rode to the Hall in the police car with the sirens blasting. We thought it was fun. Everybody came out on the porch to see what was going on. It seemed like fun when they thought it was just us, but when we told them they took Rutherford to the station, the air in the room changed.

"He's got to get rid of that hair trigger," Mrs. Carrie said. "We hadn't even planned to target the library yet."

"I guess we won't be going back up there," I whispered to Malika.

Esther and Bro Hollin left to go bail him out of jail. Mrs. Carrie inquired as to whether we'd been harmed or not. She informed us of the seriousness of it. How things could have gone awry.

The next day when we were about to leave the Hall, Rutherford opened the door and walked inside. His face looked like hog head souse.

"Don't take your coat off," he said. "Come on. Y'all going with me."

He went upstairs and came back down with the paper sack, and we headed uptown to the library. All the grown folks were at a meeting at the county seat, and he looked so pitiful, we went with him. As soon as we opened the door, the white lady picked up the phone. The whole time we waited, I kept wondering what was her name. Mrs. what? The police arrived by the time Rutherford asked to register for a library card. The chief of police came instead, and he wasn't friendly at all. He cursed at Rutherford right in front of us.

"Didn't I tell y'all not to come back here again?" Mr. Michael James King said.

He had forgotten to tell it on us.

"What's so bad about us having a library card?" I said. "We know how to read."

"I see you got a smart-ass mouth like your mama," he said. "Why is Mozelle letting you hang out down there with these agitators?"

He used the word "agitator" the same way I did when Miss Brady gave us a new word and told us to use it as many times as possible in a sentence during the day. "Use it until it becomes a part of your vocabulary," she said.

"What's an agitator?" I said. Malika nudged me.

"You 'bout to see right now."

He didn't take us to the Hall with the sirens blaring. He put us in the backseat with Rutherford, cuffed us too and took us to jail. Mrs. Carrie was right. This wasn't fun. And it was going to be even less fun when Muhdea found out I'd followed Rutherford voluntarily. Maybe it was 'cause I knew Mr. Michael James King. Even though I'd heard bad things about him, he'd always been friendly with Muhdea. And I wasn't scared. Not the for-real kind of scared anyway.

"Maybe this'll teach you gals some manners," he said.

He put Rutherford in one jail cell and me and Malika in the other one before he took off the handcuffs.

"We criminals now," Malika said.

Rutherford didn't like that at all and gave us a good talking to about the difference between a criminal and an activist.

"Don't nobody know where we at," I said after some time had passed, and me and Malika was tired of playing hand games, "Pitty Pat" to the tune of "Mary Mack," which irritated Rutherford.

"You hungry?" Malika said.

We grew hungrier and hungrier. Rutherford told us we couldn't ask for any food. I wanted to cry, but Esther had told me to never cry again.

"Rutherford," I said. "When we getting out of here?"

"Don't be scared. They won't hurt you. They're trying to teach me a lesson."

"I want to go home," Malika said. "Can I go to the bathroom?"

Rutherford told them we needed to go, and he told us to go together, hold hands.

Bro Hollin came to get us just before dark. I heard him ask if he needed to pay bail for us.

"No, take them," Mr. Michael James King said. "Next time I'm charging them with trespassing though."

"What about him?" Bro Hollin said.

"We charging him. He can't leave."

"With what?" Bro Hollin said.

"Public drunkenness to start with," Mr. Michael James King said and held up the paper sack.

We ran into Bro Hollin's arms. Malika fair out cried as soon as she got in the truck. I patted her on the back.

"We have to be brave," I said.

"I am brave," she said between sobs. "I didn't drop one tear in there."

"Y'all did just fine," Bro Hollin said.

I remembered that I planned to figure out if the chief could read and write. Folks said he couldn't. The deputies wrote tickets for him. I knew Rutherford wasn't going to give up on the library card, and decided to ask the chief for his autograph next time.

They kept Rutherford for three days. Afterward, he was more bound and determined that we get a library card. Esther and most everybody at the Hall told him to leave me and Malika out of it, but every evening he told us to get our coats. Gail saved us some of the time. She kept us in class or assigned us to teach the adults how to prepare the voter registration forms and study for the test.

Granny and Muhdea worried more than I did. I told them we were okay even though I wanted to crawl behind the library desk and hide every time I saw the police car.

"One of the deputies plays checkers with us. He taught me a couple of new moves," I said.

I started grabbing a book to read till Bro Hollin arrived to get us. Muhdea came from the café to pick us up one evening. One of the customers had seen us get in the police car and told everybody at the café. Muhdea brought a chocolate cake.

"Can you just leave them at the library?" she said. "These kids ain't got no business being in jail." She cut each one of them a big slice of chocolate cake.

"Then keep them away from the library," the chief said. "Why you letting them gallivant around with the likes of him?"

I knew it was Granny when the door opened, the force behind it, and the rush to let her inside. "Where is she?" she said, all my cousins trailing behind her. We have a system at home to keep everything in order, and dragging them kids across town wasn't part of it. Granny hated for her schedule to be thrown off. Malika walked to the front, where Granny and my cousins waited. The jail was only a few rooms, one up front with four wood desks and black swivel chairs, a kitchen where we played checkers, a bathroom and the cells, down the hall from the main room.

Granny told us to stay put while she talked to the chief, but I didn't. "These are kids," she said. "Stop involving them in your mess." She said it loud enough for Rutherford to hear her.

"You need to tell it to that boy," the chief said.

"That boy didn't bring them up here to this jail. You could've told that woman at the library to send somebody for me."

"You don't tell me what I could've done. Just 'cause your wig on too tight, don't forget your place. There's plenty room back there with that boy."

Even though Granny didn't have any use for Rutherford, she said his name so the chief would have to say it. "You mean Rutherford. Is that who you got back there?"

"Yes, Rutherford is who is at fault here. If you got a problem with me arresting these kids, take it up with him."

"We been getting along fine, and I ain't got nothing to do with them, and I know you don't want me to take up with them. We agreed to our places a long time ago, and ain't neither of us crossed the line till now."

"Why you bring that up, Pearlie?" he said.

"Why you messing with my child?" she said.

"You 'bout to forget your place, and I'm sure that boy back there be glad to have some company."

"We had an agreement. If you stick to yours, I'll do the same," she said. "Can I talk to him?"

He motioned with his head for her to go on back there. I could hear her and Rutherford's voices, but I couldn't make out the words. The chief and the deputy had huge grins on their faces. Granny came back and grabbed Malika's and my hands, and we caught hold of the other children till we were a chain.

"Can we go now?" she said.

He nodded. "I'd appreciate it if you wouldn't bring these kids up here again."

Rutherford waved to us from the window as we walked away. He came back with bruises on his face and body, and smelled worse than he looked. He refused all services from them when he was in jail, food, water and soap. Esther dabbed peroxide on his cuts and fed him clear soup till he could eat whole food again.

GOING TO JAIL had become such a regular occasion that Bro Hollin waited at the jail to bring us home. Rutherford spent more time at the jail than he did at the Hall. SNCC or the Maeby Citizens for Progress didn't have it in their budget to keep bailing him out. He stayed locked up till he worked off the fine. Some days we'd see him picking up paper on the side of the road. One cold day in February, only one deputy was there, so he let us all go home with Bro Hollin. A bunch of folks stood on the porch of the Hall as if they were waiting for us. A party, I thought.

"What's going on? Why all y'all out here?" Bro Hollin said.

"Malcolm X was assassinated."

I took off running toward home. Malika caught up to me. "Go back, Malika," I said. "I got to get home. He's Uncle Robert's friend. I got to tell Muhdea and Granny. They got to get somebody to check on him in Little Rock."

As I rounded the corner, I saw Uncle Robert's car parked on the road outside the front of our house. I ran to meet him, my book satchel banging against my leg.

I swung open the door. It slammed behind me. Granny leaned on a chair halfway between the kitchen and the living room. I ran past her to greet Uncle Robert. She didn't warn me to stop running in the house.

"Hey, Uncle Robert," I said. "You okay?"

Any other time he would've pulled a Bo dollar from behind my ear, smiled wide, and said, "Abracadabra." When he didn't answer, I pulled his coattail.

"Uncle Robert, Uncle . . ." I said.

He caught my hands and held them.

"Where your manners, Sarah?" Muhdea said. She pursed her lips. "Can't you see we talking?"

I nodded. Why was she talking to me like that? It couldn't be 'cause I was excited to see him. Maybe she'd heard about Malcolm X.

"Where's your mother?" he whispered.

I shook my head, pulled my hands away.

"I didn't see her at the Hall."

I hadn't seen him since revival. "Where you been?" I said. I saw the pictures before he could answer. "Wow, Uncle Robert, these are pretty. Is that Moses?"

I wished I'd said "spectacular" instead of "pretty." The day before, our word of the day was "spectacular," and that day it was "superior."

After I'd seen a big picture of what looked like Moses parting the Red Sea, and a bunch of other paintings and statues, I looked for my doll he'd promised to bring me. The sea looked as if it were real water. I felt as if I could get in line with the Israelites and walk across the sea behind Moses. A picture of the Last Supper lay next to the one of Moses. Behind the picture of Moses was one of Jesus sitting on a rock holding a girl with long plaits, with children sitting on the grass looking up at them.

"Robert, you trying to kill me," Muhdea said. "How much sin you going to bring in my house ? I told you before I ain't hanging it on my wall." Her eyes bulged and lips trembled.

What in the world was going on? I moved away from the pictures, startled by the tone of Muhdea's voice.

"What's come over you, boy?" She pointed her finger at Uncle Robert's chest. "Get on out of here. Get your junk out my house."

He wanted to take all the pictures of white people off the walls and replace them with colored folks. Muhdea said the people in the pictures weren't white.

"They ain't white people, Robert. That's Jesus and His disciples and President Kennedy and his brother Bobby."

"At least let me put up the Reverend Martin Luther King Jr.," Uncle Robert said.

Her bottom lip quivered as she bit on the upper one. He seemed as calm as the Red Sea. He straightened his bowtie, which was part of his uniform, a dark suit, clean white shirt, pointed-toe black shoes and close-shaven head. He was frail, and his suit hung on his body like it would on a hanger. Muhdea looked frazzled in her soiled waitress dress, thick opaque stockings rolled down past her ankles and short brown wig.

"I've done nothing here," Uncle Robert said. He placed his hand over his heart. "If you knew . . ."

Muhdea held her hand up, signaling him to stop.

"You take things too far, Robert."

Muhdea pointed her finger so close to Uncle Robert's nose I thought she might stick it up his nostril.

"Half the time I think you and Esther is plotting to drive me insane. The world might be a better place if I didn't have to waste the majority of my prayer time on y'all."

Uncle Robert stood tall and erect as if he were a soldier.

"I can't trust y'all," she said. She lowered her hand to her side. "You don't think I do, but I know things. I ain't no fool, Robert."

"I'm not hiding anything. I'm not trying to pull one over on you. The world is changing. Something serious happened yesterday."

Tears welled up in Uncle Robert's eyes. I wanted to interrupt and tell Muhdea what was wrong with him, but then he and I would be in worlds of trouble, so I kept quiet.

"Do you think I want my child roasting in Hell? Jesus! Robert." She looked dead in his eyes, her eyes blazing like a fiery furnace. "You acting like you don't know that's Jesus Christ you strutting around here with, and He ain't colored. Have you lost your ever-loving mind, child?" She brushed her hands against her dress. "It's blasphemous, Robert. Jesus Christ." She brushed her hands across her head, rearranging her wig. "Blasphemy, plain and simple."

She was mad 'cause they were colored people? Why was a painting of a colored Jesus a sin? Uncle Robert's pictures were more spectacular than the ones on our walls. The heads of President John F. Kennedy and his brother Bobby painted on a plate. Muhdea's favorite. A faded picture of the Last Supper, half the size of the colorful one propped against the coffee table. Another plate with only the head of President Kennedy and an old cuckoo clock hung beside each other on the opposite wall. The bird had quit coming out a long time ago, but it still cuckooed on the hour. As I thought about it, the old cuckoo clock chirped five times, five o'clock. Uncle Robert checked his watch, took his prayer rug out of one of his bags, walked into the hallway, spread the prayer rug on the floor, and kneeled for his afternoon prayer.

Silence blanketed the house like fog. Granny walked in the living room. Didn't smell like she had started supper. My stomach grumbled. I tried to whisper in Muhdea's ear, but she pushed me away. Esther shoved open the front door.

"Robert. Hey, bro. Where you hiding?" She looked around the room.

Granny shushed her and pointed to the hallway where he kneeled in prayer. Esther turned her attention toward Uncle Robert's pictures and statues, nodded her head, picked up the picture of colored Jesus and the children, and bucked her eyes. Muhdea cut her eyes at Esther. She placed it on the floor and remained quiet.

I waited impatiently for Uncle Robert to finish praying. He was going to tell me the whereabouts of my doll before he and Muhdea lit into each other again. I'd go to the car myself if he'd tell me where to find it. He may have hidden it behind the backseat, or under the carpet in the trunk, wherever it would bring a smile to my face when I discovered it. He loved surprising me. I never figured out why he got such a rise out of the look on my face.

I thought Esther would tell Muhdea about Malcolm X. She

couldn't be as mad at Uncle Robert if she knew he'd lost his friend. I positioned myself in the entranceway, waited, one eye on him, the other on Muhdea, but Esther walked past me into the hallway before he picked up his prayer rug.

"As-salamu alaykum, my brother," Esther said.

They grabbed hold of each other's hands. The words rolled off Esther's tongue as if she were Arabic.

"Wa alaykumu as-salam, my beautiful sister," he said.

They knew better than to laugh and grin at each other and talk in foreign languages as if we weren't in the same room.

"Oh, brother," she said. Hands still clasped together. "I'm so sorry. We heard. How are you?"

She looked him up and down. "Robert," she said as she adjusted his suit. She quickly stopped and focused on the pictures. "I love them, your work, just love them. *The Last Supper*. I want to pull a chair to the table and commune with them."

He placed his finger to his lips. I watched. Muhdea dropped into the chair.

"Nothing I've seen before comes close to what you've done. It's genius. This will help so much," Esther said.

"We did it. I see more of your strokes than I do mine," he said.

Muhdea rolled up her stockings while eyeing them. Granny leafed through the pictures as if they held the answer to Esther's rants. Uncle Robert changed the subject to something worse.

"Did you hear Malcolm's last message on race?" he said.

"No," Esther said as she grabbed hold of his hands. "What is the word concerning his death, brother? Was it his people? We all know *the man* was involved regardless of who pulled the trigger."

Granny held the statue of Joseph with the coat of many colors. Muhdea pulled her stockings up, wound the top in a knot, and tucked it so it wouldn't roll down her leg. The other one was still around her ankle. She rose up out of the chair. I felt the heat ooze out of her body, and I moved to the far end of the room behind Granny. Esther and Uncle Robert remained engaged in their conversation.

"What happened, Robert?" Muhdea said, her tone softer than cotton candy. "Who's dead?"

Uncle Robert told her as one tear at a time streamed down his face. Afterward, she no longer looked at him as a sinner with sinful paintings. She saw her son who had lost his friend, and was way too thin, and she comforted him. Before he left, she let him put two of the statues on the coffee table. Jesus and his disciples were not colored, so he might as well forget about ever hanging them on her wall.

SUMMER 1965

CHAPTER SIXTEEN

This Ain't My Fight

I WASHED DISHES while everybody else sat in the living room listening to Muhdea tell Bible stories. The Lord had created a huge storm, and when He worked, we gave Him His due respect by keeping quiet. I needed to hurry up. Granny yelled out several times "I'll be in there directly to help you," even though cleaning the kitchen after supper was my job, and it was a big one. The rain had started during the middle of supper, which didn't give us much time to settle down before it crashed hard against our tin roof and the lightning flashed through the windows. Granny had split the ground earlier with the ax, but the storm didn't pay it no mind. Certain chores needed completing regardless of the rain, and cleaning the kitchen was one of them. Dinner would've been served on time if them SNCC organizers, Mr. Bill Hansen, the lawyer Walker and some others, hadn't held Granny up telling her the details of the Voting Rights Act President Johnson was going to sign into law. I couldn't figure why Granny stood out there and listened to them. She told me the whole story when it happened, and then her and Sister Tucker talked about it at length, and I listened in. Folks on Sister Tucker's TV gave talks, and the Reverend Martin Luther King Jr. said it would change everything for the Negro. During the summer of 1965, Walter Cronkite of the six o'clock news said the United States was fighting a civil war at home and a war in Vietnam.

We were late getting supper on the stove 'cause Granny seemed to be having a good old time talking to them, which made me late washing dishes. I grouped the dishes together on the table before I started washing them, glasses, plates, silverware, pots and pans. I washed the groups in the order I had stacked them. First, the three or four fancy glasses we owned, then the baby bottles and the jelly jars. I still tried to scrape the glue off the jars even though we'd started using them as a drinking glasses months ago. Next in line were the plates. Each of us had our own plate and jelly jar. The plates, all different colors, shapes and sizes, made it easy to tell which belonged to who. We didn't have enough knives, forks and spoons for each of us, but we'd rather use our hands. Granny told us the African folks ate with their hands, and something about doing it too made me feel connected to them, Granny's kin. Food tasted better when I placed it in my mouth with my fingers, licking cornbread and turnip greens from each finger and my thumb. Granny ate from a saucer. All the food she needed could fit on it, and anything more was too much.

I rushed around the kitchen thinking about the coming revival. Me and Malika had been so busy trying to come up with a plan to get out of going to the white school that we'd barely had time to consider me getting my religion. Whether I was ready or not, it was starting on Sunday night. I'd been praying privately all summer. Nobody needed to know what I was up to. And since I'd declared myself saved regardless of what the church believed, I didn't figure I had to be as serious about it as I was last summer. I gave great thought to asking God to show me that set of redbirds, but I settled on the same sign I'd asked for last summer. He'd shown it to me once, so I believed He'd do it again. Reverend Isaiah Rich had brought in so many lost souls last summer the committee had asked him to come back again, and he'd agreed.

"We even scraped up a few extra dollars to pay him," Muhdea bragged.

I looked forward to seeing his big set of teeth paved with gold. This time I was going to try not to imagine me slipping and sliding on them like they were the streets of Heaven. I'd started praying for my sign right after school let out in May, which should be enough time since I was repeating it. Funny how I was smart enough to skip a grade in school but ended up flunking out at church.

After the last revival, Esther ignored everything and everybody. Muhdea and Reverend Jefferson tried to reason with her. Like a scratched record, pain crawled inside Muhdea for a long time after Uncle Robert left her house, but she fair broke down when Esther moved down to the Hall rather than let me get baptized, and she almost had a stroke every time Esther threatened to take me to live with her. Esther chose to go. Moved down to the Hall with the civil rights workers after she told me she wasn't ever leaving me again. A plug nickel had more value than her word. I couldn't grasp how them folks at the Hall put so much faith in her, but they did, as if her word was the gospel for the civil rights movement.

I threw the forks, spoons and butcher knives in the dishpan, almost cutting my hand. I changed the water again, poured boiling water from the pot on top of the woodstove, placed more wood inside the stove, and placed a pot of cold water on the eye. By the time the pot started to boil, I threw the old water out the back door and changed the rinse water. I washed the pots and pans. Granny's mama must've given her some of these pots. If I scraped for the rest of my life, the bottoms would still be bent and black. I changed the dishwater again before I started washing the black cast-iron skillets.

Thinking about last year's revival got me riled up again. I'd tried to get rid of that feeling months ago 'cause it didn't do nothing but get me in a whole bunch of trouble. At times the feeling snuck up on me like a rogue in the night, and Lord help the person who got in my way. I held open the screen door with one leg, and tried to hit Daddy's old hunting dog crouched beside the half-full slop barrel, with the dirty water. He howled and scooted up under the house. Thunder roared and lightning flashed across the sky, and revealed sheets of rainfall. I should've boiled another pan just to throw under the house after the old dog. No-good dog. I remembered my prayers. All year it had seemed as if the Devil and God were fighting over my soul. I poured the grease in an old lard can and made a clean pan of dishwater and added lye soap. No sense in me saying I liked washing dishes 'cause I didn't. Malika had a sink with running water and an inside toilet and bathtub in their new Jim Walter home. Running water couldn't make washing dishes any easier.

Granny finally came in the kitchen to help me with the dishes.

"What you doing in here, gal? You trying to break something? Didn't you hear Mozelle tell you to quiet down in here?" She was about to say something else, but one of my cousins came in yelling.

"Sarah. Sarah, hurry up. The sun shining, and the rain done slowed down." He pulled on my dress tail. "Come on, Sarah. You got to see the rainbow. I bet we can find the pot of gold this time. Hurry up, Sarah. We might be able to hear the Devil beat his wife too."

"Get away from me, boy," I said and snatched my dress out of his hand. "Didn't I tell you I wasn't following no more rainbows? Ain't no pot of gold. Leave me alone."

I wouldn't have said that to him if I hadn't been thinking about how Esther had interfered and stopped me from getting my religion last summer. I needed to stop carrying so much anger around with me about it and let it go like Granny said. Me and Esther got along much better since she moved to the Hall. I'd started to look up to her sometime the way the folks at the Hall did. They loved them some Esther Mae.

"Don't talk to him like that just 'cause you got a problem. You hear me?" Granny said. She told him I didn't have time today. He and the other children should go ahead. I'd be ready the next time it rained, but I had to finish the dishes now. "Save a piece of that gold for me," she said.

I washed, and she rinsed and dried the skillets.

"I hear how you been talking to everybody around here. It's time for you to let that go. Don't matter what happens to you, it's only so long that you can hold on to it."

"I ain't holding on to nothing."

"Oh, yes you is, and you better take that sass out of your voice when you talking to me. You got to find a way to get rid of it, child."

"I let it go, but sometimes it comes up again. I'll be fine."

I tried not to get mad, but it wasn't easy for me to sit in Sunday school and watch Crazy Abigail read the minutes. I filled pages and pages of lists and began to write down my pain and my joy. Esther was still on every prayer list, so it was important for me to get baptized this time.

Me and Granny washed the rest of the dishes in silence. I cherished having Granny all to myself even when she chastised me. I swept the floor, and she held the cardboard while I swept the trash up on it. Finally, she shared with me the reason why she was there.

"Esther picking you up in the morning. She taking you to Little Rock with her to pick up Carrie and that boy."

"Ma'am? What boy? Rutherford?"

"She said she'd pick you up at six."

It felt like lightning bugs were fluttering around in my chest, but I kept calm. I didn't want to jinx it.

"You mean I'm going to the Greyhound bus station?"

They must've been coming back early. I'd heard at the Hall they weren't due back till late Monday evening. If that was true, I'd miss the first night of revival, and there was no coming forth after the first night. I couldn't take a chance on it and have to wait another whole year.

"When she coming back?" I said.

"What, you don't want to go?" she said. "You been dying to see that bus station."

"No, ma'am, I want to go. I just have to be back by Sunday." I crossed my fingers. God wouldn't let me down twice in a row. Would He?

FINALLY, SATURDAY MORNING and I was overjoyed, which might fail to describe how I felt. It had taken a whole year for Granny to give me permission to go see the dog run alongside the bus, and regardless of how many times Malika told me he didn't get off the bus, not even on the highway, I wanted to see it for myself. And if it didn't happen in real life, I wanted to know how they did it on TV.

Granny checked my hair, which wasn't parted as straight as she liked it. She said I had such a bad head she didn't think she could get the parts right if she started all over again. Esther thought they were fine. They fussed over me. Granny wiped my face. Esther polished it again. Each of them greased my ashy skinny legs with Vaseline and made me stand tall while they straightened out my dress. Then Granny remembered she'd forgotten the "just-in-case" money. She tied five dollars in a pink flowered handkerchief, pinned it to my panties where the knot wouldn't show through my dress, and straightened my dress out all over again. When Granny finished, she adjusted each pleat in my dress. They greased my black patent-leather shoes with the same Vaseline they used on my legs, arms and face. Muhdea came in from washing clothes and asked if they were going to fuss over me all morning. Then she checked me again, made a few corrections, and nodded her head in approval. I was spit shined from head to toe.

Esther drove Mrs. Carrie's car. We walked out to the car as Granny and Muhdea reminded me of the dos and don'ts and continued to fix my clothes and hair. We stood next to the green and white Chevrolet.

"Mind your mama," Granny said.

"Yes, ma'am," I said before I got into the car.

For a woman who never seemed to keep her mouth shut, Esther was quiet. Driving to the bus station should've been a jovial trip, but she seemed as serious as a woman on her way to visit a man at the prison. We'd taken a class trip to the prison, and they'd shown us everything, even where the prisoners ate and slept. Much later they made the movie *Brubaker* about the horrible things that happened at that prison.

About fifteen miles outside of Maeby, Esther hadn't said much of anything. I could feel her mind churning. I wanted to ask her what time Mrs. Carrie's bus got into the station, but I didn't want to hear every detail about everything she'd ever done. I bided my time to see if she'd tell me. Before long, she asked me if I was enjoying the ride.

"It's fine," I said. I'd learned to answer Esther carefully, use the least amount of words possible 'cause she could take anything the wrong way. Next, she asked me if I'd missed her all those years. What? Where did that come from? I hadn't thought about it. People always came and went. Sometimes I was glad when they came and hated to see some folks go. After they left, I didn't think about it no more. Since she asked, I decided to study on it. After a while, I told her what she wanted to hear. I'd learned that technique from Granny. When folks ask you about themselves, give a positive answer. No point in getting in an argument with them on what they don't want to know.

"Yes, ma'am. I missed you," I said.

The real truth was, after Granny chastised me for telling my friends Esther planned to come back and get me, we continued on as if she were still there, and within a few months, it surprised me when somebody mentioned her name or asked if I'd heard from her, which I hadn't.

"Well, I missed you," she said.

"Thank you," I said.

What more did she want from me? She'd been back for almost a year. Things kept moving then the same as now. We were a family of doers. When one thing moved another took its place, and that's it, no pondering on why or how I felt about it. Didn't she know? Why did she bother me with something that had long passed?

"We have a few stops to make," she said. "First at Reverend Grinage's home. Do you know him?"

"No, ma'am. I never met or heard talk of him."

"He's one of the leaders of SNCC in Southeast Arkansas. He's done good work in Pine Bluff and Little Rock, and he is going to lend us his expertise on how to deal with this Freedom of Choice matter. I'm going to meet with him and a few other members of SNCC to discuss our plans. I want you to be a good girl and listen. You've heard a lot of this at the Hall, but pay attention anyway."

"Yes, ma'am," I said.

Muhdea had told me I didn't have to go to the white school. Not to concern myself with what Esther and other folks said. She'd take care of it. She made me promise not to get into any conversation with anybody about it. I didn't stop listening, and I pretended like I cared and paid attention. It kept me from getting riled up and saying or repeating things I shouldn't.

I turned the subject on her and asked why Reverend Jefferson was opposed to us going to the white school, which caused her to get riled up instead of me. I counted trees while she went on and on telling me about his ignorance. Nothing much else on Highway 65 except trees and every now and again a car with an out-of-state license plate. I counted them, too. Granny said I could find out more if I kept quiet than when I asked a bunch of questions.

We pulled off Highway 65 onto a side street and made a few more turns. I noticed the paved streets and two-story houses, yards with grass and roses. Within a few minutes, we stopped in front of a great big white house with a wraparound porch and a swing. I wished for a chance to sit in that swing, but since this meeting concerned me, I thought better of it. Maybe I'd get to swing before we left.

"Sarah, when we get in inside, listen closely. We have some important things to discuss, and I want you to hear them because we're going to need all the help we can get when things get started. You'll be able to relay the information to your peers. Although you can't tell everything, only what we agree upon the public should know."

"Yes, ma'am."

Esther knocked on the door, and a big dark-skinned man with curly hair greeted us. She introduced him as Reverend Grinage, and I met two other men and three ladies. I sat in a rope-bottom chair. One of the ladies asked me if I wanted a Coca-Cola.

I said, "No, thank you."

One of Granny's warnings, don't eat or drink at other folks' homes. We had enough food and drinks at home. If I got hungry or thirsty, come home. Granny believed in certain things, like burn the hair left in the comb 'cause the wrong person could get hold of it and run me crazy. Don't walk under a ladder; spit on the broom if somebody swept my feet; if a black cat crossed my trail, turn around three times and go in the other direction; don't give or let nobody take a picture of me; and above all don't eat or drink at nobody's house. There were more, and I knew them all by heart and obeyed them.

Soon after we took our seats, James and Gail, the other two SNCC workers from Maeby, arrived with Bro Hollin. They didn't mince words.

"Expect the worst when ninety-five colored students show up for class," Bro Hollin said.

"You fooling yourself if you think they don't have a plan for you. Figuring it out and then counteracting it is the problem," Reverend Grinage said. "Are the students ready?"

"If we weren't faced with them performing at least two classes above their own, I'd say yes. But at this rate, most of them are ready," Gail said. "Sarah is performing at three, four times her grade level."

"You say they've been quiet, Esther?" Reverend Grinage said.

"Not one word," Esther said. "Me and some others working with them on the transition." She shook her head. "They got something up their sleeve, but not one of them has given us as little as a hint of what it is."

"Do you have anybody on the inside?" Reverend Grinage said.

"The town is too small for that." Esther said.

"We know they're against separate but equal. We've lost that battle," Reverend Grinage said. "And they don't want you at their school any more than you want to attend, but others have come up with the most outrageous mess you can think of. With Central it was how bad they treated the students after they let them in." A sad look came across his face, and mine too.

"We've picked it apart. The way we see it, they may only allow the high school girls to attend and not the boys," Esther said. "They are extremely worried whether the boys and girls will mingle."

I scooted down in my seat till my feet touched the floor. Esther pushed me back up with her eyes. They discussed several scenarios and came up with a plan for each one. I'd quit listening by then. I'd all but fallen asleep in my chair 'cause they discussed the same thing over and over again, similar to the way Reverend Jefferson preached his sermons. Esther changed the subject to a more interesting one.

"Do you think the governor will send in the National Guard?" she said. "I believe they'll help them but not us."

I'd watched them men in uniform with dogs and water hoses on TV when colored folks protested in Birmingham. I'd watched them again in March, on horses with rifles when Reverend Martin Luther King Jr. and them demonstrated at Edmund Pettus Bridge in Selma. Why would grown folks put kids in harm's way? It scared me, and I patted Esther's leg to tell her, but she shushed me, and my fear turned into me being mad at her.

"With the attention we've gotten, it wouldn't surprise me," Gail said. "The media will be there. Maybe even the national media. We'll need to prepare. Make sure our voice is heard."

"The media hasn't paid as much attention to the school integration as they have to Gail as the only white woman living on the colored side of town. Many of the white men have insisted she leave town, and threatened nothing less than rape. We can use her situation to our advantage, but we can't forget the risk she is taking. She's started to receive more and more hate mail from out of the state," Esther said.

"Good point. I'm sure the national SNCC office is advising Carrie and Rutherford on how to handle all of it," Reverend Grinage said. "You will inform Daisy and them as well?" he said.

From the meeting, I gathered that all ninety-five of us would be attending the school regardless of what Muhdea told me. Coloreds should be prepared for whatever antics the whites might pull. Students had to be ready to be spit on, called out of their names and a whole bunch of other stuff that scared the bejesus out of me. SNCC organizers and the Maeby Citizens for Progress planned to march at the Department of Education the day after registration against the Freedom of Choice Act. I wondered if any of these other folks had children, and if they did why weren't they at this meeting with me. I supposed they were battling their own injustice somewhere in Pine Bluff.

While they were saying their goodbyes, I jumped onto the porch swing and got in a few pumps, planting my feet on the floor and pushing back so it would swing out several times before I pushed off again.

Gail held my hand as we walked down the steps. "Don't worry, Sarah. You're going to be fine."

I hunched my shoulders.

"Well, if nothing else," she said, "Mrs. Carrie and Rutherford are bringing our books back with them."

"For real," I said. "I didn't think we'd ever get them books."

Ever since the first day I met Gail, she'd promised to stock the shelves of the library at the Hall with books written by and about colored people. The SNCC national office had promised to send them last year during the "Freedom Summer." I hadn't seen any yet except the ones Gail's friends and family sent, and they only sent one copy, so we took turns reading them. Me and Malika pushed Gail to keep her word, and she swore she would even if she had to write to the president.

"I'll carry the boxes in myself," I said right before me and Esther got in the car.

I still didn't know when the bus was supposed to arrive, and the way Esther looked after that meeting I didn't want to ask her. She drove and explained the particulars of the meeting as if I weren't sitting beside her the whole time. If she didn't think I could comprehend, why was she so dead set on me sitting in on it?

A FEW MINUTES past noon we stopped at a colored café called the Fish Shack for lunch. We ate fried whole catfish, hush puppies and French fries while music played on a Seeburg. Several of Esther's friends met us there. One of them gave me a nickel and told me to go play a record on the jukebox. A picture of Reverend Martin Luther King Jr. and another one of Malcolm X giving a speech hung on the wall over the jukebox. The lady who'd given me the nickel walked up behind me. I gave her the nickel back 'cause I didn't know how to work the jukebox or know any song to play. She took it and showed me what to do.

"What's your favorite song?" she said.

"I don't know any."

"Oh, every girl has to have a favorite musician," she said.

I stared up at the picture.

"You like it?" she said.

"Yes, ma'am," I said. "I've seen them in the newspapers, but those pictures almost makes them look real."

She put the nickel in the slot and pushed the buttons.

"Your mama painted it," she said. "She was there when he spoke in DC." She pointed to Malcolm X. "Her and your uncle knew him personally. She didn't tell you?"

I shook my head. I knew she painted pictures, but I didn't know they were hanging on café walls in Pine Bluff.

"We could only afford to buy them two, but plenty of folks

around town have her paintings. Your uncle Robert is good, but your mama has the eye. You got it?"

"No, ma'am."

I didn't know if I had it or not. I hadn't ever tried to draw or paint. The closest I'd come to it was the glass me and Esther had picked up to make the mosaic. We had placed the glass around the hydrant, but she did most of the cutting and designing. Everybody who saved glass for her came to the unveiling. From time to time them and others stopped by just to see it. Esther had designed their names all throughout it. I wondered how Esther knew she could paint and draw.

Folks snapped their fingers and danced right during the middle of lunch, and when one of them said, "That's my song," she got up and danced whether she had a partner or not. I sat in the den of iniquity on the day before revival started. Help me, Lord. I didn't recognize one song, but Esther knew every one, and sang along with her friends. Where did she meet these folks? The funny part to me was the children knew the songs, too, and they could dance, not like the saints either.

"Go play with them. Have some fun," Esther said.

She couldn't have gotten me out of my seat with a pulley.

We got up to leave. She said her goodbyes. "We got to be in Little Rock by four o'clock," she finally said. In the car, she acted like her old self, talking and asking me stupid questions. "Have you thought about why colored people are in the shape we're in, Sarah?"

Oh, Lord. Here she goes again with the questions. "No ma'am," I said.

"Wouldn't you like to have as quality an education as the white people?"

She reached all the way back to slavery, tied it to the STFU, and then *Brown v. Board of Education*, the Civil Rights Movement. After all I'd endured, that Greyhound better be worth it.

"All I want is to keep going to school with my friends. Only me and Malika is going from our class. You keep talking about injustice. Snatching us away from all we know ain't just. Making us go against our will ain't just. Didn't you say that's what happened to the slaves?

And it show ain't just for them guards to spray us with water hoses and sic dogs on us," I said.

"We've talked about this. You know the sacrifice you're making is for the greater good."

"Then you go. This ain't my fight, it's yours."

We drove in silence for a long time. It ate at me when and how she knew she could paint. I knew I'd have to break the silence, and it seemed like a safe subject. I finally got up the nerve to ask her.

"When I was in eighth grade, I took an art class," she said. "Mrs. Carolyn Bolden was my teacher. The school only included an art class in their curriculum that year. Mrs. Bolden never came back after that year, but what I learned from her stayed with me. I always get the credit for painting the windows at the church, but she guided me through the whole process. If you look closely at the bottom of any of my paintings, you'll see both our initials."

"I didn't know that. Would you have known if she hadn't taught you?"

"I don't think so. I never had any reason to draw."

"Is that the reason you went to Chicago?"

"It got me there, but it wasn't the reason I left," she said and moved right past the reason to the contest. "I won a contest at an art school, which gave me a reason to leave town. When I got there, it wasn't anything like they promised. They asked for money when I thought they'd give me money and a place to stay. I hadn't wanted to take Granny's just-in-case money, but it came in handy. The place where I stayed was next door to a Baptist church that hired me to paint their windows. You see how things work out?"

I said I did, but I had no idea. She seemed to enjoy the subject and talked all the way to Little Rock. I didn't have to ask another question. Uncle Robert had taken the same class. If it was so good for them, seems like the school would've continued teaching it. Esther said they taught art at the white school. It still wasn't a good enough reason for me to want to go. She kept talking about her experience in Chicago.

"The church where I worked was the headquarters for the movement. When Reverend Martin Luther King Jr. gave his speech at the capitol, they asked artists to volunteer. My unique talent with glass was of particular interest to Reverend Martin Luther King Jr."

"Did you meet him?"

"Yes, we met, and had many conversations afterward. He inspired my interest in women's rights. It is one of major differences between me and Rutherford and Mrs. Carrie. We should work just as hard for equality for women as we do coloreds. They believe when coloreds receive equality, so will women, and that isn't true. My belief is the reason I demanded an equal number of girls attend the white school as there are boys."

We were back in the same place we'd started. I was glad we pulled into a parking lot before I got heated again. We walked up the rickety staircase with a sign on the door that read "COLORED ENTRANCE," and she paid the cashier for a ticket. Esther got us popcorn and Cokes in a cup, and we sat in the balcony and watched *The Sound of Music*. My first time at a movie theater, and I fell in love. The Von Trapp family was big like ours, the mama wasn't living with them, and the oldest was a girl. Later that night, I slept in a motel for the first time. So many firsts that day I'd never forget. Esther failed to mention what time Mrs. Carrie's bus arrived. She asked me too many times if I'd enjoyed the movie, the fish café and the talks. She tried to show me a good time, and I thought she had more fun showing me than I did having it, but I enjoyed myself just the same. Hopefully, we'd head home soon. I prayed, but not like I should've on the day before revival started.

CHAPTER SEVENTEEN

I'll Be There for You

THE NEXT MORNING, Sunday, when I should've been at church, our first stop was at Uncle Robert's shop. I was excited to see him and his shop. Esther parked the car on the curb. Storefront buildings lined the other side of the sidewalk. I opened the glass door and heard the sound of wind chimes. I'd never seen a store like his. Odds and ends covered the floor and benches. Clay, broken pottery, dust and God knows what lay scattered throughout the room. Me and Esther squished against each other, and she was close enough to Uncle Robert that her breath moistened his face when they talked. He backed away from the door, which put him practically in the second room. Esther walked to the other side of the front door. I stepped further into the room and closed the door behind me.

My eyes roamed across the room taking in the mess, including Uncle Robert's messy clothes. Didn't he know we were coming? He wore painter's pants that matched the untidiness of the rooms, which screamed for a bucket of soapy lye water and a mop and broom. It reeked of must, unwashed clothes, and I guess the stuff he used to make pottery. If Muhdea could see and smell his rank shop, she'd come up here, clean it, make him help her while fussing at him the whole time she sanitized it. I'd imagined his store as luxurious and expensive as his car. Nobody could've made me believe Uncle Robert kept a nasty place, not even God.

"As-salamu alaykum," he said.

"Wa alaykumu as-salam, and peace be unto you as well, my brother," Esther said.

I just said hi. He hugged Esther, and then me. He felt bony, too thin, no meat on his bones. I let go of him quicker than I'd ever done before. I eyeballed his bony fingers. Esther slid in front of me and wrapped her arms around his waist.

"It's so good to see you, bro. How long has it been?" she said, which was exactly what I was thinking.

"February," he said.

Esther ignored the rooms and his size and talked as usual. She handled him with respect and dignity, unlike Muhdea would've done. She'd have hauled every piece of food in her kitchen up here and forced him to eat it, pork and all. I followed Esther's lead and asked him about the bean pies Muhdea had refused to let him bring in her house.

"Where them bean pies you always talking about?" I said.

"The sisters bringing breakfast in a few, and I told them you'd disown me if they didn't bring the pies."

A few pans of half-eaten pies sat on one of the benches in the front and on a table in the back room. He'd left other moldy food in bowls and pots, which looked as if he ate a little something and forgot to come back and finish it. I wondered again if Esther'd told him we were coming today.

We moved to one side of the room when the sisters opened the door. They turned sideways to avoid hitting us with the door. They wore long dresses and hijabs. They cleared the worktable and placed eggs, steak, grits, pancakes and a bean pie, along with plates and utensils and drinks, on it. I cut the pie and bit into it, expecting the flavors to burst open in my mouth. I chewed and swallowed fast. Bean pie's texture was similar to potato pie, but the taste was a little different. It was good. I oohed and ahhed over it as if they'd given me a Christmas gift. Esther chowed down, but me and Uncle Robert picked at our food. I wasn't sure of his reason, but I had a hard time eating in the midst of dust and filth. The sisters moved in unison. They served us, but only checked in with Uncle Robert to ask if we were pleased. They left, promising to return later for the dishes.

"Wa alaykumu as-salam, my sisters and brother," they said, and Esther repeated it back to them.

He walked outside with them, and I took it as my chance to question Esther.

"How you eating this food with the way it smells in here?" I said. "And why is Uncle Robert so skinny, and what is wrong with his clothes?"

"Sarah, I'm ashamed of you," she said. "He's wearing work clothes. Can't you see this is where he creates? You know he's an artist, and if you didn't know, when an artist is at work nothing else matters, not food, or smell, or anything."

She rubbed me the wrong way. "How am I supposed to know that? You got a tone with me for something I didn't know. Either way, it still stinks in here."

"I'm trying my hardest to show you that everything isn't like it is at home. There'll be times when you will have to eat food in places worse than this, and whether you eat it out of respect for the preparer, or because you're starving, you will eat and be gracious. We don't know how long this movement will take, or what or where you or I may have to go to ensure we are granted equal rights."

I rolled my eyes at her for the way she spoke to me, which calmed her down a bit.

"Look, you crazy about Robert. Don't hurt his feelings. Let him see you eat your food. It won't kill you," she said.

"Yes, ma'am," I said. I didn't like how she said it, but she was right. I did love Uncle Robert, but I wasn't going nowhere for nobody's equal rights.

"Oh, Sarah, I see you found your appetite," he said when he sat next to me.

I placed a big piece of bean pie in my mouth and nodded. "Where is your appetite?" I said.

"I eat all throughout the day," he said. He changed the subject. "How did you enjoy the movie?"

I got diarrhea of the mouth, even sang the parts I remembered of one of the songs, "Do re mi fa so la ti do."

"Esther took me upstairs to the colored section. At least we didn't have to watch it from outside. And she didn't try to sit downstairs with the white people."

"You see how she's missing the whole point?" Esther said.

"Don't forget how young she is. She's your child, so she'll catch on in time," Uncle Robert said.

I hated when folks talked about me as if I weren't there. Uncle Robert didn't generally do it, but Muhdea said that when the two of them got together they were like two ears of corn growing in the same husk.

"I did enjoy the movie though, Uncle Robert. I never been to one before," I said. He rubbed the top of my head.

Esther filled Uncle Robert in on every detail from the meeting in Pine Bluff. She told him what each person had said, and what she thought they meant. She asked his opinion, and they debated back and forth as to the best approach. They differed on some points and agreed on others. By now, I could repeat it word for word as if in a movie.

"If Faubus orders in the National Guard. He's thinking 1957. Too much has happened since then, and it's not necessary."

"I agree," Uncle Robert said. "These pigs know what they have to do to keep the government's money. They don't want to integrate, but they know they have to do it."

"Can you get the Fruit of Islam?" she said.

He rubbed his forehead. "Oh, I don't know if that's a good idea, sister."

"The children need to feel safe, to see faces they trust," she said.

"I see your point, but the focus should be on the children and not us. Law enforcement gets antsy when we show up."

"You don't have to worry about showing up for me 'cause I ain't going to the white school," I said.

"Oh, Sarah," he said. "I keep forgetting that it's you on the front line." He placed his hand on my shoulder. "I'll be there for you either way, and I'll talk to the brothers, but I believe the FOI will see it the same as I do."

"Do this for me, Robert," Esther said.

"Don't try to pull that on me," he said. "It hasn't worked since we were kids." He chuckled. "By the way, how is your mama taking all this?"

"I wish someone would talk to her and Reverend Jefferson."

Esther stood up and walked to the end of the table. "She says the only reason she's in my face is because of Sarah. She tells me to parent Sarah, but she won't give up the reins. Her and Granny would rather be dead than give me a chance to live my life, and I'll die before I let Muhdea raise Sarah the same way she did me."

"Slow down, sis," he said. "She means well."

"But she needs to learn everything can't go her way. She didn't want either of us to leave home, but she pushed both of us out the door, me twice. I'm not going back this time, not ever. I can't live her life. I don't know how she does it."

They both needed to stop talking about Muhdea before I told them a thing or two. She put them out 'cause they didn't obey the rules, and they knew the rules backwards and forwards.

"I hear you," Esther said. "What kills me is how Granny sits back and pulls strings as if she never lived her life."

"Tell me about it," Uncle Robert said. "If she hadn't raised some hell, everything she did before she got married wouldn't be so hush-hush. Mrs. Carrie hinted at it a few times, but realized I was in the room and clammed up."

Esther leaned her head toward me. "She's just like them. Ate up all over with Granny, and Muhdea is so crazy about her. All three of them are in for a shock as soon as I get it together. I've told them over and over again, but neither one of them believes I'm going to get my own pad and take Sarah with me."

If it wasn't the day before revival, I'd tell her a thing or two about taking me with her. Granny would roll over in her grave before she let me live with Esther, and she'd said as much. They wouldn't shut up, and my feelings roared, and my earlier thoughts spilled out of my mouth.

"How would y'all feel if I talked about you behind your back? Uncle Robert, if you listened to Granny, you wouldn't look like you starving and your place wouldn't be this nasty."

"Sarah . . ." Esther said.

"Sarah, what? You think you better than Muhdea 'cause you came back home all proper, and think you know everything 'cause you hung around that Reverend Martin Luther King Jr., but you'd be a better person if you listened to Granny and Muhdea. Y'all don't know everything, and I don't appreciate y'all making fun of them."

I got up and tripped over one of the broken pots. Uncle Robert caught me. They made me fire mad, and I'd lost control of my manners. Esther grabbed my arm and snatched me in the back room. She pointed her finger in my face. She pulled up a chair, sat me down in it, and dared me to move with her eyes. Uncle Robert kneeled beside me.

"We don't mean it, Sarah. We love them as much as you do," he said.

"I'm sorry," I said. "I didn't mean to say them bad things to you."

Esther finally quit pacing back and forth, and ranting and raving. Uncle Robert promised her she could count on him and his presence at more of the meetings.

"You got to keep your strength up. I need you," Esther said as she held his hand with both of hers.

We meandered toward the door, but neither of us wanted to leave him alone. He gave me an armful of newspapers and a whatnot of a girl sitting in a chair reading a book.

"It's you, Sarah," he said.

He opened the trunk of the car, and I placed the newspapers inside. I held on to the whatnot. As soon as I shut the trunk, he pulled his hand from behind my ear and showed me a Bo dollar.

"Where did this come from?" I said as he handed it to me.

As always, I was as surprised as if it were the first time he'd performed the trick.

"How'd you do that?" I said. I loved our game. "I'm sorry," I said again and held him around his thin waist.

"Alright, brother," Esther said. Then she whispered, "You taking care of that? You got to eat, man."

"No worries," he said. "I got it under control."

Esther opened her mouth as if to say more, but decided against it. She shook her head and got in the car.

"Give my love to Mrs. Daisy and John. Know that I'm always here for you," he said as we drove off.

"Who is Daisy and John?" I said. It was better for me to ask Uncle

Robert than to ask Esther 'cause I wasn't up for a lecture, or a whole bunch of questions.

"You know," he said. "Daisy Bates and John Walker."

I didn't know, but I kept quiet cause I'd find out soon enough.

At two o'clock, we drove away from his shop. Revival started at seven o'clock. I added the time in my head. As long as I got there before Reverend Jefferson said the benediction, I could take my seat on the Mourner's Bench with the rest of the sinners. I crossed my fingers and toes that Mrs. Daisy and the lawyer John Walker were meeting us at the bus station and the bus would be on time. I fixed my mouth several times to ask Esther what time the bus arrived, but each time I decided against it. She might still be mad at me for the foul tone I'd used with Uncle Robert.

She turned the car into a neighborhood. There were only houses on each street we turned on. We pulled up to the curb and stopped in front of one of the houses. Before we got out of the car, a pretty lady walked out the door and stood on the steps, then came and met us at the car. She and Esther hugged as if they hadn't seen each other since Eisenhower was president.

"Is this little Sarah?" she said. "Oh, I'm so happy to finally meet you."

She knew a lot about me for me to only guess she must be Mrs. Daisy. She shook my hand.

"I'm Mrs. Daisy Bates," she said.

She and Esther had a similar style, except hers was for an older woman. They looked out of place in Arkansas, as if somebody had pulled them out and cleaned them up with store-bought liquid soap, and placed them back in the middle of us who washed with home-made lye soap. Sort of like the actors on Sister Tucker's TV, the ones who turned colors on her black-and-white set 'cause of the cellophane paper. Wavy black hair like the kind where you go to the beauty shop and the beautician places clips in lines over your whole head, and then sits you under the dryer till your hair turns as hard as a marble. The top of her head lined up with Esther's neck. And even though she painted her face, she didn't look Indian like Mrs. Carrie and Granny. Once a college professor came to our church to speak to us about water sanitation, and Reverend Jefferson said she was refined. I thought of that word "refined" as I stared at Mrs. Daisy.

"Come on in," she said. "Sarah, have you ever visited John's office?"

I shook my head. Esther gave me the eye, and I straightened up. "No, ma'am," I said.

She told me it was more than a law office. "It is a catchall for the movement. John is the attorney for the NAACP, but he handles practically every civil rights case in Arkansas." She pointed to the long tables with papers stacked from one end to the other and across.

"Volunteers will be in to collate the papers," she said. "We'll deliver them next week." She showed me the mimeograph machines. "My husband and I ran a weekly colored paper, the *Arkansas State Press*. Have you heard of it?"

"No ma'am," I said. "The only colored newspaper I've read is *Muhammad Speaks*. My uncle Robert gives them to me." I said the words in my head, first. I wanted to speak only the King's English with Mrs. Daisy.

I tried to read the papers strewn across the table while she talked to Esther.

"I'm only here for a few days," she said. "I'm happy we have a chance to meet. Why didn't Robert come with you?"

In another room were two lines of desks with typewriters on top. I accepted the short Coke Mrs. Daisy offered to me.

"Look around, Sarah. See if you find anything of interest," she said. She rolled a sheet of paper in the typewriter. "Feel free to type if you want." She must've noticed my apprehension. "You can't break it," she said.

The whole time she talked to me, as I admired her more and more, I wondered where I'd seen her. I knew we hadn't met. Why did her name sound familiar? Pictures lined the walls of every room, mostly framed articles from newspapers. Attorney John Walker stood beside white and colored folks. Then I saw pictures of her with Governor Faubus, Mayor Morse, and President Kennedy. I figured the folks in Little Rock had already won the equal rights Esther was still trying to get for us in Maeby. I ran my fingers across a picture of

Reverend Martin Luther King Jr., and then I saw pictures of Esther with him and other folks I'd seen on TV, and Mrs. Carrie was in the pictures, too.

While my mind reeled from thoughts of why Esther and Mrs. Carrie were in the news, I saw it, a picture of her, Mrs. Daisy Bates, the National Guard, a group of colored children, and some mad white folks. The caption read, "Equality Comes to Central High School." I remembered. Miss Brady had shown us that same picture and told us the story of nine children who integrated Central High School. Instead of typing, I read the newspaper stories next to the pictures. Stories where colored folks marched and demonstrated for their right to ride the bus, sit at the counter at Woolworth's, and one of a little girl named Ruby all alone walking to her first day of class at a white school. I read stories where coloreds all over Arkansas, Mississippi and Alabama went to jail, many of them hung from trees or found shot to death. Men dressed all in white sheets, masks and dunce hats as if they'd all decided to wear the same outfit to a Halloween party. Esther had talked about most of this stuff before she left home. I'd forgotten all about it.

I couldn't take my eyes off the photo of a boy named Emmett Till. To my surprise, Esther, Mrs. Carrie, Mrs. Bates and the lawyer Walker had demonstrated alongside these folks. I lost myself in the stories as I did sometimes when I read the Bible, especially the story of David and Job, but they were people from a long long time ago, and these were people I knew. My eyes bucked when they landed on a picture of Mrs. Carrie, Mr. Stith and Granny. I read the caption "Southern Tenants' Farmers Union," but before I read the story, I saw the photo of a bloodied, beaten white man named James Zwerg, and next to him a colored man who didn't seem as badly beaten, but bloody too, named John Lewis. I read, "Freedom Riders beaten by a white mob for riding the Greyhound bus."

I shook all over, shivered as if I were freezing cold. My legs all but folded. Rutherford and Mrs. Carrie were in danger, and we needed to be at the station to help them fight. The police in Maeby beat Rutherford and James at least twice a week, but not bad enough to put them in the hospital. Poor Mrs. Carrie was too old to take a beating. Why didn't the Greyhound dog bite those bad men? Lassie would've barked at them till they stopped. I'd waited all this time to see a scared dog that didn't help folks in distress. I steamed with anger at the greyhound. I hit the picture of it on the bus with my fist. I didn't care any longer if he could do magic, get off the bus and run beside it; I didn't ever want to see that stinking, scary-looking dog.

Esther touched my shoulder. I pointed to the picture. "Will they do this to Mrs. Carrie?" I said.

She showed me the date of the article. It had happened years ago. "The buses are integrated now. Coloreds aren't getting beat on them any longer," she said.

I heard her, and I saw the date, but I couldn't shake the feeling. I sat beside her, and listened as she finished recapping the meeting in Pine Bluff to Mrs. Daisy and the lawyer Walker. When the lawyer Walker spoke, I perked up 'cause he was asking about me.

"Esther, are you prepared? Is Sarah ready?" he said. "When we put the ball in motion, we won't turn back." Mrs. Daisy nodded in agreement. "I've prepared all of the briefs," he said. "As soon as we know how the school board reacts to the students, I'll fill in the blanks and file with the Eighth District Circuit Court."

"You will feel as if you're on your own after that," Mrs. Daisy said. "Only you and Rutherford will be aware of this plan. We can't afford to have a leak. Are you willing to create an even larger wedge between you, your mother and your church?"

"I'm the only person in a position to do it, but Mrs. Carrie will have to know," Esther said.

"She's on board," Mrs. Daisy said. "I spoke to her myself."

I balled a piece of Esther's dress in my fist. I wasn't ready. I didn't even know what I needed to be ready for. They shouldn't tell me 'cause I'd promised Muhdea to tell her every single thing that happened on this trip. I patted my left foot fast, and then faster. Esther placed her hand on my knee and pressed down on it for me to stop.

By the time we left the lawyer Walker's office, a little after five o'clock, I still didn't know what Esther planned for me to do. If we rushed, we could get to the bus station and make it home in time for revival.

"Sam's is right around the corner," Mrs. Daisy said. "Just follow me. John will join us as soon as he finishes."

Lord, please don't tell me that Esther was going to meet with Sam. Maybe his place was next door to the bus station, and coloreds waited there 'cause they couldn't go inside the terminal, but that didn't make sense to me. Somehow she knew I wanted to get back home for revival and had decided to stall so I wouldn't get my religion again.

"Do you like barbeque? Sam's has the best ribs," Mrs. Daisy said to me.

I couldn't answer Mrs. Bates. Barbeque? I wanted to go home now. "What time we picking up Mrs. Carrie?" I said as calm as possible.

Esther didn't answer me right then. She was busy tying up things with the lawyer Walker. Mrs. Daisy gave me a lot of old copies of her newspaper, the *Arkansas State Press*. There were stacks of them off in another room. She gave me a copy of a book she'd written, titled *The Long Shadow of Little Rock: A Memoir*.

"What's a mem-mo . . ." I couldn't pronounce it.

"A memoir," she said. "It's okay if you don't know it. It's a French word. It's a book I wrote chronicling my participation in the integration of Central High School."

"Is that what they're asking me to do at home?" I said.

"Yes. Yes, it is."

"What happened to them kids? How they doing now?"

She paused. "They're doing okay. I believe they're doing fine."

Esther came and got me, and we walked to the car. "I thought I told you. Their bus doesn't arrive until eight o'clock tomorrow morning. We're staying at Daisy's tonight."

I forgot my manners for the second time that day. I remembered Malika saying, "If you throw a tantrum, you can get anything you want."

"What's a tantrum?"

"You act like a crazy person, act wild, scream words that don't make sense, fall down on the floor, and pound it with your fists."

At the time she told me, I thought Granny wouldn't give me anything, but she'd take me straight to Benton and have them lock me up in the crazy house. Now I slid the rubber bands down to the ends of my ponytails and wrapped them around my wrist. Esther and Mrs. Daisy got out of the car. I didn't. Mrs. Daisy walked toward the building. Esther came around and opened the car door.

"Come on. Aren't you hungry?"

"I want to go home. I want to go home right now," I said, still calm.

"That's impossible. Now, come on," she said.

"No, take me home right now."

She caught hold of my wrist, pulled me out of the car and slammed the door. I pulled back.

"Don't start with me, little girl," she said as she eyeballed me.

"You don't have to take me. I'll walk," I said and turned to leave the parking lot.

She grabbed the neck of my dress, dragged me back, and then pushed me across the gravel, up the steps and into the barbeque joint.

"It's easier to get your way if you have an audience," Malika'd said.

"And you did this? Didn't you feel like a fool?"

"Yeah, I felt real crazy, but I still got my way."

As soon as we got to the middle of the room, I mussed my hair. It fell across my face, and I dropped to the floor and began screaming and hitting the floor with my fists.

"Home, home, home, home," I said over and over again and walled my eyes to the back of my head till only the whites showed.

I acted a fool at Sam's, knowing full well Granny had ingrained in me to never embarrass myself or anybody else in public. Afterward, I vowed, I wouldn't speak another word, not to Esther or any of them civil rights folks. Even though I liked Mrs. Daisy Bates, she wouldn't get so much as a grunt out of me. She tried, but I pointed to my throat as if it hurt too badly to talk, and she finally left me alone. Esther made gestures that I ignored, and she looked as if she wanted to strangle me right in front of all them folks at Sam's. I knew she was in a pickle, so I kept it up, knowing full well she couldn't do nothing to me, not in front of all these folks. I went to the bathroom without asking her. I splashed water on the front of my dress.

"Sarah," she said when I returned to the table, and then maybe she thought better of finishing what she'd started to say. I imagined flashes of my episode. Grown people thought they knew more than children, but I knew how to turn things around on them, too. I ordered food and didn't eat it, wasted money we didn't have. I smiled inside. No, I grinned like the Devil. I paid Esther back for causing me to miss revival. She tried to chastise me with her eyes, but whenever our eyes made contact, I rolled mine at her, and she flinched. I vowed to never cry again. I was going to stay mad from now on.

WE PICKED UP Rutherford and Mrs. Carrie at eight o'clock the next morning. Esther told me to stay in the car. The bus arrived fifteen minutes early. After seeing those pictures at the lawyer Walker's office, I didn't ever want to see a Greyhound bus station, and if that Greyhound dog ran up to me, I'd haul off and kick him back on the side of the bus.

Rutherford had walked up by the time Esther locked the door. He fussed at her while he threw the bags in the trunk of the car. Mrs. Carrie opened the back door and sat next to me. She sighed. I peeped around the corner just to see where the dogs were, and they were all on the side of the bus, even on the buses that were coming down the street.

"Can you ever be on time?" Rutherford said as he slammed the door.

I opened my mouth to greet Mrs. Carrie and then remembered my vow to not talk to any of them. I closed my eyes and pretended to be asleep. Rutherford ranted on and on. He disagreed with the national office wanting to handle the particulars of the coming school term. As far as I could tell, the national office had experience and believed their organizers from Atlanta should handle things leading up to and after the first day of school. Rutherford told us the entire trip home how he'd told them why he could lead the efforts.

"They act like it's Little Rock or Birmingham," he said. "What do they think is going to happen?"

Mrs. Carrie rocked her legs from side to side. I'd seen her do that before when she was mad.

"Did you tell them I'm leading our efforts here with the help of Bill and John?" Esther said.

He acted as if he didn't hear her and kept right on talking. Mrs. Carrie placed her hand on my knee.

"What can they do that I can't?" he said. "They're promoting their own interests. It ain't about us in Maeby. Damn, they can't even get us the books they promised."

"Maybe if you had told them that I was leading the efforts," Esther said. "Mrs. Carrie, do they know I'm here?"

"They know," she said and closed her eyes as she patted my knee.

I didn't want to see Gail's face when Rutherford showed up without any books, but right then I didn't care if we ever got any books. Missing revival overrode my interest in any books that might not exist in the first place. I'd never quite believed enough colored folks wrote enough books to fill up our whole library anyway.

"I tell you what," he said. "I'm going to make it my personal mission to integrate the public library. Why should we have to wait for books?" He turned around to face me. "You want to help me, Sarah?"

It sounded more like a statement than a question to me. 'Cause I didn't answer him, he started fussing at Esther about my behavior. "Can't she talk? Why doesn't she respect me?" Their voices elevated higher and higher. Mrs. Carrie told them to calm down. Esther challenged him with her college vocabulary. He couldn't keep up with her.

"You and your mama got plenty book sense," Muhdea'd said, "but your mama ain't got no common sense like you."

Esther and Rutherford talked at each other till we got home. Me and Mrs. Carrie rode all the way there with our eyes closed. I didn't know why she chose to keep her eyes shut, but I did 'cause I didn't want either one of them asking me any questions. I tried to calm my nerves. I'd told Granny before we left home that I'd let go of my anger from last year's revival. Nobody knew my plans to sit on the Mourner's Bench, so I sat in that backseat with my eyes shut, and suffered in silence. What was I going to do now?

CHAPTER EIGHTEEN

One Day You Will Be Ready

WHEN I GOT back from Little Rock, I was hotter than fish grease. Muhdea and Reverend Jefferson were always sneaking around whispering to each other. I watched them cup their hands together, and place them around each other's ear where nobody could hear a word. I figured they were trying to come up with a plan to outsmart Esther and baptize me without her permission. Folks watched them murmur back and forth, and they speculated and gossiped to the point where his wife came by the house without him to talk to Muhdea. They told her their secrets, and she started whispering, too, which everybody at First Baptist agreed was bad manners. I wondered myself, and made up a few stories in my head, which primarily ended with Esther headed back to Chicago toting her brown-striped suitcase.

Muhdea got more interested in the goings on at the Hall, down to the last itty-bitty detail. She'd started after I got back from Little Rock. She followed up with four or five questions after every answer I gave her. And when both her and Reverend Jefferson cornered me, it became much worse. My whole being mad and not talking didn't work with them. They were relentless.

"Who was there? What was his name again? What he have on? Did she say it exactly that way?"

"Yes, sir" or "Yes, ma'am," I said, at times unsure if I'd made up my own version of the events. When they seemed real interested in what I was telling them, I embellished a whole lot. I enjoyed my role, but as often as I turned it over and over in my brain, I didn't know what they planned to do with the information. Children answered questions. They didn't ask them. I'd memorized Easter speeches like I did my lines in the Christmas plays, and chapters for the test at school, but Muhdea and Reverend Jefferson asked me to recall verbatim conversations I'd only heard once, and half the time I had listened half-heartedly. If their plans included getting rid of Esther, I didn't mind stretching the truth a bit, especially since no matter how good I acted, she and God refused to let me get my religion. I decided it was easier to be bad, to tell stories, than it was to be mad and silent.

One day while in the pastor's study, they talked a little too much, enough for me to read between the lines. They'd been using me so they could gather information to save the colored students from going to the white school, and if they couldn't rescue all the children, they'd save me first, and then the other ones who attended First Baptist next.

"Sarah, you know how at times you may tell Malika she better not tell something on you or you will tell an even bigger secret about her?" Muhdea said.

"Well, we want you to listen for a secret like that on Esther down at the Hall," Reverend Jefferson said.

"Like what?" I said.

Reverend Jefferson seemed a little uneasy. He kept wringing his hands. "Just anything they say about the white school. Any papers that may be laying around with their names on it, bring them to us."

"Ain't that stealing?" I said.

"Not really, Sarah," Muhdea said. "We ain't keeping them. You can take them back."

"What you planning on doing with them?" I said. "What if I get caught?"

Muhdea walked over and took a seat on the couch and started fiddling with her stockings. "Oh, Sarah, you making it too hard. If you see or hear anything, just tell us."

I knew when she started messing with her hair or her stockings to let it alone, be obedient. Esther had told us we had no choice; the courts had ruled on it. We could either go to the white school or go to jail for breaking the law. I figured since they were making us go over there, the law should've made some of them come over to our school. Do an even exchange. Us trotting over there just seemed one-sided.

When Esther first stood at the podium during revival last summer and said the Freedom of Choice Act might require many of us go to the white school, nobody, not even me, believed her. Now we were getting close to the start of the school term, and everything was in place for us to go.

In the beginning, all anybody knew was the school board had won. The lawyer Walker had filed more briefs, but the wheels of justice turned slow, he said, and even slower for colored folks. I figured whoever took it to court in the first place should be the ones who honored the law. One of the older boys told us the way the law worked. Somebody committed a crime, the prosecutor took him to court, the jury found him guilty or innocent, and the judge sentenced him. In our case, I didn't know who'd committed the crime, or why it felt like we were the ones going to prison. The juniors and seniors complained more often than the rest of us, especially the boys who played sports.

"Why they go start it and expect us to finish it?" Red Bobber said.

Whenever one person brought up the white school, we spent the whole recess trying to figure out who to blame. In the end, and probably 'cause of the grown folks' influence, we blamed Esther and Mrs. Carrie for bringing them SNCC organizers to town, but mostly we blamed Esther. She'd led the efforts at the Hall and tried to get the rest of the town to follow her. She'd divided us: folks for and against equal rights argued in the middle of the road.

And Granny said that white girl living down at the Hall brought extra attention on our town from white men all over the nation. "Carrie could've put her up at her house," she said. "And your mama moving in with them only threw oil on the flame. I don't agree with Carrie on much, but she is right that the playing field needs to be level before you can go and ask for women's rights too. It ain't all the same. Them white women far more advanced than us."

But it was all stirred up in the same pot now, equal rights, children's rights, women's rights. I'd tell Muhdea whatever I knew on Esther, but if it was information I figured Mrs. Carrie or Uncle

Robert didn't want me to repeat, I couldn't share that with her. It was going to be hard 'cause all I knew was mixed up together. Instead of probing me for information, Reverend Jefferson should've asked Esther directly. Go to the source, was what Granny always told me.

THEN ONE MORNING, during the middle of the week, before I headed down to the Hall, Muhdea told me to go put on my school clothes and shoes and meet her on the corner. I was happy to be doing anything other than trying to integrate the library with Rutherford.

"Don't let nobody see you," Muhdea said.

How was I going to do that? She had spies all over town who reported back to her about me. I knew she meant the corner on the far side of the church. When I got there, she was sitting in the front seat of Reverend Jefferson's truck. She told me to slide across her and sit in the middle of them. I wished Malika could've seen this covert mission. It was more exciting than any one we'd planned to catch the train.

Reverend Jefferson drove across the tracks, passed by the stores uptown where the streets changed from graveled to paved, through the white side of town with white picket fences and yellow and pink rose bushes, and to the white school with huge windows and lines and lines of classrooms, nothing like ours. We got out of the truck and walked down the sidewalk to the superintendent's office. Walkways led to every building, separate areas for high school and elementary school, books in every nook and cranny, a grand place for learning. What were we doing over here? Had they changed their minds and planned for me to register early?

Muhdea's voice sang in my ear. "As long as I'm alive, you won't never go to no white school," she said. "Just listen when we get in here and speak briefly only if you spoken to."

We stood in front of a door with a sign marked "Superintendent Sam Ray Blackburn" in capital letters. I thought he only owned the store on the colored side of town. I didn't know he had two jobs. Mr. Michael James King opened the door. Mr. Sam Ray Blackburn sat behind the desk, slouched in a brown leather chair off to the side.

He didn't stand or offer us a seat. When I attempted to sit in one of the many chairs lined around the dark wood table, Muhdea grabbed my hand and pulled me forward. Mr. Michael James King sneered at me and then winked his left eye.

"Well, speak your piece," Mr. Sam Ray Blackburn said.

"You know Sister Mozelle," Reverend Jefferson said. They lifted their eyes up. "This is her grand-daughter, Sarah Jones. She the one they signed up to come to school here."

"We all know each other," Mr. Michael James King said. "Go 'head. We ain't got all day."

Muhdea held my hand, and squeezed it whenever I fidgeted. Like the chief, I wanted Reverend Jefferson to get on with it, too.

"Well, like we talked about. Little Sarah here goes to their meetings," Reverend Jefferson said.

My eyes bucked, and my mouth fell open. Mr. Sam Ray Blackburn looked up from his papers and swirled around once in his chair, which matched the ones around the table, the one the chief sat in and the other two just like it. Pictures of hunting dogs hung on each wall, four, no, five, all different. "We know that or we wouldn't be here," he said.

"She hears most everything they planning," Reverend Jefferson said.

"Reverend," Mr. Michael James King said in a nasty tone. "You ain't at First Baptist. Quit wasting our time. I checked out the things you told me and found them to be accurate."

"He's right, Reverend. You trying our patience," Mr. Sam Ray Blackburn said. "Is what she told you credible enough for us to make a deal? Is that what you come here to tell me?"

"Yes, sir," Muhdea said. All three men cut their eyes at her, and she shut up, too, and squeezed my hand tighter.

"Well, what you got?" Mr. Michael James King said.

Muhdea and Reverend Jefferson snitched. As Rutherford said every week, they'd dropped a dime on me. They'd used me without my knowledge, low, very low. Granny couldn't know nothing about it. She wouldn't stoop this low. I shook my head.

"The national organization coming from Atlanta. They expecting trouble. That lawyer ready to file papers. We don't know for what yet. Depends on what y'all do on the first day of school," Reverend Jefferson said. Sweat poured down his face. He dropped his hat twice. He spoke like I did when I was scared of getting a whipping.

"Generalities. You got anything solid?" Mr. Sam Ray Blackburn said. He stood up. He was a whale of a man, unlike the chief, who was scrawny. He parted his hair on the right side, and it lay flat to his head, slicked with grease. "How does Gail fit into all of this? Why haven't you forced her to leave your side of town?" Mr. Sam said.

"She's stubborn. You know the last plans we laid backfired on us," Reverend Jefferson said.

I looked from one person to the other and shook my head. I couldn't even tell Malika about this. All I could do was write it on my list.

"That was more the chief's fault than yours," Mr. Sam Ray Blackburn said. "Shit, he barely scared her. We got to do something about it. It's a sin for her to be living over on the colored side. We can't allow that. You hear me, Chief? You got one more time before we bring the county boys in on it."

"We'll figure it out," he said. "I got some things I been thinking up."

I couldn't figure if they were more worried about Gail or about us coming to their schools. Was I supposed to snitch for both of them? The superintendent turned back to Reverend Jefferson.

"They ramping up voter registration since the president passed that law. If more coloreds start voting than the ones we let vote, we will be in a heap of trouble," Mr. Sam Ray Blackburn said. "I seen niggers try to rise up before, and it wasn't pretty. You get my drift, Reverend. I need something to stop this school integration, and I need it now."

"They planning to bring the colored Muslims for security," Reverend Jefferson said. "Sister Mozelle's son is mixed up with them. They a scary group of men."

He'd dropped a dime on Uncle Robert, too. No wonder God wouldn't allow me to get baptized. I was Lucifer incarnate.

"You sure about that?" Mr. Michael James King said. "If that's

214

true, we better warn the National Guard." He rubbed his gun holster. "They kill they own leaders."

"Is that true, Sarah?" Mr. Sam Ray Blackburn said.

"Speak up, Sarah," Muhdea said.

I zipped my lips. I couldn't in good conscience tattle to these bad men. Didn't Muhdea and Reverend Jefferson know better than this? The Bible must say something about snitching being wrong. I rolled the chapters through my head, and nothing came to mind. Jesus is a man of principles. Whether the Bible said it or not, this stank to high Heaven. When I didn't answer, Muhdea squeezed my hand hard enough to crush my fingers.

"And you getting your information from her?" Mr. Sam Ray Blackburn said. "She's too scared to talk. You sure she's one of the smartest they got over there at the colored school?" He stared me up and down. Eventually, I flinched. "Just like I thought. These children won't do anything but slow down our students. We'll need to set up more special education classes than I originally thought if this is one of your brightest."

"She just a little nervous," Muhdea said. "This her first meeting."

"Can you talk, girl?" Mr. Sam Ray Blackburn said.

"What's a nigger?" I said.

"Get her out of here," he said. "She might not be bright, but she too sassy."

He could call me all the names he wanted to, but I wasn't going to tell any more on Uncle Robert or anybody else than I already told. I got my nerve back.

"I am as smart as your students, and the other kids are, too. We don't need special education. We don't want to come over here."

When I was in regular classes, a few students required an awful amount of help, but the teachers didn't place them in no special class. We helped them as best as we could, and they probably learned more from us than they would've in a class by themselves.

"Well, she can talk," he said. "What is your uncle planning? You better answer."

"He is not planning anything," I said, placing emphasis on every syllable.

The base of his neck had turned red, and it oozed up to his face.

"Is she your informant?" he said.

"There's others too," Reverend Jefferson said.

What others? I was the only person from our end of town who attended the meetings at the Hall. Preachers couldn't tell stories. He must know somebody else.

"There'd better be, or this plan won't work," the chief said. "I generally wouldn't go into this type of deal. I usually get my payment up front, but this situation presents a whole different set of problems. You putting us in a situation where I have to trust you, and overall I don't trust niggers or preachers."

Muhdea placed her hand over my mouth and pushed me behind her where they couldn't see me.

"You can trust us," Reverend Jefferson said. He fidgeted with his hat.

He'd called us an ugly name, and neither Muhdea nor Reverend Jefferson had called him out on it.

"You'd better keep your word," Mr. Michael James King said. "You don't want to see what will happen if I find out you lying to us."

"No need to worry about us," Reverend Jefferson said.

"You rolling your eyes at me, girl?" Mr. Sam Ray Blackburn said. "Is she rolling her eyes at me, Mozelle?"

"No, sir. Her eyes do that at times. She be alright."

"Y'all wasting my time. She's the one you worried about, am I right?"

Muhdea and Reverend Jefferson nodded.

"Is there anybody else?"

Reverend Jefferson read the names of the students who were selected to attend the white school that were members of First Baptist Church, and then he handed the list to the superintendent.

"I'll keep them out of this school," he said. "If one thing happens on your side of town that I don't hear about from you first . . ." He paused and pointed his finger at us. "Mozelle, I think you should join up with them, act as if you supporting that daughter of yours. I'd feel better about this if I knew you was on the inside."

"If it becomes necessary," Muhdea said.

"I don't want to mince words with you. You know what's at stake. I'll do my part, and you damn well better do yours," he said. "Y'all go on and get out of here. I got work to do."

I braced myself for a tongue-lashing from Muhdea or even a whipping when we got back to the church, but instead she talked to me.

"I won't try to explain to you what just happened," she said. "You way too young to understand it. Take my word for it, though. It's not as black and white as it seems. Me and Reverend Jefferson ain't doing nothing different from what he teach you at church."

"She right, Sarah," Reverend Jefferson said. "Folks crucified Jesus 'cause they didn't understand him. You need to be more like the disciples and help us. We can't have your grandma mingling down there at the Hall. You got any questions?"

I thought on it a minute. "What are niggers?" I said.

When I got home, I wrote all the questions from that day on my list of "Things I'll Know When I Get Grown," and I wrote down the things I remembered from our meeting. For the first time, I wrote out the word "nigger." I didn't like the way the letters laid on the page. I scratched it out, and wished I'd written it in pencil. Years later the NAACP held a formal funeral and burial for that word, but some people refused to let it stay buried. Instead, they tried to redefine its meaning, and use it in another context, but if any one of them had been there to see Muhdea's face, to see the fear in Reverend Jefferson's eyes, or to feel the air change as the word circled around the room, they would not try to resurrect anything that bad.

I thought of everybody I could seek advice from, but then I imagined the disappointment on their faces if I told them what me, Muhdea and Reverend Jefferson planned to do. I needed to warn Uncle Robert, but I didn't know how without telling on Muhdea and Reverend Jefferson. I came to the conclusion that I was a sinner now, just as bad as Esther, so it didn't matter what I did from now on. I was Hell bound.

As I sat on the steps, I saw Granny coming across the church ground from Sister Tucker's store with all the children trailing behind her. It hadn't occurred to me when we got home that she wasn't there. Muhdea hadn't said nothing about it either. She was probably as distraught as I was. I ran to meet her, to relieve her of one of the babies she carried. What was she thinking to take all of these children out by herself? She didn't tell me thank you, or ask where I'd been, or whom I was with. We walked slowly across the church ground back to the house. Muhdea met us in the living room.

"I lit the stove," she said. "Got some fire under them eyes. What did you have to run out and get from Sister Tucker?"

Granny didn't have any packages. She told the children to go out in the yard and play. I placed my baby in the baby pen. Granny sat on the edge of the chair. Bro Hollin walked in without knocking.

"Sister Tucker sent for me. The man on the other end of the phone said Robert passed just before noon."

Bro Hollin caught Muhdea before she fell to the floor. She screamed a few times, and nothing came out of her mouth, but on the last time it did, and she shook back and forth and wailed so loud the babies started up too. Granny wrapped her arms around herself and rocked in the chair.

"Go get Esther," I said to Bro Hollin.

He looked around at the scene of crying women and children as if to say I can't leave y'all like this. Sister Tucker pushed her way through the children and placed her arm around Muhdea.

"Go get Esther," I said, and he left.

MUHDEA WENT TO work making arrangements for Uncle Robert's funeral. They took up a collection at church to help with the expense. I walked around dumbfounded, somewhere between knowing it was true and not believing it, not Uncle Robert. I didn't cry. I'd kept that one vow since I boohooed at Sam's. I wondered over and over how Uncle Robert would want me to act. What was important to him? I carried the Qur'an he gave me around with me and read from it whenever I could.

After a few days, Muhdea went to Sister Tucker's store to call the telephone number Uncle Robert had left her for emergency. She wanted to set up a time to come pick up his body from the funeral home. When I got home, Granny and Esther were comforting her. The Muslim brothers had buried Uncle Robert without her consent. She was broken. I'd never seen her so weak, so sad. Granny ran the smelling salts under her nose, and Esther fanned her like the ushers did at church.

"We should've went up there," Muhdea said. "I left my baby alone. Let them bury him without me."

Muhdea couldn't believe they would go ahead without her consent. She'd thought they were going to wait for her instruction. She'd kept his burial insurance paid up. She'd told the man on the other end of the telephone that. Why hadn't they listened to her? Robert was bound for Hell.

"Esther, go get Bro Hollin. We going up there and dig him up," Muhdea said.

Esther took over like she did at the Hall. "Listen to me, mother," she said. "I'll go find Reverend Jefferson and get him to hold a service for Robert after church on Sunday. We won't have a casket, but we'll have flowers, and we can place one of his pictures on display."

"That ain't good enough. What about his soul?"

I got down on my knees and placed my head in Muhdea's lap. "He fine, Muhdea," I said. I placed the Qur'an in her hand. "He with his folks. They did right by him."

She got up out the chair and told Esther that she would go with her to find Reverend Jefferson. When they left, I asked Granny if Uncle Robert's soul was bound for Hell.

"I ain't got no authority on where a person going after he dies," she said.

I checked her eyes to see if she was telling me a tall tale, but she wasn't, and if Granny didn't know, I assumed Uncle Robert had as good a chance as any of us to go to Heaven. As a matter of fact, I planned to meet him up there one day and ask him personally what was the difference in an Islamic and a Christian funeral.

That Sunday after church, we held a whole funeral for Uncle Robert at the church as if his body were there. The mothers cooked, and they gave us the same type of repast in the church kitchen as they had all the other mourners before. The whole town showed up like they'd always done, and we celebrated and mourned Uncle Robert's life.

A few days later two of Uncle Robert's Muslim brothers drove up in a truck and brought us his belongings. Everything was boxed, taped and addressed as if he were going to take it to the post office and mail it to us. The biggest packages were for Muhdea and Granny. I was glad Muhdea wasn't home when they came. Granny was kind to them, offered them water, instant coffee. When Muhdea got home she sent for Esther so we could all open them together like it was Christmas morning.

Included in the packages for Muhdea were the pictures he'd tried over and over again to get her to put up on the wall, *The Last Supper*, *Moses*, and others. He'd included a note that read, "One day you will be ready." And for me, he'd sent a colored doll that looked just like Chatty Cathy, but she didn't talk. We helped Muhdea carry her boxes out to the junk house in the backyard.

CHAPTER NINETEEN

Give Me My Money

I THOUGHT RUTHERFORD would see I was still in mourning and give me and Malika a rest from the library, but that would be too much like right. He was obsessed with getting a library card. It took up most of his attention. Whenever Esther asked him to work on voter registration or the Freedom of Choice plan for the school, he claimed he was busy with his plans for the library.

"You act like this ain't important," he said.

She said "isn't" under her breath. "Go with him, Sarah. He'll get tired of it pretty soon."

"I don't like him, and Malika don't either. He scares us when he gets real mad."

I told Malika again that she didn't have to go with me. "If your sister wasn't about to have a new baby, you wouldn't be here for him to push around," I said.

"You'd go with me," she said.

The police were on to us and knew we were coming sometime during the day. They circled the library, and on some days, they saw us while we waited to cross the highway, and warned us not to go inside the library.

"You go in there, we hauling y'all to jail."

"Do what you got to do, and let us do what we got to," Rutherford said.

Me and Malika rolled our eyes at him. I pleaded with Rutherford to stop taking us with him.

"Why we got to go? We could be helping Mrs. Carrie and Esther," I said. He eyed me as if I'd flat out cursed him.

The second part of the plan, after we were enrolled in school, the one Esther believed in wholeheartedly, was for her to run for city council. She believed she needed to be in a position to change policy. "Remember when we had to move all our farm animals, Sarah? That's how policy works." The sitting councilmember was Mr. Cox, the owner of the café. She knew he'd play dirty and give Muhdea hell at work when he found out that she was running. She had to get some things in place before she was qualified to get her name on the ballot. She took a job at the sewing factory in Star City as a bottom hemmer, where she could make enough money to buy one of Mrs. Carrie's houses. She couldn't vote or run for office unless she held a steady job, regardless of what the federal law said. She might have to get married, 'cause a family looked better in the public eye.

Rutherford treated us like children. He didn't ask us to go to the library to help him integrate it. He told us to come with him, to obey him like the grown folks demanded I do at church and at home. That day me and Malika made up our minds to make it hard on Rutherford, create so much trouble he'd quit taking us with him. I was getting sick and tired of him dragging us up there with him. I hadn't even seen a book up close, much less checked one out.

We heard the train blowing as we ran across the track, looked back and waved at the engineer. "Come on. Stop slowing around," Rutherford said. He didn't know we secretly planned to tie our belongings up in a red handkerchief and jump through one of those open doors. We knew how fast to run to catch the train; we needed to run about thirty seconds faster to be able to leap on when it slowed down, right before it made the turn in the bend to come into town.

That Friday Malika wore her plaid culottes, and I wore my blue ones. Granny had made mine from a Simplicity pattern she got from the dry-goods store. She'd made me three pair, red, blue and yellow. Rutherford didn't catch our hands. Like always we held hands, and looked both ways before we crossed Highway 65. We bowed our heads and said a prayer.

"Come on," he said. The air stood still. There wasn't a car in sight. We let him go first. When he got to the middle of the road, he looked back and saw us still standing by the side of the highway.

"What's wrong with y'all? Come on," he said.

We checked both ways and walked slowly. When he saw us coming, he turned around and carried on. We got to the white line in the middle of the highway, turned and faced each other, and sat in the middle of the road. He was on the other side, and a car was coming when he noticed us sitting Indian style, straddling the single white line dividing Highway 65.

"What the hell y'all doing?" he said.

Cars came from the north, but nothing from the south. We stared into each other's eyes to keep from being scared as the swish of the cars and the gasoline fumes came too close to us. Sweat poured down my back. Malika's navy blue shirt was soaking wet. We squeezed each other's hands tightly.

"I ain't going back," I yelled over the sound of a black Ford truck. The driver laid on his horn as he passed us.

"He got pretty close," Malika said.

"They won't hit us," I said. "They can see my red and yellow shirt."

Our physical education teacher had told us that if we rode our bikes at night to wear bright colors like red and yellow so that vehicles could see us, and to wave a red or yellow handkerchief if we were in danger.

Rutherford ran back to us. He tried to pull me up, but we used the technique he'd taught us in case the police tried to move us. We wrapped our legs around each other, continued to hold hands, went limp, and sang "We Shall Not Be Moved."

"Sarah, get your ass up. I ain't your mama," he said. His breath stank, and his dashiki covered my face. He straddled me from behind, placed his hands under my armpits and pulled.

More cars passed by us from both sides of the highway. Horns blared. He thumped my head.

"Let go of her hands, Malika," he said.

I shook my head. "Go on and do what you got to do. We ain't going no more," I said.

Malika repeated, "We ain't going," just above a whisper.

Seemed like forever. A few people coming out of the café walked to the side of the highway.

"Leave them girls alone 'fore they get hurt," one man said. Soon afterward, two police cars blocked off the highway, sirens blaring. Without murmuring a word, one of them handcuffed Rutherford and pushed him into the backseat of their car. And before the chief said anything to us, we got up and ran toward home. When we got to the split in the road, where Malika went her way and I went mine, we high-fived each other.

"Don't forget. Tell your mama Rutherford went crazy. He made us sit in the middle of the road," I said.

"I know," she said and took off running home, and I did, too.

So far it had worked out the way we'd planned it. I stopped at the steps before going into the house to make sure I panted hard and looked as if I'd never been so scared. I slammed the screen door, and Muhdea and Granny came running to the front room. Muhdea was still wearing her field clothes, hat in hand. Granny wiped the sweat off my face with her apron.

"Rutherford gone crazy," I said.

By the time I'd finished saying that, Reverend Jefferson knocked on the door, and finished telling the story.

"He gone too far," he said. "I don't know what else to do to put a stop to his shenanigans."

Muhdea brought him a cup of coffee and a slice of German chocolate cake. "We got to figure it out," she said. Granny and Reverend Jefferson agreed, but neither of them knew what to do. He left without them coming to any conclusion.

That Saturday, when we all went uptown, Granny bought me a hoe at the dry goods store. I had a garden hoe and didn't know I needed another one.

"Why do I need that?" I said.

She didn't answer me when I asked in the store. I knew better than to bring up anything when we were uptown. Later that day she took me over to Bro Hollin's and told him to cut it down for me.

"She going to the field with y'all on Monday," she said.

Bro Hollin looked as if he'd seen a booger bear, and I did, too.

"You sure?" he said.

"As a heart attack," Granny said.

I'd asked Granny ever since I was old enough to chop in the garden to let me go to the field with my friends. They all went except Malika, who usually spent her summers in Chicago with her sisters and brothers, and I stayed home to help Granny with the kids. They chopped alongside their mamas till they could carry their own row. The closest I got to the field was listening to their stories as I counted change for them at Sister Tucker's store.

"If I can help it, you will be the first in the family that won't slave in the field," Granny said.

We went round and round, but there wasn't nothing I could say or do to get her to budge. My friends talked to her. Muhdea told her we needed the money.

"What she brings in would be a big help," she said.

"If you need the money, I'll go," Granny said.

"I know how you feel about her going," Muhdea said. "We can't always protect her though."

"She don't need to know nothing 'bout that, and as long as I'm living she won't."

Now me and Granny stood in the yard with Bro Hollin. He lived across the street from us, and grew the best garden in town. His vegetables were richer in color and tasted better than the rest of ours. I preferred to eat a cucumber or a radish from his garden any day of the week, and sometimes, if a tomato hung out into the road, I grabbed it, wiped it on my dress, and ate it before I went in the house. I didn't call that stealing.

"Sarah," he said. I looked up at him. "You be ready at three o'clock in the morning."

Granny assured him I would. I couldn't recall ever getting up that early, but my stomach and heart turned flips and leaped with joy. I'd waited for this day all my life. Bro Hollin measured the hoe against me.

"Don't worry," he told Granny. "We'll look after her. I'll put her on a row between Muhdea and Martha. They'll have her trained before lunch."

Right after lunch, I could chop beside my friends, and get in on all the fun and jokes I'd missed all these years.

"How bad is the field?" Granny said.

"We ain't had a bad field yet. We is starting a new field on Monday, but I don't even go out to check no more. She'll be alright."

I'd heard talk of them bad fields, weeds so thick it was hard to tell them from the cotton. When I saw my classmates and friends like Mark and Matthew Graves and Arthur Lee at Sister Tucker's store after they'd chopped in a bad field all day, they wouldn't be laughing and telling jokes. They just wanted to get their lunch for the next day and get home, snapped at me if I counted too slow or asked them to fill me in so I could get the joke. But on their good days, I didn't mind counting change for Sister Tucker on those evenings. When I left her store after they got their sandwich meat and bread, I felt as if I'd gone to the field with them till one of the older boys rubbed the top of my head and told me to stop dreaming.

"Granny ain't ever going to let you chop in no man's field. You might as well be satisfied with chopping in the garden," one boy said.

But here I was with one day and a few hours left before I climbed on the back of Bro Hollin's truck with them. I should surprise them on Monday morning, not tell nobody, let them see it firsthand.

"Pearlie," Bro Hollin said, "everybody will ask me."

I felt sorry for him. He knew better than to ask Granny about her business. He better brace himself for a good cussing out. I rested my hand on my hip and leaned in to listen to Granny set him out. It was the kind of story that even the older kids would pay attention to, and Bro Hollin knew he was crossing the line, so he dressed it up by calling her Pearlie instead of Granny.

"That boy," she said. "The civil rights worker Esther all caught up over, Rutherford." She squeezed his name through her throat as if she'd rather cuss in church than say it out loud. "I don't know what else to do. I'm tired of fighting with Esther. And if I don't do something, I'm afraid of what might happen. He ain't paying Sarah no attention, letting her cross the highway by herself, getting himself arrested and then leaving her alone with them lawmen. I couldn't forgive myself if I sat back and let something happen to her." She seemed to go someplace in her head, and then she told Bro Hollin why she'd come to that conclusion. "I studied on it, you know, and this is the only thing I could come up with. If she's out in the field with you, she won't be accessible to him. But far as everybody else will know, we need the money. You hear that, Sarah?"

"You don't think Esther will come get her?" he said. Bro Hollin was pushing it, but at least my plan had worked. I hoped to God Granny never found out I'd told her a story about Rutherford going crazy. I didn't do it to get her to let me go to the field. We only wanted to stop going to the library every day. After I saw all of those rows of books, I wanted to read some of them more than Rutherford. Maybe they carried the one about Mr. Stith, but going to jail every day, and seeing Rutherford's face when he got out, wasn't any fun, and somebody needed to put a stop to it.

"Ahh, Esther don't care. She knows Sarah is in harm's way. This way Esther can keep the peace with him, and I'll be the devil who did it."

Granny explaining her actions to Bro Hollin or anybody wasn't heard of in our town. Folks around here took her at her word and didn't ask any questions. Maybe she wanted it to get back to Rutherford and Esther. That way they'd know not to come around asking her nothing about it. When Granny finished, Bro Hollin changed the subject.

"You think you can carry a row?" he said.

"Yes, sir. I been ready for a long time."

ON MONDAY MORNING, Granny walked me over to Bro Hollin's. Him and Muhdea were already stacking water kegs and hoes on the bed of the truck. We spoke to him, and then me and Granny climbed into the back of the truck. She told me to sit in the middle at the back of the truck. Bro Hollin was watching her.

"That's Sister Martha's seat," he said and smiled as if it were an inside joke between him and Granny. "You trying to get me kilt first thing this morning?"

It was cold in the back of that truck and pitch dark outside. Bro Hollin carried an oil lamp from place to place as he worked. Muhdea climbed in the back of his green and white Chevrolet truck and sat on the floor. I sat between her legs. I'd layered my clothes, a raincoat placed on backward and buttoned down the back, two flannel shirts, a tee-shirt, two pair of jeans, a pair of rain slicks, two pair of tube socks, tennis shoes, rain boots, bandana, gloves and a straw hat. We didn't carry our own water. I held my belongings in my lap, a paper sack with a frozen bottle of Coca Cola, Lay's potato chips, five Pixy Stix, a can of Vienna sausages, potted meat, pork and beans, a sleeve of saltine crackers, pressed-ham sandwich, no sandwich spread, plain, two chocolate chip cookies, five pieces of caramel candy, a spoon and a can opener.

"Eat your own food. Don't give any away either," Granny'd said.

We picked up folks along the way to the field. Dinah Anderson and her mama hooked their hoes across the tailgate and climbed on board.

"That you, Sarah?" Mrs. Anderson said.

"Show is," Dinah said. "What is this world coming to? Is Granny feeling alright?"

I heard a version of that from every person who climbed onboard, Mrs. Martha, Mrs. Rebecca. John, Mark and James cracked jokes all the way to the field. I felt happy and scared at the same time. I'd seen fields all my life, but I'd never chopped a row. They were much, much longer than a garden row, and there was no hiding the plants I cut down in the slop can. It was still dark when we reached the field. Bro Hollin got out the truck and lit the oil lamp.

"Y'all hang here for a minute and let me check this field since it's our first time out here," he said.

He walked parallel to the rows, and then he walked a few paces down three or four rows. While he checked out the rows, the waning moon made its way from high in the sky and shed some light across the field.

Bro Hollin made his way back to the truck, shaking his head.

"This ain't no cotton. It's soybeans, and it's bad," he said. "Muhdea, put Sarah between you and Martha. If she can't make it, I'll take her back to town with me."

Even though the moon hung low, we could barely see our way down the row. When Muhdea saw her row, she told everybody to come in. "Sarah going to help me carry my row till the sun comes up," she said.

Everybody moved over one, and I stood at the edge of Muhdea's row, not knowing what to do next. She instructed Mrs. Martha to go on up ahead of us, and then placed me on her row.

"You chop that side of the row, and I'll chop this one. Mimic me. Don't go off on your own, or you'll cut down all of this man's plants." She checked my clothes. The plants were soaking wet. I realized why we wore our raincoats backwards.

After daylight, we settled down in the field, and Bro Hollin waited for us to get back to the truck before he took the kegs back to town to pick up ice and water. It gave him a chance to see if anybody got sick, forgot food or any number of things. That day he also waited to see if I waved him off or got back on the truck.

"She ready to carry her own row?" he said.

"Sarah?" Muhdea said.

"I'll be alright."

Working next to Muhdea was easy. She showed me what to do and then I did it. She chopped more on my side than I did. The whole time I only cut down a few weeds, then she gave me my own row. Pigweeds mingled in with the soybean plants on the row and stood almost eye-to-eye with me. They crowded the plants, which were drenched with dew. Leaves with water on them slapped me in the face as I tried to untangle them. I cut down more soybean plants than weeds. I knew this 'cause Mrs. Martha told me twice.

"We both going to help carry your row," she said. I spent a half hour on one section. When I looked up, she and Muhdea were way down in the field. They'd left me by myself.

"Come on," Mrs. Martha said. "We got you down here."

I placed the hoe between my legs and dragged it as I pulled most of the weeds with my hands. They chopped my row to where I'd skipped a patch to catch up to them. Shame smothered me. I knew how to hoe a row. I chopped all the rows in the garden within a few hours, but they were nothing like this field. Bro Hollin even said it looked as if nobody had attended to it all summer. Muhdea showed me how to hold my hoe again, said this wasn't like no garden, get that out of my head. She stood behind me on my row while Mrs. Martha carried hers, and chopped with me, as if I were a baby.

"You got to be able to tell the difference between the stalks. See, look here." She pulled a kelly weed away from the soybeans. "Grab the stem and then cut it with the corner of your hoe. You can't use the whole blade on it, or you sure to cut the bean." I tried and cut halfway through the soybean stalk. "Don't get frustrated," she said. "This here ain't easy, and this your first time."

I cut the weed. Don't get too excited, I thought, or I might make another mistake.

"Be patient now, or you going to cut down too many of this white man's beans."

I laid the weed between the rows and tried to replant the soybean. A row seemed as long as walking from the country to the other end of Maeby, but it took me much longer to walk it. When I looked out across the field, I saw green as far as I could see, like everybody in town had decided to grow collard greens and stacked their gardens next to each other. I stood up straight. The field stretched out before me in a deep gorgeous green patch. But when I bent my head, I saw the ugliness of the pigweeds and kelly weeds choking the beans. My job was to make them let go so the beans could breathe.

"Quit daydreaming, Sarah. Hide that bean under the weeds. We don't want Bro Hollin and the owner to walk your row and find his beans scattered about. He ain't just seeing beans laying there. He seeing his money," Muhdea said. She cut down a bean plant, and I felt a little better.

BY THE TIME Bro Hollin got back with the water, the sun had risen high in the sky. My clothes were dry. I took off the raincoat and tied it around my waist. Other folks knew how to time it to be at the end of the row near the road, instead of way down in the field, when Bro Hollin came with fresh water. Mrs. Martha chopped on ahead of me and Muhdea. My friends passed by me all morning and faced me going the opposite way, heads down, occasionally throwing me a few words of encouragement.

"It'll get better. This a bad field to start on. You'll get the hang of it."

Fifteen field hands in all, eight grown folks and the rest of us were kids, all from the same end of town, all members of First Baptist except me. John and Mark Graves, the Sunday-school superintendent's sons, chopped the fastest. They competed with each other the same as they did in basketball, counting every pigweed and kelly weed and soybean cut, and every time one touched the end of the row first. They drank water out of the long-handled tin cup. Mrs. Anderson and her daughter Dinah walked up behind them, and peeled off their raincoats and hats. Mr. Graves and Mrs. Martha weren't far behind.

"You coming in slow today," John yelled.

"You worry 'bout yours, and let me worry 'bout mine," Mrs. Martha said, and waved her hat at him. Everybody laughed.

After John and Mark finished drinking, they picked up their straw hats and started chopping on our row. When the others saw them, they did the same and helped us bring our row in in no time at all.

"If Mrs. Martha wasn't carrying you, she'd be racing with us," John said. "Thanks for slowing her down before she hurt herself."

I wanted to say something smart back to him, but figured it'd be better to wait till I knew how to carry my own row.

"You boys the ones glad I'm helping her," she teased, "'cause I can beat the both of you with one hand tied behind my back."

When we reached the truck, Bro Hollin handed me and Muhdea our lunch bags.

"Shed some of them clothes, eat fast, and get on back in the field," he said. "How she doing?"

"She catching on," Mrs. Martha said.

"Did I ask you?" Bro Hollin said, and they laughed.

"She'll be alright," Muhdea said. She sat on the ground and rested her back against the truck.

"How you feeling, Sarah?" he said. "Think you'll make it?"

I scooted between John and Dinah. "I'm fine, sir. I'll make it."

I folded my raincoat, long-sleeved shirts, two tee-shirts and a pair of pants, and laid them on the back of the truck. Then I put on my straw hat and gloves, picked up my hoe, stuck my tongue out at the boys, and started on my row.

"Can we have the rest of your food?" Dinah said.

"Yeah, but leave me some snacks for break," I said.

I got the knack of it, not nearly as good as the others, but I moved down the row, and I was less afraid of cutting down the soybeans. Shedding some of the clothes helped me feel lighter as well.

"Look at her go," Mrs. Martha said as she came up behind me.

The others encouraged me as they passed. A while later, Bro Hollin came down the field and helped me. Within a couple of hours, I held my head up and asked John how he was doing as he and Mark raced to the opposite end of the field.

My throat parched and my body drenched with sweat, I picked up speed as the day went by. Bro Hollin went back to the truck and brought a bucket of cold water. We all drank from the same pail and ladle. He checked each one of our rows. He picked up the soybean plants I'd cut down and placed them way over in the rows that we wouldn't get to till days later.

"Throw some of them bean plants over yonder like I did," he said. "Mr. Sam Ray Blackburn won't let us leave till he walk y'all's rows."

John and Mark helped me hide the soybeans. Bro Hollin walked a few more rows, warned us of the time, and walked to the truck. Later, he tooted the horn a couple times.

"The man coming," Muhdea said.

We saw the dust from his truck way before Mr. Sam Ray Blackburn arrived. I felt proud of my work. I'd tried to keep up on my own, but the field was too bad. Whenever I felt as if I were getting too far behind, I'd come upon a long patch that Mrs. Martha and Muhdea had cleared for me. I'd come a long way since that morning. I wondered how Granny and the kids were doing at home. Had anybody stopped by to help her cook and do the housework?

"Alright now, cut out all the foolishness. He'll be here directly, and he can smell foolery," Mrs. Martha said.

How did they work like this every day and then laugh and joke about it? Muhdea's muscles bulged through her long-sleeved shirt.

Mrs. Martha took off her straw hat, fanned with it, and stared up toward the Lord. John and Mark teased her as they passed by us on their home stretch. My legs felt like grape jelly, and my arms ached, but inside I felt like a new dollar bill.

"You coming back tomorrow, Sarah?" Dinah said.

Tomorrow? I'd made it through the day. There hadn't been any time to think about tomorrow.

"Yeah, sure."

I made the turn at the end of the row and headed toward the truck.

"Don't get too confident," Muhdea said. "The man up there."

Bro Hollin and Mr. Sam Ray Blackburn were walking the rows.

"We can't help you now the man in the field. Stay slow and steady. We ain't leaving you back here by yourself," Mrs. Martha whispered.

Everybody in the field chopped at a slower pace; a few folks stayed beside me, a few more up front, and some behind me. John and Mark quit racing. I wanted to say thank you, but I didn't know how, and I didn't want to lose my concentration, chop down any more plants.

We made it to the truck while Bro Hollin and Mr. Sam Ray Blackburn walked the rows. Each person shook my hand one at a time and said, "You made it," or "Not bad for your first day," or "You a field hand now."

I nodded my head and thanked them for their help. "I couldn't have done it without y'all."

We lined up and waited for our pay. Bro Hollin patted me on the back as he walked to Mr. Sam Ray Blackburn's truck. He took out two stacks of money, ones and fives. Mr. Sam Ray Blackburn peeled off a five first and handed it to Mrs. Martha and then gave her a one.

"Good job, Martha," he said.

He paid Dinah, John and Mark. Muhdea stood behind me. He reached over me and paid Muhdea. He held the five in his hand while she waited. Bro Hollin fidgeted with his shirt.

"That Esther's child?" Mr. Sam Ray Blackburn said.

Muhdea nodded and withdrew her hand.

"How she do?" he said.

I knew Muhdea well enough to know she was tired and wanted to go home, clean up, and get to the café on time. He gave her the one-dollar bill first, toyed with her as if he weren't going to give her the rest of it. The other hands sat on the truck ready to go.

"You sure?" he said before he finally gave her the five.

She released her breath. "If you don't mind, sir, I'll take Sarah's," Muhdea said.

I'd worked for it. I wanted him to pay me. The sun burned the back of my neck. I rubbed it and felt the sun on my hand. A grasshopper jumped into the back of the truck, causing the others to scatter before it hopped out. They moved around, but nobody made any noise. Muhdea scratched the top of her hat. The air changed. I couldn't see the field hands, but I knew they didn't want me to start nothing, and I could feel they were scared. He could take all their money back. Didn't matter they'd worked the whole day.

"She worked for it, didn't she?" he said. A smirk came across his face.

Muhdea nodded.

"Go on and get on the truck."

Muhdea touched my hand as if to say, *I'm right here.*

He didn't bend down to talk to me eye to eye. I held my head back, and looked up to him.

"How you think you did today?"

"Fine, sir," I said. I placed my hand in my pants pocket. A yellow and black butterfly flew overhead. There was no wind blowing, or birds chirping, or mosquitoes biting. It was too hot, almost the heat of the day. I stirred my toes in the brownish red dirt.

"You sure? I saw some plants on the ground. You saying one of these folks chopped down my plants?" he said. "Go on and get on the truck, Mozelle. You too, Hollin."

"I can't leave my hand," Bro Hollin said.

He glared at Bro Hollin, and he went to the truck. I never thought Muhdea or Bro Hollin would ever leave me to fend for myself. I turned around, and they looked as if Mr. Sam Ray Blackburn said boo, they would all take off running. I recognized that I was in the field with field hands, and church folks, and not at the Hall with civil rights activists, and I needed to straighten up..

"You saying them folks cut my soybeans down?" Mr. Sam Ray Blackburn said.

"No, sir." I lowered my eyes toward the ground. I shook inside, but hoped it didn't show on the outside. I smelled the fresh-cut grass. What if he refused to pay me? Would Bro Hollin make him give me my wages? "I put in a day's work, sir," I said and held my hand out to get paid.

"You think I should pay you the same amount I paid them? Ain't this your first time in the field?"

I dropped my hand down by my side, and didn't answer 'cause I didn't know how to answer him. Everybody there knew we were in trouble. Mr. Sam Ray Blackburn might make an example out of me, or he might take their money back, or no telling what he'd do.

"Ain't I seen you walk past my store with that pretty white girl?"

I humbled myself and remained quiet. Mr. Sam Ray Blackburn had let it be known many times he didn't like it that Gail lived on our side of town. Gail couldn't leave the house alone for fear of what he might do to her. He threatened to load her in his car and take her home, stared her up and down, beat whatever silly guy she walked down the road with. Gail threatened him right back. He asked her to the café, and she wouldn't go. Esther had warned her to be careful. She wasn't allowed to walk anywhere alone.

"I know what your mama doing. Ain't she too proud to send you out here?" He held the five in his left hand and the rest of the money in his right.

I tried to muster the same courage Gail displayed, or Rutherford, even though they beat him for sassing them.

"We running late," Bro Hollin said. "Muhdea got to get to the café."

"I don't think you ever chopped before. You and Hollin trying to pull a fast one on me," Mr. Sam Ray Blackburn said.

"No, sir. I wouldn't do that to you. No, sir."

My first mind said snatch the five out of his hand and run. Let him keep the one. If I knew he was going to act like this, I would've chopped down more of his soybeans than I did, embarrassing me before everybody on my first day.

"I don't like my hands lying to me," he said as he placed the five on top of the others and put them in his pocket. Then he peeled off three ones and handed them to me.

"Here," he said. "Next time tell the truth."

Three dollars, half a day's pay. Was that it? I made eye contact with Muhdea. My eyes pleaded for her to do something, anything to get me the rest of my money. She sat silently on the back of the truck. Her eyes pleaded for me to take the money he'd offered me and shut up. The rest of them didn't make eye contact with me. They looked away as if to say, *It's your problem.* We got to come back here tomorrow, and somehow I understood it, but I wasn't backing down. Right was right.

"I worked all day," I said. "May I have the rest of my money?"

"You mean give you the rest of my money," he said.

He laughed, and he gave the folks in the truck a look that they should be laughing too. Everybody except Muhdea laughed with him. Rutherford wouldn't have thought it was funny.

"Give me the amount I worked for," I said. I bristled up like I'd seen Rutherford do many times, as if a cat move might scare him.

Bro Hollin walked up beside me. "Go on and get in the truck, Sarah. What he gave you is just fine." He nodded his head and told Mr. Sam Ray Blackburn, "It's fine, sir. That's all she worth."

He'd tied my worth into it when he said earlier that I'd done a fine job, a six-dollar job like everybody else. I pleaded to Muhdea with my eyes. She motioned with her head for me to get on the truck.

"It ain't fine with me." I placed my hand on my hip and leaned on it. I held the other hand out toward him, palm up. "You pay me what I'm worth or else."

He turned as red as the evening sunset.

"Give me my money."

He walked away from me toward his truck. I walked fast enough to get in front of him. I held out my hand and motioned for him to give me my money. When he laughed at me, and placed his hand atop of my head, I pulled back my leg to give him a swift kick in the shins, but Bro Hollin picked me up and carried me to his truck right before my foot landed. I kicked both my legs and pulled on his arms.

"Let me go, let me go, Bro Hollin," I said.

When I saw the scared look in his eyes, mine welled up with water. I'd never seen that side of Bro Hollin. He looked after us. He wasn't scared of nobody, not Reverend Jefferson, or the schoolteachers, or the men on the low end of town. But here he was shuffling, letting the white man take my money, and nobody, not one single person on the back of the truck, said a word, not even Muhdea. Fear loomed through the hot summer air, and rolled down their bodies like sweat.

"Don't you bring her back to my field again, Hollin," he said. "If I ever see you with her or Esther Mae, don't you or your hands come back either."

Bro Hollin handed me over to Muhdea. She pointed for me to sit down, and when I didn't she pushed me down in Mrs. Martha's lap. She was mad, too mad to speak. I got right back up and leaned over the side of the truck.

"Give . . ."

Bro Hollin placed his hand over my mouth and put me in the cab of the truck on Mrs. Anderson's lap.

I leaned my head out of the window. "I'm telling Granny. You wait and see. She ain't scared of you."

Bro Hollin sped down the dusty road. Soon afterward he said I'd gotten all of them in a heap of trouble. It was going to be hard for them in the field for the rest of the summer.

"You work at the Hall for equal rights. You think what he did to me was equal?" I said.

"No, Sarah," he said. "I have to eat, and so do all these folks. You got to know when and what battle to fight. Today, you didn't think about them when they carried you all day, so whose money was it?"

I felt bad and tried to give him my three dollars to share with the others.

"You earned it," he said.

"Naw, she didn't," Mrs. Anderson said.

All three of them burst out laughing. He leaned his head out of the window and yelled to the others, "Give me my money."

They all split their gut laughing at me.

"What happen to all your nonviolent training?" Mrs. Martha said. They couldn't quit laughing. After a point, I didn't think it was funny. Mr. Sam Ray Blackburn had cheated me out of a half day's pay, and I still wanted my money.

"I'll get my money from him tomorrow," I said.

"You have to chalk that up as a loss," Bro Hollin said. Silence came over all of us in the cab of the truck. After a while he reiterated. "Yeah, Sarah, look at it as a lesson learned."

What lesson? I'd messed up Granny's plan to keep me away from Rutherford. A half day's pay was all I deserved for a day's work. What lesson? I'd embarrassed Muhdea and disappointed Granny and myself. I remained quiet the whole way home as the others joked at my expense. Bro Hollin stopped to let each person off at their house. Mrs. Martha got out and pulled her hoe off the back of the truck. She leaned her head through the window.

"You did good today," she said. "If you don't start bowing down to the white man, you won't ever have to do it." She patted me on the shoulder.

John and Mark pulled their hoes off the back of the truck. Before Bro Hollin drove off, Mark held his money in his hand like Mr. Sam Ray Blackburn, and John said as if he were me, "Give me my money." They fell to the ground laughing. "You bold, Sarah," John said, and everybody in the truck thought it was funny, even Muhdea. I realized they had turned the bad things into something funny, and that's what they were laughing at when they came to Sister Tucker's store.

CHAPTER TWENTY

A Whiff of Freedom

I BARELY HELD my head up when I walked down the road, too ashamed to defend myself when folks brought up what had happened to me in the field. Most folks sympathized with me, but we wouldn't be colored if there weren't any signifying. Then Granny got sick of folks meddling with me. She told Mark not to ever say another word about it. Later that evening when Granny got home from the field, Granny caught hold of my hand, and we walked down Back Street to Mr. Sam Ray Blackburn's store. I was taken aback 'cause we never shopped at his store. Granny always said if Sister Tucker didn't have it, we'd wait till Saturday. Granny told me to sit in one of the chairs out front, and she went inside. I peeped through the window and saw her and Mr. Sam Ray Blackburn giving each other word for word. She caught me and motioned with her hand for me to turn my head. A few minutes later, she came out of the store and handed me three crisp one-dollar bills. She didn't tell me nothing, and I didn't ask her.

The next week when I went to the Hall, Rutherford took me right back to the library. Granny said she would have to come up with another idea, but she didn't know what. Then a couple of days later Rutherford and Gail told us SNCC had sent enough money to pay six students to go out in the country and register folks to vote. It paid ten dollars per day. Four more than they paid the field hands. Me and Malika made a good case for ourselves, even though everybody at the Hall agreed we were too young.

"You said we the same as everybody else, so why can't we make money like them too? We ain't too young to teach and picket, and do most everything else," I said.

Esther and Mrs. Carrie finally came around. Two girls would go together to different parts of the county. When they told us we would have to be separated, me and Malika threw a fit. We convinced them to send us on the roads where we knew folks, wouldn't nothing happen to us. Malika rode the bus to Chicago by herself and didn't nothing happen. Esther finally gave in.

"They know more about registering people to vote than most of us in here, and they know the test better than all of us," she said.

I crossed my fingers and hoped there wouldn't be no white man on the other end waiting to short my check.

I couldn't wait to get home to tell Granny I'd found a new job. I could hold my head up in town again. I burst through the door, excited to tell her the good news. Let folks know that Mr. Sam Ray Blackburn might've taken me down, but he didn't have his foot on my neck. Granny was in the kitchen stirring a pot of turnip greens with turnip bottoms mixed in, my favorite.

"Good news, Granny," I said. "Sit down here at the table and let me tell you."

"What you up to now?" she said. She wiped her hand on her apron, and I pulled out the chair for her to sit down as if I were a waiter at the café.

"No, don't sit down. It's too good. You might shout." I couldn't hold it. "No more going to the library with Rutherford. Esther gave me a job. Me and Malika going to work for SNCC."

"Got you what?" she said. "Doing what? With who?" She sat down in the chair.

"With SNCC. We making ten dollars per day. That's more than the field hands make."

She still didn't know what I was talking about. "You sit down," she said, "and tell me exactly what this is. Who got ten dollars to pay you to do what exactly?"

I sat in the chair next to hers, and looked her directly in her eyes. "You know how I been teaching the folks at the Hall how to take the test and to fill out the voter registration form. Well, now they paying us to go out to the country and do the same thing. Me and Malika going out past Cole Spur."

Granny reacted differently than I thought. I'd imagined her grabbing my hands and swinging me around in a circle.

"And Esther said you can do this?" she said.

"Yes, ma'am. We starting tomorrow. No more going to the library. Ain't you glad?"

She walked over to the stove. She wasn't happy.

"Esther needs the folks registered. She got to get enough signatures on the ballot to run for city council." I placed my hand over my mouth. "Oops."

I had been very careful not to tell Granny or Muhdea that Esther planned to marry Rutherford and run for city council. Esther wanted to tell them at the right time. The lawyer Walker and the other men from SNCC didn't want the white people to know before she bought Mrs. Carrie's house, married Rutherford, and signed the forms to run for office. If they kept it close to their vest till they dotted all the I's and crossed all the T's, nobody could stop them. I'd kept my mouth shut. I knew that if I told Muhdea and Reverend Jefferson, they'd go straight and tell the man.

Granny insisted I tell her the whole story, and I told her every word I could remember and some I made up to make the story better. But when I pleaded with her not tell Muhdea a single word I'd said, she wanted to know my reasons. I rubbed my eyes and started coughing. Granny was asking me to tell purposely, and if I told on Muhdea it would be one of them "peace-breaking lies." It didn't have to be a lie; it just had to be messy enough to get others in trouble. She let it go, sent me to the hydrant to wash my face. She stared into the distance, and looked straight through me. I called her name three times before she answered.

"Granny," I said.

"What is it, baby?" she said as if she were returning from another world.

"Esther told me to wear school clothes and shoes, comfortable shoes 'cause we doing a lot of walking."

"Where is Esther?"

I hunched my shoulders. "At the Hall, I guess."

"Get my shoes, Sarah, and go tell Sister Martha to come watch the kids for me," Granny said. "You think Esther still down at the Hall?"

Granny was going to the low end, to the Hall. What could that be about? I wondered, as I pulled her shoes from beneath her bed. Mrs. Martha took her pots off the stove and came back with me.

For the second time in one week, we would be headed down Back Street. "Was Carrie down there when you left?" she said.

Granny had said less than two words to Mrs. Carrie my whole life. They acted as if they didn't really know one another. Me and Malika went round and round trying to figure out why. I'd asked Granny why they weren't friends since they were so much alike, same long, mixed-gray hair, same color, and pointed nose, same way they chastised us.

"Who said we weren't friends? Mind your business," Granny'd said.

I'd asked Mrs. Carrie, and Malika had, too, and we both pretty much got the same answer. We weren't stupid. We knew something had come between them, but nobody in town seemed to know what it was, and neither one of them was telling.

"Yes, ma'am, she still there."

"Come on." She grabbed her straw hat. She didn't bother to put on a bra or panties. Maybe 'cause she wasn't going to the doctor.

"Walk down there with me," she said.

"What about my clothes for tomorrow?"

She put out the fire under the pot of turnip greens. The smell of fat meat and greens hung heavy in the air. Granny was about to do two things that left me with all kinds of questions, go to the Hall and talk to Mrs. Carrie. What had I said to bring about all that?

GRANNY STOOD IN the middle of the living room. She held my hand. When they saw her, everybody stopped. The folks working in the other rooms, and all the way back to the kitchen, walked to the front when they heard her name.

"Mrs. Granny, what you doing down here?" one of the boys said.

Esther came from the back with Mrs. Carrie, Rutherford, Gail and James Harel trailing behind her.

"I thought I heard somebody say Granny," Esther said. "Is everything alright at home?"

"Pearlie," Mrs. Carrie said, and Granny nodded her head. "I wondered if you'd make an appearance."

Granny took out her toothbrush and moved it to the other side of her mouth. The others stood in place as if they didn't know what to say or do. They waited.

"Well, I'm here, so you can put your mind to rest," Granny said.

I turned my head to the right and gave Malika the "any idea what's going on" look, and then the "why aren't you at home getting your clothes ready" one.

"Is there some place we can talk?" Granny said.

"Sure, we can talk in the library," Mrs. Carrie said. "May they join us, or is this just you and me?" There was a little bit of frost in her tone.

"They welcome," Granny said.

Granny scoped the place out as we walked back to the library with the ten or twelve books on the shelves, certainly not from a lack of Gail trying to get them for us. We'd resorted to writing a letter to President Lyndon Johnson. We'd asked him for help in stocking the library with books by and about colored folks. It didn't seem like the national SNCC office was ever going to get around to sending them. Gail said the civil rights movement would be over before we got even one book from SNCC. We'd laughed, me, Malika and the other students, but she didn't think it was funny. The few books she'd brought with her were ragged from use, which made her both happy and sad.

I was so used to being seen and not heard, making myself invisible to grown folks, I walked right on in behind Gail, in front of James, and slid to the floor between the bookshelves. Malika sat between my legs. With the heat exuding from Granny, she probably forgot I was with her, and she surely couldn't see me squoze between the bookcases. Early on, when the Hall first opened, Esther and Mrs. Carrie had established that children were equally important to the movement as adults, and they wanted us to know and understand everything they knew.

"Transparency is essential to our success," Esther had said, and they spent as much time as needed to explain everything to us till we understood, or pretended to 'cause we were tired of trying, and tired of listening.

"Why you here?" Mrs. Carrie said to Granny, snippy.

"As if you don't know," Granny said.

"It's not the same thing," Mrs. Carrie said.

"I'll be the judge of that since it involves my child."

What ain't the same? I nudged Malika in the back with my knee. She elbowed my knee.

"She's my daughter," Esther said.

"What is it, Pearlie?" Mrs. Carrie said. "You've been quiet all this time. Why speak up now?"

They duked it out with words. It was Granny's time. The other folks' heads moved back and forth from Granny to Mrs. Carrie. Malika tried to turn her head around to look me in the eye, but she bumped me in the lip with her big head. I pushed the back of it with my hand.

"Esther is grown. She can decide for herself if she wants to be involved with your foolishness," Granny said. "Sarah ain't, and I ain't letting y'all put her in harm's way. One thing you right about, Carrie, I been quiet long enough. Did you tell Esther what she was really getting into?"

"It's 1965, Pearlie. This isn't like before. And, yes, Esther knows. Not everything, but most of it," Mrs. Carrie said.

"So you say," Granny said.

The room was sparsely decorated. An eight-foot piece of shellacked wood lay across three wooden horses, one on each end and one in the middle to help balance it. Eight steel folding chairs, three on each side, and one at each end of the table. Several uneven bookshelves with cardboard under the bottom, made out of the same wood as the table, almost fit against the wall. Granny sat at the far end of the table, Mrs. Carrie sat with her back to the door, Esther's and Gail's backs were to me, and Rutherford and James sat across from them. I wasn't worried whether or not they'd warn them I was in the room.

"Did you tell Esther about us?" Granny said.

"No, not about you. I kept my word. George did, too," Mrs. Carrie said.

Right when I was about to try to figure out George who, and what word, the door opened, and Muhdea and Mr. George Stith walked in.

"What's wrong?" Granny said. "Is it one of the kids?"

"I was about to ask you the same question," Muhdea said. She and Mr. Stith took a seat at the table. "Sister Martha told me you were down here. I thought somebody must've done something to Esther. Stith passed by, and I got him to bring me. What's going on here? What you doing down here, Granny?"

I pushed Malika to the side so I could stick my head out and see Muhdea and Mr. Stith.

"Pearlie was about to tell us why she's here," Mrs. Carrie said.

Everybody turned toward Granny. Rutherford picked at his beard and straightened his dashiki, the same one he'd worn yesterday.

"Carrie and Esther talking about sending Sarah out to the country by herself," Granny said.

I wanted to correct her. To tell her Malika was going with me. I was shocked when Malika didn't raise her hand. I pleaded with her in my head to not tell Muhdea the rest of it. Please don't spill that Esther was running for city council.

"No, Esther, you can't do that," Muhdea said. "Sarah is way too young, and with the marching and whatnot y'all been doing, no telling what could happen to her on them back roads."

"So you want her to grow up like you, afraid of her own shadow," Esther said.

"Let's not do this today," Muhdea said.

I'd heard Muhdea and Esther bicker about their shortcomings many times before. Let Granny share why she's here, I thought.

"Your mama is right, Esther. It's not safe." Granny turned to Mrs. Carrie. "Sarah already had a run-in with Sam Ray Blackburn in the field. How could you agree with this? You know what can happen."

"I know more about what can happen if we sit idly by and do nothing," Mrs. Carrie said.

She got everybody in the room stirred up, and they bickered back and forth. Mr. Stith defended Granny's and Mrs. Carrie's positions. I stretched out my leg. No need to worry whether they'd see me. The tension in the air was thicker than a handmade quilt stuffed with wet cotton. I could prop myself up on the table and cross my legs and they wouldn't notice. Instead, I stayed on the floor hidden between the bookshelves.

"Don't be forced from your position, Pearlie," Mr. Stith said.

"Can you take my word for it, Esther, and know that y'all are covering road that's already been covered more than once? Believe me when I tell you that all your good intentions can go awry, and I don't want Sarah smack dab in the middle of it when they do," Granny said. She turned her anger toward Mrs. Carrie. "And if Carrie had any sense at all, she'd be telling you the same thing."

"If you won't tell us, leave now. We know the dangers, and we're willing to make the sacrifice," Esther said.

"You going to make me do this?" Granny said.

"I've always known it was something, Granny. You just refused to tell us what it is. Instead, you give us orders, and then dare us to question you as if you were God." Esther seemed as if she wanted to take back her words, but she'd gone over the boundaries, and the rest of it was pressed against her lips. "Time out for that, Granny. Whatever you've been keeping hush-hush, things Mrs. Carrie and Mr. Stith, for whatever reason, don't want to reveal, tell us now."

At the least, I expected a grand gesture from God, lightning, thunder or a flood. Footsteps walked up and down the hallway outside. Probably going to the kitchen for water or to the restroom. It was quiet all of a sudden, and I imagined their heads pressed against the door listening. I was afraid to breathe, and I waited for the wrath of Granny, but instead she spoke just above a whisper.

"We were there," she said. "Carrie and me, in Phillips County around Elaine, Hoop Spur, actually, back in 1919. We didn't meet up with George till the 1930s."

"Fifteen years later," Mr. Stith said. "In Poinsett County, Tyronza, 1934, to be exact."

"You were in Elaine? I know you ain't telling us y'all were at the massacre," Muhdea said as if Granny and them had attended a movie.

"Well, that ain't what we thought it was when we went up there," Granny said. "We hoped to get better payment for our crops. My mama told us the only difference between slavery and sharecropping was slaves didn't go hungry."

I knew hundreds of coloreds were killed in Elaine back in 1919 'cause the white folks believed they had guns and was fixing to kill them. Some said it was more than two hundred. It was hard to tell 'cause the white people dumped the bodies in the Mississippi River, and the current took them down the river. I spelled the state out in my head the way I did aloud when I jumped rope, M-I, crooked letter, crooked letter, I, crooked letter, crooked letter, I, humped back, humped back, I, Mississippi. Sister Tucker had told me about the massacre, but she'd never mentioned, not even once, that Granny and Mrs. Carrie were there. Was Sister Tucker with them? I thought, and I placed both hands over my mouth as Granny continued.

"We lived out on the levee back then, five miles from here, on the Maeby East Road. We worked from pitch-dark morning to pitch-dark night, and everything we made, we owed it to the plantation owner before we even cleared the fields for planting," Granny said.

"She's right," Mrs. Carrie said. "We were tired and hungry, and getting more and more fed up every day."

I folded my arms across my knees, laid my head atop and braced myself for what was to come next. I could tell by Granny's tone she'd rather stick her hand in a vat of hot grease than be explaining herself to us. Somebody was frying chicken in the kitchen, and Little Stevie Wonder's song "Fingertips" played on Gail's record player. I didn't think Reverend Jefferson would mind me listening to Little Stevie Wonder's songs 'cause he wasn't much older than me. I didn't see how singing along with him could be a sin. Granny's words broke into my thoughts.

"We heard folks was organizing in Elaine, about a hundred colored farmers, being led by Mr. Robert L. Hill, called the Progressive Farmers and Household Union. They met at a church in Hoop Spur in Phillips County, near Elaine. We wanted better payments for our cotton crops.

"If we wanted to get in on it, there was a wagon that would circle the lake three times every Wednesday night for the next three weeks, till the moon was highest in the sky. We figured it was up to us to put a stop to the unfairness of the plantation owner before our families starved to death. Carrie and my husband, Ozelle, talked it up till I agreed to go along with them.

"One Wednesday night we packed a sack and waited, and sure enough, the wagon came. We climbed under a tarp and lay on our sides to give the impression of a sack of cotton. 'Member that, Carrie?"

Mrs. Carrie nodded, and Granny went on. Muhdea kept shaking her head. Mr. Stith held her hand.

"I couldn't have been no more than nineteen or twenty years old. We went to work as soon as we got there, coming up with scrambled code words on flyers, and disguised catcalls so that folks would know we'd dropped a message with the date and time of the next meeting. That was sometime during the beginning of September. Ozelle and a lot of the men who came back from the war got a whiff of freedom over there, and they weren't scared no more."

We all nodded our heads as if they'd told us so themselves. Granny was the best storyteller, and folks rarely interrupted her when she got started.

"That night in question, the night before the massacre, the whites wouldn't ever own up to the reason they took the few men who lived to jail, but I know. We had jest made a fresh pot of coffee. The men took turns keeping watch around the church. As soon as I opened the door to hand them a cup, I heard one shot, and the shell hit the facing of the door. Before I could shut the door, a few more shots came from the woods, and then I heard Ozelle scream, 'Return fire.' Later, we found out one of the white men was dead, one was wounded, and a colored snitch hightailed it off to Helena to tell the law."

She looked as if she were still back there standing in the doorway of the church, still holding the coffee cup.

"What ensued in the following days wasn't nothing short of slaughtering hogs. They came from near and far with death in their eyes. The government sent the federal troops to protect us, but they fought with them. When it was over, they killed and floated down the river an ungodly amount of men, women and children. Ozelle was one of them. We never found him."

Not one of us in that room was prepared to ask for any more details than what she told us. We didn't, not even Muhdea, who looked as if she'd been wrung out like a sheet. Granny skipped right past to the years leading up to meeting Mr. Stith. I smelled grease burning in the kitchen, and somebody ran down the hallway. It was hot, and I was sweating. Rutherford opened his mouth as if he were going to speak to break the silence, but Esther cut her eyes hard at him, and he got the message. We sat still and waited for the three who knew the details to talk, or we'd eventually disburse with knowing only what Granny told us, and know to never bring it up again. She'd lost her husband. How could anybody ask her to relive that?

"Let's jest say there was enough work to keep us busy in Phillips County for a long time. They'd captured all the colored folks who didn't scatter and locked them up. Trials started a month later, and folks turned on each other to save their lives, others were convicted of murder, and some were placed on death row. I remember Ed and Frank Hicks. If memory serves me well, I believe there were twelve of them on death row. Eventually the ones on death row got Scipio Africanus Jones as they lawyer. Carrie stayed and continued to organize the fight against the landowners. I helped put together an organization to raise funds for Ed and them, to secure their freedom. I moved closer to the river so I could keep an eye out for Ozelle. I couldn't leave him out there in that water. The sharecropping got worse, nothing changed, folks was scared, and with good reason.

"I was back and forth," Mrs. Carrie said. "We felt hopeless, but we persevered."

Muhdea fanned herself with her hand. Rutherford placed his

hand on Esther's knee. I felt bad for her and Muhdea. All these years, and Granny never told them, never said a mumbling word.

"One day, a few years later, Scipio stopped by my house, and sat for most of the day talking to me and asking me questions surrounding them days in Elaine. I had pretty near pushed the whole incident somewhere in the back of my mind so I'd be able to live with it and keep hunting for Ozelle. But Scipio had a way about him. We sat, talked and drank coffee as if we was old friends. Pretty soon, I told him things I forgot I knew and one I never spoke of again 'cause he didn't need to call me as a witness to get them men off like he thought he would, and I drew him a picture of the man who I seen shoot a bunch of folks, including Ozelle."

Everybody in the room gasped. Granny saw the man kill her husband. Malika hit my leg, and I told her I was listening. Tears raced down James' face quicker than he could wipe them away. I smelled Muhdea's lavender water. Gail handed James a Kleenex and wiped her face with another one. We all wanted to know what had happened to the man who killed Granny's husband, and she told us.

"See, Sarah done already had a run-in with Sam Ray Blackburn, and I'm afraid he done forgot what I know, or he just think he bigger than the law now. Scipio caused me to remember that Sam shot at Ozelle, and he shot another man in the face with his shotgun. The man grabbed hold of Sam's mask, and held it in his bloody hand as he slipped down to the ground. Sam eyed me, and I ducked into the woods, never to see him again till I moved back here, and walked in his store. The only good to come of that was them men Scipio represented didn't have to die."

Granny held her head down. She choked up when she tried to talk, so Mrs. Carrie took over the telling.

"Years later George and I found Pearlie in Tyronza. She'd stopped looking for Ozelle by then, but I still believed somebody would find him, and she didn't want to be too far away when they did. Did you say it was some fifteen years later, George? We came to convince her to join up with us. We believed she still had fight in her. I let George do the talking."

"We got a chance this time," George said. "Coloreds and whites organizing together. I'm the treasurer. I been in meetings with coloreds and whites sitting right next to each other. Tell her, Carrie."

"They sat on my porch as we rocked and talked," Granny said. "I studied on it. Carrie wore a lilac floral print. As hot as it was, George sported a dark wool suit. He didn't look much different than he does now, still brighter than the sun, so excited he lit up the night sky, and his smooth convincing voice, he could talk anybody into anything. It didn't take them long to get me off the porch. I'd grown weary sitting and waiting, and the meeting was right there in Tyronza."

Bro Hollin opened the door and brought in a tin of water. He was pleasant, speaking to everybody, asking if the water was cold, were we hungry. I wanted to ease out the door behind him. Even though I wanted to know what happened, it was too sad in here. Instead of him leaving, he took a seat in front of the door. Granny seemed to have gotten so caught up in the life she'd lived that she didn't even use Bro Hollin's interruption as a reason to change the subject.

"I doubted them from the start," Granny said. "But I went along with it. We did organize. We got President Roosevelt's attention. Me and Carrie rode the train out west to California, and signed up folks for the STFU, jest the same as you registering them to vote today, Sarah. Jest now I'm thinking we argued so much 'cause we were tired, tired of the train, of being away from home, of organizing. But one day as we sat on a family's porch in Pine Bluff after we'd passed out flyers all week for the meeting that night, there was word of snitches, and for some reason, I believed the white man in that family was one of them. He was much too agreeable. Our faces were on wanted posters as if we were criminals, and he showed us a copy. Carrie thought he was being helpful, and I was sure he was up to something. We disagreed with each other right there on that man's porch.

"After the meeting, I moved back to the levee. I'd spent the better part of my life accomplishing nothing, and losing folks I loved along the way. Carrie and Stith saw it differently. I take my hat off to Carrie even though for the longest time after I moved back to the levee, took up sharecropping again, I blamed her for my troubles. She never quit and never gave up on trying to pull me back in with her. The last time she tried, the time the NAACP requested her and Ella Baker to cross the South counting bodies of the dead, I blew up at her, and we agreed to never speak of my involvement with any efforts she had ever been a part of. Let me live my life as a wife and mother, and she did.

"You see what can happen, Esther Mae," Granny said.

A type of silence I'd never heard before or since draped the room. Nobody moved or breathed, or fidgeted. No birds chirped, no Little Stevie Wonder, no walking up and down the hall, just a thick silence filled with anger and grief.

"You should've told us, especially Muhdea. Don't you see what you did to her, to me?" Esther said.

Muhdea got up and slammed her hand on the table. One of her stockings had come unwound and fallen down around her ankle. She didn't bother to pull it up.

"You told me nothing. You raised me to be afraid, to stay away from things." She walked out and slammed the door.

Mr. Stith followed her. The snitch in Elaine reminded me of what might happen here. Is that why Muhdea had left? Was she shamed that we were snitches? It was probably 'cause Granny had told her stories all of her life. Was everything she'd said a fib? Did she really not sit on the right-hand side of God?

"You got to let me go, Granny," I said. "I'll be careful. I ain't scared. I have to be brave like you."

I ran out of the room and down the road to see if I could catch Muhdea and tell her I didn't want to be a snitch no longer, and even if I did want to I couldn't do it. I needed to stand up for equality by attending the white school.

CHAPTER TWENTY-ONE

Colored School Is Good Enough

ESTHER ASKED ME if I still wanted to work for SNCC after hearing all of what Granny had to say. I hated what those men did to Granny, but most of all I was sad that she'd gotten scared and given up. I wasn't afraid. Malika said she wasn't either.

On the first day, all six of us girls loaded up in Mrs. Carrie's station wagon with Esther. Esther told us she was going to drop each of us off at our first home before she went to work, and she'd pick us up at the same house when she got off at four o'clock. Granny made a good case to keep me from going, but it fell on deaf ears. The SNCC office in Atlanta expected us to start work that day, and Esther wasn't changing her mind about it.

I watched Granny as she hummed "Swing Low, Sweet Chariot" while she laid my clothes out on the bed for me. Granny hung my book satchel across my shoulder and readjusted the rubber bands on each one of my plaits as she uttered a list of dos and don'ts.

"Be mindful, look both ways before y'all cross the road, keep an eye out for anything out of the ordinary, don't get in the car with nobody you don't know, and if you see any white man following you, hide behind the bushes or lay down flat in the ditch."

I nodded and gave each one of her warnings a number on my fingers so that if anything she told me came up, I'd remember exactly what to do.

I pranced out to the road like a little soldier. When I looked back and saw Granny still standing on the porch holding open the screen door, I turned around and marched right back up to her. She seemed surprised, as if she thought I'd changed my mind and decided not to go. I stared her straight in the eyes as if I were as grown as she was.

"I ain't scared one bit, Granny," I said. "I'm proud to help Esther. But most of all, I'm proud that I'm growing up to be just like you. So don't you be scared for me either."

She shook my hand like I was a little lady. "Well, I won't be, and you and Malika do your very best out there," she said.

And since I was already being grown, I told her, "Maybe if you hadn't kept things from Muhdea, she wouldn't be scared either." I took off running, feeling much lighter than I had a few minutes ago.

Esther dropped off two girls out on the bayou, and two more out near the levee. Me and Malika rode in the backseat for a few more miles before she stopped the car in front of an old farmhouse on the outskirts near Grandy, Arkansas.

"Y'all ready?" she said.

"Yes, ma'am," Malika said.

Malika pulled on the door handle. I slid toward the other door.

"Do y'all want me to help you get started?" Esther said. "I can see you through the first call."

"No, ma'am, we know how to do it," Malika said.

I eased over closer to the opposite door.

"Sarah, you can't get out on that side. A car might be coming," Malika said.

As if a magnet were stuck to my behind, I slid back across the car seat. For a second, I hoped Esther would change her mind and insist we stay in the car and go back home with her.

"We'll be fine. We been teaching people how to register all year," Malika said.

"Esther, don't stay here and watch us, either. Go on back home. We big enough now," I said.

The other girls were juniors and seniors in high school. Me and Malika had just finished the fourth grade. She'd turned nine years old that April, and my birthday was in July. SNCC had hired us to register voters after President Johnson signed the Voting Rights Act. Supposedly, Mrs. Carrie, Esther and all the civil rights workers said supposedly, folks should now be able to register without paying a poll tax, owning land or taking a test. Esther and them had gone straight to work on their plans for her to run for city council. Some folks had tried to register at the water house, but them white folks acted as if they hadn't heard the news. Esther said they'd all be educated by November, she'd see to it personally.

We stood on the side of the long gravel country road, our schoolbook satchels sparse with registration forms and pens.

"Try not to make any mistakes," Gail had said as she organized our bag. "These forms have to last until we can get more from the SNCC office."

We watched Esther drive off. Granny would've driven around the corner and snuck back to check on us. Everything stood as still as we did, no wind blowing, no birds chirping, no animals running across the road. The only sound I heard was the gravel crackling as the car tires rolled down the road.

We jumped across the ditch and walked a piece to get to the first house. A little bitty shotgun house in need of paint with rusted screen around the porch held on with the help of two or three nails, and a screen door hung on by its hinges. Dust covered our shoes, and Malika wiped it off with her hand, and it reappeared with the next step. We woke the gnats up from their sleep, and they covered us. I fanned them off me and Malika, and she tried, too, but to no avail, so we picked up our speed and tried to outrun them. Then everything in the weeds came alive. Birds chirped, bugs hopped, and mosquitoes bit us.

We talked back and forth as we walked. "I didn't think Granny would let you go after all that stuff she told," Malika said.

I took my face towel out of the book satchel and fanned away the bugs we'd stirred up. "She probably wouldn't have if it was left up to her. But you know Esther gets the final word when it comes to me," I said.

Malika acted as if she just now recalled the rules of the Bible and First Baptist Church.

"Even though it's the rule," I said, "she don't like it none at all."

Malika shivered as if she were cold. I laughed at her even though it wasn't funny. We walked up to the front of the house.

"We got to make sure we keep an eye out for Mr. Sam Ray Blackburn," I said. She agreed, no telling where he might be lurking around.

"How you want to do this?" I said.

"You do the talking, and I'll fill out the forms," she said.

"You do this every time. Why I got to do all the talking?"

"You talk better than I do. I like to keep an eye out so I can have your back."

I cut my eyes at her and winced. I knocked on the screen door, hoping it wouldn't fall off its hinges.

"You remember what to say?" I kept knocking.

Nobody answered. We walked around to the corner of the house and peeped into the backyard. Nobody stirred back there either. We walked around to the other side of the house and looked, Malika in front and me right behind her. Not one soul, nobody home. We went back and sat on the front porch. I pulled the yellow pad and a pen out of my book satchel.

"You marking it down?" Malika said.

"We have to record it."

"How?" She walked around the porch. "I don't see nothing that say who live here." She turned the knob on the door to their house.

"Don't go in there, girl. You know better." I studied on how to record it for a minute. "What if I write road number one and house number one—nobody home?"

Malika walked down to the mailbox. "They last name is Johnson, but ain't no address," she yelled.

I met her, and we walked down the road and talked as gravel dented the soles of my school shoes. Somebody was always home. Most families had children, and somebody had to be home to watch them. We tried to recall if we'd ever been to an empty house. "Where could they be?" Malika said. It wasn't uncommon in Chicago 'cause everybody went to a job at a factory or an office. It was hard for me to imagine everybody being away from home all day.

"When you going back up there?" I said.

"Mama said I might have to stay up there and go to school if these white folks start something with us for going to their school."

Neither of us wanted to go to the white school, but now we understood it was our responsibility like it was the grown folks' obligation to register and vote. Malika had given up on trying to figure how to get out of it.

We kicked rocks as we walked and wiped our shoes off with our bare hands, but the dirt reappeared even when we weren't kicking rocks. I saw the next house in the distance. We still had a ways to go. We sang songs, played hand games, and talked about when we'd get grown as we inched our way toward the next house. Malika fixed her mouth a few times to talk about what Granny'd told us yesterday. I quickly changed the subject, and she let it go for a little while and then tried again. Eventually, she blurted it out before I caught it.

"Did Granny tell you anything else when y'all got home? I just knew you weren't coming," she said.

"I knew she was done talking. That's the last we'll ever hear from her about that," I said. I jumped 'cause I thought I heard something. "Did you hear that?" She didn't, but we hid behind a huge oak tree and held our breath. It was nothing. Not even a wild boar. "See, you brought up that mess and got me skittish. I don't want to talk about it no more. We can't be scared every time the wind blow. We got to be like them other people in Alabama and Mississippi, and they ain't scared."

We came from behind the tree and walked along the side of the road till we got to the next house. We knew now to check the mailbox first. The name printed in red, capital letters was Holmes. I knocked and couldn't believe it was happening again, no answer.

"Where these folks at?" I said. "We got to sign up somebody so Esther won't lose faith in us. We should've brought our bicycles. No telling how far the next house is."

We walked around the corner of the house and peeped in the backyard. A big woman stood at the washtub scrubbing a white sheet on the washboard. We went on back there and spoke to her. She didn't seem surprised to see us.

"What y'all gals peeping around the corner of my house for?" she said. "I saw you over there at the Johnsons. They ain't at home."

Malika pranced right up to her and held out her hand. The lady dried her hand on her apron, then shook Malika's hand, and mine, too. Malika lit right in on her as if she were the last person on earth left to register.

"I'm Malika Ann Brown, and this here is Sarah Jones. We're with SNCC, the Student Non-Violent Coordinating Committee."

The woman wrinkled her face and switched her eyeballs back and forth as if Malika had said it in French, like "Bonjour, mademoiselle." She went on back to scrubbing her sheets. I knew she needed warming up. She wasn't the kind of woman whom I could talk fast to. Four little naked boys ran out to the backyard from the other side of the house. The biggest one wasn't no more than four or five years old.

"Can't y'all see I'm talking? Get on back around that corner and play," Mrs. Holmes said. They scrambled. I heard them around the corner playing tag.

She looked Malika up and down. "Who you say you wit?"

She stared me up and down, too. I stood almost a head taller than her oldest boy, but Malika wasn't much taller than her middle one. She probably wondered what Malika was doing working for a committee when she should be running around naked and playing in the yard like her boys. Malika eyed me, and I stood up proud, told her all about SNCC, and the reason we were there.

The lady said her name was Mrs. Holmes, but we already knew that. Her husband was out working in the field. Malika sat down on the back porch and took out the voter registration form and a pen. I was about to ask her for her first name when she started talking to me.

"What you got there?" she said.

She startled me a bit. Stopped me in the middle of my presentation.

Malika spoke in her uppity Chicago voice. "This is the form you have to fill out so you can be registered to vote," she said.

"Ain't nobody said I was registering for nothing," she said. She pulled another sheet out of the tub while she pushed the other one back into the water.

"Well, if you let me finish," I said.

She burned a hole through me with her eyes. "Won't matter if you finish or not. I'm done listening. I got work to do."

Her water was getting cold. I checked my Mickey Mouse watch. We'd been there over thirty minutes. What could I do to get her attention again? What did Rutherford teach us? She picked up a sheet and started wringing it out at one end.

"Let me help you with that," I said and grabbed the other end out of the tub before she could say no. We wrung the sheet out tightly and hung it across the clothesline. The sun hit it just the right way, and the rays scattered across the white sheet. I gave her my spiel the whole time we wrestled with the sheet. She turned away from me and addressed Malika.

"Your friend speak real good. She said it just like an Easter speech."

I thought Malika would back me up, but no words came out of her mouth. She stood frozen in place, so I stressed the importance of why colored people must vote again.

"Mrs. Holmes," I said. "We got to vote. If we don't, we won't ever be able to do nothing but work in the fields. Don't you want better for me and your boys than a broke back from bending over a hoe and pulling a cotton sack?"

She side-eyed me as if to ask what else was there for us to do. We went round and round with Mrs. Holmes for more than an hour. Every time we came up with a good reason for her to vote, she told us another one why she didn't have no use for it.

"What about better schools for your boys?" Malika said.

"Colored schools is good enough," she said and propped her hip to one side.

My thoughts exactly, but I pushed forward.

"I know you want your boys to be able to sit in a café right next to the whites instead of ordering ice cream at the window," I said. One up for me.

"I make my ice cream right here. See that old bucket over there? I makes it right in there." She got me again. *Help me, Malika.*

We tried all the tactics and asked every question the civil rights workers had taught us, but Mrs. Holmes believed her family was doing just fine. Mr. Holt paid her husband a fair wage for driving a tractor from sunup to sundown.

"And he ain't carrying no hoe or pulling no cotton sack," she said.

I dropped my head. "I didn't mean it like that," I said.

She touched my shoulder to let me know she didn't take it that way. "Who y'all folks over there in Maeby?" she said.

"I'm Deborah Brown's daughter," Malika said.

"She work at the café?"

Malika nodded, and I did, too. The leaves on the trees swayed back and forth, and dust from the dirt yard blew in my face. That sheet might get dirty before it dried.

She stared straight at me and asked, "Who your folks?"

"I'm Esther White's daughter. She the reason I told you why we need you to register. If we register most of the colored folks, she can win the city council office in November 'cause we outnumber them."

Again, the look. The boys wanted water, and she drew them a cup from the hydrant.

"Your mama running for city council? Is she crazy? What you say her name is?" she said.

"Miss Esther White, and no, ma'am, she ain't crazy. She's real smart."

She scratched her head. Her bosom shook. "Is Elworth White her daddy?"

"Yes, ma'am. Mr. and Mrs. Mozelle and Elworth White are my grandparents."

She grinned real big. I noticed snuff stains on the few front teeth she had left.

"I know Elworth. He stops by here and picks up slop for his hogs every Saturday." She dropped the second sheet into the rinse water and rested her hand near her lower back, right above her hip. "Did he register?"

Shame crawled up my body and showed through my eyes. "No, ma'am. He works out of town all week," I said.

Before I could drop my head all the way down, I heard Granny's voice scolding me: *Don't make me snatch your head up, Sarah. If you don't get it up high right now, I'll do it for you.*

"See there," Mrs. Holmes said. "Elworth ain't like his daughter. He got sense. He ain't trying to register to vote, and he owns his land outright. He ain't worried 'bout feeding his children or getting put out of his house, and he ain't registering. The truth is, and you go back and tell your mama this, hear? We ain't in no position to cause no ruckus out here. Mr. Holt owns this house and this land, and my husband works for him. You tell your mama to put herself in our shoes and see how quick she be signing her name."

Malika didn't pay Mrs. Holmes no mind. She made her voice real sweet and pleasant like the civil rights workers had taught us and said, "President Johnson signed the Voting Rights Act, and you don't have to own land or pay poll tax no more to register. Can we come back and talk to your husband when he gets home?"

They had taught us at the Hall to get some type of confirmation, register them, set a time to come back, leave something so we'd have to come back. We'd learned there wasn't any such thing as a no answer. Whoever came up with that big idea obviously hadn't met Mrs. Holmes.

"Y'all children can come back as many times as you want, and the answer be the same," she said. "I'm glad to see y'all be so smart though. Makes me feel right proud. Come on back around anytime. Maybe you can teach my boys a thing or two."

She started wringing out the sheet. We folded the sheet in half and twisted it from each end. By the time we wrung out the third sheet, Malika'd caught hold of my end. We helped her wring out four more sheets and hung them on the clothesline.

"These belong to Mrs. Anna up the road there in case you was wondering why I got so many."

It was the first time the tone in her voice held a hint of shame. We'd begun our day around eight o'clock that morning; it was almost noon, and we hadn't come close to registering anybody.

"I'll be feeding my boys in a minute. Y'all want to stay and eat?"

"No, thank you, ma'am. We've got our lunch in our bags," I said.

Mrs. Holmes walked us out to the road and pointed us toward Mr. Wilkes' store.

"Y'all girls might have better luck with Mr. Wilkes," she said. "He owns the store and the land it's sitting on. Y'all tell Elworth I say they're raising some good little girls, and good luck to your mama, but she is crazy to go up against these white folks. Tell her I'm putting her at the top of my prayer list." Oh Lord, even she knew Esther was a sinner. She waved to us as we walked down the road and yelled, "And tell them I think y'all brave, too."

The boys ran behind us, and she called them back before they got to the road. Malika pointed out that our clothes were soaking wet.

"We can't go in that man's store looking like this. Let's eat our lunch under that tree over there and dry off first."

We walked along beside the ditch. I heard a car in the distance. We threw our book satchels in the ditch and lay on top of them. I covered my eyes with the top of my dress to keep the dust out. The truck slowed as it got closer to us. Malika squeezed my hand. The truck stopped right in front of us. Mr. Sam Ray Blackburn sat in the passenger's seat. I prayed he wouldn't see us. I wondered if he did. His driver got out and kicked the tire on his side.

"It's fine," he said. "Must've been a bump in the road."

He drove off, and we lay there quietly for a good while before we got up.

"I'm not brave," Malika said, her voice shaky.

I pretended to be brave, but my knees wobbled. I stood up, my dress a muddy mess. I reached my hand out. She grabbed hold of it, and I pulled her up.

"I know we'll get Mr. Wilkes to register," I said. "But let's eat first."

We sat under a big oak tree. Malika started taking her food out of the paper sack. I took out my yellow pad, placed it on my knees, and wrote, *Road number one, house number two, did not want to register, Mrs. Holmes.*

CHAPTER TWENTY-TWO

We're Getting Married

GAIL DISMISSED US from class an hour early. I should've known something was up when she didn't keep me and Malika for French lessons. Most of the other kids went home to do their chores. Miss Flora and Miss Pastel's cooking swirled through the air from the kitchen, and their girls stayed at the Hall after class, too. Funny how all four of them were short when their mamas were so big and tall.

Gail asked me and Malika to help Mr. Thomas and Mr. Jonas prepare their voter registration forms. They would try to register on Monday. So far six folks, not counting Mrs. Carrie, Granny and Mr. Stith, had been able to get their voter registration cards, two couples, both schoolteachers who owned their own land and could afford the poll tax, Bro Hollin, I tutored him, and Esther after she bought Mrs. Carrie's house. Others tried, but for one reason or the other, they came back to the Hall feeling dejected or bruised and with blackened eyes from the beating the white men gave them. It was awful the way they beat poor Rutherford and James. Mrs. Carrie said it was part of the reason Rutherford was always mad lately. Esther tried to get Muhdea to agree to register, promised her the Maeby Citizens for Progress would pay the poll tax, but Muhdea said no, and her answer wasn't going to change, so stop, please stop, coming to her with her foolishness. But Muhdea's words fell on deaf ears, and Esther asked her again whenever the mood hit her.

Gail beckoned for me not long after I started working with Mr. Jonas. She'd forgotten to show me some papers.

"Mr. Jonas, fill out this section, and I'll check it when I get back," I said.

When I got to the classroom, Esther and Gail were sitting at the table looking through a small stack of papers. I sat next to Gail. She placed her arm around me and gave me a hug, and then she took her arm away.

"Sarah, do you remember me telling you I went to a boarding school?" Gail said.

I nodded. Her parents had sent her off when she was in the third grade, and she was only allowed to come home on breaks and holidays. Granny and Muhdea wouldn't ever go for nothing like that, and I wouldn't ever want to leave them either. I couldn't ever stay away from them like Esther did.

"Gail and I filled out an admissions application for you to go to the same school Gail attended in Boston," Esther said.

"What for?" I said. "I ain't, I mean, I'm not leaving home to go to school."

Gail tried to place her arm around my shoulder again, and I shook it off. "It's an alternate plan. One day you may want to go. It doesn't mean you have to go."

"We're applying for scholarships, and we both believe you're smart enough to get in," Esther said.

I stomped my foot. "You always trying to change things, Esther," I said. "Why don't you mind Muhdea and leave well enough alone? I ain't leaving town to go to no school. I ain't even going to the white one across the tracks, so y'all can just leave me alone."

Gail seemed shocked that I didn't think this was a good idea. "We're not trying to get you upset," she said.

"Gail is right," Esther said as she pointed her finger at me. "And one day you're going to learn I make decisions for you. Not you or Granny or Muhdea, but me. The sooner you understand that, the better."

I didn't have to say much to get her riled up. She got up from the table and slammed the chair against it.

"We wanted you to know, Sarah. That's all is going to happen right now," Gail said as if she were the peacemaker.

I walked around to the backyard, madder than Esther, and tired of her and her big ideas. Rutherford and Reverend Moses, the

Methodist preacher, sat on the steps passing a brown paper bag back and forth, and drinking out of it.

"Hey, Sarah," Reverend Moses said. He beckoned me with his long brown fingers. I stood in place. He turned the bag up to his lips. "You stubborn, ain't you?"

"You hear him talking to you, girl," Rutherford said. "Come see what he want." He turned the bag up to his lips.

"What y'all drinking?" I said.

"None of yours," Rutherford said as if it was all one word.

"Fine," I said and turned to walk toward the front yard. I tried to stay as far away as I could from Rutherford and his dashiki-wearing friends. Every time I tried to talk to him, I ended up at the library or the jail, causing Granny to take time away from the children and her work to come and get me. She never raised her voice at Rutherford, but at home, she always said that one day he was going to find himself at the butt end of her .22, which was her pearl-handled pistol she kept under the mattress, and probably wouldn't fire even if she put bullets in it. He wore a new dashiki, and so did Reverend Moses, who never wore nothing but a white shirt and black tie. Rutherford was bringing him on over to the cool, colorful side of dressing with him.

"Come on back here, Sarah," he said. I kept walking.

"And that's going to be your daughter," Reverend Moses said.

"Not hardly," I said as I picked up speed.

"As if I'd want you," he slurred, and they both laughed loud as if what he said were funny.

Mr. Thomas, Mr. Jonas and Malika were seated at the conference table when I came in.

"Where you been?" Malika said. "Mr. Jonas been waiting for you."

"What it matter to you anyway? " I said.

"'Cause you always late," she said. Mr. Thomas and Mr. Jonas looked at us with disapproving eyes.

Mr. Thomas grew sick of our bickering. "What's wrong with y'all girls?" he said. "That ain't no way to behave."

"It's not me, Mr. Thomas," I said.

"Come on and finish helping me. I ain't got all day," Mr. Jonas said.

"Mr. Jonas, what they cooking in there that smells so good? Is it cake?" I said.

"I done smelled all kinds of things coming out of there. At one point, I thought I smelled smothered steak, but I know better than that," he said.

"Hard to tell. Them smells is all twined together by the time we got here," Mr. Thomas said.

"Well, look here," I said and pointed to the signature line on the form. "Pretty soon all you'll need to know is how to sign your name or mark an X on this line, but that day ain't quite here yet, so let's go through the questions."

He frowned and told me to go ahead and ask him. "They'll never be able to turn me away for not knowing, Sarah," Mr. Jonas said, "but I'll be glad when the day come when we don't have to take this test or pay a poll tax."

"I'll be glad when you shut the yapping and get to work," Mr. Thomas said.

We were about finished when we heard Gail yell from the living room. "Finally," she said. "Oh, God, come in here. I can't believe it. Everybody come see this."

The mailman carried box after box from his truck and set them on the porch. Gail pulled the flap open on one of the cardboard boxes and held up a book. The mailman shook his head at her, as if he didn't understand what all the excitement was about. He set another box on the porch.

"Bring them inside," Gail said, but he wasn't coming any further than the porch.

Rutherford and Reverend Moses came from around the side of the house. Miss Flora and Miss Pastel wiped their hands on their aprons. Esther ran down the stairs, and Mrs. Carrie wanted to know what all the commotion was about. Mr. Jonas and Mr. Thomas picked up a box and carried it to what we'd always hoped would be the library. Gail opened the box, and me and Malika pulled out the books. We caught hands and swirled around yelling, "We got books." Gail's face was apple red, and every so often, she covered her face with her hands. She and Esther hugged Mrs. Carrie.

"I can't believe it," Mrs. Carrie said.

"All this commotion over nothing but books," the mailman said as he placed another box on the porch and shook his head again.

It seemed as if he wasn't ever going to stop taking books out of his truck. James and Reverend Moses started helping him.

"Where'd all these books come from?" the mailman said. He wiped sweat from his splotched red face.

"The president," I said. "We wrote to President Johnson, and he sent them to us."

"Well, that can't be true," he said. "The president wouldn't send y'all no books."

"Yes, he would, and he did, too," I said as we danced around the boxes. "Me and Malika wrote the letter, and everybody signed it."

"Then this letter must be yours," the mailman said as he handed me an 8x10 yellow envelope addressed to me and Malika.

Malika caught the other end of it. "Let me open it, Sarah. Don't just stand there."

"Let go before you tear it," I said and jerked it out of her hand. She slapped the back of my hand. "That hurt." I shook my hand.

"Give it to me," Rutherford said.

I placed my hand that held the envelope on my hip. "Does it have your name on it?" I said, and that set him off.

"You need to check your child," he said. "And Gail, this ain't nothing. Don't think that you done something big here. They just books. It ain't no fucking revolution."

"Rutherford," Esther said.

"Hey, you better shut up before I bust you in your lip. Who you think you are calling me out like that? You better check yourself."

Reverend Moses caught onto his elbow and tried to guide him away from us. He jerked his arm away.

"Don't touch me, man." His eyes were bloodshot. "These women are trying to phase me out." He switched the brown paper bag from his right hand to his left, and pointed at each one of us as he backed down the steps with Reverend Moses. "Ain't neither one of you nothing without me. Remember that." They walked around the corner of the house as Reverend Moses consoled him.

I'd seen Rutherford get mad before, even twist Esther's arm, but not like that. Me and Malika eyed each other. I handed the letter to Esther. She pushed my arm away, and went after Rutherford. Gail took the letter.

"Come on, girls. We've got boxes of books to open," she said. We opened the letter together once we were in the library. Both our full names were written in the heading, mine first, Miss Sarah White, and Malika's right under mine, on official paper, Gail said, and signed by the president himself.

"You girls should be proud," Gail said. "This letter is very, very special."

Overall, the letter said he didn't have the power to integrate the library, but it seemed we were serious about reading, and he did have the power to send us more books than we would have time to read before we graduated high school and went off to college. Miss Flora's and Miss Pastel's girls jumped up and down as if he had written the letter to them.

"He said y'all was going to college. He said y'all going to college," they repeated as if it were a song. "Can we go, too? Can we go, too?" they sang.

"He's talking about all of us," I said. "We're all going to college."

Gail, Esther and Mrs. Carrie had told us many times they were preparing us for college. One day Malika asked Gail if students at college spoke French, and if not where would we use it if we were separated.

"France, of course, preferably Paris," she said, which seemed more like a fairy tale than "Snow White and the Seven Dwarfs." We played along with her when she placed boas around our necks and berets on our heads. "It's all in the clothes," she said as we spoke French to each other.

Me and Malika were the only ones who kept at it, and according to Gail, we'd gotten pretty good. But when President Johnson stated so matter of fact that we would go off to college, it became real to me, and that day I no longer planned to graduate high school. I became a girl who was going to college.

When Esther came in the room, I asked her what was wrong with Rutherford. Why did he cuss in front of us?

"He's frustrated," she said. "He doesn't want to be left out of things. Be nice to him, Sarah. He's going to be your father."

"No chance," I said. "I don't even like him."

Along with many other harsh words, she told me I had to change my mind about him. "We're getting married, and we're all going to live under the same roof."

Every time I started to like her, she went and did something to turn me totally against her, like not telling me we were staying in Little Rock on the first night of revival. I tried to see in her what the folks at the Hall saw, and not what the folks at the church said she was, which always confused me 'cause right afterward Reverend Jefferson told us to see the good in everybody. They didn't see any good in Esther. It wasn't that I couldn't see why they said some of those things about her. Esther could get under my skin and scratch harder than a stray cat. I wasn't going to live with them. Esther could marry who she wanted to, but she couldn't believe Muhdea and Granny would let her take me away from them, and I told her as much.

"Get that out your head, Esther. I'm down for the cause." I liked using slang phrases that I'd learned from Rutherford. "But that ain't happening, man. You know, see you when I see you. Peace out." I held up my middle finger and forefinger, indicating a peace sign. "Y'all do what you want, but I'm going to the crib," and I walked toward the door.

Esther caught the neck of my shirt and snatched me back to her. She pointed her finger so close to my face it touched my nose. "Listen to me, little girl. I am your mother. Don't you ever, ever forget it. Now get your little ass back over there and finish putting those books on the shelf, and don't say another word until I tell you to."

Tears formed in Malika's eyes as if Esther were talking to her. "Here, Sarah," Malika said. She handed me a book called *The Fire*

Next Time by James Baldwin. "Help me," she whispered, and I did without saying a word.

Later we ate sandwiches and drank Cokes on the front porch, talking to each other with our eyes. Miss Flora's and Miss Pastel's girls, too. One of them who was prone to making us laugh at the wrong time said after about fifteen minutes of silence, when she was sure nobody was around but us, "We still going to college. You can talk then, Sarah."

We all laughed, silently, and the more we tried not to laugh loudly, the more it wanted to come out. We placed our hands over our mouths, and then over each other's mouths, and held our stomachs, and when we couldn't hold it any longer, we laughed out loud.

Soon afterward, Esther called me to come upstairs. It was the first time I'd seen her bedroom. She wore a long white dress with yellow daisies all over it. Her hair was pulled back with the same color band as the one tied around her dress. She was the prettiest person I'd ever seen. Esther told me I had the looks, and the beauty came with age. I didn't believe her.

A smaller replica of the dress she wore lay on the bed. "Who is that for?" I said.

"It's yours, Sarah," she said. She picked up the dress and held it against my body. "Looks like it's going to fit you."

"Where we going?"

She smiled wide. "We're doing it today," she said. "We're getting married. Me, you and Rutherford are getting married today."

"You playing, right?" I said. She kept that big stupid grin on her face. "You ain't playing? I ain't marrying nobody. I'm going home. Did you tell Muhdea and Granny? I bet they ain't coming."

"Sarah, as smart as you are, why do you choose to continue to use that word?"

"What word?" What was she talking about? This was when she chose to correct my English. "Is Granny coming?" I was sure that she'd give up on marrying Rutherford after the way he'd been acting. Was he the only one she wanted to marry?

"They're not coming." Her smile looked plastered on her face. "But we'll be okay. Don't you like your dress? Isn't it pretty?" She rambled. "Let's be happy today, Sarah. Go wash up, and let's see if your dress fits."

There wasn't anything else I could do. I was trapped the same as I was in Little Rock, and I wanted to scratch her face like a stray cat. I felt that I couldn't scratch her at all 'cause even though she didn't say it, her eyes begged me not give her any trouble, to please behave just for today, and I did. When she finished, we looked like twins. My dress was too big, but it was a shift dress, and Esther said it didn't matter. I would grow into it next summer. She dabbed a little bit of pink lipstick on my lips and stroked my cheeks with her blush brush.

Malika came up and told us the lawyer Walker and the other folks had arrived. "You look pretty, Sarah," she said. I wanted to cry.

It wasn't a big wedding. Only a few folks who was always at the Hall, members of Maeby Citizens for Progress, a few of the civil rights workers from Little Rock and Pine Bluff, the lawyer Walker, Mrs. Carrie and Malika. Nobody was dressed up like folks generally did for a wedding. It was Saturday afternoon around three o'clock.

I walked down the stairs a few steps ahead of Esther. She gave me a basket filled with the same small daisies that were splashed over our dresses, and told me to sprinkle them on the floor as I glided down the stairs and across the living room to stand beside Rutherford. Then I remembered Rutherford's dashiki was yellow and white, and wondered why I hadn't put two-and-two together when I saw it, and then sneaked home so I wouldn't be dropping flower petals as I walked across a creaking wood floor.

I threw a handful of flowers on the floor. Gail faced me. She placed her fingers at each end of her lips telling me to smile, and I did.

I stood right next to Rutherford while Reverend Moses said words over them, and then asked Esther if she'd take Rutherford to be her lawfully wedded husband.

"Yes," she said. "Of course I will."

Rutherford said yes, too, but he didn't ask me if I took either one of them, so why was I standing up there? The whole wedding lasted around five minutes. Unlike the weddings I'd attended before that lasted hours, with singing, reading poems, lighting candles, jumping brooms and crying family members.

All kinds of food covered the table in the library, and a white wedding cake sat in the middle of it. They'd removed all the boxes of books we hadn't opened to another room, and decorated the library in yellow and white, including the tablecloth. Mr. Thomas had smelled smothered steak, and greens, and mashed potatoes, and meatballs, and ham, and chicken wings, and a lot of other food. I wasn't hungry, and I didn't eat that day, not even a piece of wedding cake.

It was getting late, and I was ready to go. The festivities died down. Just us kids were running around and playing. The lawyer Walker was educating Esther and them on what to expect when she filed her papers to run for city council. I remembered the meeting at his office and wondered if Esther had married Rutherford so it would look right when she ran for city council. They'd talked about it at that meeting, but at the time, I didn't think they meant it. Mrs. Carrie told us to go out on the porch and play so they could hear lawyer Walker talk. I was surprised she didn't tell Malika and me to come in and listen to him. Malika would rather go play. I preferred to stay and take notes, but I was on good behavior and went on out to the porch.

Mr. Michael James King pulled up in his police car, and he and Mr. Sam Ray Blackburn got out and walked up to the porch before any of us could warn Esther and them. They both wore the same type of boots with spurs. The chief wore his uniform, and Mr. Sam Ray Blackburn had donned his usual outfit, Tuf-Nut jeans and a white shirt with silver studs around the collar. They walked straight to the door and opened it without speaking to us. We followed them inside. As soon as they got to the room where Esther and the others were, the chief started talking.

"What y'all doing up in here?" he said.

"Officer," the lawyer Walker stood up, "this is a private event, and unless you have reason to believe we are disturbing the peace, then you aren't welcome here."

"Who the hell is he?" Mr. Sam Ray Blackburn said. "We can go to any place we want to."

Gail acted overly proud to tell him. "He's attorney John Walker from the NAACP in Little Rock," she said.

Most folks at the Hall were familiar with the NAACP's role in the integration of Central High School. White people called them rabble-rousers. I didn't know if it was because Mr. Sam Ray Blackburn heard that the lawyer Walker was an attorney or that he worked for the NAACP, but whatever the reason, he went haywire. He picked up one of the folding chairs and slammed it against the wall. For the second time that day, a man cussed in front of women, children and Christians.

"What the hell you doing, Gail? You coming with us. Arrest her if you have to, Mike," he said.

"Sir," the lawyer Walker said.

"Don't sir me, boy. Who the hell do you think you talking to? Mike, get Gail and let's take her on out of here. Handcuff her if you have to." He slammed another chair against the wall, and spit flew from his mouth.

Mr. Michael James King looked as if arresting her were the last thing he wanted to do. He caught hold of Mr. Sam Ray Blackburn's arm and tried to lead him carefully toward the door. By then everybody had come to see what all of the commotion was about. They circled the walls of the room and stood in the doorway.

"We don't want no trouble," Mr. Michael James King said. "Let's go, Sam. We'll see to this at another time."

"Get her out of here, Mike. You got to do it now," he said.

"I will. I told you I would," the chief said. It sounded as if he were talking to a crying baby.

It took a while, and much cussing and fussing by Mr. Sam Ray Blackburn.

"Do you know how you disgracing your race over here with these bucks? You should be ashamed to call yourself a white woman. You just a nigger lover."

Eventually the chief's words seemed to soothe him, and he followed him toward the door. They both looked back at us while they walked to the door as if they were walking away from a set of wild hogs. Mr. Jonas told us they were gone, and the lawyer Walker tried to convince Gail to go back to Little Rock with him, but she didn't agree with him.

"Sam's rage is escalating," he said.

"Am I supposed to run every time I'm threatened?" Gail said. "Does that sound like freedom to you?"

The lawyer Walker threw up both his hands and walked away from her. He eyed Esther and Mrs. Carrie as if to tell them to talk some sense into her. I waited to see what they would do. Malika elbowed me to let me know she was paying attention too. They'd taught us to not be afraid, to stand up for what we believed and to die for it if we have to.

"We're all in danger, John," Esther said.

Esther didn't only talk the talk, but she walked the walk. Mrs. Carrie patted her on the shoulder. The lawyer Walker said his good-byes and warned us to be careful.

"Esther, Rutherford, congratulations. We have a good plan, as good as any, if you know what I mean," he said. "Those boys are stirred up, and we don't want any trouble here tonight. I don't think any of you should sleep here. I hope you heard him. They got a plan too."

"You right," Rutherford said. He started folding the chairs and placing them against the wall. "Let's get this place clean, and get all of y'all home."

Mrs. Carrie, Esther and Rutherford walked the lawyer Walker to his car. I stood at the screen door.

"You know we can't let fear rule us, John," Mrs. Carrie said.

Esther came over where me and Malika were standing.

"Are you girls okay?" she said. "We can take it from here. You run on home before it gets dark. I'll come and get you when we're done."

"Okay," I said to her, and then thanked God 'cause I was so ready to get out of there and go home.

I moved fast, getting my things together. She caught up with me to tell me the rest of it. "We're spending the first night in our new home, and we want you there with us. We might as well start our new life all together."

"Oh, hell, no," I said.

I placed my hand across my mouth. I hadn't meant for those words to come out, but I meant what I said. She'd sprung the wedding on me, and now this. She was crazier than Mr. Sam Ray Blackburn. I tried to talk, but nothing came out. I swallowed, and breathed hard till I collected myself. Then I told her what I'd been thinking all day.

"Esther, I don't mean any harm. Please forgive me for stepping out of my place, but I think your marriage to Rutherford is going to break Muhdea's heart into so many pieces she won't ever be able to fix it. And then if you say you taking me away from her, she will die. As for Granny, she just plain ain't going to stand for it." I turned the knob on the door and opened it. "I'm going home, and don't you even think about coming after me."

Malika caught my arm, and I pulled it away. She knew I was burning up and left me alone. Her, Miss Flora, Miss Pastel and their girls came out to the porch and watched as I stomped down the road on my way to tell Granny everything before Esther got there.

CHAPTER TWENTY-THREE

Miss Ora Bea Is Preaching

ESTHER FORCED ME to live with her and Rutherford. Granny and Muhdea didn't like it at all, but they didn't put up much of a fuss 'cause of what the Bible says. Esther threatened to get the courts involved, and calling in the law never turned out in favor of any colored person.

"It ain't much I can do till you turn thirteen," Granny said. "Bide your time till I figure out how to get you out of this mess."

I wanted to be as mad at them as I was with Esther, but I was tired of being mad, and it never helped me get my way.

Muhdea said their hands were tied. "If they weren't, believe me, you would be home with us. God and the law got us bound."

I didn't bring any of my toys, books or clothes, except a few of my everyday clothes, not even Chatty Cathy, who I kept with me whenever I was in the house. She read with me, played with me, helped me put the kids to sleep. Every night Esther tucked me into my wrought-iron twin bed, read me a story I could've read myself and wished me a good night's sleep, I felt alone even in the twin bed. I'd never slept in a bed by myself. I slept with Granny. I pushed my back up against the wall and rolled myself in the covers. When Esther went back to her room, Rutherford fussed at her. He fussed from the time they walked in the house, and all through dinner. I heard knocks against the wall and scuffling. Then when it quieted down, I heard them grunting, and then they fussed again before he started snoring. Esther crept to the bathroom and washed up. Running water in the house made bathing before I went to bed a whole lot easier. I'd still rather be at home with Granny, helping her bathe and change the babies, putting them down for the night, and kneeling beside her to pray before we turned in ourselves.

I waited a while after Esther came from the bathroom before I left. I unrolled myself out of the quilts, crawled across the creaky wood floor to the living room, feeling for splinters and Rutherford's African statues strewed across the room. While still on my knees, I opened the front door in the dark and crawled across the front porch and down the steps. As soon as my foot touched the ground, I got up and ran through the backyard, between the rows of Granny's garden and across her backyard to the back door. Granny left the door unlocked and waited for me in the kitchen.

"That you, Sarah?" Granny said every night.

The next morning, before anybody rose, I sneaked out of bed and back to Esther's house.

IT WAS THE fifth Sunday, and I went to the bedroom to get ready for Sunday school. Granny's dress was lying on the bed, the same dress she'd worn to the doctor that day we met the civil rights workers. She liked pleats, so Mrs. Martha made all of her dresses from the same pattern, but with different colors, plaid dresses, floral, solid blue and lilac. She made belts to match the dresses. She made her a new one every year, and since Granny never gained or lost weight, she owned quite a few of them.

I laid my white lace dress with the petticoat underneath on the bed next to Granny's dress. My dress buttoned down the back, and her buttons lined the front of her dress. Her panties lay next to her dress. I placed my white satin panties next to her white cotton ones. I wondered how long it would take me before I'd be able to fit into a pair of her bloomers. I picked up Granny's and held them to my waist. The tag inside her brassiere read "Playtex 34-C." I didn't own a brassiere. Mine were as flat as the bottom of a skillet. Some of the girls in my class wore training bras. I'd asked Granny if I could get one, but she said I didn't have nothing to train yet. I held her bra to my chest and figured it would be a long time before I needed that size. I picked my notebook up off the dark brown, wood dresser with a crack in the mirror from the left top corner to the bottom right, and wrote, *How many years will it take before I'll be able to fit into a size 34-C bra and a big pair of bloomers?*

Granny walked into the room wearing a faded peach robe with a raised applique of yellow and green flowers covering it, and hanging on by a thread.

"Sarah, put down that book and get your clothes on. I thought you'd be ready, then I come in here and find you sitting on the bed writing in that notebook."

She sat on the other bed and started greasing her legs with Vaseline. She handed the jar to me, and I did the same. Granny picked her panties up off the bed and put them on without taking off the robe. She picked her breasts up from hanging down near her waist and put them into the bra cups one at a time. "Hook me up," she said.

I pulled the robe down her back till I saw the bra and fastened the hook and eye. I got dressed exactly as she did, then asked her to button my dress. Watching Granny made me think of all the things I might not ever know. Things I didn't know whether she'd be around to tell me when I was old enough to understand. Like what women did with the red rubber bag with the long white cord hanging in the bathroom, and those pads in the lilac box that read Kotex, and why did they have strings at each end. When I asked, she said I was growing up too fast, and I should wait and let things come to me.

Granny slipped on her shoes. "Why you getting dressed up?" I said.

"I'm going to church."

"Sunday school, too? What for?"

"Yes, ma'am. Ora Bea preaching."

We called Miss Ora Bea and Mr. Stith jackleg preachers, meaning they didn't have no church of their own. Mr. Stith visited other churches and preached when the regular minister was sick or out of town or sometimes for no particular reason. Mr. Stith had ministered at our church before, but not Miss Ora Bea. She didn't even sit in the pulpit like the other preachers did when she visited. Why was Granny making an effort to go hear her? What could that be about? Granny only went to church on what she considered a special occasion. "God and me already handled our business here on earth," she said.

Granny didn't particularly care for being involved with a crowd of folks. She liked them plenty enough, but if too many of them got together weren't nothing but a whole lot of pretense and lies. Now she was putting on her newest dress to go hear Miss Ora Bea.

"What's so special about Miss Ora Bea preaching?" I said.

"Nothing much. There's been some folks saying they ain't going if she preaching. I like Ora Bea, and she got as much right to give the message as Jefferson or any them other men," she said.

Muhdea called me, and I left Granny sitting on the side of the bed putting on her shoes. As I walked in the living room, Mahalia Jackson was belting out "Go Tell It On the Mountain" from the portable radio. Muhdea told me to cut it off. Before I could turn the knob, Esther came through the door singing along with Mahalia. Her voice sounded just as good to me, which was one thing I didn't get from her. I couldn't sing a lick.

"Where you going?" I said.

She looked fly. Either red was her favorite, or it was the only color them short shorts and skirts came in. She wore a red miniskirt with three big silver buttons on each side. She couldn't have gotten a fourth button on there if she'd tried. Her blouse was white chiffon with the same smaller buttons, and she wore a pair of white boots. I didn't understand her wearing boots in the summertime, but she said, "These boots are made for walking," and since, according to her, me or nobody else in town had any fashion sense, I let it go. As far as I was concerned, even though they were white, my feet would sweat and eventually stink in them.

"Where you going?" Muhdea said.

"Church," Esther said.

"Ump," Muhdea said. "It might burn down today since the Devil going to be there." Muhdea didn't have a good word for nobody since she got mad at Granny for keeping secrets from her. "My whole life was one big story," Muhdea said.

"Takes one to know one," Esther said.

"You calling me the Devil? Honestly, Esther, the Lord don't want to see you looking like that in church. It's disrespectful."

Granny's voice came from the back room. "Esther, stir that pot of greens for me, and check to see if that stick of wood burned out. All the food should be done," she said. "We'll be able to eat as soon as we get back. You staying for supper? 'Cause if you is, Muhdea won't be able to invite Jefferson and his wife."

Granny hoped Esther would say she was having supper with us. Reverend and Mrs. Jefferson ate at our house every first, third and fifth Sunday, when service was held at our church. It was the fifth Sunday of the month. If I'd gotten baptized, I would already be at the church practicing with the choir. The young adult choir sang every fifth Sunday. I just knew by now I'd have my gold robe with my name written on a tag at the neck, as if it were store-bought. But no, 'cause of Miss Hot-Pants-Wearing Esther, Crazy Abigail (sorry, we can't call her crazy no more) got my secretary job, and I wasn't ever fitted for a robe. I got hot just thinking about it.

"Esther, you burning the greens," I said.

She took the pot off the stove when Granny told her, but some of the greens and liquor dropped on the wood. "I got it, Sarah," she said. "Step back before one of the sparks lands on your dress."

I didn't know why Granny told her to do it. She acted as if she never put out no coals before.

"It'd probably be easier if your pants weren't so short," I said. I knew one thing didn't have anything to do with the other, but I wanted to be sassy with her anyway for having the nerve to wear that outfit to First Baptist. Reverend Jefferson just wouldn't be Reverend Jefferson if he didn't mention it, and Muhdea wouldn't be herself if she didn't get embarrassed and seek sympathy from the other mothers in the church. Esther insisted on peace and nonviolence down at the Hall, but she seemed to come in our house stirring up nothing less than the war over there in Vietnam. I might have to live with her and Rutherford, but neither one of them could make me bring my clothes to their house.

"Come on, Sarah, we ready to go," Granny said. "Esther, be sure to drown out the fire before you leave. We'll see you over there. You look nice."

I grabbed my book satchel. Now that Granny had started asking questions about what I was writing, I'd better keep it with me wherever I go.

"Ump," Muhdea said as we lined up and marched outside, me and Granny each carrying a baby on our hip. I'd be glad when Muhdea stopped being mad at Granny. She would've told me, "Don't hold on to it. Water under the bridge." We left Muhdea and Esther at the house arguing. Muhdea wanted to know why her husband wasn't going to church with her.

We were early, and still there was hardly a seat left. More folks than Granny thought had come to see Miss Ora Bea preach. Granny told me to save Esther a seat beside me. When Esther got there, Reverend Jefferson dismissed us to go to our appropriate Sunday-school classrooms.

"What took you so long? I thought you were right behind us." I said.

Miss Ora Bea taught the adult women's class that Sunday. Esther was in her class. They received the banner for the most money collected, and the number of people present. For people who didn't want her to preach, they show collected a lot of money.

Reverend Jefferson stood at the podium and told us we would be going promptly into the eleven o'clock service 'cause of our special guest speaker. He read the benediction for Sunday school, and then read the opening verses to begin church service. Deacon Allen rang the church bell as Reverend Jefferson continued to read. So many folks showed up at church that Reverend Jefferson asked some of the children to take a seat in the choir stand, and in the balcony. I was one of them. I sat on the last row of the choir stand, where I would have sat every Sunday if I were a member. A room was on each side of the pulpit. On the right side was the choir room, where the mothers kept the grape juice and crackers for sacrament. They set up before service started and covered it with a white tablecloth. Wearing white caps, dresses, stockings and shoes, they marched out of the choir room and took their seat on the first row of pews.

The choir sang two songs before taking their seats. By chance, I sat next to Crazy Abigail. Reverend Jefferson read a few scriptures from the book of Ruth. He said she was a heroine. I generally fell asleep right after he finished reading the scriptures.

The visiting ministers walked out of the pastor's study on the left side of the pulpit and took their seat in the pulpit. Where was Miss Ora Bea? I elbowed Crazy Abigail in the side, and asked her. She shook her head. I rose up and looked around the whole church. Miss Ora Bea was sitting on the pew with the mothers. She wore the most beautiful deep purple robe with gold and red tassels hanging down her chest. I was in awe of how royal she looked. I pointed her out to Abigail.

"She ain't preaching?" I whispered.

Abigail placed her finger to her lips and shushed me. I rolled my eyes at her. Reverend Jefferson finally came to the podium and introduced Miss Ora Bea as if she were sitting in the pulpit with him. I turned my head back and forth from him to her, looking as if she were a fairy godmother seated between the church mothers. When Reverend Jefferson finished giving her very high praises, which included her studies at AM&N College, Miss Ora Bea rose in her velvet robe and walked to the announcement podium. I stood up. It was hard to see her from the choir stand. I turned to Abigail again, and she put her finger to her lips before I could get out a word.

"Women can't sit in the pulpit. It's a sin," a choir member said.

I knew it was a sin for us to play in the pulpit, and only preachers were allowed to walk or sit up there, but Reverend Jefferson had just called her a preacher. Mr. Stith was the same type of minister as she was, and he was in the pulpit. I perked up to listen to what she had to say. Her style was similar to all the preachers I'd heard before. She read a scripture from the book of Ruth, and then announced her topic. Her voice was so light I couldn't make out what she was saying, till she got toward the end, and banged her fist on the podium, and got louder and louder like Reverend Jefferson did.

I noticed the usher whisper to Muhdea, she passed it on to Granny, and they left the church at the height of Miss Ora Bea's sermon. What had she said to them? Within a few minutes, the entire men's side of the church was empty. Miss Ora Bea stopped right in the middle of an "uh-hump."

One of the ushers whispered to her, and another one walked toward the pulpit, holding up his right hand and index finger. He wore black pants, white shirt, black shoes, white gloves and a black bowtie. Reverend Jefferson rose out of his chair, where he had half gotten up and down all during Miss Ora Bea's sermon, and met the usher. Then he stood at the podium and wiped sweat beads from his forehead with his white handkerchief.

"I'm going to give the benediction now. Please repeat after me," he said. "May the Lord watch between me and you while we are absent one from the other." He raised his hands. "Now let us all say, amen." As soon as we said amen, Reverend Jefferson said, "The Whites' house is on fire. We all need to get over there and help out right now. Deacon Allen went for the fire department." Everybody was almost out the door when he said, "Men start a water line. We all need to pitch in."

By the time I found Granny, most every colored person in town had surrounded our house. Thank God, we lived next to the church. I stood between Muhdea and Granny. The mothers took care of the rest of the children. Esther came up behind me. I hadn't seen her since Sunday school.

"Did you drown the fire in the stove?" I said. I moved nearer to her.

"What?" she said.

Tears formed in my eyes. Our house burned faster than newspaper. I asked her again.

"Don't start," she said.

Muhdea broke away from the mothers, who were fanning and comforting her, and ran toward the house screaming, "My children, my children."

Me and Esther caught her by the arm. She thought one of us was inside. We pointed out every child before she settled down.

The men started two water lines, one from our hydrant and one from our next-door neighbor's. I didn't know where they got all of the buckets. Young men traded out with the old and vice versa when they got tired. Their work didn't have much effect on the fire.

"Looks like it started in the back," one of the men said when he came off the line.

I shivered for Esther. She was going to be in a whole bunch of trouble.

"We think we can manage it if the fire trucks hurry up," another one said.

From where we stood, I choked on the smoke, and it burned my eyes. Other folks coughed and rubbed their eyes. Folks from the low end of town and the civil rights workers came to help, but the fire department was nowhere in sight.

"Where's the fire department?" Rutherford said. "They should be here by now."

Around the same time, Deacon Allen returned. "You might want to go talk to them. They taking their time," he said to Reverend Jefferson.

"Did you tell the chief?" Reverend Jefferson said.

Deacon Allen nodded. "He said he couldn't make them leave church. They be here as soon as he could get enough of them rounded up."

White men volunteered at the fire department, and colored men helped out once the truck arrived. Flames blazed from the back of our house and out the top of the tin roof. Pieces of tin curled back. Whenever the men controlled one area, fire broke out in another one. Then after a loud boom, black smoke and flames whooshed up over the house and covered the blue sky. Every available man ran and got in the water line. The faster they threw buckets of water on the house, the quicker it burned. The heat scorched my face.

Reverend Jefferson came off the line with Deacon Allen. "Come on," he said. "They got to do something before any more houses catch fire." They headed toward town.

I prayed the fire wouldn't get anymore out of hand.

Esther started hollering and crying, "We're losing everything. Help us, Lord. We're losing everything."

She scared me. Granny held my hand real tight. Muhdea turned and, without saying a word, walked toward the fire department. Miss Ora Bea followed her.

In one big swoop of fire, the tin roof broke loose and dropped to the ground. I loved listening to the rain tap on the tin. I looked up at Granny and saw the reflection of the fire in her eyes. I smelled the tar and brick siding burn. Sparks flew out everywhere. Women backed away in fear, and the men couldn't get close enough to throw water on the house any longer. It reminded me of when we burned a hog's hair after slaughter. It crackled tons louder than the fat meat we cooked down to make grease and pork skins. All anybody could do was stand and watch it burn.

"If the fire truck would just get here," a man said.

"You think they rush for us?" a lady said. "They don't care nothing 'bout our property."

When I thought it couldn't get any worse, Rutherford yelled for the men to come to the church. "The church is burning. Grab your buckets."

One man grabbed the water hose, and the others lined up with their buckets. All the women and children stood in the middle of the road. The church steeple with the bell inside fell down into the church, and lit it like it was a big match. The whole church caught fire. We watched as the choir robes and the pulpit went up in flames. Something about seeing the choir robes burn made me realize that my stuff was burning up, too. I shook my hand loose from Granny's and ran toward the house. If I couldn't save nothing else, I must get Chatty Cathy and the whatnots Uncle Robert had given me. I ran toward the house, but Esther grabbed the tail of my dress and held on to it.

"It's too late, Sarah," she said.

Somehow I knew. I laid my head on her chest and sobbed. People mumbled among themselves.

"You think Esther Mae's association with them civil rights workers got anything to do with them coming so late?" one of the deacons said.

"You know it is. I bet they set fire to it 'cause of her," a woman said.

It was as if somebody lit a match to his words, and they spread like the fire from one person to the next. I knew if I'd heard it, Granny had too, but she just held my hand tighter as tears rolled down her face. I tried to get her to let go of my hand so I could tell them off, but she wouldn't, and I fought with her. I wrapped my arms around my waist. My gut felt contorted like a swizzle stick. My legs softened like overcooked rice. Tears streamed down Muhdea's and Esther's faces, and I heard the babies crying in the distance. I heard folks say our house was set on fire 'cause Esther got mixed up with the civil rights workers. It was a warning from the white folks. And if the whites didn't set fire to it 'cause of Esther, she show was the reason they were late coming and let the church burn to the ground.

Reverend Jefferson and Deacon Allen walked fast down the trail and crossed the road. They stood in front of the church and watched the fire blazing through the windows and roof. Reverend Jefferson took off his hat and kneeled, Deacon Allen followed suit, and soon we all kneeled and prayed in front of the burning church. Not long afterward, the fire department showed up, and demanded we move out of their way.

"I knew it would go fast," one of the men on the truck said. "We can't save these paper-thin shacks."

"Where were you? Is this how you treat Negroes? It was their home, their church," Rutherford said.

The volunteer firemen, and the men who were already there, went about their work and put out the fire at our house and at the church. The charred black frames leaned to the right as if they were going to topple over. Miss Ora Bea walked from person to person, still wearing her royal robe, and held their hands, or touched their shoulders, and comforted them with Bible scriptures and prayer.

It seemed as if the world went around and around with me on it, speeding faster and faster.

CHAPTER TWENTY-FOUR

Power to the People

I WOKE UP in my bed at Esther and Rutherford's house. Granny sat on the edge of the bed with a face pan of cool water and a washrag. She wrung it out and placed it on my forehead.

"Wake up, Sarah," she said. She picked up the smelling salts and placed them under my nose.

"It stinks," I said.

"Finally. You had me scared for a minute," she said. She sat with me for a few minutes, touched my head to see if I had a fever and asked me a few more questions to make sure I was fine before she let the others know I was okay. "Y'all, Sarah woke," she yelled.

"Did we save anything?" I said.

"The house burned clean to the ground. Ain't nothing left except the junk house and that glass you and Esther put around the hydrant. It still shining as if everything didn't burn down around it."

"Mosaic," I said. "We made a mosaic." She stared at me and didn't say anything. "And the church?"

"Same as the house, the grass and all. Just burned." Her voice broke.

"Ain't that something?" I said. "What about Chatty Cathy?

"I'm sorry, Sarah." I swallowed the tears, two, three times. I noticed Esther and the others standing in the doorway as I was about to doze off again.

Granny shushed them away. "Let her sleep," she said. "She'll be alright."

I beckoned them to come on in 'cause I couldn't take the sadness.

That night was the first time I spent the whole night at Esther and Rutherford's house. Granny and two of the kids slept in the twin bed with me. She and one of the girls slept foot-to-head, and me and another one slept head-to-foot. Granny's foot slapped me in the face. One of the babies rested in her arms.

When I woke up, Muhdea was agitated with somebody in the kitchen. Bacon and Folgers coffee smells swirled through the house. One good thing to come out of our house burning down was we were all back together again, Esther too. Rutherford fussed at Muhdea like he did with Esther, but Muhdea gave him word for word where Esther never said much of anything back to him.

"How you feeling, Sarah?" Muhdea said when I walked into the kitchen. She handed me a baby. "Change him and come on back and eat breakfast," she said.

"We don't eat pork in this house," Rutherford said. "If you stay here, we got to have ground rules."

"I ain't arguing with you no more 'bout it," Muhdea said. "Don't you have some work to do down there at the Hall? 'Cause you show in my way here."

Rutherford was in a battle he had no chance of winning, and he didn't know it. He'd brought up a subject that was a battle between her and Uncle Robert, and she wasn't nowhere near over him yet.

"Listen to me, Mozelle," he said.

"That's Mrs. to you," she said. "And you listen to me. It's meat, and we eat whatever meat we got. Our house just burned to the ground, and you want to be choosy about what type of meat I can cook in here? Rutherford, whatever your name is, boy, you better get out of my face right now." She focused her attention on me. I'd gotten stuck listening to their argument and forgot to take cover. "What you waiting on? You think the baby planning on changing himself?"

Unlike Rutherford, I knew when Muhdea was on a rampage, and I scattered. I knew to stay out of her way for the rest of the day, and maybe the next day, too. Thank goodness the baby didn't start crying, or she would've gotten him straight, too. Not even Granny would try to calm Muhdea down when she was like that, but Rutherford kept trying to get his point across. Stupid.

A few minutes later Rutherford slammed a plate on the table, and Muhdea came into the bedroom. "Sarah, stay here and keep an eye on things while I go over to the house to meet the insurance man," she said. "I don't know how your mama put up with that boy.".

The Georgia insurance man had come by our house every month for as long as I could remember to collect life insurance, which I couldn't understand why they didn't call it death insurance, or funeral insurance, 'cause that's what folks used the money for. Hadn't nobody died, and it wasn't the time of the month to pay him, so I wasn't sure why she was meeting him. I would've asked her, or followed her over to the house to see for myself, if she hadn't been riled up.

"Yes ma'am," I said. "I'll watch them."

Rutherford, on the other hand, challenged her authority every chance he got.

"You telling Sarah, a child, to watch over my house?" he said.

"Boy, if you don't get the hell out of my way and leave me alone before I lose my religion," Muhdea said. "Your house? Huh," she said and walked out of the door.

I'd seen Muhdea riled up many times, but she never ever cussed. I came in the living room where Rutherford was sitting on the brown velvet couch drinking from a scrunched brown paper sack like the one I saw him and Reverend Adam Moses pass back and forth. Esther's house was cute, and she kept it clean. It was shaped like most of the shotgun houses around town, but her, Rutherford and the folks from the Hall had fixed it up, and it didn't look old and run-down like some folks' did. The furniture was practically new, mostly donated. The baby rested on my hip. Rutherford stared at us as if he wished we'd disappear.

"She preparing you to get pregnant before you graduate high school," Rutherford said. "Why don't you try being more like your mother?"

"She had me before she graduated high school," I said.

"You got a smart-ass mouth like your grandmother." He turned the sack up to his mouth.

"What you got in that bag?"

"Grown folks' business," he said.

I turned my nose up at him. I didn't want to know anyway. "You a mean man," I said and headed for the door. "Now you can watch over your own house and these children." I'd rather have Muhdea fuss at me than spend one more second looking at him scratch his bumpy face and drink something that made him even meaner.

"Where you going?" he said.

"Grown folks' business," I said and slammed the door.

I ran across the backyard, pulled up the fence and crawled under it, and carefully walked between the rows of squash and cucumber in the garden. In August, the garden was dry after a good harvest and waiting for the soil to be tilled for winter planting. I found Granny and Muhdea standing in the front yard looking at black burnt wood. Before Muhdea started yelling at me, I told her why I was there.

"I got to go down to the Hall," I said.

Muhdea told me that there wasn't anything for me to worry about. We'd have our home within a month or two. I could even go to Pine Bluff with her to pick it out at the Jim Walter's home lot.

"We won't have to build it from the ground up," she said. "We go pick it out, and they'll bring it down here in two parts already put together."

"How will they do that?" I said.

"You seen them on the back of them trailers on the highway with a big "wide load" sign."

I'd seen them before. They were slower than a train. I waited for one of them to go by before I could cross the highway once. It was hot, and they were so slow I almost fainted.

"Remember when Sister Tucker told you they brought the school buildings from McGhee on a couple of them trailers?" Muhdea said.

I knew our school buildings came from the Japanese concentration camps, but I never thought of how they got there. Granny looked as if that were something she never wanted to remember.

"What I remember is the one building falling off the truck when the driver stopped short," Granny said.

"Well, I don't think that's going to happen to our house. You see how good Deborah B's house held up," Muhdea said.

"Yeah, but that one building ain't never stood up straight," Granny said. She was right about that. It leaned over worse than the

Leaning Tower of Pisa. I always wondered if it was leaning like that when the Japanese lived in it. Granny changed the subject.

"Sarah, you better get on down to the Hall before your mama have a fit. Change your clothes first."

I waved at the men over at the church. It was burned as bad as our house. Reverend Jefferson and a few of the men tipped around the smoldering wood and sprinkled water on it with a hose.

"I see you woke up," Reverend Jefferson said.

"Yes, sir," I said. "And I'm feeling just fine."

When I walked up the steps at Esther's house, I heard music coming from inside. I pulled open the screen door, and Rutherford and Reverend Adam Moses were standing on top of the coffee table singing loud. I thought they were the ones on the record player, but then I saw the little box with a round vinyl album spinning around and around. It must've belonged to Reverend Adam Moses. Both of them, Rutherford and Reverend Adam Moses, passed the paper bag as they sang along with Mr. Smokey Robinson. I knew that 'cause one or the other of them inadvertently said, "Can't that Smokey Robinson sang? And don't forget the Miracles."

When Mr. Robinson started singing the lead, Rutherford took the bag from Reverend Adam Moses, stood in front of him on the table, and sang into the bag as if it were a microphone.

"Before you ask some girl for her hand now, keep your freedom for as long as you can now," Rutherford sang loudly, words slurred, and Reverend Adam Moses said, "Go 'head there, Rutherford, sang it."

They sang the chorus together as they stepped from side to side, erasing the hand wax Muhdea had applied earlier, and replacing it with shoe prints. I didn't know how Reverend Adam Moses kept his house, but Rutherford better be ready to be in a whole bunch of trouble.

"Give it to me. Give it here," Reverend Adam Moses said when Mr. Smokey Robinson took the lead again.

"Ah, man, I was just getting my groove," Rutherford said.

Reverend Adam Moses took a drink from the bag before he stood in front of Rutherford, and this time, he sang from his gut. I couldn't move from the door. They were as funny as anybody I'd ever seen on TV, but for some reason, I didn't laugh with them. Rutherford slipped and fell off the coffee table.

"You alright, man?" Reverend Adam Moses said. He extended his hand to help Rutherford up onto the table. I shook my head and wished Muhdea and Granny could see them.

"Come on, Sarah," Reverend Adam Moses said. "Sing with us."

I thought it would be best if I didn't change clothes, got the children, and went on down to the Hall.

"No, sir. No, thank you," I said.

"You see how she is?" Rutherford said.

Reverend Adam Moses started singing "We Shall Overcome," and Rutherford joined in with him. I gathered up the kids to take to Muhdea. Then I turned and left before Rutherford could start in on me. How could he talk? He was a bigger kid than I'd ever been.

THE MAEBY CITIZENS for Progress included me and the others who came to the Hall with their mothers, and the ones who were going to attend the white school, and SNCC, NAACP and other potential members. We met every Friday night, especially since we were getting ready to attend the white school. That night Esther was supposed to address folks' gossip. Some of them said outright that the firemen let our house and the church burn down 'cause they were trying to scare us into not going to white school. Rutherford said he believed they set fire to it in the first place, so why would they come put it out, and others agreed with him, including the lawyer Walker, and other SNCC workers from Pine Bluff and Little Rock who were present at every meeting now, and would be till school started in the fall.

I was on my way to the Hall when I saw Reverend Jefferson round the corner about the same time as I did.

"You coming to the meeting?" I said.

"Well, not exactly," he said.

It was the first time I'd been alone with him since I became a snitch.

"Reverend Jefferson, folks say the white people probably burned down our house and the church, and if they didn't start it, they let it burn down anyway, but folks can't come up with no good reason why they let the church burn 'cause whites don't really have nothing against you. But . . ."

"Hold on," he said. "Stop right there. That's just malicious gossip. I'm here to put a stop to it now."

I wrung my hands together, and started my times tables in my head. "I think they might've burned it down. Maybe they thought we had information and didn't give it to them."

Twelve times five equals sixty, and so does ten times six, and three times twenty. I tried to clear my head by thinking of every number I could multiply that equaled sixty. I drew a blank and decided to try a different number to keep me from hearing whatever Reverend Jefferson might say that would keep me from telling him that the whites set the house on fire 'cause I didn't tell him Esther was getting married and running for city council. I interrupted him before I lost my nerve.

"I didn't tell you Esther and Rutherford were getting married, or Esther is planning to run for city council. That's what the white folks found out, and it's the reason why they burned down our house and the church caught fire."

His eyes all but popped out of his head, rolled around on the ground, and stood up and stared back at him.

"Esther Mae is doing what?"

I ignored his question.

"We can stop spying on Esther now. Everything is out in the open. I'll go to the white school. You and Muhdea don't have to protect me any longer."

I twisted the toe of my shoe in the rocks. Reverend Jefferson placed both of his hands in his pant pockets. He looked as if he didn't know what else to say to me. He was dumbfounded. Reverend Jefferson didn't say another word. He caught my hand and walked inside the Hall.

I looked back down the road and saw Rutherford and Reverend Adam Moses walking fast. If it were Muhdea and Granny, I would've ran back to meet them. But Rutherford wasn't one to find safety in. Running back to him was like sticking my head in the lions' den. I was surprised to see him arriving on time. Rutherford hadn't come to a meeting on time since everybody voted for Esther to run for city council, and for her to lead the meetings instead of Rutherford. Gail said the whole thing was a slap in the face to Rutherford. He wanted to run for office. He was the man, not Esther, which was what he said every time they got into a fight at home at night.

"Wearing pants doesn't make you a man, and don't you forget it," he said more times than I cared to remember. There was no mistaking Esther for a man, which was what most of the men at the Hall said at one time or another.

Esther stood at the podium in the living room. The civil rights workers called it the workroom, or meeting room. When we weren't having a meeting, picket signs and all the paraphernalia we used to make them were strewn across the floor and along the walls. Rutherford loved to say "paraphernalia" every chance he got. Me and Malika would be working on a sign, and six out of nine times we could guess when he was going to say it. Just as I was thinking about it, Rutherford and Reverend Adam Moses opened the door wide and were talking loud. They stood right behind us. Reverend Jefferson tried to shush them, to no avail.

Standing to one side of the room near the windows were some of the deacons from First Baptist Church. Mr. Peter Everett was propped up against the wall, leaning on his shoulder. He moved a dip of snuff from side to side with his tongue. Next to him was deacon and superintendent Matthew Graves. He looked smaller in stature next to Mr. Everett than he did when I used to sit next to him at the table during Sunday school. Reverend Jefferson walked over and stood near them. Deacon Graves placed his long fingers on his shoulder. He gave a brief handshake to each one of the men from First Baptist, twelve in all. I counted.

Most of the regulars were seated in front of them in folding chairs on the first five rows, along with the lawyer Walker, and the other civil rights workers from out of town. Mrs. Carrie sat on the first row next to the lawyer Walker. Gail and most of the students sat on the floor against the wall. It was a little after seven according to the clock hanging on the wall behind Esther. Malika scooted over and beckoned me to sit next to her, and I did. Bro Hollin walked in and stood near the door.

Esther said we were fortunate that both Muhdea's house and the church were insured.

"Although they were both insured, they weren't covered 100 percent," she said. She pulled her hair away from her face. A few strands stuck to her red lipstick. She took a moment to fuss with it, pulled it away as if it irritated her. It happened all the time. By now, she should've known to pull it back in a rubber band, but instead she laid it across her red blouse, and as she spoke she moved it from one side to the other. "That means we will all have to pitch in and help rebuild the house and the church."

"The first fish fry is set for Saturday and Sunday," Deacon Graves said. "There's a signup sheet in the kitchen for all y'all who need a ride to the river. We want to see plenty of poles in the water 'cause catfish biting real good right now."

When everybody was done agreeing with Esther and was sure of the whereabouts of the signup sheet, the lawyer Walker stood and talked about the fire.

"We can continue to speculate about how and why the fire started," he said. "We also have concerns as to why the fire department failed to adhere to their responsibilities. Until earlier this week, we quietly and slowly forged ahead, but now that's over. We will have to move forward cautiously but quickly."

That caused a stir in the room. Folks began to talk among themselves. They wondered whose house would be next. By the time Esther got them settled down, Reverend Jefferson made his way to the podium, and Esther stepped to the side as if we were at First Baptist Church. He raised his right hand to quiet the folks who were still talking, and they shut up the same as they would've at church. Then he told them that he would be brief, which could mean anywhere from a few minutes to a few hours.

"Me and my members came here to ask you to put an end to these gatherings before anything else happens, before somebody gets hurt," he said. "And I'm going to ask you kindly to withdraw your petition for these kids to go over there to the white school. This has gone far enough."

The lawyer Walker stood, and adjusted his navy blue suit jacket and skinny blue tie before he spoke. He told us that it was too late to revert our plans. The courts controlled whether we went to the white school or not, and they'd already spoken on it. Then he posed the question to Reverend Jefferson directly.

"Who do you believe started the fire?" he said.

Reverend Jefferson grunted and scratched his head. He eyed the men from the church. They all nodded.

"Well, I ain't here to place blame," he said. "But it don't matter who struck the match. We all know who started the fire."

"Who?" The word filtered throughout the room like dominos falling. Folks speculated, but nobody was sure of who or how it started. Reverend Jefferson had captured our attention the same as he did when he spoke at church. He reared back and stretched his neck like he did when he was close to the end of his sermon, after he reeled us in, and was near planting his message for us to chew on all week.

"Everybody in here know we were doing just fine till Sister Esther Mae come back home," he said. "She done come back with her sinning ways and brought all this evil down on us."

He went on to talk about the days of Sodom and Gomorrah, when people didn't abide by the laws of the Bible, when they thought they could go their own way and build what they wanted, leaving God smack out of it.

"You right, Reverend" and "Amen, Reverend" echoed through the room. Some folks looked shocked by what he was saying. I thought he was wrong to say Esther was the reason for the fires. Reverend Jefferson hit his stride, encouraged by his deacons and a few traitors who were new to the Hall and working for equal rights.

"Esther Mae, we tried, and there ain't no saving you. The only thing that can help you is if you pack up and leave town never to return, and take these other folks you brought here with you."

He took out his handkerchief and wiped the sweat from his brow.

"You need to leave town by the end of the week, and if you don't respect us enough to do it on your own, we won't mind helping you."

The twelve deacons from First Baptist said "Amen" in unison, and clapped as if they were in church. Folks said some nasty things, called her out of her name, and a sinner. I thought the men might pick her up and carry her off to Chicago right then and there. They moved closer to the front, caught under Reverend Jefferson's spell. He raised his hands, his palms facing them as if he were a school crossing guard. They continued to edge toward the front.

"I think she should leave tonight before we all end up sleeping in the road," one man said.

"He right," another one said.

When me and Malika stood up, I still couldn't see past the men. I crawled around their legs till I was up front standing beside Reverend Jefferson and Esther. The grown folks' eyes glared at me, and anger streamed from some of them. Malika crawled behind me and stood by my side. The lawyer Walker remained seated, but Mrs. Carrie stood up. It was a quiet anger, respectful, no voices raised, or speaking out of turn, but tension filled the room like it did when my cousins and me waited for Muhdea to punish us.

"Reverend Jefferson," I said, but he didn't hear me. I spoke up. "It's not her fault," I said louder and everybody heard me. "Esther didn't cause the fire."

He scratched the right side of his face. "Sarah, you don't know what you talking about."

"Yes, sir, I do know Esther didn't do nothing wrong. She ain't no more a sinner than you or the deacons. Don't the Bible tell us to forgive everybody? How come we can't forgive Esther? Ain't she one of God's children like you?"

"This is grown folks' business, Sarah, and nobody here gave

you permission to speak," Reverend Jefferson said. He bent down and whispered in my ear, "You better shut your mouth. Don't say another word."

I tried to tell him it was our fault. That Mr. Sam Ray Blackburn knew I didn't tell on Esther and Rutherford. He pushed my face to his pant leg to muffle my voice. I bit his leg. He yelped but didn't let go of my head. I wiggled from underneath his hand.

"It's our fault, not Esther's," I yelled. "We the ones should be ran out of town."

Before I could continue, Mrs. Carrie spoke up. "Please settle down," she said. "We don't know who started the fire or why it was started. It could have been faulty wiring. Pearlie cooks every Sunday, so it could've been a spark from the firewood. We don't know. All we do know is the fire department did not come to our rescue, and that's enough to be angry about. Please, let's stick to what we know, and not blame others for what we don't know. Isn't that right, Reverend Jefferson?"

He let go of my head and stuttered, "I reckon you got a point. I'm just so upset about the church."

Him and the deacons lowered their heads and backed down. Reverend Jefferson looked like Crazy Abigail did when she peed on herself in class. He seemed to be fishing for the words to say when I heard Rutherford's voice come from the back of the room.

"Now take that and get out of here," he said.

"You got that right," Reverend Adam Moses screamed.

Reverend Jefferson was wrong, but Rutherford didn't have no room to talk. Folks cut their eyes at him as if to tell him not to say another mumbling word against Reverend Jefferson, especially the men from the church. Whether he was right or wrong, he was our pastor. Reverend Jefferson cut his eyes back in their direction.

"Moses, now I know you know better. You and that boy need to stop acting the way y'all been around here, and please put that bottle down. It's embarrassing."

"You don't know nothing 'bout what I'm doing," Reverend Adam Moses slurred. "At least I'm standing for the cause. What you doing, Jefferson? Standing in our way as always."

Reverend Jefferson gathered up the deacons, and they headed toward the door. He turned back and pleaded with Esther.

"Please, Sister Jones, I'm begging you to put a stop to this before somebody gets hurt. We were lucky this time. We only lost material things. If you keep this up, we just might lose some lives, and don't none of us want that to happen. It ain't too late, Miss Esther. It ain't too late for y'all to leave town now."

When Esther first came home, I would've given up my religion for him to tell her to leave town. But now I understood some of what she tried to do. I might not want to live with her and that mean Rutherford, but I wanted her to help us get equal rights. After Reverend Jefferson and the church members left, Esther closed the door behind them and settled down the regulars. She reassured us we would be alright, and we should remember we were working toward a greater good; whatever happened to us individually, we needed to persevere without fear of the unknown. Regardless of Reverend Jefferson's request, we were proceeding as planned.

"Power to the people," Esther yelled and held her fist up high.

We repeated it. "Power to the people."

"We fear no one," she said. We repeated it.

Rutherford came and stood by her side. She whispered in his ear. He didn't seem to like what she said. "I can stand wherever I want," he said.

She whispered in his ear again.

"You don't know nothing. You can't tell me what to do," he said. He stormed across the room, stepped over and on some folks who were seated on the floor, and slammed the door behind him. Reverend Adam Moses followed him. Esther continued as if he hadn't interrupted her.

"I have a confession," she said. "Please settle down." It seemed as if she were going to cry. I got up and stood beside her. She held my hand.

"Go ahead, Miss Esther," Mrs. Carrie said.

"I can't allow you to continue to believe the white man set Muhdea's house on fire. It wasn't them," she said.

Silence fell over the room. "Who was it then?" a voice said from the back, and folks started mumbling among themselves. Esther squeezed my hand tighter.

"I did it," she said. She lifted her head and looked out at them. "I got a light off the stove to burn the trash outside in the barrel. I thought I saw a piece of the paper fly off, but when I looked for it, I couldn't find it. I assumed I didn't see it and went on to church. I believe now it did happen. As a matter of fact, I'm quite sure of it," she said.

"Why didn't you say something in the first place?" a man said.

"I wasn't sure, and I didn't think the community would be so afraid. I'm sorry, very sorry," she said.

LATER THAT NIGHT, when everybody left the Hall, me and Esther walked home together. She held my hand as we strolled down Back Street toward home. I looked up at her stained red lipstick.

"I wasn't scared like the other folks," I said.

"What, Sarah?" she said.

"I wasn't ever afraid to go to the white school. I just didn't want to go. I wanted to stay at the colored school with my friends, but it's okay now. I still don't want to go, but I guess we have to. We have to, like the children did in Little Rock," I said.

"Sarah," she said as she held my face between her hands. "I should've allowed you to get baptized. I shouldn't have pulled you off the Mourner's Bench. I should've known you were smart enough to figure it out. I'm sorry. Will you forgive me?"

We talked about all kinds of things as we held hands, swung our arms back and forth, and walked home. She explained her reasoning. She'd thought I was too young to get baptized. She didn't think I knew what I was doing. She didn't know me. She thought Granny and Muhdea were wrong for allowing me to do it in the first place. She was angry at them, but mostly she didn't know our ways, she didn't know me.

"All the wrong reasons," she said. "But then I turned around and put you in the same position with the movement. You're too young to fight this battle, too. I don't know what I'm doing anymore. Nothing seems to be working."

When we got home, Granny and Muhdea were sitting at the table talking. Muhdea hadn't spoken a word to Granny since she found out Granny was a civil rights activist when she was young. Granny had tried to talk to her, explain, but Muhdea looked at her sideways, rolled her eyes, and sashayed away. I wondered if Muhdea was ever going to talk to her again. When I tried to talk to her about forgiveness, which was what she preached most of the time, she shushed me, and told me to mind my own business. Even during the fire, and afterward, she barely said a word to Granny. When Granny tried to get her to talk, she blew her off. I tried to intervene, and Muhdea stopped talking to me for a few days. After that, I stayed out of it. Granny said she'd come around. Give her time. Watching them laugh and talk at the table that night made me feel everything was alright again.

"Good, y'all talking," Esther said.

They sneered at her and then laughed about it.

"Don't say a word, Sarah," Muhdea said. They found that funny, too.

I hugged each of them around the neck.

"Took y'all long enough," I said.

"Didn't I say don't say a word?" they said.

Esther came back to the kitchen from the bedroom.

"Has Rutherford been here?" she said.

Me and Esther sat down at the table. I laid my head on Granny's lap.

"No telling where he and Reverend Adam Moses went," Esther said. "He is becoming impatient with our lack of progress."

"It can't help that we all piled in here on you," Muhdea said. "But we getting one of those prefab Jim Walter homes. The man said we can move in a little over a month from now."

I hugged Granny around the neck again. She stirred her tooth-brush in the snuff jar and placed it in her mouth. "The other good news is we talked to your sisters, and two of them coming home in the next few days to pick up the kids."

I almost fell out of my chair. I raised my head up out of Granny's lap. "You can't let them go. They ours now," I said. "They should come home and stay like Esther did."

Muhdea rubbed my back. She was still wearing her waitress uniform, and her eyes were red from the smoke coming off the stove at the café. "I'm learning that things change, Sarah, and you will have to learn it, too. I promise you we'll find a way to see them all the time."

Esther's house felt dark and cold even though the lights were on, and it was hot outside. I laid my heavy head back in Granny's lap. My arms, legs and body were heavy, too, and I didn't know what to feel.

"Go on and get ready for bed," Esther said. "It's getting late."

I went and crawled between the two of my cousins who slept in the bed with me and Granny. I pulled them all close to me. I watched the others in the bed across from me. What was I going to do without them?

CHAPTER TWENTY-FIVE

We Demand Equality

ME AND MUHDEA hitched a ride with Reverend Jefferson. He was going to a Baptist meeting in Pine Bluff. I needed store-bought school clothes to wear to the white school. Muhdea was going to help me find clothes and to check on our new house. Granny, Muhdea and Esther gave me a few dollars each. I added it to the money I made from registering folks to vote, and the one day I chopped soybeans. Granny had made Mr. Sam Ray Blackburn give her the rest of my pay, three dollars. She had told colored folks to stop shopping with him. She worked out a plan with Sister Tucker where she carried more of the items folks had purchased from him, and the fish man now came by twice a week instead of just Saturdays. Mrs. Carrie carried the credit for the folks Sister Tucker couldn't help.

After a couple of weeks, Granny saw this was becoming a big inconvenience for most folks. Some of them stopped by our house and asked her how much longer she wanted them to stay away from his store. The fish man and Sister Tucker felt the strain as well. One day Mr. Sam Ray Blackburn stood out in the road and talked to Granny for a good while. A day or two afterward, Granny put the word out that one more week would teach him a good enough lesson. Folks agreed, but Mrs. Carrie, Esther and Rutherford threw a fit. They went round and round with Granny, but she didn't budge. Rutherford called Granny names even Mrs. Carrie and Esther didn't agree with.

I hoped to use the extra three dollars to buy a purse like Malika's. I planned to keep a running total in my head so I wouldn't over-spend, and then when it was all said and done, I'd ask Muhdea if I could use what was left over to buy a purse. Sister Tucker had said

I'd thank her one day for knowing how to count in my head. This might be the day.

I sat in the front seat between Muhdea and Reverend Jefferson. I couldn't see why Muhdea was taking me to get new school clothes if I wasn't going to the white school. I asked her and Reverend Jefferson if they'd changed their minds.

"Muhdea, why y'all taking me to get new clothes?" I said. "You change your mind about me going to white school?"

I knew better than to question grown folks. Children were supposed to wait and see what happened. I braced myself for a scolding.

"We have to keep up the appearance," Reverend Jefferson said.

I kept quiet and waited for the rest of the answer.

"If anybody get wind of what we doing, you will be in trouble," Muhdea said.

Reverend Jefferson began to hum "His Eye Is on the Sparrow."

I sat up tall in my seat. Since I'd spoken up, I might keep going, I thought.

"I told Reverend Jefferson I'd go to the white school. I don't want to tattle any longer," I said.

They eyed each other and shook their heads as if to say, poor child, she doesn't know a thing.

"You can't stop a car in motion," Reverend Jefferson said. "This is a lesson to all of us. All we can do is pray on it."

He pushed down a little too hard on the gas pedal. "Oh, shoot, Sarah, I'm going too fast," he said.

After he eased up on the pedal, the blue and white Ford slowed down a bit.

"Now I'm within the law," he said and cleared his throat.

Muhdea cleared her throat, too. She squeezed my hand.

"I know you believe we wrong, child," Muhdea said, "but we did what we thought was best. I do know and want to express to you that . . ." She paused for a long moment before she spoke again. "Ain't nothing either one of us did to cause them fires."

Reverend Jefferson agreed with her and reassured us that God took favor in what we did, and He would see us through it. I peeped around Muhdea and saw the lake at Pine Bluff. It was the same as it was the first time I saw it, still, quiet and serene. Trees lined all the way around the lake as far as I could see. I wished we could go put our feet in the water and forget about shopping for clothes. A car blew its horn at Reverend Jefferson, shaking loose my dreams of riding on the boat that sailed slowly across the water. Reverend Jefferson could say we were doing God's work all he wanted to, but these knots wouldn't be in my stomach if he were right.

"Reverend," Muhdea said. "You know Esther took the responsibility for the fire just to settle folks' nerves. She left the house when I did, and wasn't nothing on fire when we left."

He grunted. I didn't know if that meant he saw the good Esther done or not. I was going to "keep up appearances" with Muhdea and Reverend Jefferson the same as they were doing with everybody else. I guessed we were all in for a surprise, come September.

Not much later Reverend Jefferson dropped us off at Haim's Department Store. "I'll be back in an hour," he said. "Y'all be standing right here on this corner."

We waved at him as he drove off. Plastic girl and boy dolls, taller than Muhdea, were dressed in clothes I'd never seen before. They were posed in the window. Muhdea said they called them mannequins, and they made them specifically to show off the clothes.

"It's a window display," she said. "Do you see anything you like?"

It all looked good to me, even the clothes on the mama and daddy.

"Where's the grandmother and the great-grandmother?" I said.

"Leave it to you to remember us," Muhdea said. "I imagine they wear the same outfits as the mama."

"Not if the mama is Esther," I said, and we both laughed at the thought of Muhdea wearing Esther's hot pants.

"I'd look a mess," Muhdea said. She changed the tone of her voice when she spoke again. "Sarah, we don't want to take up these folks' time in here lollygagging around. If you see anything you want in the window, we can go in here and ask for it. We can point to it in the window." She thought for a minute. "Yes, that's the best way to do it." She seemed jittery, as if she were ready to go, and we hadn't even gone inside. "If you don't see it in that window, they have displays set up in the store. I don't want you putting your hands on the clothes on the rack. You hear me?"

"Yes, ma'am," I said. The way she talked scared me.

"You see anything you want?"

We stared at the window. I was dumbfounded. I'd never chosen my own clothes. Granny gave me another dress when one of mine got too little for me or shoes when my feet outgrew my old pair. Three girl mannequins stood in the window, one of them dressed in more clothes than I'd ever worn at one time, and they wore winter clothes when it was summer. One girl wore a red and black skirt, with a red sweater and a black patch on the elbow, a scarf wrapped around her neck, a black coat with her arm in one sleeve as the mama helped her into the other, and her mama wore a similar out-fit. The father and son stood off to the side watching them as if they were ready to go someplace fun. They all wore red and black. I wasn't sure if wearing the same colors was the style for window dolls, but it looked sort of corny.

"Can I get that whole outfit that girl standing next to her mother is wearing?" I said.

We gazed at the clothes in the window a while longer. Muhdea let out a long sigh. "Well, Sarah." She grabbed my hand and squeezed it. "Let's go get this over with."

She opened the door, and I saw lines of clothes of all colors and all types. Rows of the same skirt and next to it more rows of the same sweaters and dresses. To my left a set of stairs led up to more clothes. Over to the right, men's and boys' clothes lined the floor. Granny would love the way everything was organized. Muhdea pulled me along beside her. About five steps inside the store, a white lady greeted us.

"Good morning," she said and smiled way too wide. "How can I help y'all today?"

"We looking for school clothes for her," Muhdea said and nod-ded at me. "She likes the outfit in the window."

"Oh, that's from our Buster Brown collection. I don't know if you'll be able to afford the whole outfit," she said.

I knew Buster Brown's name. It was written on most of the clothes and shoes Malika brought back from Chicago.

"Well, you may be right, but let us see," Muhdea said. "Less coloreds ain't allowed to be in here?"

The white lady seemed surprised at what Muhdea asked. "Yes, yes, of course you can be here," she said. "I'll show you where your cash register is."

We passed by the shoes, purses, perfume, makeup and the outfit in the window. We walked down the stairs to a room without windows or mannequins, and it was dimly lit. Two colored ladies greeted us. The white lady called them by name, but I didn't catch it. All the clothes were on two long racks, one rack for girls and one for boys.

"Y'all look around, and let me know if I can help you with anything," one of the colored ladies said. Their clothes didn't look like the ones upstairs. Even though they were in the same store, the dresses looked more like my school clothes, floral pleated dresses with a high waist and belt to match. Mine was homemade. I wondered if the two colored women sewed all of these clothes. Why did that white lady bring us here? We didn't come all the way to Pine Bluff to buy these clothes. Muhdea didn't seem to be put off by it.

"Don't you see nothing you want, Sarah?" she said. Both women held dresses up to me for her to guess how I might look in them.

"Muhdea," I said, "can we just ask them to tell us the price of the outfit in the window?"

With the money I'd earned working for SNCC and chopping soybeans, Granny's change and the collection from the church, we figured I could buy a coat, a pair of shoes, socks, two dresses and seven-days-of-the-week panties to match. I kept the purse in the back of my mind with my fingers crossed. Folks expected me to come back with something spectacular. I'd be a laughingstock if I bought clothes that weren't even as nice as the ones I'd left home wearing.

"These the only ones you can choose from," one of the colored women said. The other one went off to help a woman who was already shopping when we got there.

"What size is she?" the woman asked Muhdea with a hiss at the end of her words as if she were trying to shush her.

"I don't know. This is our first shopping trip," Muhdea said.

She pulled a tape measure out of her pocket and took my measurements. Afterward she showed us the place on the rack that should be about my size.

"Get it a little too big," she said. "You'll be able to take it in if it don't fit, but if it's too little you out of luck," she hissed.

"Yeah, you right," Muhdea said.

I looked upside the woman's and Muhdea's heads. I wasn't spending my money on these clothes. I knew Muhdea was playing a joke on me, and pretty soon we'd go back upstairs and get the outfit in the window.

"Can't I just try it on?" I said. When Granny made my dresses, she fitted me two or three times before it was ready. "I don't want any of these. I want the outfit in the window. If I don't have enough money for all the pieces, I can still buy some of them."

Now the woman looked me upside the head. "Don't you know?" she said. "Didn't you tell her?" She looked at Muhdea. "Honey, you can't even try on these clothes down here, and you show can't buy the ones upstairs. I don't care how much money you got."

"Muhdea?" I said. "She's just playing with us, right? We didn't come all the way up here for nothing, did we?" My voice cracked. I was about to cry. I thought Pine Bluff and Little Rock already had equal rights. The lawyer Walker and the SNCC men talked as if we were the only ones left behind.

I imagined the kids making fun of me. My clothes were good enough. I didn't even want store-bought clothes, but Esther insisted on it. Since Reverend Jefferson had to come to Pine Bluff on business, she'd talked Muhdea into going with him, and taking me to this store that was supposed let coloreds come inside and buy clothes. Esther couldn't have known about this hole at the bottom of the stairs, or she wouldn't have sent me up here to be shamed. Did she want me to stage a sit-in? I couldn't do it by myself. Were some other folks coming? Were these women in the store part of it? When Rutherford took me and Malika to the library, and the clerk refused to give us a library card, we sat Indian style till the police came, picked us up, and took us to the police station while we remained cross-legged. Rutherford said to hold the position as long as they would let us. It was the best way to protect the sensitive parts of our body if they wailed on us. He demonstrated.

"See, if you fold your body over your knees and place your arms across your head, mostly all they can hit are your back and arms. You can take those blows longer than getting gut punched, or head banged," he said.

Nobody ever hit me or Malika, but they beat Rutherford like he stole something. It was fun when the two deputies picked me up by each arm and swung me back and forth like I was one of the swings at school. They made a game out of it to see who they could swing the highest, me or Malika. All the while, they were taking us to the police car, to jail.

"Look here, Sarah," Muhdea said. She held up a blue and white checkered dress. "This one is pretty. We ain't never seen no material like this."

She tried to hold the dress against my body. I pushed her hand away, hard. She checked me with her eyes, but I was too far gone.

"I don't want any of these dresses."

"Don't act like that, Sarah. These are good dresses."

"I don't want them. Let's go, Muhdea. I don't want them," I whispered so as not to embarrass her in front of the store clerk. "Tell them," I said. "Insist on it."

She placed her face in front of mine. We were nose to nose. "You behave," she said. "I won't make you buy it, but we can't change these folks' rules."

"We can protest. We can demand equality," I said. "Esther would do it."

I knew that was a gut punch harder than the ones the police gave Rutherford.

"You getting beside yourself, young lady," she said. "I could care two cents 'bout what Esther would do. Come on, let's go."

She reached for my hand. I pulled it away from her. She caught my arm, and I jerked it away from her and ran up the stairs. I didn't know where I was going. Maybe I'd go outside and pout knowing that she would snatch a knot in my behind when she caught up to me. But as soon as the red and black outfit, the one like the display in the window, caught my eye, I walked up to it, touched the hem of the skirt with my hand, and sat in the middle of the aisle Indian style. Muhdea and two white women reached me about the same time. Muhdea pulled on my crossed arms. She couldn't get me to unfold them.

"What is wrong with this girl?" one of the white women said. Other white folks in the store came over to see what was going on. "A colored girl is sitting in the middle of the aisle," I heard one woman say. More and more people gathered. There were way more white people shopping upstairs than colored folks downstairs.

Muhdea looked more helpless than the clerk at the library when me, Malika and Rutherford did a sit-in. The white ladies stared at me as if I were the three-headed man at the county fair. I began to sing "We Shall Overcome" quietly, mostly to calm my nerves. As more and more folks came to see the commotion, and Muhdea pleaded with me, begged me to get up, I got more frightened than ever. Malika wasn't there to squeeze my hand, or Rutherford to encourage me to demand my right to shop in this store like anybody else. I didn't know what I was thinking, but this wasn't it. I was in it knee-deep now and couldn't turn back.

I changed songs and hummed "I Need Thee Every Hour." Why, I didn't know, 'cause that song had failed me once before. I heard the store manager trying to break up the crowd.

"I'm the manager," he repeated as he moved the people out of his way. The only people I could see now were Muhdea, who was still whispering in my ear, and a different white store clerk, who wore rose perfume, her hair pulled back in a bun. She was young like Esther.

She whispered in my other ear, "Don't move. I won't let nobody hurt you. I called the police, which means the media will come with them." She rose up and looked around as if to see if anybody other than me could hear her. "Tell the police what happened. Can you do that?"

"Yes," I said.

Muhdea said I was going to get her locked up. "I'll use my school clothes money to bail out," I said.

"Sarah, please, let's go while we can still walk out of here," she said. I shook my head. "You will be sorry you did this when we get home."

"Sit with me, Muhdea," I whispered. "I'll show you how to do it."

"I won't let anything happen to you," the white lady said. "My husband is a lawyer. He's on his way."

Soon afterward, three police officers made it through the crowd, and one of them started disbursing the crowd.

"So you thought you'd disturb the peace today," the one with the bump on his nose said.

I shook my head.

"Y'all had your fun," the police said. "Get your daughter and get out of here before I take you across the street."

They must teach them to say that at police school; the police in Maeby said the same thing every time they came to the library to arrest Rutherford. The white lady kept her hand on my shoulder. Muhdea was on her knees in front of me with tears forming in her eyes. I hadn't ever disobeyed Muhdea, not once, not ever. I'd shamed her in public. I had better get up before I embarrassed her any further.

"A preacher is outside," another policeman said. "Says he's your ride to Maeby."

As I was about to unfold my arms, a man stuck a microphone in my face with the number seven written on it. Another man with a camera stood behind him with a light shining in my face.

"Can you tell me what you're doing here?" the man with the microphone said.

The white lady nudged my shoulder, encouraging me to tell him. I remembered what Rutherford said at the library.

"I'm not moving until I can buy that outfit," I said. "I have rights."

Felt like flapjacks flipping in my stomach. His face was too close to mine, and his breath smelled like fried liver.

"What outfit do you want to purchase?" he said.

"This one," I said and pointed to the red and black skirt.

"Why do you want that one?" he said.

"My mama said I need it to wear to my first day at the white school." I said.

"What's your name, and where are you from?" The look on his face changed from blank to knowing.

"My name is Sarah White, and I am from Maeby, Arkansas," I said.

"And who are you, ma'am?" he said to Muhdea, but she didn't answer. "Is this your daughter?"

Muhdea shifted her eyes from one side to the other. She looked as if she'd been cornered like one of our hogs before the slaughter. I held my head down. She didn't answer. What was I doing? I wanted to run out of there. I'd taken this further than I knew what to do.

"Is this your child? Do you support her?" he said.

"No, no, sir," she said. She stood up and brushed the front of her dress with her hands.

Had she disowned me? The store manager told the man with the microphone to leave the store. The policeman encouraged him to leave as well.

"She wants to buy a school dress." the man with the microphone said as he held it to the mouth of the store manager. Like Muhdea, he didn't answer either.

The policemen didn't pick me up and swing me like they did at the library. They were serious. One of them told me he wasn't playing, and he would haul my little ass to jail and lock the cell if I didn't get up and get out of the store that minute. The way he said it forced me out of my Indian position, and if so many people weren't in my way, I would've run out of the store. Muhdea held onto the neck of my dress as we walked.

I heard a man say, "Coloreds need to learn to stay in their place. Give me a minute with them, and they wouldn't be walking out of here upright."

"Mozelle." It was Mrs. Cox from the café. "Mozelle, is that you and little Sarah causing all this commotion?"

Muhdea didn't even look up at her. The policemen pushed us on toward the front door. Reverend Jefferson stood in front of the truck waiting for us. As soon as the policeman handed me and Muhdea over to him, Reverend Jefferson told me I was in trouble.

"You alright, Mozelle?" he said as he helped her into the truck. Then he came around and got in on the driver's side. He paused after he started the engine. "You in a bunch of trouble, Sarah."

A white man knocked on the window before he backed up. He was the store clerk's husband. He handed Muhdea his card, but she refused to take it. I took it out of his hand.

"What's your name?" he said. I told him. "How can I get ahold of you?"

Reverend Jefferson pushed his foot on the gas. The truck rolled backwards. I tried to think of how to tell him to get in touch with me, but nothing came to me. Then as my eyes scrolled across his card, I remembered.

"Call the lawyer Walker," I said. "He knows me."

We rode in silence, which meant Muhdea was too mad to speak. If she did, she might get mad enough to bust me upside of my head or something worse. Ever since I could remember, she'd warned me that she'd bust my head wide open, but she'd never done it to me or nobody else as far as I knew. Esther called it an empty threat and told her as much to her face, but Muhdea walked off and left her standing there. If Esther mouthed off to me the way she talked to Muhdea, I would've hurt her badly, but Muhdea shook her head and left Esther up to Jesus Christ 'cause she was beyond reproach. It seemed to me she should be mad at them folks who wouldn't let us buy any clothes when we came all this way, instead of eyeing me like I stole something. I was the one who should be throwing a fit. I couldn't say one word about how frustrated I was that I couldn't buy the outfit I wanted.

We were almost halfway home when she finally spoke to me.

"What in God's name did you think you were doing back there?" she said. "What's got into you, girl? Have you lost your mind? We could've been thrown in jail or worse."

"I been to jail before," I said.

She eyed me as if to say if I said one more word, she'd slap me through the back of this truck. Then she told Reverend Jefferson blow by blow what had happened in the department store. When she finished, silence blanketed us again like a heavy fog. I had no place to go. I was trapped between her and Reverend Jefferson. Surprisingly, he was quiet for a change. He knew Muhdea better than I did, so he was probably scared to utter a word the same as I was.

"I thought you knew better than to take on that foolishness like your mama and that boy she with. Do you think they done brainwashed her, Reverend? I heard tell of them doing that to folks," she said.

Her question opened the door for Reverend Jefferson to start preaching, and what a sermon he gave us for a good ten minutes about evil, and how the Devil could be walking around looking just like us. He didn't necessarily have to be red with eyes of fire and a long tail.

"Is the Devil done taken over you, Sarah?" he said.

I shook my head.

"Then what is it, child?" He continued before I could respond, and if he hadn't, I wouldn't have known how to answer him anyway. "I been worried, as I know you have, Mozelle, 'bout what we got ourselves mixed up in, but seeing Sarah today, knowing what you just went and done, I have to believe we done the right thing."

"You right, Reverend. No telling what Sarah would turn into if she went to that white school. I thought she had a strong mind, but I see now she ain't as smart as I thought. One minute she wants to get baptized, and the next she following Robert and them Muslims, and what she did today was just not the Sarah I raised."

"We have to pray them demons out of her," Reverend Jefferson said. "I'll gather a prayer group as soon as we get home."

There wasn't any way I was going to let the mothers and every other Christian with holy water start praying over me again. I'd done everything I could after Esther left to be in their good graces, to show them I wasn't like Esther, and they didn't need to waste their prayers on me. It wasn't my fault Esther wouldn't let me get baptized. I was smart enough to know the deal we'd made with Mr. Sam Ray Blackburn was wrong. Snitching and telling on folks behind their backs was wrong, and probably a sin even if I couldn't find the exact words in the Bible. Instead of arguing with them, I held my peace, and I sat between them with steam coming from me so hot they should've been able to feel it. I was ashamed of Muhdea. I was glad she didn't tell the reporter she was my grandma. And she'd called me dumb, and said I wasn't smart. My eyes lowered. My head hung down on its own.

"I ain't dumb, Muhdea," I said. "And I ain't no follower."

"Then stop acting like you dumb, Sarah," she said.

I didn't see the lake when we passed by it, or peep across Muhdea to see the different license plates on the cars, or count how many passed us.

"Bring her to the church around seven," Reverend Jefferson said. "We'll pray it out of her."

I rolled my eyes and pouted the rest of the way home. I slammed the door when I got out of the truck. Granny and Esther stood on the porch as we pulled up. How did they know I was in trouble? Reverend Jefferson waved to them as the gravel crackled under the weight of his truck. A redbird perched on the roof of the house.

FALL 1965

CHAPTER TWENTY-SIX

Speak the King's English

ON THE FIRST day of school, we lined up in front of the Hall at seven o'clock in the morning. All of us students, along with the members of the Maeby Citizens for Progress, the NAACP, SNCC, the in-town and out-of-town civil rights workers, Mrs. Carrie, Mr. Stith, Bro Hollin, the lawyer Walker, the news reporters, some onlookers from town and a whole lot of other folks I'd never seen before in my life. The day after Labor Day, 1965, our first day of school, and purple-blue clouds overhead hung low and threatened rain. Hurricane Betsy was headed to New Orleans, Louisiana, and we were concerned tornadoes might spin off and head our way. Malika admired my red and black outfit, which was just like hers except it was yellow and black.

"Is it new?" she said. "You even got a purse." She twirled me around. "Is it store-bought?"

"Yes," I said. "I'll tell you the whole story later. But you see that white man over there with the lawyer Walker?" She nodded. "Well, he came by our house with the clothes early this morning. He was with the lawyer Walker and said his wife wanted me to wear this to school today."

She eyed me. She knew me and Muhdea had gone to Pine Bluff on Saturday to buy clothes. I told her again that I would tell her the whole story later.

"He gave them to you?" she said.

"He tried, but I wouldn't let him," I said. "I untied my handkerchief and gave him all the money I took to Pine Bluff with me, and I gave him my just-in-case money Granny always pins to my panties."

"You finally used that money, and you give it to a white man. You crazy, Sarah. How you know you didn't give him too much?"

"I saw the tags and added it up."

She seemed to be satisfied with my answer. But just in case she wasn't, I took the crinkled empty handkerchief out of my patent-leather purse and showed it to her.

Esther's voice came over the loudspeaker she held in her hand. She looked gorgeous in a khaki-colored safari dress that buttoned down the front, with the same color belt. Muhdea would be proud that it was long enough, below Esther's knee.

"We don't know what's going to happen when we get over to the white school," she said, "but keep your eyes on me, follow my orders, and do not be afraid."

She handed the horn over to the lawyer Walker. He wore a navy blue wool suit and a thin black tie. I'd seen him wear it many times before.

"If for any reason you can't see or hear Sister Esther," he said, "take your direction from me. You are prepared. Don't be afraid."

I whispered to Malika I wasn't scared till they told me not to be afraid, and she said, "I know." We held hands. We were fifth in line. Esther lined us up from the first grade to the twelfth grade. There were three or more students in the other grades, but only me and Malika from the fifth grade. Reverend Adam Moses said a prayer. Reverend Jefferson stayed clear of anything having to do with civil rights, but he still drilled us in history and math. After the prayer, he handed the bullhorn to Rutherford, who came from nowhere. It was my first time laying eyes on him in days. He looked as if he'd rolled out of a ditch. Not that he ever cared whether his clothes were pressed or that he'd worn the same dashiki yesterday. I whispered to Malika when he started talking and didn't hear a word he said. He shied away from Esther's stare like a chicken. Then Mrs. Carrie spoke with tears in her eyes. She choked up on every word.

"Be brave," she said. "I never thought . . ." She placed her hand across her mouth. "Just be brave."

Afterward, we walked single file down the gravel Back Street, came up between the Esso gas station and the café, crossed over Highway 65 while the men held up traffic coming both ways, crossed the railroad tracks, passed by the cotton gin onto paved streets and manicured grass lawns, not dirt yards and gravel roads like on our side of town, and strolled down the sidewalk till we reached the Maeby Elementary and High School. Colored men turned off lawn mowers and waved at us. A few white women stood on their porches with both hands on their hips. One colored woman came from the backyard and swirled her dishtowel in the air. Esther, Mrs. Carrie, Gail, James, Rutherford, Reverend Adam Moses and Mr. Bill Hansen led the way. Esther stopped us about a block from the school and spoke to us without the bullhorn.

"Remember, we won't sing or chant," she said. "We march in silence in honor of all the children in other cities who traveled this road before us."

A tall wire fence surrounded the school, with barbed wire atop and a padlock on the gate. I wondered if this was new, put up just for us, or if the kids were so bad they locked them inside. We stood on the outside of the fence.

We stood along the side of the fence on the grass, two by two, with the oldest in front. The school was two long one-story buildings separated by a circular building and sidewalks. I imagined the circular building was the cafeteria they'd told us about, with a stage for plays and musicals. The entire front of the building facing us had large windows at the top and the bottom. The ones at the top were pushed open. I would have to stand atop a desk to stick my head out of the window, but one of the boys from our basketball team could do it standing flat foot. I figured for as many kids whose heads were stuck out the windows as if it were a school bus, they must be standing on something. From where I stood, I only saw the big kids and not the elementary students like me. Other white folks like Mr. Michael James King and Mr. Sam Ray Blackburn stood on the school grounds, behind the locked fence.

Their school didn't look anything like ours. I could gaze out those windows till I eyed the Pyramids or climbed Mount Kilimanjaro. The windows at our school were small and spaced out across the building. Sometime in 1944, our buildings were tarpapered barracks with cotton mice running around like students.

I wanted to meet the girls and boys whose names were written in the front of my books, and those who'd marked out the words, torn out the pages, written, "Niggers can't read" throughout. If they didn't think I could read, then why write it?

Me and Malika held hands. We clasped our fingers one between the other so tight the side of them was dented and red, and we swung our arms back and forth. We swung them the same way every year as we waited for the judges to call our names as the winners of the 4H competition at the Lincoln County Fair on colored day. They never did. The judges chose the white girls and boys every year, but we didn't give up. We raised a fatter cleaner pinker pig every year. I told Malika our pig would have to stand on its hind legs, turn around, and tell them judges to "kiss my ass" before they let us win. She thought it was the funniest thing she'd ever heard, and they put us out the ring that year for disrupting the contest. Malika opened the gate, and I patted my ass at them the way I imagined our pig would've done.

Now Esther walked up and down the line. She talked to the lawyers, the reporters, the civil rights workers, especially Rutherford, the citizens of Maeby and everybody else who called out to her with a question, caught her arm, or pulled the sleeve of her new dress. Every time she walked past us, she checked on me and Malika.

"Stand up straight, Sarah. Are you girls okay?"

We told her we were doing fine. I inquired about Mrs. Daisy Bates. She'd told us she might be able to lend her support. Esther stooped down and spoke very low.

"Sarah," she said. "Why are you asking me that? You know she had a stroke. She wishes she could be here with us. We'll go see her one day when this is over."

She checked my face, looked into my eyes, and walked on. After what seemed like a real long time, and nobody had come to unlock the gate, the lawyer Walker and Esther with Rutherford in tow met with the three or four white men through the fence. My shoe rubbed the side of my little toe. I asked Malika if she wanted to play the word game to take my mind off things.

"Let's practice enunciating words," I said. Our teachers had told us to do this to settle our nerves.

"Okay," Malika said. "Say 'elevator.'"

She knew I couldn't say that word. For some reason, I wanted to add an R after the second E, which threw me 'cause I had trouble rolling the R. Gail had brought it to my attention last summer, soon after we started our French lessons. My tongue was flat, which made it hard to carry a tune to a song, and to roll an R.

"Phonate," Gail had said. "Purse your lips, stick your tongue through them, and pull back quickly." After much practice, I'd pronounced my own version of "bonjour."

Malika nudged my side. "El-e-va-tor," she said.

"Why?" I whispered. "Why in God's name would I ever have to say that word? We ain't got none in this town. I ain't never seen one and probably never will, so why, out of all the words we know, would you want me to say that one?"

"Speak the King's English," Malika said. Her voice quivered.

I pursed my lips and tried to pronounce each syllable of the word "elevator."

"Don't worry, Sarah," she said. "If they ever ask you, I'll say it."

Esther had said the white folks didn't want us in the same classroom with their students. They thought we were slow and would hold them back. They never said it aloud, but they took the money out of my hand when I went to the stores uptown and counted it for me as if I didn't know how to make change. Now Esther told us we had to wait outside till the lawyer Walker got the ruling from the judge as to whether or not we all would be placed in special education classes. Them calling us slow always made Gail madder than a mad hatter.

"You're smarter than the girls in my prep school," she'd said to me and Malika. "If there's anything that can heat me up it's the thought of you girls in special ed."

The crowd parted to let Esther through. She strutted toward

us with Rutherford and the lawyer Walker in tow. Other than the students, there were about forty people from town who'd come to watch, mostly women. They wore church clothes, whether they belonged to a church or not. They stood to the right of us. About twenty-five members of Maeby Citizens for Progress stood to the left of us and wore church clothes as well. Sister Tucker and Mrs. Martha had on the same purple hat. I knew both of them wished any other woman had worn it. They competed for best dressed every Sunday, from their shoes and stockings to their dress and hat. The winner was the one who got the most compliments. Reverend Jefferson had told folks to stop complimenting them before they ended up with the Devil. Twenty or thirty people came from surrounding towns, and they mixed in with either group. It seemed like a lot of people to us. I hadn't ever seen that many white people mingled in with colored folks.

People moved to the side as Esther's long legs came toward us again. In a funny way, I felt the red hot pants and miniskirts fitted her better than that long beige button-down dress, but she looked pretty in it all the same. Rutherford still wore his Kente-cloth dashiki, and carried a pick as if he had an Afro instead of straight hair like white folks. Whenever Esther moved, he followed her, touching her booty, and catching ahold of her hand. She shook it loose to write on the clipboard she carried as if she were an insurance collector. She came to check on us again and placed her hand under my chin, so I looked up at her.

"It won't be long," she said. "What's wrong? Are you okay? What about you, Malika?"

"My feet hurt," I said. "They don't want us here anyway."

She stared me up and down as if she didn't know who I was. "Don't start, Sarah," she said. "Don't act like you don't know what's at stake here." She walked away.

The white students peered out at us from behind the open windows of the classroom, girls and boys. I hunched Malika when I saw Mr. Sam Ray Blackburn's boys. One was a year older than the other one, but they looked like twins with their black hair greased flat to their heads and parted on the left side. As hot as it was, they both wore black leather jackets. There must've been an open gate behind the building 'cause more and more of them stuck their heads out of the windows, and more grown people filled the parking lot. One lady with a silver bun on her head yelled at Mr. Michael James King that he should disperse the colored folks. They had no reason to stand in front of the school.

Colored folks lined the street behind us now. Seemed like an equal amount of people on the inside and outside of the fence. Where most of the colored folks wore their Sunday church clothes, the whites seemed to be wearing their work clothes, simple cotton dresses and khaki pants.

We waited as students and grown folks whispered back and forth to each other as if we weren't outside, and at times our heads were bowed like we'd taken a moment to pray. Wind blew hard through the trees, causing the branches to sway, and every now and again, we heard a clap of thunder.

"Tornadoes going to be here directly," one woman wearing a loud yellow and blue hat said. She wasn't from around here, or she'd know those were just rain clouds.

I peeped around one of the boys to see the children's heads hanging out every window, two or three heads to a window. They didn't seem to be dressed any better than us. The girls had on plain, pleated, floral dresses, and the boys wore khakis. I don't know why Esther was so concerned about my clothes. Their hair was all different colors, black, white, blond and red. A girl with long red hair hanging outside of the window stuck her tongue out at me. I stuck my middle finger right back at her. She pointed me out to some of the other students. I ducked back behind Malika, and stuck my finger up again. The space around me seemed smaller. I smelled the churchwomen's perfume. Over the years, I'd learned to tell who they were by their lilac, rose, musk and floral fragrances. Mrs. Mary wore fresh-cut roses, and Sister Tucker wouldn't be caught without her lilac. It was comforting to know they were there with us.

Nobody yelled profanities at us, no fire hoses plugged into fire hydrants spraying us with water, no National Guard needed for our protection. Three of Uncle Robert's Muslim brothers stood at attention in front of the gate. They'd already been there when we arrived, dressed the same as he always did, in a dark-colored suit, skinny bowtie and close-cut hair. We all bided our time: Esther and the lawyer Walker waiting for the judge, and nosy folks itching for gossip, colored and white, news people filming and writing on pads, civil rights workers feeling as if they'd accomplished something, and us, who would rather be back at our own school. I wondered how long them boys and girls they called the Little Rock Nine stood outside before they let them walk into Central High School, and poor James Meredith all the way down there in Mississippi integrated that school all by himself, but it was little Ruby Bridges whom I thought about the most. She was younger and smaller than me and Malika. I bet she was real scared as she walked beside them grown folks, and like me, she probably just wanted to go home, and never set foot in an all-white school. Up till now, I'd believed them boys and girls wanted to attend the white school. It had never occurred to me their mamas and daddies made them go, the same as mine made me.

I couldn't feel my fingers 'cause Malika squeezed them so tight.

"Let's recite all fifty states and capitals backwards," I said.

Malika started first. "Wyoming," she said.

"Cheyenne," I said. My voice trembled. "Let loose a little bit." I pulled my fingers slightly. The blood began to circulate through them again.

"You scared, Sarah?"

I shook my head. "Naw, these white people ain't scary."

"King's English, Sarah. You can't keep forgetting to use it."

Esther's voice rang out over the crowd. "Mary Sue, John Raymond and Carrie Ann, please come forward."

They were all first-graders. I touched Mary Sue's shoulder as she walked by. She caught my hand, and looked at me with tears in her eyes. A few drops slid down her face. I wiped them away with the back of my hand.

"Don't let them see you cry," I said. "I'm coming right behind you. Don't be scared."

Rutherford called the names of the second-grade students. Esther called the third-graders, and then it was quiet again. The strangers who didn't know us inquired as to who and how many children were going inside. I couldn't see where they went once they let them inside the gate. Uncle Robert's Muslim brothers opened and closed the gate after Mr. Michael James King unlocked it. Mrs. Carrie walked in with them. I prayed they wouldn't send them to the special education class.

"Why they stop calling them?" the lady in the blue and yellow hat whispered.

Thunder roared, but there wasn't any lightning yet. I figured it would pour within the hour. Folks mumbled to each other. It sounded like bees buzzing. Mrs. Carrie came back, and reporters began to question her as soon as she was on the other side of the gate. The brothers kept them from rushing her. We were first in line now, and could see all around us. We stood in the center, and there was plenty of space between us students and all the other people.

"Did they put them in the special education class?" a reporter said louder than the thunder clapped.

"I wasn't allowed back to the classrooms," Mrs. Carrie said. "The kids are in good spirits," she said, but it didn't sound right.

I checked my Minnie Mouse watch, eleven o'clock. We carried our lunch pails with food we liked to eat 'cause we wasn't sure what white folks ate for lunch. I wished I could be in general assembly with my old classmates pretending to listen to the principal give out instructions for the upcoming year, and arguing with Malika about which one of us would be first in our class that year. Now I was stuck in limbo. There wasn't any way I could go back and face my friends at the colored school, and I sure didn't want to go inside the white school.

Esther walked toward us. Some folks patted her on the back, some whispered in her ear, and others asked her about the students. She checked on me and Malika.

"You're shaking, Sarah," she said. She straightened my skirt. "Come on now. Be brave for mama." She placed both hands on my shoulders and looked into my eyes. "The other kids are okay. There isn't any reason to be afraid."

I shook her hands away from my shoulders. My fear turned to

anger. I'd tried to think differently of her. At times, at the Hall, she acted like she was just as smart as Granny. But now, I felt like Granny was right. Esther didn't know shit from shinola. I wasn't scared. My feet hurt, and I told her as much. All this was her fault.

"When we going in?" Malika said. Her teeth chattered.

"In a few minutes," Esther said. She held Malika's face in her hand, and then she pulled her close and hugged her.

She knew better than to try and hug me.

"Are we next?" I said. "Otherwise, I can run home and get my old shoes."

"Soon, Sarah," she said and started talking to a reporter who was impatiently waiting for her to finish with us.

Not long after Esther left us, she called the sixth-graders. At the rate they were going, we would be there all day.

"Do you want to run for it?" Malika said.

"Where to?" I said. My dogs were barking. "Naw." I tried to move my toes around in the shoes. "I'd get caught in these shoes anyway."

Malika lowered her eyes. She squeezed my hands tighter. "Sarah, I don't want to be a part of this no more," she said. "Ain't no telling what they'll do to us once we go inside."

"King's English," I said with a smirk on my face, which changed back to serious before I spoke. "They can't hurt all of us." She looked even more afraid, so I used broken English. "All we gots to do is be dumb."

She pushed my shoulder and nodded. "Stop it, Sarah. I'm not acting dumb for nobody." She remained solemn. "Do you know what happened to the other children who integrated the white schools? What are they doing now?"

I didn't know, but I knew she was scared. "They attended college and went on to do great things," I said. "Mrs. Daisy Bates said so."

"What great things?"

I changed the tone in my voice to sound authoritative like the lawyer Walker. "Big great things," I said. "Real big great things like lawyers and doctors." I didn't think Reverend Martin Luther King Jr. would appreciate the way I'd phrased it. "You know what? When

I meet that Dr. Martin Luther King, I'm going to ask him why he made his English so challenging for us to write and speak."

We laughed, and every time one of us tried to talk, we laughed again. We couldn't stop. Malika tried to answer as if she were Reverend Martin Luther King Jr., but she couldn't get a word out before we cracked up again.

Esther saved me from having to come up with any other answer. She began to call more students. I wondered why she'd skipped our grade, the fifth grade.

"Arizona," Malika said.

"Phoenix," I said. "Like the bird. We just like the bird, too."

We finished with the states and capitals, and started our time-tables. When we finished them, I asked Malika if she wanted to practice speaking French or doing fractions.

"You know we're supposed to forget we know those," she said.

"Do you really think they'll single us out 'cause we know something they don't?" I said.

Esther had told us to wait, pace ourselves, and watch what they did before we acted. She said white folks were funny acting, and to test the water before we even put a foot in it.

"They ain't out here," I said. "We can practice in private."

"No," she said. "You'll forget and get us in trouble."

I let it go 'cause the whole idea was foolish to me.

It was getting late, and me and Malika were getting hungry. A few drops of rain landed on my face. Thunder clapped louder, almost roared. Esther called more students. We multiplied. I took out my pressed-ham sandwich first. Malika was afraid she might drop sandwich spread on her sweater. I wondered if Mary Sue was still crying. Was she looking for me? Mr. Stith noticed my feet hurt. He picked me up while Sister Tucker loosened my shoestrings.

"If you take them off, you won't be able to get your foot back in them," she said.

Mr. Stith held me for a good while, long enough to give my feet a rest. I didn't want him to put me down, but I couldn't leave Malika by herself any longer. He set me down and picked Malika up for a little while. We weren't the kind of girls who generally needed picking up.

By the time the rain came down hard enough for us to notice it, only the fifth-, eleventh- and twelfth-grade students were left outside. It was two-thirty, and the bigger kids, especially the boys, threatened to go back to the colored school. They'd had enough.

"I'm sick of standing out here," one of the older girls said.

"I'm hungry," the basketball player said.

I wanted to offer him the other half of my sandwich, but it was all I had, and I wasn't sure how long it would be before I got to go home.

Malika went to the Port-a-Potty again. Esther's voice came through the loudspeaker. I was surprised most folks were still there. Some let up their umbrellas, and some held theirs over our heads.

"The superintendent won't allow any more students inside," she said. "The classes are overcrowded."

"This some bullshit," the basketball player said. "Y'all had me over here all day for this shit."

Folks mumbled like an out-of-tune church song, a call-and-response song. A few droplets of rain fell on my hand. The basketball player and two other boys left. Three girls followed soon afterward. I longed to go with them, but I'd told Mary Sue I was going to be there for her. Some who could care less about civil rights started to disburse, patted us on the back, and wished us well as they meandered back home to their chores. The white people started walking away, too. Other folks seemed to not know what to do. They said they knew something like this would happen. White folks always had something up their sleeve. They wouldn't be surprised if they'd figured out how to send the other students back to the colored school by tomorrow. I was floored. Esther and Rutherford tried to explain.

"Are we going to school?" I said.

The first day of school was always a big day in Maeby. Hardly anybody ever missed a day of school anyway, but nobody missed school on the first day. It wasn't like we hadn't seen each other all summer. I didn't know what it was, but for me, the day after Labor

Day was exciting and filled with hope and expectations of learning something new.

"We're working on it, Sarah, but we can't get it done before three o'clock," Esther said.

"I got to go to school today," I said.

"Why can't you act more like Malika?" she said in a nasty tone.

What was so wonderful about Malika? Esther turned around to answer questions for the reporters. The lawyer Walker pulled her to the side. Folks who didn't care much for civil rights and the nosy ones were gone. The members of the Maeby Citizen for Progress, the reporters, the civil rights leaders and Uncle Robert's Muslim brothers were still at the gate. Thunder clapped, lightning flashed, and the sky boohooed. Esther told whoever was left to disburse.

"We'll come back tomorrow," she said kindly, but I could tell she was fire mad. Malika noticed it, too.

"Hope she isn't mad at you," she said.

I waited till wasn't anybody paying much attention to us. Not many people were left on either side of the fence. Esther told us to head back to the Hall with the other students and grown folks. I couldn't leave without telling Mary Sue I was gone. Me and Malika started toward the road. I looked back at the white school. I snatched my hand away from Malika's and walked fast to the locked gate. I walked straight up to the Muslim brothers and said, "As-salamu alaykum."

"Wa alaykumu as-salam," they both said.

"Is Uncle Robert doing fine where y'all buried him?" I said.

They seemed taken aback by the question.

"Would you tell him for me, when you visit his grave, that I miss him, and I would've come to the funeral, but Muhdea wouldn't let me?"

They looked as if they were trying to figure out what I was talking about, but said they would tell him anyway. A flash of lightning shimmered across the sky. They looked in the direction of the lightning, and I slid through the opening in the gate. The white people didn't seem to notice I wasn't supposed to be inside the gate. I made it halfway across the schoolyard before people started to try to catch me. One person after the other tried to catch my hand, but I snatched it away from them and kept right on walking fast. Like Esther, I was bound and determined. I picked up speed and then began running down the sidewalk. Esther and Rutherford called my name from the other side of the fence. Mr. Sam Ray Blackburn was closest behind me. He promised to snatch a knot in my ass when he caught me.

"Crazy nigger," he said. The second time he'd called me out of my name. One more time, and I'd have to figure out how to kick his ass. Everybody knew three times was the limit.

I turned to the left and ran down the waxed hallway. I got to a round building, stuck my head in to see if there really was a stage in the cafeteria, and there was, thick red curtains and all. I kept running, sticking my head in every room and yelling Mary Sue's name.

"Mary Sue," I yelled. "You in there?"

Before anybody could catch me, I kept running. White men and women ran behind me. I could tell how close they were to me by the click of their shoes. After I opened three or maybe four classroom doors, I found Mary Sue.

"Mary Sue, you in there?" I yelled.

I heard a tiny scared little voice. "I'm back here," she said.

She stood up. I ran back to the last seat on the last row and stood next to her.

"Well, I declare," the teacher said.

The rest of the white people, including Mr. Sam Ray Blackburn, came in the room behind me. All the students raced to the front of the room, and those close enough wrapped their arms around the teacher's legs. A boy with white hair pulled my plait as he walked by me. I hit after him with my fist, but he was too far for it to land in his back.

"You come to get me?" Mary Sue barely said.

Mr. Sam Ray Blackburn reached for me, and I backed away.

"You come to get me?" Mary Sue cried.

I didn't know what to do. Mr. Sam Ray Blackburn grabbed me. Bro Hollin wasn't there to stop me that day like he did when we were in the field. I stomped his foot, and then I bit him on the hand that held my arm.

"I didn't come for you," I said to Mary Sue. "I won't be coming to school here."

Mary Sue boohooed harder than the rain did outside. Mr. Sam Ray Blackburn let go of me and told me to shut her up. I placed my forehead against hers and whispered to her to calm down. We looked at each other eye to eye.

"I can't stay here," I said, "but you have to stay and do good for me, okay?"

She whimpered. "Okay?"

"You have to be the smartest in the class," I said.

She nodded between whimpers. "Stop crying and don't ever cry again," I said. I wiped her eyes dry. She raised her head and held it up high. She would be alright without me. They would never break her down.

Mr. Sam Ray Blackburn handed me over to Mr. Michael James King and a man he called the principal. Mr. Michael James King dragged me down the hallway and across the schoolyard. He unlocked the gate and handed me over to Esther.

"Here, take her," he said. "Now you see why we don't want y'all niggers over here."

Esther, Rutherford, the lawyer Walker and the three Muslim brothers were soaking wet and speechless. The lawyer Walker and the three Muslim brothers all reached out to grab me after Mr. Michael James King let me out from behind the fence, but the lawyer Walker got to me first. He picked me up and wrapped one arm around my head, covering my ears as if he wanted to protect me from hearing another nasty word.

CHAPTER TWENTY-SEVEN

We Must Continue
to Push Forward

BRO HOLLIN CAME back to get us in his truck. We piled in it, soaking wet. Esther repeated over and over again, "Heads up, please." She seemed not to know what else to say. "We don't have anything to be ashamed of."

It was hard for me to hold my head up. Nobody'd told us they might not let us attend the white school. All that hard work we did all year, and nothing to show for it. I wondered if the grown folks would think it was our fault and be mad at us. They mumbled under their breath. Esther or Mrs. Carrie reminded them, "Hold your peace until we get to the Hall." I bet our teachers and all the other folks who'd helped us get ready were going to be upset with us, too.

Muhdea and Reverend Jefferson wouldn't be though. They'd be glad the scheme they'd concocted worked. I'd changed my mind about it a long time ago. I'd made peace with going to the white school. It was going to happen one day. It might as well have been today, couldn't put change off forever. Granny had whispered that to me one evening, long before the church and our house burned to the ground. When she told me, I figured it all made sense; religion, family and equality could all thrive in the same garden like okra, tomatoes and corn. But when I told Reverend Jefferson and Muhdea, they didn't want to hear it. Maybe I failed to explain it to them the way Granny told me. Muhdea said a tomato vine could wrap around the okra, and choke it, and kill it. They gave me a tongue-lashing for not appreciating what they'd done for me, the scheming, snitching,

337

sinning and God knows what else to keep me safe. Of course, they didn't use any of those words to describe what we did, but I saw it that way from the start.

Nobody was on the road as we drove to the Hall. My feet hurt. I wanted to take off my shoes and go barefoot. Granny would have to press my hair again for school tomorrow. It was getting darker, and the clouds looked angry when the thunder roared.

The stores uptown were closed. I couldn't tell if the lights were on or off. There wasn't anybody on the sidewalks. I wondered if all them white folks had marched to another hall to reevaluate their situation like we were going to do. I peeped into the window of the dry goods store. If it were open, I'd march up to the door and trade in these shoes for another pair. I bet Sam Ray Blackburn was over there at the white school making plans to keep the rest of us out for good. The thought of it made my heart hurt worse than my feet. I imagined everybody else's did, too.

We passed Morning Star Methodist Church. I hadn't ever been on this end of town during the middle of a school day. It was way too quiet. I remembered when Esther painted their stained-glass windows. Their Jesus was much bigger than ours at First Baptist. He covered the entire window.

I looked back at Highway 65 to see an eighteen-wheeler and a blue and white Ford truck swish by. Gas fumes fouled the air. Malika almost bumped me from behind. I was used to her being in front of me, but for some reason today she was walking behind me, fussing at me every chance she got.

"What's going to happen to us now?"

I hunched up my shoulders. She bumped into me.

"You can't just stop and daydream."

I looked back at her and rolled my eyes.

"You mad about this shit."

I shook my head.

We went straight to the Hall. It looked lonely to me, as if it missed us. Gail opened the door. Esther had painted the glass that covered over half of the door with grown folks and children carrying picket signs. As soon as the last person came through the door, the

Hall woke up. The mumbling and whispering that were simmering came to a head. Tempers flared. Esther blamed the lawyer Walker, and he blamed the civil rights workers, mainly Rutherford, and they blamed Esther and Mrs. Carrie, and the rest of the folks lined up on whatever side they chose, leaving us, the students, standing in the middle of the floor. Nobody seemed to care that we got put out of school before we even started. The lawyer Walker was at the podium. He waved a handful of papers at us.

"I'm filing these in the Eighth District Circuit Court first thing tomorrow morning," he said. Everybody kept talking to each other and wasn't listening to him. He slammed the podium with his fist. "It's not over yet," he yelled. He got our attention.

"You all know I prefer to continue to fight for separate but equal schools," Esther said. She stood at the podium next to the lawyer Walker. "But we lost that battle. John will ask the courts to immediately instate total integration."

The lawyer Walker nodded. Folks wanted to know what that meant for us, for the students who weren't allowed to register. I felt the hair on my head turn back to natural and tried to smooth it out with my hand. I couldn't go back over to the colored school with a nappy head.

"I hope I can trust you this time," Esther said. She paced across the front of the room, sneering at the lawyer Walker as she spoke. "If you had done what you were told in the first place, we wouldn't be in this mess now."

"Just wait a minute," he said.

Esther walked away. He tried to grab her, but his hand missed her dress sleeve.

Mrs. Carrie shushed him and steered the conversation in a totally different direction. "How we coming along with Esther's bid for city council?" she said.

SNCC was supposed to send campaign funds, but they hadn't the last time he gave us an update. "Well," he scratched the back of his head with both hands.

I thought of Granny when she said he was a cool drink of water, and Muhdea sang out yes, Lord.

"Don't take this the wrong way, Esther, but not even the coloreds will vote for you as long as you are married to Rutherford."

Rutherford strutted toward the podium carrying a brown paper sack and scratching the bumps in his beard.

"I don't want to hear it. Stay back there," the lawyer Walker said. "The truth is I've bailed you out of jail three times for DUIs." I scribbled "DUI" across my brain so I'd remember to write it in my book. "The community may be forgiving of a DUI, but not the domestic abuse. You shouldn't have put your hands on Esther."

I wasn't there when he beat her, but she came home looking like he did after the police turned him loose. Granny wanted to whip him, but Muhdea convinced her it wasn't the Christian thing to do. I would've helped them, but Esther said leave him alone, and she doctored on his bruises before she let us look at them.

"You don't know what you talking about, John," Rutherford said. "I have . . ."

The lawyer Walker cut him off. "I don't want to hear a word out of you. You knew what we were up against, and you hit her anyway. I don't remember the last time I've seen you without that bag in your hand."

His eyes cut Rutherford up into tiny little pieces. Rutherford lowered his head and walked out of the door. The lawyer Walker continued as if Rutherford didn't mean any more to him than a plug nickel.

"I'm fed up with his shenanigans," he said and pointed his finger at Reverend Adam Moses. "And I'm sick of yours, too."

Reverend Adam Moses followed Rutherford outside.

Malika nudged me in the side. "Don't they see us standing here?" she said.

"They don't care," I said.

Mrs. Carrie gave me the eye. I was mad enough to get smart with her, but my home training rushed into my mind and stopped me. The last thing I wanted to do was be disrespectful to her.

"What do you suggest?" Esther said.

"Rutherford needs to leave town," the lawyer Walker said. "He can come back after this is all over, but he needs to go right now."

Rutherford cracked the door and stuck his head inside the room.

"She's my wife, man, not yours," he said. "Are you really serious? You got to be kidding me." He lit a cigarette and opened the door wider, where half of his body was between the door and the room.

"SNCC isn't going to send any money as long as you're in town, man," the lawyer Walker said.

Rutherford slammed the door without saying another word. It was a mess. They told us to sit on the floor and wait. We were the ones who were hurt and mad. We did all the work. Our friends talked about us at school every day. They would get to us. Wasn't this whole thing supposed to be for us?

Miss Pastel and Miss Flora, wearing dresses to match their names, handed out sandwiches and short Cokes. "Hold on to that bottle. We can get a nickel for it," they took turns saying as they handed them to us.

Sometime late in the evening, when all the grown folks had said more than their piece, they told us we were picketing at the Education Building in Little Rock the next day.

"Strike while it's hot," the lawyer Walker said. And the day after that unless the courts decided to reverse its decision.

We, the ones who weren't allowed to attend the white school, would return to the colored school ASAP.

"No, oh no, that's not happening," one of the boys from the eleventh grade said. He shook his head and got up off the floor. "I didn't do all that work for nothing. Y'all better come up with something 'cause this right here ain't happening. Man, I ain't going back to no colored school. I ain't taking that."

John and Mark Graves, the superintendent's sons, got up and stood beside him. "Me either," they both said.

The girls stood beside them. "Me either," we repeated one after the other. I was too taken aback to mumble any more than that in our defense.

"You all better sit back down on the floor," Esther said. "You knew we were up against the system. It just happened that the system won this time. This fight isn't over yet. Tell them, John."

The lawyer Walker agreed with her, and eventually we sat down and remained quiet the remainder of the evening. Except we grumbled to each other, but the volume in our voices was below a whisper, and we couldn't make out what the other ones said, but we nodded our heads as if we did. I knew whatever was said was against returning to the colored school to get ridiculed every day.

Esther told us it wasn't necessary to keep us out of school. We would go to Little Rock with them for the march, but our presence wouldn't help their lawsuit. What would help them, I found out later, when Esther and the lawyer Walker called me into the classroom and shut the door, was for me to sign my name on them papers as the plaintiff.

"John is going to file the lawsuit in your name," Esther said.

I didn't know what that meant, but I was cautious about signing my name to anything. Granny had told us not to take any pictures or sign our names for fear of what people might do with it.

"There isn't anything for you to worry about," the lawyer Walker said. "It's only for the record. You won't have to appear in court with me."

I held the pen in my hand for a long time. I eyed him and then the papers lying on the table. That day was getting worse by the minute. A fly landed on the line where I was to sign my name.

The next morning we realized Rutherford hadn't come home. He wasn't at the school bus when we left for Little Rock to march around the Education Building. We marched for a couple of hours before the police made us dismiss, but not before the news reporters took our pictures and asked questions as to why we were marching. Esther and the lawyer Walker pushed me in front of the camera. We circled the front of the brown brick building. People peeped out at us through the window, but they didn't come outside. Between the folks from Maeby and the civil rights folks from Little Rock, there were about fifty of us. We were the only students. It was an ordinary day, no thunder, no lightning or dark clouds like it was the day before.

A white man who said he was the attorney for the Health, Education and Welfare Department came out of the building to talk to us.

"I don't know what you are expecting to gain by protesting

here," he said. "We don't make those decisions. You have to take it to the courts." He saw the lawyer Walker and addressed him. "John, you should know that."

"Publicity," Esther said. "We want to pressure the courts to integrate the schools in Maeby. We're asking for public support." She gazed directly into the TV camera and smiled. "I'm running for a city council seat this November. I need financial support to win." Her voice changed to that of an announcer. "I'm reaching out to all the people of Arkansas to get involved, especially financially. I invite you to come to Maeby and see for yourself what we're up against."

She wasn't tugging at her dress, a blue safari dress that was made just like the one she wore yesterday, buttoned down the front, belted, and hemmed below her knee. She still didn't look as if she belonged with the rest of us. She belonged on TV. Afterward, she sat down and talked a long time with a few of the reporters. They held tape recorders, and some of them took notes.

A few minutes after the police told us to move on, we got back on the bus. We sang freedom songs. Some of us tried to accept the fact that all was lost and we would return to the colored school. We discussed what we'd say to the kids who teased us. We decided that sticking together and defending each other was best. Gail and James stood up at the front of the bus as if she were going to lead us in another song. They held on to the two silver rails as the bus rocked them from side to side, and tears rolled down her face and James' too.

"We've done all we can do in Maeby," Gail said. Her voice broke, and James took over.

"Our time has run out, and although we're sad, we're taking the afternoon bus tomorrow back to our homes," James said.

Silence smothered the bus. They took their seats. Esther's face was long, and Mrs. Carrie hung her head low.

Mrs. Carrie took their place at the front of the bus. "We knew this day was coming," she said. "They're leaving us, but we must continue to push forward. You all know what's happening with SNCC since Stokely Carmichael's voice is becoming louder than John Lewis'. The writing is on the wall, and Gail and James need to get in front of it. They'll still be with us in spirit."

Esther stood next to Mrs. Carrie. "Everybody come down to the Hall tomorrow morning so we can give them a proper sendoff," she said.

We all remained quiet for the rest of the ride home. It was one of those times where words didn't count for nothing. Whatever words came to mind wasn't enough. I figured the others were like me, shocked and too dumbstruck to speak. Gail could've told me she was leaving. She'd told me I could become fluent in French. I'd be able to talk to them in their language the same as I did with Malika. I'd assumed she would be there to teach me. Who was going to teach us French now? She never let on that one day she'd leave us. Never let on. I wiped my eyes before any water fell. Malika nudged me in the side.

"She could've told us, first," she said. Her eyes were red.

When we got home, I checked throughout the house for Rutherford. I asked Esther if she knew where he was. Was she worried about him?

"He'll show up," she said. "Probably still cooling off from the meeting."

"If he believed in the Lord, it wouldn't take that long," I said.

"Some things take longer," she said. "His pride was damaged."

"My pride was damaged at the white school, and I need a little longer to get over it," I said.

"You got until tomorrow morning," she said.

My face dropped. The thought of going back to the colored school made me sadder than I was when I found out I had to go to the white school. I should've been happy to attend school with my friends, see my teachers, get back to a regular routine, and establish myself as the smartest in the class again, or fight with Malika over it. But I knew my classmates would make me pay for trying to leave. They would call me names, say I wasn't smart enough to get into the white school, not good enough for them whites to let me in the door, they didn't want me, and now I was back with my tail between my legs. There was no way I could defend any of it.

I knew why they'd cut the line off at the white school and sent the rest of us away. I'd heard Mr. Sam Ray Blackburn tell Muhdea and Reverend Jefferson. The others had suffered so I wouldn't have to go to the white school. He couldn't just send me back alone. It would look too suspicious. Reverend Jefferson was the one who'd suggested there probably wasn't enough room for all of us at the white school.

A lot had happened since we first found out. I'd changed my mind, but Muhdea, Reverend Jefferson and Mr. Sam Ray Blackburn hadn't changed theirs. Mr. Blackburn had followed through on his promise in return for us giving him information on Esther and her organization.

By the time I got dressed for school the next morning, Granny and the kids were in the kitchen, no sign of Muhdea, Esther or Rutherford. Granny set a fried egg and biscuit sandwich in front of me at the table.

"Where's everybody?" I rocked one of the babies on my knee.

"They all down at the Hall. Nobody was hurt, but it caught fire 'fore day this morning and burned down," she said.

I got up and tried to hand her the baby. She placed her hand on my shoulder and told me to sit for a while longer. "Finish eating first, and then you can go," she said. I gazed at her with questions in my eyes. "I don't know any more than that."

I pushed the food down my throat as quickly as possible. Then I ran down the empty road to the Hall. Nobody was sitting on the porch rocking and waving good morning. Halfway down the road, I saw Malika running toward me.

"Where is everybody?" I said when we finally met.

She took time to catch her breath. "Gail and James spent the night at Mrs. Carrie's. Thank God."

We passed the juke joint. The padlock was on the door. The gravel parking lot was empty. Nobody was sitting on the back of a truck inquiring whether I was too far away from home.

"Did the whole thing burn down like our house, like the church?"

"Yes. Folks saying Mr. Sam Ray Blackburn was trying to scare Gail."

I didn't smell any bacon and eggs coming from the houses as I passed by each dirt yard.

"Everything's gone. Can't hardly tell nothing was ever there.

When the fire truck finally came, all they did was spray water on our house and some of the other houses to keep them from catching on fire," she said.

"Is Rutherford down there?" I said.

"Ain't nobody seen him or Reverend Adam Moses."

I stopped cold in front of the Hall. There wasn't anything left of it except smoldering charcoal and ashes. A sharp pain shot through my stomach and bent me over. I wrapped my arms around it. Too many fires in too few days. I knew from when our house burned down that it might take two or three days before the fire went completely out, and whatever was left turned cold. The burnt folding chairs and tables were scattered around the yard. By the time I arrived, folks had somewhat settled down. Malika had said by daylight it was all over, which was at least a few hours ago. Gail's face was red and covered with smut.

"The saddest thing is we lost the books," she said. She held a book in her hand that looked as if she'd tried to save it from the fire. Most all of the pages and the front cover were burned. She walked across the street to Malika's house.

My eyes burned from the smoke, and the smell was worse than a rotten skunk and a dead rabbit mixed together. Bro Hollin started to round up all the children. He told us to go home before one of us got hurt. I spotted Esther sitting on the steps of Malika's house with Gail. We slipped around Bro Hollin and went over to where they were. Gail hugged both of us together as if she hadn't just talked to us, and then she caught James' hand.

"Let's get changed before we miss our bus," she said.

The police car rolled down the road and almost came to a stop in front of Malika's house. The window was cracked a little bit, enough to see it was Mr. Sam Ray Blackburn behind it. Gail turned her back to the road. She took my and Malika's hands in hers.

"Keep fighting for justice," she said. It was all she had the strength to say.

They left, and I waved at Malika. "See you at school tomorrow." Esther told me I could miss the rest of that day. Gail called me and Malika back as if she'd forgotten to tell me something.

She placed her arm around our necks and whispered in our ears, "I'm going to check on the school as soon as I get home. I'll write to you," she said. "You girls have outgrown this town, and you need to be in a place where you can flourish."

We looked at each other after she left. "She must be crazy," Malika said.

I agreed. My eyes watered from the smoke. "See you at school tomorrow," I said and headed out running toward the east road. I wanted to swing my feet at the spring that pumped clean water to the water tank in town and returned it fresh to us through the faucet. Nobody would be there today. There was too much going on in town.

"Where you going?" Malika said. The sound of her voice came from behind me. I turned my head around, but kept running.

"To the spring," I said.

"You want some company?"

I waved my hand in the air and picked up my speed.

CHAPTER TWENTY-EIGHT

Run as Fast as You Can

IT WAS THE weekend of the Turtle Derby. Me and Malika didn't have any trouble out of the kids at school when we returned that first week. I wasn't sure why they didn't tease us. Maybe they knew we were already feeling down. We were all somber after the fire at the Hall, and Gail and James left town, and nobody knew where Rutherford had gone off to. The teachers might've warned the students not to tease us or they'd get in trouble. I didn't know, but whatever happened, I was glad they left us alone.

Muhdea had told me to come to the café after school. She needed help with the overflow of customers from the Turtle Derby. I ran into Malika on the corner. Her mama had asked her to help out, too. We were both running late, but she asked me to wait a minute.

"I got to tell you something," she said.

"Tell me inside," I said. "Muhdea hates it when I'm late."

I pushed open the door, and Muhdea was standing there with our white aprons in her hand.

"Fold it in half and put it on," she said. "You late."

It was 4:01 p.m. on Friday evening. Mrs. Deborah Brown, Malika's mama, was flipping hamburger patties on the grill. The whole grill was covered with patties.

"Hurry up," Muhdea said. "We backed up already."

Soon, we were running back and forth from the kitchen to the dining room, clearing tables, mopping up spills, and grinning at white people as they slipped us a nickel or a dime, and sometimes even a quarter.

"Look at these little girls work," one man said. He stretched out his arm for the entire café to see. "Here." He held a nickel between his forefinger and thumb. "Here's a little something for your trouble."

I stuck the money in my apron pocket, thanked him, and kept right on cleaning. Muhdea had warned me to get back to the kitchen with the dishes before they got too heavy. The last thing I wanted to do was break a pan full of dishes.

"Stick together," Muhdea had said. It was easy for us to stay together. We'd done it all our lives.

White tablecloths had replaced the regular yellow and white daisy ones on account of the derby. New, white slipcovers with wildflowers and matching seats covered the yellow vinyl chairs. Ours and the waitresses' aprons were the same color as the slipcovers. The owner had warned us to not get them dirty, which was nearly impossible when we were bussing tables. Mrs. Martha, two ladies from First Baptist Church and two other ladies from the low end of town were the waitresses. I knew Mrs. Martha could move fast from the time I spent with her in the field, but watching all these women together, moving in concert with each other, placing their hands on our backs to direct us one way or the other, was like watching a dance recital. I watched Mrs. Martha slide a plate away from a man who looked as if he owned a pig farm and ate up all of his profits by the time he raised his fork and took the last bite of chicken-fried steak and gravy. She placed the plate in my bin and guided him to the cash register without him feeling as if she rushed him.

"Come on, sir," she said. "Let's see how much damage you done."

He followed her as if she cast a spell on him. All the waitresses did that time after time.

"Go 'head and eat that last bit of pie," one of them said with a smile. "It's good, ain't it? Now, come on to the register 'cause that man over there at the door looks like he real hungry."

Afterward we pounced on that table and cleaned it in nothing flat. I'd learned that any job could be fun if I did it with friends. Esther and Mrs. Carrie never got that. They would rather see us slop hogs than work at the café, but we had fun, racing each other, competing for tips, and dodging the waitresses.

We were dog tired, and the end of the night was near when Muhdea and Mrs. Brown sat us at a table in the kitchen to eat our favorites, hamburger, fries and a chocolate shake. We split the tips without them having to tell us to.

I'd tried many times to get Gail and James to come to the café to see us work before, but they'd refused to go anywhere that didn't serve colored folks.

"I'll buy y'all a cone of vanilla ice cream," Malika had said, but we knew they weren't coming, and we'd worked at the Hall long enough to know why, but that didn't keep us from teasing them, trying to goad them into coming to the café. Muhdea said they probably hadn't ever seen a hard day's work in their lives. I wondered if they'd made it home safely.

"I got something to tell you," Malika said.

Muhdea came and took our plates before we finished eating and before Malika said another word.

"Y'all got tables," she said.

We raced to the front. "What you got to tell me?" I said. She acted as if she didn't hear me.

We cleared the dishes for the last few patrons. It wasn't fun any longer. My legs and feet hurt. We'd slowed down from a quick run and slide across the floor to barely making it.

"You take them two tables, and I'll clean the two over there," Malika said. We weren't together. We were tired, and we carried two tables full of dishes in our pans. We passed Muhdea as she headed to the front with a mop and pail.

"Y'all be careful," she said.

We set our pans on the kitchen floor, and then stacked them on the counter to be washed. They wouldn't allow us to mess with the water hose. The water was too hot and could scald us. We heard the bell on the front door tinkle, but I didn't pay it any attention. Finally, Muhdea came to the kitchen and handed Mrs. Brown an order for a hamburger and fries with a short Coke in the bottle.

"I was 'bout to cut off this grill," Mrs. Brown said. "Who that coming in here this late, the chief?"

"A man passing through on his way back to California," Muhdea said.

"Can he take it with him? We closed, and I'm ready to go as soon as Mr. Cox pick up his money and these receipts."

"He eating at the counter," Muhdea said and walked back to the front.

We kept unloading the dishes. A few minutes later, Muhdea stuck her head through the door to see if the food was ready.

"You go on back. I'll bring it out," I said.

All of the other ladies had left earlier. Muhdea and Mrs. Brown and me and Malika stayed to close up. Malika helped clean the grill.

I cleaned the front while I waited for the plate, and Muhdea counted the receipts. I glanced at the clock. Only fifteen minutes before Mr. Cox would be here. Fifteen minutes before Muhdea would be in a whole lot of trouble. I acted as if I didn't see what she was doing. She pranced around as if that man weren't colored and she weren't doing anything wrong.

I went back to the kitchen when I thought his food was ready. I pushed open the swinging kitchen door with my hip, carrying the burger and fries.

Mr. Cox didn't come in to close the café that night. He sent his wife and daughter.

Malika hit me in the back with the kitchen door. I'd forgotten the short Coke. "Move, Sarah," she said. Then she saw Mrs. Cox, her daughter and the colored man sitting at the counter, and she stopped next to me.

"Y'all give the customer his food," Muhdea said. "We ain't got all night." Then she turned to Mrs. Cox. "I got everything ready for you. It's alright here in this bag." She rushed over and handed the bag to her as if it were any other day and there wasn't a colored man sitting at the counter. "Go on, girls," Muhdea said. "His food is getting cold."

We walked side by side. I set the plate on the counter. Malika handed me the short Coke, and I set it next to the plate. His fingernails were clean, and he wore a white buttoned-down shirt. He was dark, but not the same dark as Muhdea or any kind I'd ever seen before, and his hair was curly, clean and shiny, but not greasy like the white men around here. He smiled at us, and thanked us, and called us pretty, real pretty, and said he bet we were smart, too. Muhdea smiled from across the room. Mrs. Cox finally came to her senses.

"What in the world y'all doing, Mozelle?" she said. She talked through her nose, and so did her daughter, who turned several different shades of red as she stood next to her mama.

"You need to take your food and leave right now," Mrs. Cox said.

"You sit right there and eat," Muhdea said. "Sarah, go get him a piece of pecan pie."

Muhdea followed us to the kitchen. "Sarah," she said as soon as we were out of earshot of Mrs. Cox. "Y'all run as fast as you can over to Carrie's and tell your mama and whoever else is up there to get over here to the café."

Living in the country, timing was everything, a time to plant and a time to uproot, a time to break down and a time to build up, a time to ask questions and a time to shut up and get moving. Me and Malika took off running as if the law were after us. We saw Mrs. Martha and the other waitresses first. They were standing on the corner under the sycamore tree, smoking cigarettes and gossiping.

"Muhdea said get back to the café right now," I said, catching my breath.

"What for?" Mrs. Martha said. She threw the cigarette on the ground and put it out with the heel of her shoe.

"She said right now. We going to Mrs. Carrie's to get Miss Esther," Malika said.

They didn't ask us any more questions, and we didn't stay around to answer them if they had. When we looked back, they were heading toward the café. It was a time to make haste, and they did. If Muhdea or Granny made a request, folks knew they didn't mince words and got to it. They'd dropped their hoes in the middle of the field, and were ready to take orders when they got there without question.

We slammed on Mrs. Carrie's door with our fists. She opened it, and I was surprised to see Esther holding a meeting since the Hall was gone. We were out of breath.

"Muhdea said everybody get to the café right now," I said. They got up, Mrs. Carrie, Bro Hollin, Miss Pastel, Miss Flora and a few others, and moved as if the Lord had called them.

"What's going on, Sarah?" Esther said. She put away her papers and got up to leave. "Never mind," she said. "This is as good a time as any to start a debate with Bo Cox."

We got on the back of Bro Hollin's truck. One of the women mentioned that Mr. Cox didn't see Esther as a threat to him in the race for city council. He was the owner of the café and the incumbent. We were back at the café in no time. Muhdea met us at the kitchen door with our aprons in her hand.

"Y'all go around to the front door," she said to the others. "Hurry, Mr. Cox will be here directly."

Hamburger patties sizzled on the grill like they had earlier that night when the café was packed with people from the Turtle Derby. Fries hissed in the basket of hot lard. By the time we'd tied our aprons and gone out front, Mr. Cox, Mr. Sam Ray Blackburn, Mr. Michael James King, other white people from town and the folks from Maeby Citizens for Progress were all coming in the front door. The waitresses directed the folks to their seats as if the café were open for business, and the colored man from California was still sitting at the counter on the swivel stool with the plastic seat. Malika's sister and her husband from Chicago were the last two people to come in. She hadn't told me they were in town.

Mr. Cox sent his wife and daughter home, all but pushed them out the door. The wife was as pretty as Alison on *Peyton Place*, but her daughter put me in mind of the wicked witch in *The Wizard of Oz*. As soon as they left, he got to cussing, and threatening to send us all to jail, especially Muhdea.

"Mozelle, you done loss your freaking mind," he said. "You can't take over my café."

He grabbed the left side of his chest. He tried to continue, but he was gasping for air. It was hot. He was sweating. We all were. As he tried to talk, the waitresses began serving the patrons, and me and Malika brought them their short Cokes. We acted as if Mr. Cox and his boys weren't throwing a fit and screaming at us, and calling us out of our names. Muhdea gave us orders as if she were a choir director, and in no time at all, folks had been served, and we were picking up their plates. Bro Hollin smacked his lips as if he'd just eaten the best burger and fries of his life. Mustard hung on his top lip, and looked as if it were about to fall off.

Esther surprised me most of all. It was the first time I'd ever seen her listen to Muhdea, and do what she said without giving her any lip. She wore a light blue miniskirt, and the man from California couldn't keep his eyes off her. She sat next to him at the counter and looked more like she should've been traveling with him instead of living in Maeby with us. Folks acted as if they'd been coming to the café for years, and they looked mighty fine sitting there at the tables. Mrs. Brown and Muhdea washed the dishes as we brought them in the kitchen. They didn't even ask us what was going on out front.

Mr. Cox got in Esther's face. "This is all your fault," he said. "You should've got on the bus with them others." He pointed his finger in her face. The colored man from California stood up. "We ain't changing nothing in Maeby. Get that through your thick skull," Mr. Cox said.

Esther swiveled on the stool. "Look around you, Bo," she said. "Something is already changing."

He held his arms by his sides and balled his fists. His knuckles were red. It looked like he was trying with all his might to keep his hands at his sides, and not hit Esther or have to fight the man from California. All eyes were on them now. Esther got up slowly and stared him down eye to eye.

"We'll see what happens at the polls," she said, and strutted to the cash register.

Folks went back to what they were doing, but he stood there with his fists balled. The waitresses refused to take any tips from the colored folk. Mr. Michael James King couldn't get hold of any of his deputies. I imagined they were out having fun due to the Turtle Derby. Nobody answered when he called on his walkie-talkie, and that made him real mad.

"Joe, James, come in," he said. "Can't you hear me, damn it?"

There was nothing they could do except threaten and cuss at us. We moved in unison, picking up dishes, taking up money, and giving out change. Mrs. Martha came back to the kitchen.

"Mr. Peter ain't got enough money," she said. "Y'all put your nickels together. I don't want him to feel embarrassed."

I went in the bathroom, unpinned the handkerchief from my panties, untied the knot, and unfolded the five-dollar bill and a dime Granny never let me leave home without. Malika came in while I was unfolding the money.

"You giving him your just-in-case money," she said.

"If this ain't the time to use it, it won't be one," I said.

The handkerchief was hard to get untied. I went out to the front and slipped the five-dollar bill to the waitress, and she smiled.

"This here ain't over," Mr. Michael James King said. "I will arrest all y'all tomorrow for trespassing. You can count on that. Write they names down for me, Bo."

Mr. Cox rubbed his hand back and forth across his forehead. "You know everybody here," he said.

When all of the dishes were cleared and washed, and all of the money and receipts were counted, right in the middle of their ranting and raving, Muhdea walked up to Mr. Cox and handed him the money bag and receipts, and then she untied her apron and handed it to him.

"This my last day, Mr. Cox," she said, loud enough for us all to hear.

Everybody, except the white men, clapped for her. We, the workers and patrons, left through the front door. They all piled in Bro Hollin's truck. Me and Muhdea decided to walk. The man from California drove off. Bro Hollin said he was going to follow him to the edge of town to insure his safety. Malika stood in front of her sister's black Lincoln Town Car.

"See you later, alligator," I said.

Malika didn't say, "After 'while, crocodile." She put her hands in her pockets and hunched her shoulders up. "I'm leaving with my sister tomorrow morning," she said. "I'm going to school in Chicago."

I walked over to the car. "You mean for good?" I said. The back car door was open, and I closed it. "You leaving me now? You leaving me all by myself?"

Cars whizzed by on the freeway. A few of the drivers blew their horns. Malika looked around and up at the sky as if God might pull her up. I turned the toe of my shoe in the gravel.

"I don't want to go," she said. "I'll be by myself, too. Chicago schools started in August."

Mosquitoes covered her legs but not mine. I wished for them to bite her good. She didn't even fan them away. Her sister opened her door and told Malika it was time to go. There was plenty to do before they left the next morning.

"I'll write to you only in French," she said. "And my sister said you can come visit us this summer." She rambled on, hoping I would let the wind go out of my chest. I couldn't let her leave thinking I was mad at her. God would be mad at me if I did. Muhdea walked up beside me and placed her hand on my shoulder as if she knew I was struggling.

"I ain't going to cry, Sarah," Malika said.

"King's English," I said. "You better not cry."

We curtsied like we thought they might do in France.

"Au revoir," she said.

"Adieu, mademoiselle," I said and slammed the car door for her.

It seemed as if the crickets were trying to outsing the frogs, or was it the sound of the turtles? Muhdea held my hand, and we walked home without mumbling a single word. When we reached the porch at Esther's house, she let go of my hand.

"I won't ever leave you and Granny," I said. She stared at me as if what I said might not hold true and kissed me on my forehead.

Granny opened the front door. The news spread fast, and she knew Muhdea had integrated the café, and stood up to the white men. She gleamed with pride. I'd never seen her look so pleased with Muhdea. We sat at the kitchen table and listened to Muhdea tell what happened again, and again. Every now and then, she asked me to cosign on what she said, and I nodded my head or added my two cents.

"You going to miss Malika," Muhdea said when she noticed

my thoughts drifting off. "Ain't no getting 'round that, but hold Ephesians 3 near your heart, and you'll get through it."

Muhdea told us she didn't know what it was about the man from California that caused her to integrate the café and quit her job.

"I saw my old tired reflection in that man's eyes. I saw the same one in Sarah's eyes when we were at the department store. I didn't want to be that woman no longer," she said.

Muhdea was telling her story for the fifth time when I opened the door for Reverend Adam Moses. I peeped behind him expecting to see Rutherford, but he wasn't there. I hadn't seen the reverend or Rutherford since they stormed out the door at the Hall after the white people refused to let us attend their school.

He sat at the table, and Granny poured him a cup of coffee. He congratulated Muhdea, and she told him what had happened at the café even though he already knew.

I rocked back and forth in my chair to calm the thoughts swirling around in my head, like where was Rutherford, and where y'all been for so long without telling nobody. I bided my time. Sooner or later, Granny would pull it out of him.

"I thought Esther would be home," he said.

Granny assured him she wasn't home and was probably still at Mrs. Carrie's house.

"I stopped by there," he said. "Carrie said the meeting broke up over an hour ago."

He waited around for a while longer expecting Esther to show up, and when she didn't, he finally got around to telling us why he'd stopped by.

"You know Rutherford got a hot temper," he said as if he were beginning a sermon, and I wasn't in any mood to hear a long one.

"Whelp, he was fire mad that day. We started out walking to clear our heads, and the next thing you know, we'd hitchhiked all the way to Rutherford's home in Mississippi," he said. "I stayed with him awhile to help him get his head straight, but when it was time for us to go, he decided not to come back."

I thought Granny was going to jump up out of her chair and do a sanctified shout.

"I came for his belongings," he said. He took a clean handkerchief out of his coat pocket and rubbed it across his head and then wiped the sweat off his face. "Basically, his clothes and photos. He don't want nothing else."

Granny got up from the table and slammed the chair under it. She took her toothbrush out of her mouth. "I always knew he was yellow," she said. "Come down here telling us to fight for our rights, and he too scared to pick up his own shit."

I went with Granny to Esther's bedroom. I knew the photos he was talking about. Rutherford had pulled them out and showed them to me enough times, and I knew the stories that went with them by heart. It made me mad to think that the first time he told me I was impressed with him. He'd walked beside the Reverend Martin Luther King Jr. He was at the March on Washington, but didn't cross paths with Esther. There were a lot of pictures of him smiling, his head thrown back, and both his arms around women's shoulders. He looked happy, and not at all like he looked the day he left town. Granny placed all of Rutherford's stuff in a pillowslip and handed it to Reverend Adam Moses.

"Good riddance," she said.

We sat back down at the table, where Muhdea seemed as if she were still playing the night's events over in her head. Granny poured her another cup of coffee and gave me a glass of buttermilk. There wasn't any leftover cornbread to crumble up in it. They agreed it was best Esther wasn't here to see Reverend Adam Moses take away Rutherford's belongings. We got up to go to bed. Esther still hadn't come home.

"You get up early in the morning and go say goodbye to Malika," Muhdea said. I was planning to go anyway.

REVIVAL

CHAPTER TWENTY-NINE

It's a Ritual, a Rite of Passage

I STAYED UP all night. I sat on the back porch and broke up pieces of glass and glued them together. I made a picture of two girls, me and Malika. I put it together on top of a piece of a cardboard box. I knew I didn't have time for it to dry. For early October, it was still quite warm outside. Within a few weeks, I'd need to wear a winter coat. It was the time of year when the fall and summer competed for attention. There was warmth in the air even though fall was lurking around threatening rain and cold weather. At daylight I went into the house and got my notebook, my list of "Things I'll Know When I Get Grown." I laid the cardboard with the mosaic on top of it and left to say goodbye to Malika.

She was standing on the porch when I got there.

"What you doing up?" I said.

"I wanted to look around by myself. What if I don't ever come back, Sarah?"

That made me feel a way I'd never felt before, and I was sad. "Don't mean we won't see each other again," I said.

"You swear?" she said.

I set the notebook down on the porch. I handed her the mosaic. "I made this for you. It's us."

We laughed. It barely looked like girls, lessen us. "It's ugly, but I'm keeping it forever," she said.

I gave her my notebook.

"Why you giving me yours?"

"I did a whole lot of things I didn't tell you about. I wrote them in here. You can take it and read it so you will know the bad things I did."

"I don't need to know that, Sarah," she said. "I know you."

We sat for a while and watched Mr. Peter burn trash on the lot where the Hall used to be. We talked about some of the questions we'd written in our notebooks. Malika went inside and got hers. We read from the first pages of the list. We didn't even understand what the questions meant. After a while, we both knew that for whatever reason we'd started keeping our lists, we didn't need to any longer. We got up and walked over to where Mr. Peter was burning the trash and threw them in the barrel.

"We moving into our new Jim Walter house today," I said. She wished she could be here to help me. "I got to go. Granny will be needing my help." We shook hands, and I left running toward home.

"Sarah," Malika said.

I stopped and turned around. She waved her hand, I waved back to her and took off running again.

Our new house was ready, and most everybody came to help us. Granny fried cracklin' over a fire in a black witch's pot. We cleaned and gutted fish on the picnic table. Bro Hollin and some of the other men carried in the furniture. Granny gave me strict orders to make sure that anybody who wanted a plate of food got it right away. They were doing us a favor, and the least we could do was to keep their bellies full. I ran food back and forth all day while I listened to them tell me how good it was, except it would've tasted better if the cook had added a little bit more salt or taken out a little bit more pepper. Sister Tucker closed her store and brought over a jar of pickles and pickled pig feet. Mrs. Martha and Bro Hollin wanted another piece of fish, and the Graves boys asked for a dipper of water. Whoever asked for food or drink, I went and got it.

The men put up the beds, and we dressed them with sheets and bedspreads. We set the table with placemats, matching dishes, glasses and utensils. Our Frigidaire hummed in the kitchen, no more waiting on Saturday to pick up ice at the icehouse. Some of the furniture was brand-new, and a lot of it was hand-me-down. I'd never seen Muhdea so happy, and Granny was too, except she didn't show it as much. Folks talked about what they would do when they got their new houses.

"I'd get a bigger refrigerator and keep my meat in it instead of in the smokehouse," one woman said.

"I sure wouldn't want all Coppertone appliances," another one said.

Some couldn't wait to get all indoor plumbing, but every one of them wanted Esther to make them a mosaic, the only thing of beauty left after the fire.

When everything was in place, Muhdea and Bro Hollin went out to the junk house and got the boxes Uncle Robert had sent her. They put all of his pictures on the wall, including *The Last Supper*. When all of the food was about gone, we all gathered around the mosaic, and Reverend Jefferson blessed our house.

"Look what we built out of the ashes," he said.

He was right, everybody from the smallest child, to Mrs. Carrie and the civil rights workers, even the ones like Dick Gregory, Julian Bond, the lawyer Walker and Bill Hansen, had hammered a nail or painted or done something for us to see this day. Reverend Jefferson thanked every one of them.

"This is what love is, children," he said. "And don't you ever forget it."

He went on to tell us our house was built out of love, the kind of love Jesus represented, which was the same type of love being put into building the church. Volunteers from all over the county and out of state had come to help rebuild the church. It took longer to rebuild it from scratch, and our house came mostly ready. They called it a prefab home. The men installed a baptismal pool under the church pulpit. Reverend Jefferson had baptized the last converts at the river that summer.

After Reverend Jefferson finished praying, and everybody went their separate ways, we sat down at our new yellow table. We all gave a sigh, one after the other.

"Esther, we'll pick up our things from your house later this week," Muhdea said.

I laid my head on the table. Esther rubbed the top of it with her hand, something Granny generally did. Our house smelled like brand-new. Esther made a motion to get up but decided against it.

"Why don't you stay here tonight?" Granny said.

Esther declined. She still needed to make campaign plans for the next day.

"Sarah can stay," she said. That led to them trying to convince her to move back in the house with them. She could have her own room since the kids were gone. Esther tried to convince them that she was fine on her own, and Muhdea reminded her that women shouldn't live alone. Even having Rutherford around was better than being by herself.

"I lived alone in Chicago," she said. "A lot of women are on their own these days."

Granny placed the teapot on the stove, and got a Lipton teabag and a cup from the cupboard.

"If you're worried," Esther said, "Sarah can move back in with you. We shouldn't have forced her to live with us in the first place."

Granny looked pleased. I didn't want to slip out during the middle of the night anymore, and I couldn't imagine Esther living over there all by herself.

"What's wrong, Sarah?" Granny said. "Ain't that good news?"

I rubbed my eyes with the back of my hand. The teapot squealed, and Esther got up to get it. I wasn't sure how Granny and Muhdea would take it, but it was the right time to tell them.

"I'm going home with Esther," I said.

They all looked shocked. Muhdea opened her mouth as if she were going to protest. Granny placed her hand atop of Muhdea's, and whatever she was going to say she didn't.

"Are you sure, Sarah?" Esther said.

A FEW WEEKS later, me, Muhdea and Granny were sitting at the table eating supper. I came to their house after school and waited for Esther to pick me up when she got off work and finished campaigning. She met her supporters at Mrs. Carrie's house. The grown folks did most of the work now. I helped out one or two evenings a week and on weekends. There wasn't as much for us to do since the other kids were settled in at the white school, and only the lawyer Walker worked on the lawsuit to get us full integration. Esther came in the kitchen looking as if she'd registered all the coloreds in Maeby. She sat down and laid an envelope in front of me. I read my name printed on it. Granny set down a plate of fried corn, turnip greens with the bottoms mixed in and a baked sweet potato with fresh butter, cinnamon and sugar sprinkled on it.

"Open it," Esther said. She was way too excited to wait for me "The school accepted you. They gave you a full scholarship." She didn't touch her plate of food. She pulled the letter out of the envelope and showed it to us. "This is wonderful news. They want you to come right away."

I knew what she meant, but Muhdea and Granny didn't have a clue. They didn't know Esther and Gail had insisted that I sign an application to go to school in Boston. We didn't share in her excitement. Here she was again changing the program when we were getting along just fine. Granny wrung her hands. Esther eyed each of us in disbelief. There wasn't any reason to discuss it since I wasn't going anywhere, and typical of Esther to mess with our lives, get Muhdea mad at her again. I got up from the table and left the room. Let her explain it to them.

I walked out the door without telling them where I was going. I didn't even know. I did know they wouldn't agree with Esther. Granny would put up a fight this time, and I knew what happened when they disagreed, and I didn't want to be in the middle of that again. I started out walking down Back Street. The sun was still high in the sky, and it was warm outside. I glanced at a few of the houses as I passed by, but nobody was sitting on the porch. I remembered it was suppertime. I ran up the east road and headed to the spring, where nobody would bother me.

When I got there, I sat at the edge of the spring and took off my socks and shoes. I let my feet dangle in the water. I heard a noise further down the path and thought it was the last of the grasshoppers jumping across the weeds. A few minutes later Reverend Jefferson walked up on me and darn near frightened the mess out of me.

"You almost scared me," I said.

He said I did scare him. "What you doing out here today?" He wore overalls and a flannel shirt. He sat next to me, rolled up his pant legs, took off his socks and shoes, and put his feet in the water beside mine. "I reckon you missing them SNCC workers, and Malika," he said. "Don't worry. You'll adjust to it."

I kicked the water. "I miss my cousins, too," I said. I lowered my eyes and hung my head a bit. We kicked the water and sat a while in silence.

"What is it, Sarah?" he said. "What's worrying you?"

I told him about the letter, the school, and about my feelings toward it. He sat on it for a long time before he spoke, and when he did, it wasn't what I wanted to hear. He agreed with Esther. After all he'd done to keep me from going to the white school, he thought I should go thousands of miles away to a place where I didn't know anybody. I picked up my shoes and started to get up. I got madder at him than I ever was at Esther. He took the shoes out of my hand, and asked me to wait a minute.

He tried to explain, but the more he said, the angrier I got, and I questioned him as if he weren't a grown preacher. I wanted to know why he and Muhdea went against their own race and put me in the middle of it. He talked to me man to man, and not like he was God standing in the pulpit giving out orders.

"I tried on many occasions to explain that whole thing to you," he said. "Like the children of Israel, we were lost at the time, but as you can see now, we found our way."

"Sir," I said, "can you tell me in your own words?"

His body shifted from the inside out. He didn't only look at me; he studied me as if I were a person in the Bible, as if he were getting ready to deliver a message to the congregation he wasn't sure they were prepared to hear. He scratched his head.

"It was wrong," he said. "I tried to come up with a softer way of telling you, but we shouldn't have done that, and we never should've brought you in it. Yes, the reason the other kids weren't allowed to register for the white school and why your mama is still up to her ears in court cases is 'cause we didn't want it to look as if we were protecting you."

We sat next to each other for a long time, letting what he'd said marinate. I'd thought it, but knowing was like being hit in the chest with a fastball.

"Well, Sarah?" he said.

"We can't change it now," I said. We sat quiet for a long time, staring at the overcast sky and the water stream. I thought of several different ways to push him further, but the answer would've been the same: they were wrong, I was dishonest, what we did was reprehensible. We moved to a space where there was nothing left to say. He was probably ready for me to leave, but my feet felt too heavy to move.

"Well, Sarah, you enjoy that school, and write to us," he said. "I will certainly place you on the top of the prayer list. But I must get back to work unless there is something else I can do for you." He rose from the bench.

It occurred to me this might be the last chance I get to ask him for advice about my religion. "Yes, sir, there is one more thing."

He looked startled. He'd dismissed me as kindly as possible. It was getting late. He'd shamed himself by sharing the truth with me, a child. But I was feeling myself, and he was feeling guilty, so I went for it.

"Will you baptize me?" I said.

He studied on it for a while, scratched his head, moaned, sucked in his jaws. "Sure," he said. "I'll be happy to baptize you. You can be the first one I dip in the new baptismal pool. If you sit on the Mourner's Bench and get saved next summer, I'll baptize you first."

"I'm already saved," I said. "I ain't going through that no more."

I didn't know if it was the authority in my voice, or if God was working with him. He hesitated, and then he asked me to tell him my testimony. The one I didn't get the chance to tell back then.

"Give me the short version. It's 'bout to get dark," he said.

I'd put him in a position for the second time that day he was uncomfortable with. I spoke quickly before he changed his mind.

"I asked the Lord to let choir sing 'I Need Thee Every Hour.' It was the same song Granny asked for and her mama asked for it before her. I was outside with Esther, right where the stained-glass window used to be, and they sang it. Don't you remember? It was

369

the last song." I left out the details where Esther disagreed with me and I peed all over my shoes. He knew what happened.

"You promise you telling me a true story," he said.

"Yes, sir. You can ask Muhdea and Granny."

"I'm going to take your word for it." He climbed down into the spring and stood with his arms outstretched like John the Baptist. "Come on," he said, and I did.

He placed his hand across my eyes and nose. "Sarah White, has God forgiven you for your sins?"

"Yes, sir."

"Is your testimony true?"

"Yes, sir."

"Then I baptize you in the name of the Father, Son and the Holy Ghost."

He dipped me in the water as if we were dancing. He brought me up quickly.

"I didn't choke," I said.

It was said that folks who weren't saved coughed up the water. The water was cold. I was shivering. I wiped the water away from my face. We were soaking wet. I didn't shout, or cry, or run around in circles, but I did feel relieved. What, I didn't know when I sat on the Mourner's Bench, and I didn't know fully at this time, but I did know a portion of it and I told him.

"The praying, the sign, the Mourner's Bench, the revival, none of it is all it's set up to be, is it?"

He looked puzzled.

"I mean getting baptized is just a symbol, a ritual, a rite of passage," I said. "The real meaning is inside me. Isn't it?"

He stared me dead in my eyes. His face showed signs of disappointment, loss. He didn't say a word. He walked away from the stream without me.

CHAPTER THIRTY

Bye, Mama

ESTHER WAS RUNNING for city council, but the whole community voted for me to go to that school in Boston. My teacher, Miss Brady, Sister Tucker and all of the students signed a petition. The mothers of the church and the deacons gave a fish fry every Saturday to raise money for me. One day as I passed Mrs. Carrie's house, she called me to come sit with her for a minute. We talked a long time about this and that, the fire, the movement. She was stalling. She sifted through the papers on the table while she talked. Her face was long and tired. She was solemn.

"Sarah," she said, "I'm getting too old, and Esther is taking my place. You and Malika are the next in line. The way the world is changing, you're going to need much more education than we can provide you here in Maeby. One day the two of you will blaze a trail similar to the way Pearlie and I did. If Esther is able to run for city council, think of what's ahead for you. My only hope is that we've given you a good foundation, and I believe we have."

"Thank you, Mrs. Carrie, I said. "I truly don't want to leave home."

Everybody else had tried to convince me to go, but nobody gave me a reason why until Mrs. Carrie sat me down. I didn't tell her that day, but I knew then what I was going to do.

A few days later, while we were eating dinner, I told Granny, Muhdea and Esther.

"I'll go to Boston," I said. "But may I wait until after the election?"

That November Esther lost her bid for city council in the primary. She knew it would happen long before it did. Her running was a symbol as well, one that opened the door for other elections, for the one a colored person would eventually win.

On January 5, 1966, Granny, Muhdea and Esther walked me to the highway to catch the bus. I carried the same brown-striped suitcase Esther did when she left years ago. We walked down the same trail next to Mr. Peter's house. Two redbirds were perched atop of his roof in the middle of winter. They followed us down the trail and up the road till we turned to go past the café, and then I didn't see them anymore. I blew them a kiss with my free hand. Nobody was at the water house, but everybody I knew was at the Esso station, waiting for us. All of the church members, the members of Maeby Citizens for Progress, the teachers, the students, Mrs. Carrie and even the lawyer Walker.

Granny gave me a paper sack with fried chicken, biscuits and all kinds of store-bought goodies. All she could say was "Sarah," then she straightened my ponytail. Sister Tucker gave me a bag of two-for-a-penny caramel kisses and several bags of Bugles. Muhdea pressed a fistful of balled-up money in my hand. "Make us proud, Sarah," she said. Esther gave me a box. "Open it on the bus," she said. Reverend Jefferson said a short prayer, his first. They stood next to each other and waved slowly as I got on the bus. I took my seat and placed my face and hands against the window. Esther walked up to the widow. "Bye, Mama," I mouthed. I waved until long after the bus left the Esso station.

I settled on the bus, and opened the box from Esther. It was a mosaic of two girls, a pretty one. The girls looked just like me and Malika.